Kill Squad

A Trouble Thriller

Matthew Doggett

Five Brothers Publishing

Contents

Get Your Free Novella

VISIT **MATTHEWDOGGETTAUTHOR.COM/TROUBLE** FOR A **free** action-packed novella (while also signing up for my awesome email list).

Prologue

THE GATHERING WAS HELD in a community center in Cleveland in a predominantly Black neighborhood. Prominent members of the Cleveland Jewish community attended, the milling audience an almost equal mixture of Black and Jewish people of all ages. If it weren't for the coming together of the two communities, the two terrorists surely would've been noticed.

The two white men, John Winston and Nathan Fox, were twenty-two and twenty-three, respectively. They showed up in two cars, which they parked three blocks away on opposite sides of the community center. They wore semi-formal clothing that matched the occasion, and they carried their explosives in backpacks. Although they saw each other in the auditorium, they did not acknowledge each other's presence.

Working their way through the milling crowds, they smiled politely at these people they'd come to hate. They did not know any of these Black people or Jewish people personally, but they hated them, nonetheless. They hated them for their skin color or their religious practices or their heritage. They hated them because they'd learned to hate them over long periods of time and with considerable help from conspiracy theories, half-truths, and outright lies.

John Winston took a seat in a folding chair near the right side of the large room. He glanced over and saw Nathan Fox do the same on the left side. Winston placed his backpack between his legs and pushed it under the chair with his feet. His armpits were drenched, but he kept his jacket on. Winter was almost upon Cleveland, and it was chilly outside. He wouldn't be sitting here long, anyway.

There was a banner up on the stage behind the podium that said, "Celebrating 100 Years of Jewish-African American Relations." John tried to keep himself from grimacing at the thought of these people conspiring to oppress the white man.

He felt no doubt about what he was doing. None at all. Although he was nervous, he felt giddy, his head swimming with purpose. He was a proud member of The White Power Alliance, and he wanted nothing more than to kill people just like the ones who were chatting inanely around him.

A Black man in a suit came out on stage and asked everyone to take their seats.

That was John's cue. He stood up and murmured something to the old Jewish lady next to him about hitting the bathroom. He was out the door and into the chilly afternoon air a minute later.

Winston didn't wait around to see if Fox would leave when he was supposed to, exactly two minutes after him. He hurried back to his car and pulled out the phone that had only been used once before, to test the phone that was now connected to the explosive device sitting under a seat in the auditorium.

He sat in the car with the engine running and watched the clock. When the time was right, he selected the only number in the phone's call history and pressed send.

He heard the explosion even through the closed car windows. Smiling, he shut the phone down and put the car into drive. But he didn't take his foot off the brake pedal. He leaned forward over the steering wheel and listened. Then he heard the second explosion, and his smile turned into a grin.

As John Winston drove away, he rolled his windows down so he could listen to the screams coming from the community center.

***

Ethan Lee Bove turned on the news at 12:30 his time—3:30 Cleveland time—his stomach fluttering with excitement. The story didn't hit the airwaves until nearly an hour later. But when the first rushed reports came on his television, it was worth the wait.

He was so excited to see the aftermath of his plan, that he watched several minutes of a report delivered by a Black reporter before he changed the channel to find a white one from a different network. Once that was done, he sat back in the chair in his living room, the sounds of his two young children and his wife on the other side of the house mixing with the news report.

Absently, Bove reached out and grabbed his prized SS dagger off the side table. It was in its nickel-plated scabbard, the black hardwood handle comfortable in his hand. As he watched the television, he used his thumb to push the scabbard away from the dagger hilt, making it click slightly. Then he pulled it back into place. This was his habit, so ingrained it was almost unconscious.

Dagger in hand, a sense of calm swept through him. He still had a couple of distasteful tasks ahead of him, but he put those out of his mind, allowing himself to focus on an accomplished mission.

The short black hairs creating a horseshoe around his balding skull dragged on the leather of the chair as he sank deeper into the recliner. He pursed his thin lips and let his always-droopy eyelids close over his dark eyes. He moved his thumb down to the widest part of the dagger's grip, rubbing it gently over the solid nickel Nazi eagle embedded in the wood there. Half-listening to the news report, he imagined what it must have been like in the auditorium when the first explosion went off. He pictured all the Blacks and the Jews being blown apart. He could hear their screams in his head. They sent pleasurable tingles through his body.

He imagined those who were still ambulatory rushing away from the site of the first blast, gathering in panic on the other side of the auditorium. Maybe some of them ran outside. But not many, he thought. The shock and confusion would've been too great. And then he pictured the second blast. He breathed heavily, a little giggle escaping him.

It had been a target of opportunity that Ethan Lee Bove could not pass up. And he had no shortage of men willing to do the work of placing the bombs after they were built carefully by a man who worked in demolition, collapsing tall buildings with expertly placed explosives.

But it was just the beginning. A test run of sorts. Something to strike fear into the Black and Jewish communities that were invading America like termites invading a house. They had to be dealt with in the only way that worked. With force.

Bove was not so naive to think that he could rid America of all the Blacks and Jews and Hispanics and Asians and Arabs. Of course not. But he could do the next best thing. He could carve out a swath of land free of the inferior races. A place where white men and women could raise white children without the degradation of having to share their communities with *people of color*. A place where Aryan values and the Aryan way of life could thrive uninhibited. It was the way things were supposed to be. The way things were *meant* to be.

And he had a plan to make it happen. Many, many people would have to die along the way, some of them white race traitors. But that was okay. In fact, it was more than okay. It was the icing on top of the cake.

As the news went to commercial, Bove went deeper into his meditation. He felt the power of the bygone Nazi war machine coursing through him from the dagger in his hand. They had come so close. Oh, what the world would've been like if the Nazis triumphed during the great war. They could've made quick work of all the subhumans in America. The Blacks had already been rounded up in ghettos. Arabs hadn't really been a problem back then. Hell, the American government of the time had already imprisoned most of the Asian population. It would've been easy enough to ship them back to where they came from. Or better yet, exterminate them like the Nazis did so efficiently to six million Jews. It had been a start. But it wasn't enough.

So now it was up to Bove. He'd been working so hard, and now the gears were turning.

He let his thoughts drift back to the bombing at the community center. The imagined sounds of screams echoed in his head, making him smile.

Chapter 1

I KNEW WHAT I was doing. I may have been drunk and pissed off, but I knew exactly what I was doing.

That's not to say I felt good about it. But sometimes the things you have to do aren't the things you want to do. Sometimes, you've just gotta grit your teeth, pull out your lighter, and burn it all down.

"Please," Hoffman said, kneeling next to me on the lawn. He clutched at my pant leg, and I kicked him away, sending him onto his scrawny ass. "Please," he whined, "it's all I have left."

His face was bloody from where I'd hit him while getting him out of the house. It wasn't a hard hit. I wasn't in the habit of beating up old men just for the hell of it. Even if they really fucking deserved it.

"You don't remember me, do you?" I asked him, looking down at the bottle in my hand. I was busy shoving a bandana down into the mouth so it would touch the gasoline I'd poured in there before riding over to this nice neighborhood. Even though it was a liquor bottle, the vodka that had once been inside wasn't what I'd consumed to get drunk. No, I'd poured it out before filling the bottle up at a gas station.

"What?" Hoffman said. "What? Who are you?"

I'd never been a fan of vodka. What I'd had was a pint of Jameson whiskey while I waited for Hoffman to come home. That bottle was in pieces on Hoffman's kitchen floor.

Besides, vodka won't burn well enough to start a proper fire. You might get a clean blue flame, but that's it. Easy to put out with a bit of water. Hell, you might not even need water. It might just go out on its own.

If you really want to start a structure fire, you need something a little more robust to use as an accelerant. And nothing beats good old gasoline.

"It's probably impossible for you to remember how many people you've wronged in your life, isn't it?" I asked, looking down at him. He looked old in the evening light. Decrepit. His skin was sallow, and his cheeks were covered in patchy gray hair. All the hate and evil had rotted him from the inside out. It was no more than he deserved.

"Listen," he said, getting on his knees and clasping his hands together. "Listen, if you—" Something caught his eye, and he turned his face toward the street. The next words he spoke weren't directed at me.

"Help!" Hoffman shouted. "Help, he's crazy! He's gonna burn my house down!"

I figured we'd have company sooner or later. *Better get this show on the road*, I thought.

"Hey!" A man called from behind me. "I called the police."

"Good," I said, low enough that the man wouldn't hear it.

But Hoffman heard it. And he looked up into my face, his mouth parting to reveal too-white dentures as he gaped up at me.

I'd shoved enough bandana into the mouth of the bottle to get a good portion of the cloth soaking. It was ready. But as I reached into my pocket for my lighter, Hoffman lurched to his feet. He was going to run away. I couldn't have that.

I pulled my hand out of my pocket and grabbed him by the collar of his lime-green polo, yanking him back down onto the lush grass of his front lawn. He didn't weigh much at all. He certainly wasn't the imposing figure from my childhood memories. I was pleased to feel none of that old, bad fear upon seeing him again after all these years.

"Hey!" the man from across the street said. Only he wasn't across the street anymore. I could hear his footsteps. He was running toward me. Using the same hand I'd pulled Hoffman down with, I reached into the right pocket of my black leather jacket and grabbed the Sig Sauer P320 pistol. As I pulled it out, I turned around and pointed it at the man. He wore jogging pants and a muscle shirt. Probably just finished his evening workout. But he made a nice show of sprinting quickly back into his house when he saw the pistol. Probably hadn't run that fast since he was a kid.

A look around the upper-middle-class neighborhood told me that several Concerned Citizens were interested in what was happening to their neighbor. But they clearly weren't Concerned enough to confront the guy in the leather jacket with a menacing-looking gun in one hand and a Molotov cocktail in the other.

Smart people. They'd go far in life.

As I put the gun back in my pocket, I moved over to Hoffman—who was hyperventilating on the grass—and put a foot on his chest. "Don't move," I said, pulling out the lighter.

Hoffman's house was a nice Tudor with two steep, front-facing gable roofs on either side, flanking the central portion where the front door was. It was brown and white, with a brick-timber-and-stucco facade. Two chimneys poked up from the roof. It was a much nicer house than the one Hoffman and his wife used to live in, back when they were acting as foster parents to unfortunate kids like me.

He'd done well for himself, apparently.

I hope he forgot to pay his insurance, I thought as I lit the red-and-white bandana sticking out of the bottle. I dropped the lighter onto Hoffman's face. He made no move to stop it, and it bounced off his bulbous red nose. He whined as I transferred the cocktail into my right hand.

The sound of sirens came to my ears, faint but growing.

I'd showed up at his house with two vodka bottles full of gasoline in my motorcycle's saddlebags. And I'd used one full bottle on the interior, dumping it around the entryway and the rooms directly off it. Then I'd extended the trail further into the house with half of the gas from the bottle I was currently holding. While I'd been doing that, I'd been asking him questions. Hoffman told me that his wife had been dead for two years. He promised me there was no one else in the house, but I'd checked anyway, escorting him around at gunpoint to make sure.

So as I hefted the bottle in my hand and took aim at the open front door, I knew exactly what I was doing.

The sirens were louder. Not long now.

"You used to make me call you King," I said to Hoffman. Then I threw the bottle. It smashed to bits directly in the middle of the open doorway, and the flames spread like wasps from a downed nest.

I watched the fire and smoke for a long moment before looking down at Hoffman again. He was staring up into my face, a knowing look in his eyes. "Rubble?" he said. "Terrence Rubble?"

"It's Trouble now," I said.

A moment later, screeching tires, sirens, and a lot of yelling competed with the roaring sound of the growing house fire.

Chapter 2

THE COP SHOVED ME into the small holding cell, shutting the door behind me. There were two other guys in the cell, sitting on a bench against the wall. There was a low block partition separating the single metal toilet from the rest of the space. Otherwise, that was it. A bolted-down bench, a partition, and a toilet. And two men. I met their gazes, hoping I was hiding any glimmer of recognition that might have come across my face.

"Back up," the cop said. I did, sticking my cuffed hands through the rectangular gap in the bars so the guy could retrieve the cuffs.

As the cop turned to leave, he said, "I'm sure you fuckheads will make fast friends." Then he was gone, leaving the three of us alone.

The two guys were white, like me. The guy in the corner was the older of the two. Mid-twenties. Broad shoulders. Muscular arms. He had a high-and-tight haircut that made him look like a jarhead. Brown eyes watched me as I paced back and forth in front of the cell door, muttering softly. I knew I stank like whiskey, and I wasn't trying to hide my drunkenness.

The second guy—the one closest to me—looked like Hitler's idea of perfection. Blond hair, blue eyes, fair skin. He had the skinny body of a runner. I pegged him for twenty-two years old.

Both of them were dressed like frat guys. They had polo shirts and khaki pants on. But they both wore combat boots on their feet. The older guy had random tattoos on his arms.

I kept the pair in my peripheral vision as I paced. The younger guy looked away after a few minutes, but the older one didn't. And it wasn't something I could let slide.

"What?" I said, stopping and raising my arms as I faced him. "What are you staring at?"

The guy got up without a word, stretching his spine toward the ceiling and puffing his chest out. The younger guy got up a moment later, although he looked reluctant. It took him a moment to get his game face on as he stood behind and to the side of his buddy.

I stepped up and got in the older guy's face. He was about as tall as me. Just over six foot. "You wanna do something?" I asked him, our faces inches apart. "I'll fuck you *both* up."

There was no going back now. I knew he wouldn't back down. And if I wanted his respect, I couldn't back down either. And getting this guy's respect was all I wanted. It was why I was here.

But I also knew something about him and his friend. I knew I could take them both, even drunk.

If there was any doubt in my mind about this, it disappeared a moment later as the guy opted for the worst possible move. He shoved me.

I could never understand the shoving thing. Not in a situation like this. If you were going to commit, commit. Shoving someone was wasting your first move, as far as I was concerned. And in many fights, the first move is the most important.

As he pushed me, I stepped my right foot back, allowing my body to turn slightly, putting myself in optimal position for throwing a punch. I whipped my right hip forward as my arm rocketed up, fist clenching as it came. His reaction time wasn't too bad, but it wasn't enough to save him. He pulled his head back, but my fist still caught him in the cheek and nose as it continued its arc. I felt his nose crunch under the blow.

Then he was stepping back, and I was moving forward, crowding him toward the younger guy in the small cell. I faked a left to the gut and, when he reacted, hit him with a right jab to the face.

The younger guy sidestepped and moved around, coming at me from the right. I twisted that way, sending the point of my elbow into the middle of his chest, knocking his breath away. I shoved him to the ground and then turned back to greet a fist. My head whipped backward with the blow. It was a good hit. But not good enough.

The older guy came forward, but he hesitated. He should've gone berserker on my ass while I was momentarily dazed. But he didn't. And I took full advantage.

He tried a weak left roundhouse, which I knocked away easily. I went for a right jab, and he turned slightly to his left, which was what I'd been hoping for. I stepped toward him, scything my left elbow up and slamming it into the side of his head. He stumbled and fell onto the bench, then onto the concrete floor. I got on top of him, straddling him and grabbing a fistful of shirt with my left hand while I readied my right elbow for a blow to the face. But I didn't deliver the blow.

"You done?" I asked. "You ready to treat me with the respect a brother deserves?"

I could hear the younger kid catching his breath behind me. I could hear him moving.

The older guy nodded, blinking dazedly.

"Tell your friend it's over," I said.

"Ty, it's over," the man said.

"You hear that, Ty?" I asked without turning around or lowering my elbow.

"Yeah," Ty said. "I heard it."

I let go of the guy's shirt and stood up. "What a fucking waste," I said with disgust as I stepped away from him. "White men fighting each other. That's exactly what *they* want."

Ty came around to help his buddy up while I got out of the way, sitting on the other side of the bench to catch my breath. I'd have a black eye. I could already feel it.

"The fuck do you know about it?" the older guy said, stepping around the partition and grabbing some toilet paper for his nose.

"What do you mean?" I asked. "Anyone with half a brain can see what's going on in this country. I know you've seen it. Unless those tattoos are just for show. If that's the case, I might have to finish beating your ass after all."

"I'm right here, motherfucker," he said, but his heart wasn't in it. He was done, and we both knew it. He sat down on the bench and held the wad of toilet paper to his nose.

"They aren't just for show," Ty said, coming to his buddy's defense. "We're actually doing something about it. What are—"

"Shut up, Ty," the older guy said. "Just shut up."

"Oh, are you?" I asked, leaning back. "Watch the news tonight—if you get out of here. You'll see what I did to some rich Jew's house."

That caught their attention. They both studied me for a moment. "What did you do?" the older guy asked.

"Like I said. Watch the news."

There was a long moment of silence before the older guy spoke again. "My name's Spencer," he said, his tone heading toward friendly. "What's yours?"

I looked at him, considering. "Terrence. People call me Trouble."

"Trouble, huh? That's a hell of a nickname."

"Suits me," I said.

"So is that why the cop said we'd make fast friends?" Spencer asked. "Are you down for the cause?"

"I don't know what 'cause' you're talking about. I just don't think it's right what's happening to whites in this country. In this *world*."

"So you, what? Painted a swastika on a kike's house?"

"Listen," I said, "I knew this guy, okay? He deserved whatever he got. He was a greedy piece of shit."

Ty and Spencer were silent. I stared out through the bars of the cell at the concrete wall across the way. And I knew it had worked.

I was in.

Chapter 3

I GOT MY PHONE call about an hour after being put in the cell. I made a show of coming back to the cell dejected, slumping down on my side of the bench and shutting my eyes. The truth was, I didn't call anyone. I didn't need to. I was confident the ploy had worked.

And after about twenty minutes of silence, Spencer spoke. "You know the fourteen words?" he asked.

I still had my eyes closed, and I pretended not to hear him.

"Hey, Trouble," he said, raising his voice. "You know the fourteen words?"

I opened my eyes. My left eye only opened halfway, thanks to the swelling from the blow I'd taken. Both guys were looking expectantly at me. "What?" I said. "Why do you care?"

"I might be able to help you get out of here," Spencer said. "Just tell me the words."

"How would that help me get out of here?" I asked, sitting up.

"We could post bail for you," Ty said, whispering.

"You don't even know how much my bond will be. Hell, *I* don't even know yet. I haven't seen a judge."

This didn't seem to dissuade either man. "Still," Spencer said. "We might be able to help."

I sighed. "We must secure the existence of our people and a future for white children," I said. "There. You happy now? I said your magic words. Can we leave now?"

Spencer smiled. "If we get you out of here, you'll owe us a debt," he said.

"If you can get me out of here, I'll do whatever I can to pay you back." I said this without much emotion. Like I didn't believe they could do it. Even though I knew they could. I slumped back on the bench and shut my eyes again.

Time passed.

I straightened up when a cop came to the cell. "Clark, Fisher, let's go," he said, unlocking the cell.

Ty and Spencer filed out of the cell and waited while the cop closed and locked it again. They both glanced in at me and gave me a nod before walking off toward the front of the station. I made no move. Just watched them leave.

Then I was alone in the cell.

A half-hour later, the same cop who'd brought me to the cell came back, stopping outside the cell door. "Hook up," he said.

I stood up, turned around, and put my hands through the gap in the door. The familiar and anxiety-inducing feeling of steel tightening around my wrists followed. Then I was walking ahead of the cop as he told me where to go.

There was nothing special about this jail. If you've seen one, you've seen them all. Heavy doors. Thick walls coated in glossy paint. The smell of industrial cleaning chemicals.

I soon found myself in a windowless interrogation room with two chairs and a table. The cop sat me down in one of the chairs and uncuffed me. He left without a word, closing the door behind him.

A minute later, a man and woman walked into the room and shut the door. The man, tall, Black, and friendly-faced, was Special Agent Hudson. The woman, slender, American Indian, and trying to hide her excitement, was Special Agent Nez.

"How'd it go?" Nez asked, focusing on my swollen left eye.

I looked up into their faces for a moment before casting my eyes down and slumping on the table. "I don't think they bought it," I said.

I risked a glance up. Hudson, the older of the two, had managed to keep his face impassive. But Nez looked like her favorite show had just been canceled. She made like she was tucking a strand of hair behind her ear, but there was no strand. Her shoulder-length onyx hair was arranged in a bun at the back of her head. She pulled out the other chair and sat down with a sigh. Then she looked at me. Something on my face gave it away.

"I'm gonna beat your ass," she said, standing up again, the metal chair scraping loudly against the concrete floor.

I grinned. And despite their best efforts not to, both Hudson and Nez smiled.

"I think we're good," I said.

"Don't *do* that to me," Nez said, putting her smile away. "I'm serious."

I put my hands up. "Hey, I'm just trying to keep things light. It's not like there are lives depending on us or anything."

With that, both special agents looked at me without a trace of humor.

"Jeez. Can't take a joke?" I said. The truth was, there was something about feds that made me want to mess with them. Granted, Hudson and Nez were only the second and third feds I'd met, but it was still hard to resist. Three out of three is a hundred percent, last I checked. But there was also the fact that I needed to keep things light for my own sanity. Spewing nonsense hate about Jews and protecting the white race made me feel downright dirty. I couldn't let myself get infected by that hate—the kind I felt coming off of Spencer. Not so much Ty—he wasn't there yet. But Spencer exuded hate like it was sweat.

And in my experience, even if you don't believe the things they're saying, just being around that kind of stuff was soul-sucking. So messing with these two feds was a defense mechanism of sorts.

Plus, it was fun.

Nez settled back into the seat while Hudson leaned against the wall. I told them about the interaction. They'd been watching the cell on a camera, but the feed didn't have sound. So they hadn't heard anything. They didn't want to risk sending me in with a wire or hiding one somewhere in the cell. I'd agreed completely.

Now, I told them, it was a waiting game. See if they really would post my bail. If not, then we'd have to try something else. Maybe even something that wouldn't involve me. And if that happened, I would be going to prison for a long while. Which was not something I particularly wanted to do.

Nez and Hudson wanted this little charade to succeed for different reasons. They didn't care if I went to prison. They wanted to prevent any further home-grown terrorist attacks.

Of course, I was all for that. I'd seen the coverage of the bombing in Cleveland. And although no one had taken credit for it, you didn't have to be Sherlock Holmes to deduce who the perpetrators were. When Black people and Jews are attacked, it's a good bet there's some Hitler-loving psychopaths involved. And if I could save some lives while keeping my own ass out of jail, I considered that a win-win.

But, like I told the feds, only time would tell.

Chapter 4

Coakley caught his breath as he leaned over the sink. The water ran pink as it washed the blood off his hands and down the drain.

"Holy shit," Dyer said from behind him. "Holy shit, I can't fucking believe it. You know how long I've known that guy?"

They were in the mudroom, and Dyer was leaning against a rack of open shelves with hooks for coats at the top and cubbies for boots near the bottom. He didn't have any blood on him. His hands were clean.

Coakley glanced over his shoulder. "Longer than you've known me," he said, rubbing his hands with soap to create a pink lather.

Dyer nodded. "Yeah. Longer than I've known you." He crossed his arms and stared at the floor, lost in thought. Coakley turned back to focus on his hands.

Dyer was in his late twenties, just a few years younger than Coakley. He had the fair skin of an Irishman and a boxy reddish beard jutting from his ruddy cheeks. His head was shaved to the scalp. He wore a Kimber 1911 pistol on his right hip.

"Well, you never know in this business," Coakley said. "You just never know."

"I just don't understand how someone could lie like that," Dyer said. "He should've told me as soon as the feds swooped him up. But he didn't. He lied. How the fuck do you get like that? What makes a person do that?"

"This is a war," Coakley said, turning off the water. "The feds know it. It's about time we know it, too." His hands weren't completely clean yet, but he wanted to stop this conversation as soon as possible. Dyer clearly hadn't noticed how Coakley had subtly influenced the interrogation they'd just performed. That was good. It meant his secret wouldn't come out this night. *One* of his secrets, anyway. He had too many to count, it seemed like. But the two biggest ones *couldn't* come out. Not if he wanted to go on breathing.

Using several paper towels from a roll on a dispenser on the wall, he dried his hands.

"Oh, I know," Dyer said, uncrossing his arms and standing up straight. "I fuckin' know it's a war. Believe that."

Coakley fixed his copper-colored eyes on the other man. "Don't say it like that."

"What?"

"'Believe that.' You sound like a monkey when you say shit like that."

Dyer said nothing, just cast his eyes down. Coakley tossed the ball of paper towels in a trash can and stepped out of the mudroom, into the hallway. He pulled out his phone and drafted a call. Bove picked up after two rings.

"Yeah?"

"You better come over here," Coakley said.

"It's him?"

"It's him."

Bove hung up the phone.

Coakley put the device away and leaned forward, placing one hand on either side of the kitchen doorway. Staring down at the slate tiles, he breathed deeply and wondered if he was crazy for doing this.

It was too late now. There was no turning back.

Like he'd said, this was a war. And it was one he was determined to win.

He stood up and said, "You want to smoke?"

Dyer came out of the mudroom. "Yeah."

They moved through the house and to the front door.

Stepping out onto the porch, the two men looked through the gloom and across the small valley at a house nestled into the opposite hill. The Cape Cod-style house featured two dormers facing out toward the valley. It was dark blue with white trim. It was less than a year old, like most of the homes tucked into the narrow valley just ten miles away from the rocky Oregon coast.

As Coakley took a smoke from Dyer, he waited for the door to open. Dyer lit his smoke and handed the lighter over. Coakley took it without looking. It was winter in Oregon, and chilly out. But he knew they wouldn't be outside for long.

The Cape Cod's windows glowed orange with inviting light. As Coakley lit his cigarette, the front door opened. A man stepped out, the sound of children's laughter spilling out after him. It was a sound that gave Coakley a badly needed dose of confidence. After all, that was why they were doing this. For the children. For the future of children like the ones laughing in the house across the valley.

Coakley had seen what was possible under Ethan Lee Bove's leadership. He knew they could win this war. But they had to be smart. They had to fight dirty. And Coakley was determined to be an integral part of that.

Bove, a man of average height and below-average weight in the Land of the Fat, walked down the sloping dirt driveway from the Cape Cod. He took his time. He never seemed to be in a hurry. When he got to the dirt road that ran down the length of the narrow valley, he looked up and saw the two men waiting for him. He raised a hand in greeting. Dyer and Coakley returned the gesture.

Bove kept the hair flanking his bald crown short and neatly trimmed. He was wearing brown slacks and a black collared shirt with the sleeves rolled up over thin forearms. No jacket, Coakley noted. A pistol sat snugly in a worn leather holster on his right hip. On his left hip, he kept his prized SS Dagger, attached to his belt with a clip. He moved up the steps on the hillside made of wooden railroad ties. The moonlight made the going easy. When he came up the porch steps, he looked at the two men, deep-set and heavy-lidded eyes under thin black eyebrows. "Let's see what we got," he said.

After Coakley and Dyer disposed of their cigarettes in the porch ashtray, the three men went through the house. Coakley opened the door to the garage and ushered the other two men inside.

Mark Hearn was unconscious in a metal chair in the middle of the space. His arms were strapped to the arms, his legs to the legs. The chair itself was affixed to the slab with concrete anchors and L-shaped flanges. Two work lights on tripods blasted him with white light. His once-handsome face was swollen and lacerated. The index and middle fingers of his right hand had been severed at the middle knuckles. The tops of these two fingers lay on the concrete where they'd fallen. The fingernails of his left hand had all been pulled out. Nearby sat a rolling workbench with an array of tools on it, some of them still bloody.

Bove crossed his arms and looked at the mess of the man before him. "Is he dead?"

Coakley moved past Bove and felt for a pulse. "No. Want me to wake him?" he asked.

Bove contemplated that for a moment before shaking his head. "No. You both heard him confess?"

Coakley nodded. Bove looked over his shoulder to see Dyer's answer.

"Yes, sir," the younger man said. "Took him a while, but he finally admitted it."

"But he's not a federal agent?" Bove asked, turning back to face Coakley.

"No. An informant," Coakley said.

Bove sighed. "What about the information? Is there anything other than the recording we found at his place?"

"He said the recording was all he had," Coakley replied. "He said it was a new thing. That they approached him less than a month ago."

"So what do they know?"

"Nothing. He hadn't had a chance to give it to them yet. And he didn't even know about this place. But we better be very careful from now on. If they got to him, you can bet they'll be trying to get to others."

"Do they know my name?" Bove asked, turning to Dyer. "I understand this was your friend, but I need to know the truth. Did you tell him about me? Did you tell him my name?"

Dyer swallowed and shook his head. "No, sir. I followed orders. I never talk about you to anyone other than the people in this room."

Bove looked at Coakley, who nodded. "I asked him what he told the feds. He said nothing yet. He just made the recording, and there wasn't much on that. But if we'd brought him into the inner circle . . ."

"Yes, well, that's why we do these kinds of checks beforehand," Bove said.

"I'm sorry, sir," Dyer began.

Bove put up a hand to stop him. "Not your fault, Dyer. Not your fault."

Hearn made a small moan and moved his head. Bloody saliva dripped from his mouth.

"Step back," Bove said to Coakley as he pulled his dagger out of its scabbard. Coakley did as he was told. Bove stepped up behind the bound and beaten man, grabbing a handful of his hair in one hand while positioning the blade at the left side of his neck. He yanked the man's head back so he could look into his face. Hearn's swollen eyelids struggled up. Finally, he got his eyes open as much as he could and looked up to see Bove standing there. Bove knew him, but he didn't know Bove. Although Coakley was sure he could guess who the man was. Hearn's mouth moved.

Bove jammed the dagger into his throat and dragged the blade under his jaw. A torrent of blood spewed out of the wound. He had to work a little harder to get through the cartilage at the front, cords of muscle standing out on his forearm. Hearn struggled ineffectually against his binds. When Bove got the blade to the right side, having opened both carotid arteries, he pulled the dagger out and straightened.

Coakley grabbed a roll of disposable shop towels from a nearby shelf and tore off several. He stepped around the still-twitching Hearn, avoiding the large puddle of blood on the smooth concrete floor, and handed the towels to Bove.

"Sorry to leave you with the cleanup, but I need to get back across the street," Bove said as he cleaned his dagger off.

Coakley nodded. Dyer said, "Yes, sir."

Bove walked to the same door they'd come through, now working to clean off his blood-coated hand. As he got to it, he turned around. "I know this wasn't easy," he said. "But you two did good." He tossed the bloody shop towels down and pointed at them. "My DNA is all over those," he said. "I'm trusting you two to get rid of them. And of him."

He opened the door and stepped out of the garage, shutting it behind him.

Coakley looked up at Dyer. The two men smiled grimly at each other.

Then they got to work.

Chapter 5

FIVE DAYS BEFORE I ended up in jail with a couple of white suprema-cists, I had been paying a little visit to my old friend Mr. Hoffman. I'd rented a car from a used car lot with a handful of cash, leaving my motorcycle parked on the lot for a hefty fee. I wasn't in the habit of carrying credit cards, and I didn't want to leave any sort of paper trail. I needed the car because it's much easier to perform a stakeout in a car than it is on a motorcycle.

Through some combination of drug use and good old-fashioned repression, I'd managed for many years to blank out memories of my time at the Hoffman household as a child. But time has a way of bringing these things back to the surface. Nothing stays buried forever.

Despite being wanted by police in California, I felt it was my duty to come back to my home state and see how the Hoffmans were doing. Once I remembered their treatment of me and the other foster kids under their care, there was really no other choice. Checking up on the two child abusers wasn't something I wanted to do. It was something I *had* to do.

Truth be told, I wasn't entirely sure what I would do if I found them. And as I sat down the street from their house, watching Mr. Hoffman leave the place in his Lexus, I still didn't know. As far as I could tell, they were no longer acting as foster parents to any kids. That was good. Priority number one, check. I could breathe a little.

When trying to locate the Hoffmans, I'd come to the realization that I didn't know either of their first names. It had been nearly thirty years since I'd seen either of them. And if I'd ever known their first names, they were gone now, lost to the sands of time. In public, or when a social worker was present, we were told to call them Mr. and Mrs. Hoffman. But when it was just us and them, we were instructed to call Mr. Hoffman King and Mrs. Hoffman Queen. They treated us about as well as monarchs across all recorded history treated their lowest subjects, so the self-aggrandizing nicknames made sense.

But after a little digging, I learned that King Hoffman's name was Lyle. Lyle Hoffman. And his wife's name had been Shelly. My search—I say mine, but it was really my tech-savvy friend Dylan who did the heavy lifting—told me that Queen Hoffman had died three years earlier at the ripe old age of sixty-eight. The official ruling was death by massive coronary, but I figured it was just karma doing its thing. Better late than never.

But old Lyle was still up and kicking at seventy-two.

About an hour before he left the house in his Lexus, I watched him walk out and check the mail. The man in my memory was heavy around the waist and always seemed to have a five o'clock shadow. The man I saw walk out of the McMansion was thin and stooped. But it was him. I knew before he'd taken three steps down from the front porch that it was him. The years had made him lean, but not in a healthy way. He looked sickly, the stubble on his face gray, the wispy hair on his head stirred by the light breeze. Maybe karma was catching up with him, too. Maybe the walking tumor had actually grown a tumor.

Call me sick, deranged, and callous if you like, but I took some small amount of satisfaction in his appearance. But he'd lived a long life. And he'd done well for himself, by the looks of it. People like him didn't deserve either of those things, in my opinion.

He used to beat, threaten, intimidate, and mentally abuse children. He and his wife. I didn't know if they did anything else. Anything sexual. It was possible, I supposed, but I'd never been subjected to such awful things.

They had seemed to take pleasure in our discomfort. They only fed us one meal a day. They had strict rules about what we could and couldn't do, and there'd always been hell to pay if we so much as bent one of their precious rules. We kept up their yard, cleaned their house, and waited on them. And if we didn't do what they said, they would beat us. Always on the body, so the bruises wouldn't show.

But things got worse than that. I got to where I didn't mind a beating. I would take credit for things I didn't do to keep other kids from the fist or the belt. And Lyle Hoffman saw what I was doing. He saw that the threat of violence wasn't working on me. So he started threatening my friends. Other kids there. He would beat *them* instead. One girl, Melissa, got the brunt of it before I did something I'll regret forever. I ran away.

And I couldn't live with the guilt of what I done, leaving little Melissa in the hands of those two monsters. So, somewhere in my preteen or early teen years, I learned to block that time of my life out.

But a recent conflict had brought everything back to the surface. And I knew I had to do something about it.

So here I was, watching Hoffman, wondering what I should do. I had no idea as I sat in that overpriced rental car that my actions would soon throw me into a shitshow the likes of which I'd never faced in my life.

And I've had what some might call a life of conflict. My name is Trouble, after all.

As Hoffman's black Lexus sedan bumped out of his driveway and drove away from me, I decided I'd wait for him to come back home. It would give me time to decide on a course of action.

It would be no fair fight to go at him with my fists. Never mind that it would be a kind of poetic justice for him picking on kids he outweighed three-to-one. Never mind that he deserved a few broken bones. I couldn't do it. I couldn't beat up a stooped, skinny, sickly old man.

So I started thinking about making him apologize. Or getting him to confess to some of the stuff he'd done, and then handing the confession over to the police. Or maybe just breaking some of his stuff to get my anger out.

I had to do something. Even if that something was more symbolic than anything. I couldn't just let it go. I needed to close the loop in my own mind.

About fifteen minutes after Hoffman left his house, I decided I would start with a little conversation. It would be up to him how things went from there. I would have to gauge his responses. I would look into his eyes and see what was there. See if he'd changed. Repented, maybe. Then I would decide what to do with the old bastard. Maybe I was wrong. Maybe I *could* beat up a stooped, skinny, sickly old man, under the right circumstances. I wasn't yet ready to rule anything out.

But I never got the chance to find out. Not then.

A vehicle came up behind me, moving slowly. I immediately recognized it. It had driven past once before, not five minutes earlier. It was a black and silver Jeep Wrangler. The newer kind with the back windows that are proper windows, not just pieces of plastic you zip on. The first time the vehicle drove by, there had been nothing on the driver's side door panel. I was sure of that. But this time, there was. I could see the magnetic sign in the rearview mirror. And although I couldn't read it as the vehicle crept up on me, I had a good idea what it would say.

"Fantastic," I mumbled as the Jeep—which was doing maybe five miles an hour—finally came up beside me. It stopped in the middle of the street next to my rental. I ducked down and looked out the passenger window while waving hello at whoever was in the Jeep; thanks to the tinted window, I couldn't see more than a vague shape.

This also gave me a chance to read the magnetic sign. It was white lettering on a stars-and-stripes background. *Neighborhood Watch*.

Chapter 6

Despite not being able to see the person inside, I waved and gave a thumbs-up, hoping they would just leave.

They didn't.

The driver's side door opened and a man in his fifties stepped out. He wore black cargo shorts and bulky white tennis shoes. His oversized Hawaiian shirt did an adequate job of hiding his gut. He left his door open, bent at the waist so he could see me, and then gestured for me to roll down the window. He had a thick head and salt-and-pepper hair in need of a trim, but my first impression was he had a friendly face. He had his lips tucked together and his brow slightly furrowed, like he was sorry to bother me.

Instead of rolling the window down, I opened my door and stepped out. It was still winter in Southern California, the temperature a downright chilly mid-sixties.

"Sir, stay in the car please," the guy said as I got out.

I pretended not to hear him, wondering if he would say it again. He did.

"Sir, I need you to stay in the car."

I looked at him over the top of my rental—a pale blue Toyota Camry. I was standing on the sidewalk, so I was now considerably taller than him. Donning my best confused-but-harmless look, I glanced at my car and then back to him. "What? Why?"

The guy exhaled loudly, but he dropped it. "Do you live here?" he asked.

"No."

He waited for more information. I looked at him.

"What are you doing here?" he asked.

"I was just sitting in my car."

"Why?"

"Seemed like a good place to sit. I was tired of driving." I could've made something up. About a dozen things came to mind. But, for some reason, I wanted to see how far this guy would take it. Maybe it was some spillover anger from seeing Hoffman. Maybe it was the power trip the guy was clearly on that made me angry. Maybe it was the fact that if I'd been in a nicer car and not dressed in a leather jacket and worn jeans, he probably wouldn't have given me a second thought.

No matter the reason, I was going to make this guy work for it.

"If you don't live here, I'm going to have to ask you to leave," the man said, raising a hand toward the quickest way out of the neighborhood.

I leaned forward and propped my elbows on the roof of my rental. "You're going to have to ask me to leave . . . a public street?"

"That's right," he said. "Or I will be forced to call the authorities."

"And tell them what? 'I'd like to report a man sitting in a car.' Come on, man. Give me a break. I'm not doing anything wrong." Okay, maybe I was planning the possible assault of one of the residents of the neighborhood this man took it upon himself to watch. But he had no way of knowing that. I wasn't breaking any laws. Yet.

"I really don't want to have to call the authorities, sir. Go find another neighborhood to sit in."

"What's your name?" I asked him.

His eyes narrowed.

"Not like that," I said, waving a hand. "Your first name. My name's Terrence. What's yours?"

"Gary," the man said warily.

"Hey, Gary," I said. "Listen, I have a perfectly legitimate reason to be here, okay? I also don't feel like I need to tell every complete stranger who happens to come up and ask me what that reason is. I think that sitting in a car on the side of a public road—without a red curb or a 'No Parking' sign in sight—is something that's allowed. Don't you think so?"

While I spoke, I could tell from Gary's body language that he was doubling down. I wasn't convincing him, which was a shame. So when he said, "Leave now or I'll call the police," I was not surprised. He then got back in his Wrangler and drove off down the street, quickly getting up to thirty miles an hour in the twenty-five.

I got back in the sedan, knowing I hadn't seen the last of Gary. Or if I had, I would soon be talking to the police. I didn't want to do that. I also didn't want to give in to Gary's completely ridiculous order to leave.

It took me the better part of five minutes to decide to leave, but I didn't think there was a big hurry. A call like Gary's would be low on the list of priorities for the local police station. But my slow decision-making process soon came back to bite me.

As I turned the keys and fired up the engine, Gary's Wrangler and a dark green Chevy truck sped around the corner ahead of me at the end of the block. I turned the wheel and pulled gently away from the curb, thinking if they saw I was leaving they would just let me go. But before I'd even made it to the right side of the road, the vehicles were on me.

The Chevy blocked my path forward while the Wrangler bounced up onto the sidewalk on its way to stop behind my rented Camry.

I put the vehicle in park, surprised at this turn of events. Gary hadn't struck me as the action-taking type. This seemed all wrong. Normal people operating under normal circumstances try to avoid confrontation. But it was clear these guys were itching for a fight. And guys they were. Two men got out of the truck, both of them carrying baseball bats. In my rearview mirror, I saw Gary getting out of the Wrangler. He had a pistol in his hand.

What the hell? I thought. It wasn't like I told him to fuck off—at least not in so many words—so why the sudden escalation?

I reached for my right jacket pocket, sticking my fingers inside and feeling the butt of my Sig Sauer P320 pistol. But I came to my senses and pulled my hand back out again. I hoped I could de-escalate the situation.

But as it turned out, I was wrong.

Chapter 7

"GET OUT OF THE car!" the driver of the Chevy yelled, standing next to the front left tire and gazing through the windshield at me. He had a narrow black mustache on a face red with anger. He wore khaki dress pants and a white dress shirt, tucked in. His buddy was a bit younger—maybe late thirties—and more casually dressed in jeans and a blue button-up. He stood near the other tire, looking in at me, his aluminum baseball bat hanging down by his side. Gary was still behind me, looking around nervously with his gun held by his thigh.

I rolled the window down a crack and said, "I'm good, thank you. I don't want any."

Stupid. Sometimes, I just can't help myself. My mouth has a way of getting me into trouble. And I'd been through a great many confrontations in the last couple of years. I'd gone up against people much more serious and frightening than this little ragtag crew. My senses had dulled, I guess.

The guy with the mustache brought his baseball bat up and smashed it down on the side mirror, busting it off with the dry crack of snapping plastic.

"Come on, man!" I said. "This is a rental."

"Get out!" the guy shouted.

I opened the door and stepped out, letting the guy come around the door and grab me by the collar of my leather jacket.

I held my hands up, letting him lead me away from the car and onto the sidewalk. "Search it," he said to his buddy.

"What for?" I asked. "What the hell do you think I have in there?"

The guy didn't answer me, and his buddy propped his bat against the front of the car before stepping over and yanking the passenger door open.

"Gary, what's going on here?" I asked.

Gary looked momentarily apologetic before getting control of himself again.

"Shut up," Mustache said, pulling on my collar.

The younger guy—but still older than me—pulled the paperwork out of the glove box and tossed it on the floor.

"Hey, that's not even my stuff," I said. "It's a rental."

"Shut up," Mustache said again.

It took Mustache's friend a few minutes to go through the whole car. When he was done, he looked up at his buddy from the open trunk and shook his head. "Nothing."

"What were you looking for?" I asked.

"Search him," Mustache said.

"That's not going to happen," I said.

Mustache's buddy hesitated. I looked him in the eye and shook my head.

"Do it!"

"Why don't you just let me leave, huh?" I asked, talking to Mustache. "That's what I was trying to do when you rolled up on me."

"What are you hiding?" Mustache asked.

"Nothing," I said. "But I draw the line at the neighborhood Gestapo violating my personal space."

Apparently, something I said really pissed Mustache off, because the next thing I knew, his baseball bat was crosswise against my throat. He was behind me, a hand on the bat on either side of my head, choking me with the thing. I reached up and grabbed the bat, my hands next to his, and tried to push it off. But I couldn't get enough leverage. I could feel my throat collapsing under the hard metal of the bat, and I knew that even if he wasn't trying to, he could end up killing me if he went too far.

Still holding onto the bat, I jackknifed my upper body forward, looking to throw Mustache over my head and onto his back on the sidewalk. But he dropped his weight just in time, preventing me from getting the momentum needed. So I did the next best thing. I flopped over onto my back, in the grass of someone's front yard. And since Mustache was hanging on my back, I landed on top of him, making sure to throw my head backward on impact. I felt the back of my head smash into his nose. His hands loosened on the bat, and I shoved, breaking his grip and freeing myself.

Scrambling up, I yanked the bat away from him as blood flowed out of his nose and into his narrow mustache. It was clear he was dazed from the blow to the head, so I turned my attention to his buddy, who was coming at me with his bat up and ready to swing. Gary was the bigger threat, but I could see out of the corner of my eye that he hadn't lifted the gun. Yet.

When Buddy was still two steps away, I whipped my right arm and the bat forward, sending the top of it hurtling toward the guy while loosening my grip and allowing the body to pass through my fist without actually letting go of it. Like halfway between throwing it and jabbing with it. The knob at the bottom hit the base of my palm, and I gripped it tightly again—but my arm still had some more of an arc to travel toward the guy's head. A split second later, the top of the bat hit Buddy in his mouth. The result was exactly what I'd hoped for. I still had the bat in hand, while Buddy was stumbling backward, momentarily distracted from bludgeoning me to death. Win-win.

But then I turned to see Gary. He'd brought the gun up. He was pointing it directly at me. And he had his finger on the trigger.

Chapter 8

"GARY," I SAID, DROPPING the bat and putting my hands up. "I'm done, now, okay? I was just protecting myself, but I'm done now."

He was taking shallow breaths, his eyes as wide as close-range bullet wounds. I watched his trigger finger, waiting for the pink skin to go white as he squeezed. Meanwhile, both Mustache and Buddy were coming around. I knew if I made another move, Gary would shoot me. And when his pals were ready to fight again—which would be soon—I would be out of options.

But that old saying about cops never being around when you need them was proved wrong as a squad car turned onto the road. I didn't see it at first, because it came from behind me. But I saw Gary's face change as he looked over my shoulder. And I saw Buddy, who had both hands clamped over his damaged mouth, look that way too. I glanced over my shoulder, never so happy to see a black-and-white in my life.

That happiness was short-lived because I knew I would be going to jail. And probably prison soon after that, thanks to the warrants I was sure I had out in the great state of California. Whether that was better than being dead, I wasn't entirely sure.

The cop worked quickly to take control of the situation. The first thing she did was to make Gary put the gun down. I was kind of surprised she didn't just start firing at him. That seemed to be the default move for a lot of cops. I was thankful for her cool head, considering I might've been caught in the crossfire.

Soon enough, two other squad cars showed up and started sorting through the mess of which I'd been a major part. I sat cross-legged on the curb with my hands cuffed behind me while the police officers interviewed the other three men, one at a time, out of earshot.

I was searched and arrested, although the officers didn't tell me what exactly for. I figured several things. Assault, for one. Possession of a firearm without a proper license, probably. It didn't matter. The woman had clearly run my name through the system. I should've known better. The last time I was in California, I'd been arrested by sheriff's deputies. It was a whole thing. And definitely not one I was keen to relive.

I was taken to the local jail and processed, and there I sat for a little over a day, wondering when I'd get my phone call. I didn't know who I would call, though. I had no idea who could help get me out of the mess I was in.

Then, on the afternoon of the day following my arrest, one of the cops came and got me from the single-person cell they'd put me in. The guy led me to an interview room and sat me down. I waited for about fifteen minutes before two feds walked in and introduced themselves as Special Agents Hudson and Nez.

"You're currently facing at least ten years," Nez said to start the conversation off. "How would you like to bring that down closer to zero?"

I narrowed my eyes. "I'm listening."

***

Despite my best efforts to avoid it, I sometimes read the news. So when Hudson and Nez started talking about white supremacist organizations, I knew what they were referring to. I'd read the headlines. I'd heard about the Cleveland bombing and the too-many-to-count mass shooters who'd been steeped in the racist bullshit for so long that it was all they thought about.

Of course, this was nothing new for America. Anyone who knows history knows that. Every country has to deal with a different flavor of home-grown terrorist at some point. In America, you had idiots running around wearing white sheets and other idiots running around talking about how a German madman's vision of the world sounded hunky-dory to them.

But in recent years, it seemed like it was getting worse. What had once been relegated to dark corners of the internet or whispered conversations among closet racists seemed to be invading the mainstream. Blatantly bigoted conspiracy theories were parroted by talking heads on major news networks and written into the permanent record in Congress by members of the House and Senate.

And the ranks of these homegrown terrorist organizations were growing.

Nez and Hudson started explaining this to me like it was a class on sociology.

"Yeah," I said finally, cutting Hudson off. "I read the news. What do you need me for? How can I possibly help some willfully ignorant dipshits see the light?"

The two special agents seated across the metal table looked at each other, then back at me. "We want you to infiltrate a white supremacist organization we think is planning a string of major attacks," Nez said.

I just stared at them, my mouth hanging slightly open. "How the hell do you propose I do that? I don't have any ties to racist organizations. In fact, I've been known to come down pretty hard on those kinds of people."

"On paper, you're an ideal candidate," Hudson said, placing his perfectly manicured hand on a closed leather file folder in front of him.

I thought about asking him if all FBI agents had hands like his, but I could see Nez's hands, and they weren't anything like his. Her nails needed trimming and her hands had seen plenty of hard work. Maybe that was indicative of why they made a good team—if they did. I had no idea. I'd only known them for about five minutes. I was still trying to get a read on them. But at a glance, they seemed to complement each other.

"What does that mean? 'On paper'?" I asked.

"It means you're the type of person they're looking for," Nez put in.

"And what type of person is that?"

"A history of violence. Facing some prison time. Disregard for authority. Willing to get his hands dirty," Nez said. "With a little tweaking, we can make it look like you've been on the path toward violent extremism for a long time. It won't be hard."

"I'm flattered, I guess," I said. "But you think they'll actually check my criminal record? And—not to look a gift horse in the mouth—why don't you just get a professional to infiltrate this organization? Isn't that what you guys do?"

"They *will* check your record," Hudson said. "They have their tentacles in law enforcement and military institutions around the country. It's impossible to keep them all out."

I waited for him to answer the other question. Once again, the two of them shared a look. Then, on some invisible signal, Nez took over again. I was starting to think these two *were* a good team.

"We were working an informant already," she said. "We think he was compromised. Which is why we need someone like you."

"Holy shit," I said, leaning back. "Is your guy dead? You think he spilled that you guys are onto them?"

"We're not telling you any more until you agree to our terms," Hudson said, opening his leather file folder and retrieving a thin document. "I've put it in writing."

He slid the document over. It was three pages, with the final page being the place for me to sign. I read it over twice, then I looked back at the two agents. "Did you guys talk to Murke about me?"

Murke was a guy I'd done some work with in the past. He was a spook, and I wasn't sure if the two three-letter organizations spoke to each other. But I was willing to bet they did. And I was pretty sure it was why my name had even popped up in the FBI's system when I'd been arrested.

"We know about the unofficial work you've done for the US Government, yes," Hudson said.

I nodded. It made sense. I wasn't a complete amateur in their eyes. I'd had some experience. Although I'd never been undercover before. Not like they wanted me to be. Still, they were in a bind, and I was looking like a good alternative to a trained operative. And if I died on this little job, it wouldn't take much for them to wash their hands of the thing. It would probably look like I was just another prison-bound racist who gave his life for the cause.

I didn't think too much about it. Honestly, it was something I probably would have done anyway if I'd had the opportunity. There's nothing I like more than messing with idiots. Especially the dangerous ones. And these people made me sick. They were giving America a bad name. They were responsible for the deaths of innocent people.

So I signed the document and slid it back over to Hudson.

"When are these attacks supposed to go down?" I asked.

"We don't know exactly," Nez said. "But certain chatter suggests it could be as soon as next week."

I tried to hide my surprise. But by the look on their faces, I didn't do a good job of it.

"We better get to work," Hudson said. "Are you ready?"

Chapter 9

MY TWO NEW FRIENDS called one of the cops and asked him to bring my property to me. When the guy came back, he handed Hudson the plastic bag of my stuff and frowned at me. I grinned at him as he left.

"What about the guys who were arrested with me?" I asked as we stood up to leave. "The neighborhood Gestapo."

"They'll be released without charges, if they haven't been already," Nez said, opening the door.

Hudson gestured for me to head out. He still had my property, and he apparently wasn't ready to give it back yet. I walked out the door and followed Nez while Hudson fell in behind me.

"I don't think that's a good idea. Those guys might've killed me if the cops hadn't shown up when they did," I said.

"You know why they were all riled up?" Nez asked, looking over her shoulder.

I shrugged.

"Because four days ago their neighborhood was blanketed with racist pamphlets," she explained. "It's been happening more and more. Especially in upper-middle-class neighborhoods like that."

"Racist pamphlets?" I asked. I hadn't heard about these.

"Yeah. They're more like flyers," Hudson said. "They put them in little plastic bags to keep them dry and weigh them down with a little bit of dry rice or pebbles or something like that so they're heavy enough to stay put. Easier to throw that way, too."

I remembered the guys searching my rental car and not finding anything. It suddenly made sense. They were looking for a cache of racist flyers they thought I was getting ready to throw out. I suddenly felt bad about busting up their faces. Kind of.

"What did these flyers say?" I asked as we went through a door and headed into the bullpen. A couple of cops sitting at desks glanced up at us as we went through. Nez and Hudson ignored them. I smiled and gave them a thumbs-up as I passed.

"You know, the normal stuff. Blaming everything wrong in the world on Jewish people or Black people or immigrants. And, of course, advertising a website that spreads this kind of nonsense."

"You know who did it? Is it the same group that's planning these attacks?"

"All these groups network," Nez said. "Many of their members belong to more than one, so it can be hard to tell the difference. But we think that whoever's handing out flyers is a small part of a much larger problem. They're probably not exactly the same people who are planning the attacks, but I would be willing to bet they're working toward the same goal."

"What's that?"

"To collapse society and start a race war," Nez replied. "They think white people will rise up and kill everyone who doesn't have the same amount of melanin as they do."

I was speechless for a few long moments as we went out a back door and into the fenced-off parking lot behind the building. Cruisers sat around in the lot, gleaming in the afternoon sunlight. Nez led us to a black SUV. As we got in, I said, "They really think that's going to happen? Don't they realize that they're in the minority by pretty big margin?"

Nez shrugged in the driver's seat. "They think every white person is secretly racist, I guess. Or maybe they don't believe it will actually happen. Maybe they just want to cause some chaos. Wreak some havoc. Kill some Jews and Blacks and browns. They're definitely obsessed with military tactics and culture."

"Huh," I said. It was all I could think of. The reality of my situation was starting to dawn on me. And I was beginning to realize that I would have to be steeped in hate myself if I was going to be convincing. The thought made my stomach churn.

As Nez put the vehicle in reverse, Hudson reached back and gave me my property. Well, everything except my gun.

"You'll get the weapon back later," he said before I could ask.

I nodded reluctantly.

Then we were rolling through the gate and turning out of the police station. I looked out the window at the people on the sidewalks and in the cars. For the first time, I was overly conscious of the color of their skin. It wasn't something I'd really thought about before. At least not in this light, anyway. To say I didn't "see" race would be a lie. Of course I did. I had eyes. But I'd never let someone's race affect my thoughts before. I'd never let it change my attitude toward a person before I could get to know them. To judge them based on their actions and the way they treated me or those around them. I approached everyone with a certain degree of skepticism, ready for anything. But lumping everyone of a certain race together—assuming they all had the same personalities, beliefs, goals, attitudes, and outlook—seemed pretty dumb to me. Probably because it *was* dumb.

I thought for a moment what it would feel like to be angry at or frightened by someone who didn't have the same skin color as me. I tried that mindset on for size as we drove. It was like trying on a pair of shoes two sizes too small—and putting them on the wrong feet. Was this how these people actually lived? Was this how they saw the world? Was every Black person a threat to their identity? Their way of life? Was every Jewish person—and I wasn't sure how you could tell someone was Jewish by looking at them—conspiring against them?

I felt ill after a few miles of driving. But mostly I felt sad for people who thought this way. I felt a deep pity for them. It was such a narrow and ignorant view of the world. You had to willfully ignore all the everyday occurrences that negated the racist worldview. And I could see how living with this poison in your mind would drive you crazy. How it would make you miserable. And violent. And dangerous.

But most of all, I could see why these people—whoever they were—were wrong. I didn't think there was any point in arguing or debating with people like that. There was no question in my mind that what they believed was just plain wrong. And there was no question that they needed to be stopped before they caused any more damage.

Really, it made no difference to me *why* they wanted to kill innocent people, just as it made no difference what those innocent people looked like or what god they worshipped. They were people. Just like me.

The only ones who gave up their right to be left alone were the ones who went after the innocent. After that, all bets were off.

Chapter 10

"IT'S NOT LIKE ACTING. Don't think of it as acting. That's what movies and shows get wrong." Nez and I were sitting on the back patio of the FBI safe house, or rental, or vacation property. Whatever it was, it was one of the nicer places I'd ever been to—especially since having been arrested a little more than a day before. Usually, your circumstances change for the worse when you've been arrested. Luck was on my side, for a change. But I wasn't all that eager to press it.

"So what's it like if it's not like acting?" I asked Nez while looking out at the sparkling swimming pool and the landscaped border around it. There were three or four different kinds of palm plants growing up against the brick fence that enclosed the place. The grass was getting a little yellow, though. And it needed a trim.

"It's like being a different version of yourself," Nez said. I could feel her dark eyes boring into the side of my head. I could tell she thought I wasn't taking this seriously. But I was. Just in my own way. I was easing into it like a new pair of riding gloves. Trying it on for size. And considering that she was someone who was, presumably, American Indian, I figured I better work on the habit of not looking someone I was supposed to pretend to hate in the eye.

Did white supremacists have a thing against American Indians? Surely they did. I was guessing their whole philosophy could be summed up as, "If it ain't white, it ain't right." I would've laughed if it wasn't so dumb.

"Okay," I said, enjoying the winter breeze, which wasn't all that different from a spring or fall breeze in this part of California. "So you're telling me I need to find a version of myself that's racist?"

"Kind of, yes," she said. "Just use your own past. Use your own experiences but tweak them in a way that will make it seem like you've been developing a racial hatred for years that's only just now really surfacing. Just don't lie about anything unless you absolutely have to. The more lies you tell, the more likely it is that you'll get caught in one. And if you do that, you're as good as dead."

I pursed my lips and turned to look at her. "Got it. So, lie without lying. Don't act. Be myself, but a version of myself I've never been before and would never be in a million years."

"Oh, don't give me that shit," she said, surprising me. "We all have it in us. It's human nature to fear those who are different. Just tap into it. Use it to become one of them. You won't be under long enough to start having psychological problems."

"You mean *more* psychological problems?" I said. Nez rewarded me with a smile. It was a brilliant one, too.

"You said it, not me."

I smiled back.

"There's really not much to it," she said, turning serious again. "The simpler you keep things, the better. You've been a career criminal your whole adult life, right?"

"Allegedly," I said. "I've had a few straight jobs."

Nez cocked an eyebrow.

"Fine. Yes. But I've always picked my jobs carefully. I'm not some smash-and-grab idiot who goes around robbing civilians, you know."

"I know. I'm not judging you. I'm trying to make the point that you're already cut out for this kind of work. Half of undercover work is controlling your fear and anxiety. Not letting it show. You must have some practice in that area."

I shrugged. "Yeah, I guess so."

"Good. So now all you need to do is create a legend."

"What's that?"

"It's who you are when undercover. Who you'll be presenting to The White Power Alliance. The racist version of yourself, complete with anecdotes based on real events in your life that illustrate your worth to the cause."

"Okay."

"And you'll need to memorize some stuff. Like the fourteen words and a few other common sayings."

"What are the fourteen words?"

"It's kind of like a slogan used by various white power groups," Nez said. "'We must secure the existence of our people and a future for white children.' It was coined by David Lane, a member of a terrorist group called The Order."

"Great," I said. "This is going to be fun."

"I can tell you're excited," she said, matching my deadpan tone.

The sliding glass door behind us opened, and Hudson stepped out. He'd been inside the house, trying to set up a way to get me in with the group. He didn't have his jacket on, and his white long-sleeved shirt was rolled up over thin but muscular forearms. "Alright, we're on for day after tomorrow," he said.

"Day after *tomorrow*?" I said. "I thought I would have some time to learn this nonsense."

"You do," Hudson said, looking at me like I was surprised that night follows day. "You have slightly less than two days."

I looked at Nez, but her dark-brown eyes were hard. There was no support there. "Fine," I said turning my chair to face the table. "So how are we going to do this?"

Hudson remained standing. "There's a small peace march scheduled for Tuesday in Santa Clarita. It's in response to the racist fliers that have been showing up in the area. We have it on good authority that some White Power Alliance foot soldiers will be there for a counter-protest. We know that they use these marches as a rallying cry for other white supremacists to come out and join the fun. Then they recruit from the nearby jail."

"What? They recruit from the jail? Why not just recruit at the counter-protest?"

"It's kind of brilliant, actually," Nez said, taking over. "They know that any of the counter-protesters who get arrested are willing to take action. They don't want people who just show up and shout insults at the protesters. They want people who show up and start fights. So by recruiting from the jail, they know that the guys they get are serious about the cause."

"They also post bail for these guys," Hudson said. "And then they do their best to make sure they never show up for court. Once there's a warrant out for their arrest, it pushes these new recruits deeper into The White Power Alliance. They're offered protection, training, and a place to stay where they won't be arrested and sent to prison. Plus, they have the whole bail thing hanging over their heads. It's a great way to get serious foot soldiers for the cause."

I was starting to see how the system worked. If these guys knew they'd be facing prison time, then it wouldn't be a hard decision to stay with the WPA. They would have a cause to fight for and a brotherhood to do it with. But it didn't make total sense to me. "What about the money?" I asked. "If they skip their court dates, then the WPA doesn't get their money back. How can they afford to do that?"

Nez and Hudson looked at each other. "They have plenty of money," Nez said to me. "We just don't know where it comes from. They deal in various cryptocurrencies, which makes things difficult to track for us. We can track cryptocurrency transactions—anyone can—but we have to know the specific wallet addresses they use. And they do something called chain hopping—exchanging one coin for another and another in quick succession. This makes them hard to track. Regardless, it's clear they have money to burn."

My mind immediately went to work on that. Did they have a wealthy backer? Or did they have some other source of income? I didn't think that their little YouTube channels and content machines could generate nearly as much money as the feds seemed to think they had. But it wasn't my most immediate concern.

"So you want me to go to the counter-protest and, what, start a fight with some activists?"

"That's right," Hudson said.

"But I thought that's only how they recruit foot soldiers. Isn't that what you said?"

"Yeah," Nez replied. "So?"

"So if the attacks are supposed to be within the next month, then I won't have enough time to work my way up the ranks, right?"

"We'll just have to make do with whatever information you do get," Hudson said, finally pulling out a patio chair and sitting down at the table.

"There's no way they'll tell the foot soldiers everything," I said. "At most, I'll get to hear about one attack. Maybe two, if I'm lucky. We won't be able to do anything about the others."

"Maybe you can help us arrest one of the leaders. We can lean on him and get him to spill about the others," Hudson said.

I shook my head, clasping my hands together on the table. "If we're going to do this, we need to do it right. And I think I have a way to make myself stand out. You said the protests are going to be in Santa Clarita? That's where I was arrested yesterday, in Stevenson Ranch."

"Yeah, so?" Nez said.

"So I was there to pay a visit to a guy I used to know. A real piece of work. And his last name's Hoffman. That's a Jewish name, right?"

Their defenses immediately went up. Their backs straightened as they looked at me through narrowed eyes. "What's your point?" Nez asked. "What are you proposing?"

"Just hear me out," I said. And I told them my plan.

***

"No," both Hudson and Nez said at the same time. "No way."

"Think about it," I said. "If I'm willing to set a guy's house on fire, what else would I be willing to do for the cause? That would make me stand out over all the other recruits. Going in, I would be a legend. I'm betting the higher-ups would want to meet me. To shake the hand of a guy who burned a Jew's house down. Don't you think? Isn't that better than just fighting some protesters?"

When they both hesitated, I knew I'd gone a long way to convincing them.

"It's been a wet winter here, so there's a lower chance of causing a wildfire. We can have the fire department ready for it," I said. "And best of all, it would make sense that I'd end up in the same jail as anyone from the protests. With a little work, you can get me in the same cell with the WPA guys. I can do the rest from there."

"This is insane," Hudson said.

"This is the best shot we have of getting me in a position to stop all the attacks, not just one or two," I said. "You know I'm right. And, of course, I'll make sure the guy's out of the house before I torch it. I'll make sure it's empty."

"It could work," Nez said, tapping her chin with one finger and turning to Hudson. "But he is the very definition of a flight risk. We'd have to tweak his record a bit for it to look natural that the judge would give him bail. But we were going to have to do that anyway."

"And what if the bail is too much for them to want to pay?" Hudson said. "What if they don't offer to pay it?"

"Then I'll get out anyway and say I called in a favor or something," I said. "But I bet they'll pay it. If what you guys say is true, then they'll pay it."

Hudson and Nez were both looking wide-eyed at the table, thinking. I'd said all I needed to say, so I stood up and walked inside the house to look for something to eat. There was some leftover pizza in the fridge, but not much else. I figured it was what Nez and Hudson had eaten last night. I picked a couple of slices and threw them in the microwave. Then I pulled out my phone and started doing research on my new best friends, The White Power Alliance.

Chapter 11

THERE WASN'T A TON of information on The White Power Alliance online. At least not that I could find. The Anti-Defamation League and the Southern Poverty Law Center seemed to have more information on the organization than the Federal Government. Although that probably wasn't actually the case. What the feds had probably wasn't available for public consumption. Still, I wasn't worried. I figured Nez and Hudson would give me the rundown. But I wanted to see what was online about them.

Both the ADL and the SPLC referred to The White Power Alliance as a domestic terrorist organization. More than that, they called them "white power accelerationists" because they advocated for the overthrow of the government and the transformation of America into the whites-only nation they thought it should be. According to the reports I read, there were more than a few references to the WPA in the rambling, half-coherent manifestos of several mass shooters who'd targeted synagogues or communities of color.

More than anything, it seemed to be a loose and decentralized organization of several different white supremacist groups. Or that's what the reporters and researchers for the ADL and SPLC thought. But if there was someone pulling the strings to recruit new members in California, then there had to be some sort of centralized leadership.

Someone who was in charge of doling out the money, at the very least. Maybe it was a small committee, but I doubted that. These kinds of organizations always had a head somewhere. And a chain of command for issuing orders.

They probably wanted everyone to think there was no central leadership. That would only benefit them. And so far, they seemed to be doing a good job of it.

I read a piece about a reporter who pretended to be a white supremacist. He got onto one of the group chats on a social media website favored by far-right extremist organizations. Once in the chat, he saw all kinds of disturbing stuff being discussed. The people used coded language, although it wasn't very sophisticated. It was easy to see what they were talking about. Sometimes they would just replace real words with [REDACT], encouraging each other to "[REDACT] all the blacks and browns," "[REDACT] all the jews and muslims," and to "[REDACT] your local power station." Zero points for subtlety. And the refusal to capitalize Jews and Muslims was to be expected from these clearly bright and educated people who were, I had to assume, mostly young men.

Anonymous users posted infrastructure maps and documents that gave advice on close-quarters combat and how to use AR-15-style rifles and other weapons to ultimate effect. Other users posted advice on causing the most damage and sowing chaos, saying that shooting up a school or a crowded store was good, but to "make it count" it was better to target critical infrastructure.

It didn't take long for a cold stone to form down low in my guts. The casual way these people talked about mass murder was more than a little disturbing. And it made me curious. It seemed like with all these chats—the article mentioned at least a half-dozen well-known white supremacist chats that were active daily—there would be a correlation in ideologically motivated shootings or attacks. So I did a search.

Sure enough, out of over six hundred mass shootings in the US the previous year, twelve of them were done by white supremacists—a 30% increase over the year before that. They'd killed twenty-five people in those twelve attacks and injured many more.

I wasn't naïve enough to think I could stop every mass shooting in the country, but I thought if I could prevent twenty-five people from getting killed, it was a worthy cause. But I also knew it wasn't going to be just twenty-five. Not this year. If Hudson and Nez were to be believed, the coordinated attacks that were coming would kill a whole lot more people.

Somehow, I managed to get the two slices of pizza down while I read, despite the cold and heavy rock in my guts. As I was finishing the second slice, the two feds came in from the back patio.

"Okay," Hudson said. "We've got the okay to do it your way. Our boss was reluctant at first, but he knows how important this is."

"It's a good idea," I said after swallowing.

Hudson frowned, but Nez nodded. "Good," she said. "Confidence. You're going to need a lot of it in the coming days."

We spent most of the next two days hammering out the details and getting me ready to go undercover. I could've used another month or so to get ready, but that wasn't possible. And five days after I'd been arrested on Hoffman's street along with three other guys from the local neighborhood watch, I was arrested again for lighting a house on fire and giving an old man a light beating. Only this time, the arresting officers were in on it. So was the cop who'd brought me in and put me in the cell with Spencer Clark and Ty Fisher. His little comment about us making fast friends worked like a charm.

I'd had a moment of panic when Spencer had asked me if I knew the fourteen words. Even though I'd memorized them—and other ridiculous white power sayings—I had a moment where my mind went blank. So I stalled a little bit and forced myself to relax, and the words had come.

That was it. I knew I'd made an impression. What I didn't know was whether The White Power Alliance would post my bail. I went and saw a judge the day after Spencer and Ty were released. And I cringed when I heard the number spoken out loud. $200,000. I knew it could've been a lot more if my full record had been taken into account, but Hudson and Nez had talked to the judge and the DA and settled on the number. It would mean the WPA would have to part with at least $20,000 to get me out. No small amount.

And as the hours ticked by after I returned to the jail, I grew more and more sure that the ploy hadn't worked. I was put in a cell with a bed and a toilet and nothing to do but think about how I might've blown the whole thing. And I waited.

Chapter 12

"HERE HE COMES! LET'S move, move, move!" Dyer said, bringing his binoculars down.

He and Tucker, a twenty-four-year-old ex-Army private, turned and rushed as fast as they could through the fifty-yard patch of trees abutting the power plant's fence line. They were dressed in drab ghillie suits that matched the color of the mostly lifeless trees around them. There were a few evergreens here and there, but most of the trees were barren, and would remain so until spring.

They made it out to the road on the other side of the trees and pulled their ghillie suits off quickly, putting them in the Ford Explorer's trunk before jumping into the vehicle.

Tucker drove so Dyer could concentrate on writing stuff down. He could also call Coakley if he needed to from his spot in the passenger seat of the maroon-colored vehicle. The road they'd parked on intersected the road that led out of the main plant entrance. It was the same road they'd seen the guy leaving by over the last four days. And he always left around the same time. But now they needed to figure out where he lived. That was the next step.

"Just wait," Dyer said, putting a hand up. Both men stared at the intersecting road some two hundred yards ahead. Seconds passed.

Then Jeffrey Mendoza's vehicle—a silver Dodge truck—passed, going from left to right.

"Okay," Dyer said. "Just take it slow. Stay back a good distance."

Tucker was used to taking orders. He nodded and put his foot on the gas. They turned right onto Kallunki Road, the Columbia River to their left. The Dodge truck was up ahead, going maybe forty miles an hour. There was little traffic in this area, and only two cars passed them going the other way. The landscape was dull, with yellow winter grass and brown trees in between the industrial lots that dotted the roadside on their right.

They followed Mendoza all the way down to the Columbia River Highway. That was where things got tricky. There was more traffic, and Dyer grew worried that they would lose the man, so he ordered Tucker to get closer.

But it was only a two-lane highway, and Tucker managed to keep one car between them as they drove east. Then, Mendoza's blinker came on. "He's goin' to Washington. Should I follow?" Tucker asked.

"Yeah, of course," Dyer said. "I don't care if he's going to Canada. We gotta find out where he lives."

Tucker nodded and followed Mendoza onto the interchange ramp that took them onto 433 and the Lewis and Clark Bridge. The Columbia river sparkled dully in the drab afternoon sunlight as they crossed out of Oregon and into the town of Longview, Washington.

Now they needed to stay even closer. There was more traffic here, and Dyer could feel that they were getting close. Longview was a maze of suburban streets, and he felt certain Mendoza lived here.

When the silver Dodge turned into a McDonald's parking lot, Dyer instructed Tucker to follow. They parked four spots away and watched Mendoza go inside. Dyer lost sight of him as soon as he went through the doors; the reflections on the windows made seeing inside impossible. "You see him?" Dyer asked.

"No."

"Shit," Dyer breathed. "This is too much. If we follow him out of here, he's bound to get suspicious. I knew we should've had two cars for this."

"Why don't we?"

"'Cause everyone's busy, that's why. Not enough manpower. Not enough *trusted* manpower."

The two men fell silent, waiting.

"I dunno," Tucker said. "I doubt he's even noticed us. Most people are fuckin' oblivious."

Dyer said nothing. He stroked his boxy red beard with one hand, watching the fast-food restaurant.

After about five minutes, Mendoza came out. But he wasn't carrying anything. No food. No drinks. Nothing.

And he was looking right at the Explorer.

"He's comin' over here," Tucker said.

He was right. Mendoza was walking with a purpose. As soon as he stepped out of the place, he'd been fixed on the Explorer. Dyer realized that he hadn't been inside eating. He'd been inside looking out one of the windows, watching the SUV, deciding what to do. And it looked like he'd come to a conclusion.

"What do we do?" Tucker said.

"Shit. Fuckin' goddammit," Dyer said, turning and opening the glove box. He pulled out his Kimber 1911 pistol and hid it behind his body just as Mendoza stepped up to the driver's side window.

He wasn't a small guy. And he didn't look like the meek type. He had bulky arms and shoulders flanking a thick neck. Dyer figured he weighed over two-hundred pounds and stood at around six-one. He knocked on the window with the knuckle of one hand and said, "Are you following me?"

Tucker turned and looked at Dyer with the expression of a kid who's been caught cheating on the biggest test of the year. Dyer opened his mouth but said nothing. He didn't know what to do. They'd never planned for a confrontation like this.

"Hey, assholes," Mendoza said, hitting the window with the side of his fist. "You got something you want to say to me?"

"We don't know what you're talking about," Dyer said loudly. "We're not following you."

"Bullshit. I'm going to call the fucking cops if I see you again, you got me?" He stared through the window for a moment before saying, loud enough for the men inside to hear, "Fuckin' rednecks."

Before Dyer knew what was happening, Tucker was slamming the door open and lunging out for Mendoza. The two of them hit the sedan in the adjacent spot and then fell to the asphalt, grunting and wrestling.

Dyer opened his door and jumped out, running around the back of the vehicle. Mendoza had quickly gotten the upper hand. He was holding Tucker to the ground with one hand, bringing his other back for a punch. It was a punch that probably would've broken half of Tucker's face. But before he could make the move, Dyer put the barrel of his 1911 to the man's forehead. Mendoza froze without being told.

"Get up, motherfucker," Dyer said.

Mendoza put both his hands up and stood from a gasping Tucker. Dyer stepped back, creating a gap between gun and target, resisting the urge to glance around for witnesses. This was a clusterfuck, and there was only one thing to do. It was a shitty thing, but there were fuckall choices left. "Get in the back," Dyer told the man, gesturing toward the SUV.

Mendoza's eyes bounced from the SUV to Dyer. He hesitated.

Dyer, who'd been practicing trigger discipline thus far, shifted the digit inside the guard. He slid the external safety lever down with his thumb. He was sure Mendoza saw both movements.

Still, the man hesitated.

"Hit him," Dyer said.

Tucker, who was crouching between the two men, didn't need to be told twice. From his crouching position, he punched Mendoza in the crotch. The man gasped and doubled over.

"Get him in the back," Dyer directed.

Tucker stood up and yanked Mendoza back, clearing enough room to open the door. The injured man moved with little resistance. But when it came to getting him in the SUV, Tucker had to hit him again to convince him. Dyer followed the injured man in, keeping the gun on him. Meanwhile, Tucker got in the driver's seat. They pulled out of the parking lot, and Dyer risked a glance behind. There was a wrinkly old woman standing outside the McDonald's door with a drink in her hand, staring after the SUV with a shocked expression on her face.

"Goddammit," Dyer said, slamming the butt of his gun into the side of Mendoza's head. The man went limp and collapsed against the opposite door.

Coakley and Bove weren't going to like this. Not one bit.

Chapter 13

"WHY THE HELL DIDN'T you call me?" Coakley said, struggling to keep his voice level.

"I didn't wanna talk over the phone about this," Dyer said.

The two men were standing in the shade on the front porch of Coakley's house—the same porch they'd been standing on a few days ago when Bove came over to see about the rat problem. Tucker was still in the maroon Explorer, which was parked on Coakley's driveway next to the garage.

"I thought about messaging you in one of the chats, but I didn't want to risk that, either," Dyer said.

"No, you're right," Coakley said through clenched teeth. "You're right. You're right, you fucking idiot. Jesus Christ. Why didn't you stay back like I told you to?"

"I was afraid we were gonna lose him. Would you have preferred that outcome?"

"Yes! Yes, I would have because we could've tried again. Now we're locked into this course of action. At least tell me you got rid of his phone and any other electronic devices he had on him."

"'Course. I'm not stupid."

"From where I'm standing, you're the stupidest man I've ever seen in my life. You know how Bove is going to react to this? I'm not going to cover for you. This is your fuckup. Jesus Christ."

Dyer wasn't cowed. He glared at Coakley and said, "Now we can learn how to shut the whole fuckin' place down. We'll make him tell us."

"The attacks are still three weeks out, you idiot. What if they find us? What if they come here and find us and we all go to jail for the rest of our fucking lives? Did you think about that? The whole reason for finding out where he lived was so we could snag him only when we needed him. To limit our fucking exposure. Don't you understand that? Sometimes you're dumber than a nigger, you goddamn idiot."

Finally, Dyer dropped his eyes.

The two stood there for several long moments before Coakley spoke again. "I'm going across to get Bove. You and Tucker get the guy in my garage and get rid of that fucking Explorer. Have Tucker take it down to California somewhere and ditch it. At least five hundred miles from here, you got it? And make sure he torches it so there won't be any DNA evidence the cops can nail us with. Can I trust him to do that? Can I trust you to convey that information in a way that ensures he won't fuck it up?"

Dyer nodded, still looking down.

"Good. Go."

Coakley followed Dyer down the porch steps, but where Dyer turned right and walked along the dirt path to the driveway, Coakley continued down the hill. His feet crunched on the dirt road as he crossed and stepped onto Bove's property. The winter sun did little to warm his skin, and a cool breeze whispered down the valley, but Coakley was still sweating heavily from his armpits.

He climbed the steps and knocked on the door at Bove's house. He heard little feet running inside before the door opened and a little face stared up at him. "Uncle Bill!" Bove's son Brandon said.

Coakley smiled. "Is your dad around?"

"Is that Bill?" came a woman's voice from inside. "Let him in, Brandon."

Brandon opened the door wider, looking up with bright green eyes. When he was inside, Coakley closed the door and looked to his right into a room where Bove's wife Sarah was homeschooling her two boys. She had a portable blackboard set up and two old-school wooden desks for the kids, one of which had recently been vacated by Brandon.

"Hey, Sarah," Coakley said, raising a hand.

Sarah grinned back with a mouthful of perfectly white and straight teeth. Her blonde hair was cut into a pixie hairdo, making her look like Julia Roberts's version of Tinkerbell in the movie *Hook*. Brandon had her blond hair, but the older boy, Stephen, had his father's dark hair. Stephen was the less hyperactive of the two even though he was only ten, three years older than his brother. He looked up from his textbook and waved hello before getting right back to his studies.

Glancing at the chalkboard, Coakley saw it was split into two sections—one for each student. On the right, in Brandon's section, there was the heading "Handwriting." Underneath it were several quotes attributed to some of history's greatest white supremacists. Coakley read the top two. The first was from Adolf Hitler. It read, "A state which in this age of racial poisoning dedicates itself to the care of its best racial elements must some day become Lord of the earth." The second one down was from Jefferson Davis: "You cannot transform the negro into anything one-tenth as useful or as good as what slavery enables them to be."

Coakley's guess was that Brandon was supposed to copy them down to practice his handwriting. On the left side, there were some basic math problems for Stephen to copy down and then solve.

Sarah stood up from her chair next to the chalkboard and walked over. "I'll show you to him," she said. "Brandon, get back to work! You still have two quotes to write down. Then I expect you to tell me what they mean."

Brandon's shoulders slumped dramatically as he turned and headed back to his desk in the miniature classroom.

"He's up in his office," Sarah said, leading Coakley toward the staircase down the hall. When they were out of sight of the children, Sarah turned around and grabbed Coakley's hands. She looked up into his eyes expectantly.

"Don't do this," Coakley whispered. "Not while he's here. Not now. Something's come up."

"When?" Sarah whispered, pressing herself against him and kissing his neck.

She smelled like lavender. Her lips were soft on his neck, and he felt himself stirring. Coakley freed his hands and grabbed her by the shoulders, pushing her back. "I said not now, goddammit. *Never* while he's here. I don't know when. The next time he goes out of town, I guess."

The subtle creak of weight on a step caught their attention. Coakley dropped his hands, and they turned toward the staircase to see Bove emerge at the bottom of the stairs. "What's with all the whispering?" he asked, looking at his wife and his most trusted confidant.

"Sarah said you didn't want to be disturbed," Coakley said. "But I was just telling her that something's come up and I needed to see you right away . . . We didn't want to disturb the children's schoolwork."

Bove studied them for a moment with his small, dark eyes. "Well, why don't you come on up, then?" he said, talking to Coakley.

Sarah turned without a word and went back to the children while the two men walked up the carpeted stairs to Bove's office. Coakley looked at the back of Bove's head, where the thin and trim line of black hair cut a straight line across his neck. He tried to get a sense of what the other man was feeling. Had he crept down the stairs and listened, or had he really come down right then? What had he heard? Did he suspect? Did he *know*?

Bove turned into his office—it was the first door on the right in the upstairs hallway. The room was sparse and neat, much like the man himself. Everything had its place, and economy ruled all. The only evidence of any personality showed through three items. One was a picture of the Bove family on the L-shaped desk against the far wall. Ethan Lee Bove sat on a porch swing with his wife next to him. The picture had been taken when the children were younger, and they each held one in their lap. Brandon, the younger one who took after his mother, was sitting in Sarah's lap. The dark-haired older boy was in his father's lap. They must have been six and three. Everyone in the picture was grinning except Ethan. His smile was genuine, but he showed no teeth. It was a mischievous smile. One that seemed to say, "I have a secret and I'll never tell."

The other two items that passed as decorations in the room were both flags. One of them was a white flag with a black Celtic cross in the middle and the words "White Pride World Wide" set around it. Coakley recognized it from Stormfront, the white supremacist organization founded in 1995 by former Klan member Don Black. It was the first white power group to have a notable web presence, and it was the group Bove had first been involved with. It was a way to remember his roots.

The other flag was over the computer desk so Bove could lift his head and look at it while sitting there working. In the upper left-hand side of the flag was a black square with a stylized white fist in the middle. The fist was holding a knife, which was dripping blood from its tip. The rest of the flag was black and white—the red of the blood was the only other color. Where the red stripes would be on an American flag, there were lines of text on this one. There were two sayings that made up the stripes. The first was the shorter of the two, and as such, it made up the four stripes opposite the black square with the fist. These four stripes all read: "White America First." The bottom three read: "Kill Them All, Let God Sort Them Out."

There was a line of a dozen rifles and boxes of ammunition against one wall, while the other was occupied by bookshelves stacked with various survival supplies. Coakley knew this was just the overflow. There were many more weapons and many more supplies at caches around their property and across the state.

Bove's desk had three different computer monitors on it, and he shut them all off before turning to face Coakley. The men stood there, near the desk. Bove crossed his arms and sat on the edge of his desk.

Coakley's heart shuddered in his chest, but he showed no outward sign of stress. He knew he showed no sign. Even his armpits, which had been sweating heavily on the way over to the house, had stopped sweating. Even Coakley didn't know how he did it. He just did. And over the years, after being in more stressful situations than he cared to count, he'd gotten used to it. The fear never went away, not really, but he'd gotten used to it. He figured that the day the fear went away was the day he'd die.

"Dyer and Tucker fucked up," he said when it was clear Bove was waiting for him to talk. "They kidnapped the guy from the power plant I told them to tail."

Bove's jaw muscles flexed, but his eyes didn't change, and he made no other indication that he was upset. But he was. Those jaw muscles didn't bounce like that unless Bove was good and mad.

"Why did they do that?" he asked, eyes fixed unnervingly on Coakley.

"They got too close, they said. The guy came up and started yelling at them about calling the cops. So they snatched him."

"Did anyone see this clusterfuck go down?"

Coakley nodded. "At least one woman. Probably more."

"Get rid of the car. Somewhere far away."

"I already put them on it."

"What about the man?" Bove asked.

"Across the street."

Bove nodded and fell silent. He still had his eyes fixed on Coakley, but they seemed distant now. He was lost in thought. Nearly thirty seconds passed before he spoke again. "We'll have to move it up. Shorten the timeline."

A thrill of excitement shot through Coakley. "Can we do it?" he asked.

"I think so," Bove said. "But we've got to start mobilizing soon. We almost have enough people. We're close."

"Enough people for everything? For all the attacks?"

"I was just talking to McCray down in Los Angeles about it," Bove said. "And he thinks he's found us a poster boy for the movement. Someone we can use to get the troops riled up and ready to do what needs to be done."

"Good," Coakley said. "Who is he?"

"Just some career criminal who has finally had enough," Bove said. "He torched some Jew's house in the suburbs down there. A couple of our guys met him in jail."

"Want me to check up on him?"

"It's already been done. I agreed to bail him out. McCray's going to take him to the Mount Shasta camp. Then we can start the final moves."

Chapter 14

I SQUINTED IN THE late afternoon sun as I pulled my leather on outside the tidy Santa Clarita Sheriff's Station. There were a couple of cars in the parking lot, and I looked around at them expectantly. The driver's side window on a lifted and mud-spattered white Ford truck rolled down, revealing a man in his forties with a long brown-blond beard and a white wife-beater shirt.

"You Rubble?" he asked in a voice that told me this man was a die-hard smoker.

"You the one who bailed me out?" I asked, flipping my collar down as I got my leather settled on my shoulders.

"Yep," he said, rolling the window back up.

I stood there, looking at the tinted truck window for a long moment before waving once and shouting, "Thank you!" Then I started off into the parking lot. It wasn't like I had another ride, but I didn't want to seem too eager.

I heard the window roll down again. "Don't be an asshole," the guy called out. "Get in the fuckin' truck."

I looked over toward Golden Valley Road, which ran past the station, then back at the truck. Shrugging, I headed around and opened the passenger door. Spencer Clark sat in the front seat. His nose was discolored from when I'd broken it, and I could see a nasty bruise through the buzzed hair on the side of his head where I'd elbowed him. But he nodded at me with something like pride and gestured toward the back seat. I opened up the truck's suicide door and got inside.

"Name's McCray," the driver said, looking at me in the rearview mirror.

"You can call me Trouble," I said.

McCray lit a cigarette and then looked back at me. "We're going on a road trip."

"Now? I need to go get my motorcycle. And the rest of my shit from my motel room."

"It wasn't a question," he said. "Now, give me your phone."

I looked at Spencer, who was turned in his seat. He nodded.

"Give me the fuckin' phone, guy," McCray said.

I shook my head and sighed, but I pulled the phone out of my pocket and gave it to McCray, who gave it to Spencer. I watched as Spencer pulled the battery out and then the SIM card, tossing all the different pieces in the glove compartment.

McCray looked at me in the rearview mirror and laughed, putting the truck into reverse. The cab smelled like stale beer, fresh sweat, and cigarettes. And as we pulled out onto Golden Valley Road, I contemplated further lobbying to go get my stuff. I doubted it would do any good. So instead I asked to bum a smoke. McCray gave me the evil eye, but he passed his pack back.

We headed out of Santa Clarita and got on I-5 going north. I pictured a drone high above us in the sky, tracking the vehicle with the kind of fancy cameras only three-letter government agencies can afford.

I was going into the belly of the beast. And while Nez and Hudson were keeping an eye on me from the sky, it didn't quell the unease I was feeling deep down inside. If something went wrong and I was found out, there was nothing they could do to save me.

For now, I was on my own.

***

You don't know just how big California is until you drive its length. I had grown up on the rolling highways of the Golden State. I'd gotten to know my home state's intricacies while riding its cracked roadways through cities and towns and villages alike. I'd left stretches of my skin on the streets after laying down my bike. I'd been shot at, stabbed, sliced, and beaten. I'd left my blood soaking into the asphalt. And I'd been the reason other men had lost theirs on different stretches of blacktop.

And while I much preferred the more scenic and intimate Highway 1, I'd done my fair share of traveling on I-5, which traverses the state lengthwise from Mexico up to Oregon and beyond. So the trip north was like hanging out with an old friend. But like an old friend, there was little left to be discovered. We'd said most of what we had to say. After that, there was little to do but just sit and stare at each other. And that's what I did. But looking out the window only did so much for my mind. My fear burbled from a boil to a simmer because there was nothing to do but sit and wait.

I swear the same construction projects on certain stretches of highway had been started when I first got my license. As far as I could tell, they hadn't made any progress on them. It was as if the same men were coming out to the same stretch of road to move the same dirt around every day. Highway improvement projects were a family affair, spanning generations. When old dad turned gray and stooped and finally had a heart attack, falling face-first into the sandy dirt, Junior came up, picked up his shovel, and kept going. Not far behind him, with a miniature shovel and a Tonka truck, was little Junior Jr., waiting his turn.

That wasn't the reality, obviously. But this was what my mind did when left to its own devices. I'd worked construction, although never on a road crew. And in a sense, my fantasy was accurate. Keeping a country intact was hard work, and many people had given their lives to maintain the paved pathways across America. They'd worn out their joints and destroyed their backs and paid the toll associated with a life of labor.

I wondered what an America run by white supremacists would look like. Surely they wouldn't kill everyone who wasn't white. That wasn't really feasible. Maybe they would force them to do the labor of keeping the country together. Maybe instead of men and women of all colors working on the road crews across the nation, it would only be Hispanics and Blacks and Asians. There were some precedents for this type of behavior in the nation's history.

Someone had to maintain the roads, after all. *Someone* had to keep on top of the infrastructure. Would that kind of honest, salt-of-the-earth work be beneath the new white ruling class? How would it work? Would they model the new America after apartheid South Africa? Rhodesia, maybe? Would only white, land-owning men be allowed to vote? Or would they allow white women to vote, as well?

My mind grappled with these questions. With the sheer ridiculous hubris of it all. Calling for revolution was certainly romantic, no matter how hate-filled or idiotic the cause, but what about the task of running the country after the dust settled? If they didn't genocide everyone who didn't look like them, they would essentially be an occupying force. Would they expect those they oppressed to just give up and go quietly into servitude or slavery?

I'd read enough to know that the general attitude was, "we'll figure it out later." They referred to what they called the Zionist Occupied Government—ZOG—as anti-American. They thought the Jews controlled the banks and the media and the government. But what would happen when they took over all these essential institutions? Pretty soon, another group of psychos would be accusing *them* of controlling the banks, the media, and the government. Only this time, it wouldn't be a conspiracy theory. It would be true.

The whole thing was crazy. It made about as much sense to me as similar groups on the other side of the political spectrum, calling for a violent communist revolution. Granted, this latter group was much smaller and weaker and less prone to violence than white supremacists. Still, I saw them as two sides of the same ridiculous coin.

The sun went down while we drove north. McCray and Spencer weren't much for talking. And when they did talk, it was mostly to each other. Since McCray was constantly smoking with his window open, I couldn't hear half of what they said to each other, anyway.

Still, it didn't keep me from asking twice where we were going. I got non-answers both times. I also asked about getting a couple of changes of clothing, but Spencer told me, "You'll be taken care of."

We pulled over to get gas after about four hours of driving, and I bought some junk food from the gas station. I offered to drive, but McCray refused. When we got back on the road, Spencer was driving.

Finally, I stretched out on the back seat to try and get some rest. There was a bunch of random junk on the seat with me—t-shirts, oil rags, loose tools, and a roll of camouflage duct tape—but I shoved it all down into the footwell to give myself some room. There wasn't enough room for me to stretch out fully, but with my knees bent I could lie flat on my back. There was no way I could actually sleep, but I figured I'd better give it a try.

We stopped twice more for gas and restroom breaks before pulling off I-5 at ten to one in the morning. We were in the town of Mount Shasta. Although I couldn't see the mountain after which the town was named, I knew it was out there somewhere, looming snow-capped in the dark.

The town was utterly quiet, its 3,500 residents mostly at home, asleep. It was a quaint mountainside town with an economy based mostly on fishing, hunting, and winter sports on the mountain. We rolled through a blinking yellow stoplight, seeing only two other cars moving on the road once we got away from I-5.

Spencer guided us into a neighborhood, where he stopped in front of a small ranch-style house. McCray told me to stay put before walking inside. He came out a few minutes later carrying two heavy-looking duffel bags. "What're you waitin' for?" he called out. "Help me, goddammit."

Spencer and I jumped out of the truck and headed inside the house where we grabbed crates full of ammo, and boxes with MRE rations from the unfurnished living room. A craggy-faced man teetering on the edge of old age watched us from down the hall. He never said a word. When we had everything loaded up, McCray got back in the driver's seat. I got in the back again and Spencer sat shotgun.

We then backtracked out of town and turned onto State Route 89. The air was noticeably colder here, and I was glad for my jacket. But since McCray was a chain smoker, I always had cold, smoke-laden air blowing into my face.

We turned off 89 onto a smaller dirt road. After driving for nearly forty-five more minutes, we came to a simple metal livestock gate. There were trees on all sides now, and there was no moon out. Impenetrable shadows made it impossible to see more than twenty yards beyond either side of the road. And when a couple of guys with semi-auto rifles appeared out of the shadows on this side of the gate, I nearly jumped. They were dressed in all black with black gloves and face paint. Clearly recognizing McCray's truck, they came up and exchanged pleasantries before opening the gate and letting us through. As we continued on, I looked out the back window to see the two men close and lock the gate before disappearing back into the trees like wraiths in a graveyard.

Chapter 15

THE CAMP WAS QUIET. Four men came out of an army-green canvas tent, pulling coats and guns on. I caught a glimpse inside the tent, which looked to be about ten feet wide and twenty feet long. There were a few card tables set up inside with folding chairs around them. Electric lights hung from the ceiling. The four guys were all dressed in fatigues, which included the coats they fastened against the cold before pulling their weapon straps around their heads.

"Let's unload," McCray said.

Spencer got out and opened the suicide door before pulling on a black coat that had been with him in the front. I stepped into the frigid winter night and went to work unloading all the stuff we'd got from the house in Mount Shasta. I was thankful there wasn't any snow on the ground, but I wasn't dressed for this weather. My jeans had holes in the knees and all I had on under my leather jacket was a t-shirt. I was dressed for Los Angeles winter weather, which wasn't really winter weather at all. By the time we finished loading the stuff into the tent, stacking it along the walls next to similar supplies, my hands were numb and my ears burned.

It was warmer inside the tent because there were a couple of electric heaters going, and that's where we all gathered. Not far off in the distance, I could hear the hum of a generator.

"Get him all set up, would you, Weldon?" McCray said to one of the guys who'd come out to help us.

"Yes, sir," Weldon said, propping his Ruger AR-556 rifle against a stack of crates.

McCray, who'd produced a black hoodie from somewhere with a big red swastika on the front, grumbled something about going to headquarters. He walked out of the tent. Moments later, his truck roared to life and then purred as he drove off.

I exchanged what I hoped was an excited yet exasperated look with Spencer, who was watching me with a smile on his face. The other three guys, whose names I didn't catch, sat down at one of the three card tables in the middle of the room—the one nearest a heater—and resumed some kind of card game.

"Wait for me, assholes," Weldon said.

"Hurry up, then."

Weldon looked me up and down and then moved to the back of the tent. He stopped at a stack of opaque plastic storage bins, unstacking a couple of them before opening one up and pulling out a pair of fatigues wrapped in plastic.

"Try these," he said, tossing them to me. I caught them, realizing that it wasn't a whole set of fatigues, just a pair of pants. I moved over to the nearest card table and pulled out a folding chair, sitting on it to untie my boots.

"What about long underwear?" Spencer asked.

"Shit. Yeah," Weldon said. After some more digging around, he came back with a set of tan-colored long underwear made from 100% polyester. I stripped to my boxers, pulled the long underwear on, and then pulled the pants on. They fit. Then Weldon gave me a tan fleece jacket and a heavier waterproof camouflage coat in the same pattern as the pants. It was all brand-new stuff, straight out of the plastic. It was the same getup the other four guys were wearing. I wondered how they afforded all this stuff. It wasn't cheap.

"What about you?" I asked Spencer.

"I'll get changed back at the barracks," he said. "No worries."

"I'll take this stuff," Weldon said, stepping up and grabbing my pants, t-shirt, and jacket.

I reached out and grabbed the sleeve of my leather jacket. "No," I said. "Not this."

"No personal effects," Weldon said in a hurt voice. "That's the rule."

"Fuck the rule," I said. "You're not taking my jacket. That's my lucky leather."

All eyes were on me now. Weldon looked at Spencer, who told me, "He's right. That's the rule. No one else has personal stuff here."

"I don't give a shit what everyone else does or doesn't have," I said. "I'm keeping my jacket. If boss man McCray has a problem with it, he can come talk to me himself."

Spencer snorted. "McCray's not the boss man."

"Well, whoever," I said. "I don't care. I won't wear it if that's the problem. I just want to keep it with me."

Spencer shrugged. "Just let him have it," he said.

Weldon stuck his chin out, but he let go of the jacket.

"Good," I said. "Now what?"

"Now I show you the barracks and we get some shuteye," Spencer said.

We headed out, leaving the four guys to resume their game. I could feel their eyes on my back as I walked out into the cold night.

"When do I get a gun?" I asked as Spencer led the way down a path between trees. There were small garden lights spaced every ten yards or so along the trail, lighting the way.

Spencer laughed. "You ever used one before? You gotta learn to shoot first."

"I know how to shoot."

"Yeah, well, we'll see soon enough. For now, we just need to get some sleep. We get up early around here."

"What time is early?"

"Five-thirty."

"Christ, man, you serious? Five-thirty? I didn't think I'd be joining the fuckin' army when I agreed to get bailed out by you guys."

"Oh yeah? You'd rather be back in that jail, waiting to get your ass sent to prison?"

I considered that for a moment as we walked, crunching dirt and rocks under our boots. "I guess not."

"This is so much better, man, believe me," he said. "We get to have a purpose here. A reason for existing instead of just . . . existing. And we get to bust some sub heads."

I knew what he meant by "sub." It was short for subhuman. It was a term that encompassed anyone who wasn't white, along with race traitors—white people who were against racism.

"I could bust heads on my own," I said.

"Not like this, man," Spencer said. "Not like this."

Soon, we came to a domed metal building in a clearing. We came on it from the front, so I couldn't see exactly how long it was, but it looked long in the limited light. It was about fifty feet wide, army green, and it had a single light bulb next to the metal double doors.

"Who's there?" a voice called from off to our left.

"Spencer and a new guy," Spencer said.

A guy emerged from the trees, walking over with his Ruger AR-556 held at patrol ready. Like everyone else I'd encountered in the camp so far, he was dressed in fatigues. He had his coat's hood up and was wearing a tan-colored buff over the bottom half of his face. Judging by what little of his face I could see, he looked to be in his early twenties. He and Spencer bumped fists and then snapped off a Nazi salute. Considering that the other guys in the tent hadn't greeted each other that way, I figured it wasn't a requirement, so I made no move to do it.

"Who's this?" the guy asked.

"This is Trouble," Spencer said. "The guy who burned down that Jew's house in Santa Clarita."

"It didn't actually burn down," I said. "The fire department got there pretty fast, along with the pigs."

"Still, man, that's pretty fucking epic," the guy said, sticking his right fist out. He had thin gloves on that would allow him to operate his weapon without taking them off. We bumped fists. "Name's Stoll," he said. "You guys go on in. Get some sleep. Word is tomorrow's a big day."

"Why? What's going on?" Spencer asked.

Stoll shrugged. "No idea. They don't tell us shit. But the rumor is, the time for action is fast approaching. Maybe we'll go mobile. Maybe they'll actually tell us the fucking plan. Who knows? But Cotter and Halverson have been busy at HQ all day."

Spencer grinned, turning to me. "You got here just in time, man. We're finally gonna get to kill some subs!"

"You guys are serious about this shit, huh?" I said. "This place is legit. Honestly, I didn't think it would be much more than a loose collection of dudes. I didn't expect this."

"You getting cold feet or something?" Spencer asked, his smile disappearing.

"No, man," I said. "I just . . . didn't expect this. Most of the people I've met are all talk. This is all just a surprise. I had no idea. I guess I just got used to the idea that we'd have to put up with all the subs for the rest of our lives."

"I know what you mean," Stoll said. "I had to get used to the idea of actually taking meaningful action, too. I mean, the whole system is set up against us. It's all designed to make us think that the only thing we can do is vote. But that's bullshit. It doesn't work. The only votes that matter are the ones that are backed by millions of dollars. And we all know who controls the money in this country. But once you realize there's another way, then you start to get used to the idea. You realize that violence and disruption are the only way things will really change. Looking at human history, it's easy to see. But we've been beaten down, our masculinity taken away. They've tried to turn us into cucks. Pussies. Snowflakes. But you can't eliminate human nature. You can't take away who we are as men at our cores."

I nodded during this little monologue, but something struck me as false about it. It seemed practiced. Of course, that was the nature of rhetoric and propaganda, I supposed. Maybe after he repeated it enough times to himself and others, it would sink in, becoming incorporated into who he saw himself as, and his role in the world. I just hoped I didn't sound like that when I said stuff in support of the white supremacy movement. If I did, I wouldn't be alive for long.

Spencer seemed to buy it, though. He spouted some bullshit about rising up and taking our rightful place as rulers of all other races. Then we said our farewells to Stoll and headed inside the building.

The entire place was one big room, lined with cots on either side. Most of the cots were occupied by sleeping men—all white, obviously. A few of them raised their heads, looking to see who'd come in. Most of them, though, were fast asleep, breathing heavily or snoring. Everyone was sleeping in identical black sleeping bags, and each cot had a small white pillow at its head. There were military-style footlockers at the foot of each cot. I looked around for rifles like the one Stoll outside was carrying, but I didn't see any. I guessed the brass weren't ready to have these guys running around with loaded rifles. Yet.

As we passed an unoccupied bed, Spencer whispered, "That's me." He directed me down the length of the simple metal building to a small cluster of empty cots near the back. He pointed one out and told me it was mine. Then he pointed to a door in the back of the building. "Toilets," he said. "Showers are back there, too, but we have designated bathing times."

I nodded. "Thanks."

"Get some sleep," Spencer said, before heading to his cot.

I put my leather jacket in the empty footlocker, then undressed down to my long underwear. It was warmer inside the building than outside, but it was still chilly. I unzipped the sleeping bag and slipped inside, lying on my back. And as I closed my eyes, the body-odor smell of the place invading my nostrils, I wondered about my next moves.

Stoll had mentioned two people named Cotter and Halverson at headquarters. I decided if I could slip away, I would try to find the place. If these two guys—I assumed they would be men—were in communication with the head of the organization, there could be damning information there. Maybe I could find enough dirt to shut this whole rotten thing down. The first problem would be getting the information without getting caught. The second problem would be alerting Nez and Hudson that I had it.

I stared at the ceiling, thoughts swirling and sleep about a hundred miles away.

I had a feeling morning would come awfully fast.

Chapter 16

In Lowell, Massachusetts, off Liberty Street, a man named Liam Tanner was just getting home to the house he shared with two other mid-twenties men. The yellow lawn was splotchy, and the house needed a new coat of paint. Liam noted these things for the hundredth time, but neither he nor his roommates had the time or the money to address the myriad issues around the house. And he knew their slimy Greek landlord wasn't ever going to do it.

Before he even got to the front door, he could hear the music coming from inside the house. And the voices of his two roommates, Seth and Tyler.

Liam's body was sore from his barbacking job, and he wanted nothing more than to drink a couple of beers in peaceful silence before going to sleep. But tonight, like every other Thursday night since he'd moved into this house, that wasn't going to happen.

He walked in the door to see Tyler and Seth hunched forward on the couch, staring at the big screen television as they played video games while a Bluetooth speaker blasted hip-hop music. The coffee table was littered with beer and liquor bottles, and both men were spouting a running commentary as they battled in the digital world.

"Comin' through," Liam said, walking in front of the television to get to the rest of the house.

"Come on, bro!" Tyler said. "Don't do that shit!"

Liam clenched his jaw, doing his best to ignore the outburst. He'd known that moving in with a Black guy wasn't a good idea. Of course, Seth wasn't much better. And he was as white as they came.

Liam went to his room, tossed his backpack down, and grabbed the six-pack he'd stashed in there earlier, knowing if he left it in the fridge, it would be gone by the time he got home from work. He tossed two beers in the freezer and opened a third to drink warm. The other three he put in the fridge.

"Don't drink any of my beers," he called from the kitchen. There was no reply other than the ongoing commentary between the two friends.

Heading back to his room, Liam fired up his computer and sat down at his desk. He opened up a Brave browsing window and made sure his VPN was on. Then he checked the first of the three websites he checked every day, three times a day. Nothing new in the group chats there. At least, nothing of importance.

It was the second chat website he visited that sent his heart lurching into his throat. There it was, a message from the user name Extermin8ThemAll: *Stand by. It will not be televised.*

Liam's eyes went wide, and his mouth dried up. *It's really happening,* he thought. *It's coming. Soon. We're really going to do it.*

He stared blankly at the computer screen for several long moments, his conscious mind busy picturing what it would be like. What it would *feel* like. He was going to join the ranks of true white patriots. Those who'd given their lives for the greater good.

He stood from his desk chair and went to the closet. He pulled out his rifle case and opened it up, looking at all its semi-automatic beauty. Catching himself, he moved to the door and locked it. Then he got the rest of his supplies out, laying them on the bed. He had a tactical vest, ten extra magazines (all already loaded), two 45-caliber pistols, and a whole suit of homemade body armor inspired by the guys who shot up North Hollywood after robbing a bank back in the nineties.

After feeling pretty shitty when getting home from work, he now felt excited. He felt happy. He felt like he was actually going to make a difference when he donned all his equipment and headed down to Roxbury to kill himself some subs. He was confident he could kill ten or more people before the cops got him. But he knew just killing ten people wasn't likely to make much of a difference. No, his task was part of a much larger plan for White Revolution in America. He didn't know the exact details of this plan, but he trusted those in charge. He knew that it involved more people like him—people all over the country—along with major blows to the energy infrastructure. They would topple the Zionist Occupied Government by sowing chaos and terror. And in so doing, they would allow the rightful rulers to take over. White rulers.

He would just have to trust that everyone else would be doing their part while he was doing his. And with those two simple sentences—*Stand by. It will not be televised.*—Liam knew that he had a week or less before he was called up for duty.

Tyler and Seth laughed from the living room, interrupting Liam's daydream. But he smiled anyway. He knew who he would kill first before he headed to Roxbury. Their raucous laughter didn't do anything to ruin his mood this time. Because he knew he'd have the last laugh when they were lying on the living room floor, bleeding out and pleading for mercy that would never come.

He couldn't wait.

Chapter 17

JUST OVER TWO-HUNDRED MILES southwest of Liam's house, three men in a 1990 black Pontiac 6000 sedan rolled to a stop on a quiet Brooklyn street. It was nearly four in the morning, and there was little traffic in the Green Point neighborhood. They stopped on Green Street just behind a Toyota Corolla that had been parked on the side of the road since the previous evening. The man in the back wished the two men luck, got out of the Pontiac, and then got in the Corolla, pulling out of the spot so the Pontiac could pull in.

They'd chosen Green Street because it was a straight shot to McGuinness Boulevard, which they would take to the Pulaski Bridge into Long Island City, where they would take the 495 to the 278. They would be halfway back to Connecticut before the cops even showed up at the house.

The man behind the wheel was twenty-two-year-old Frank Mize. Next to him sat nineteen-year-old Aaron Slone. They were proud members of the white supremacist group called The New Order. Due to petty squabbling at the top of their organization, they had no affiliation with The White Power Alliance. Bove had tried to bring them into the fold, but the group's leader wasn't willing to give up the little power he had over his followers. Of course, neither Mize nor Slone was aware of this.

What they were aware of was the fact that two organizers for The Revolutionary Liberation Front lived in a townhouse one street over from where they now sat. The RLF was a loose collective of anti-racist, anti-government, and anti-capitalist militants who seemed to show up at every white supremacist rally across the country to antagonize proud white brothers and sisters simply practicing their first amendment rights. They also showed up at protests against police brutality and racism and wealth inequality as self-proclaimed protectors of the protesters on their side of the political spectrum.

The New Order and other white supremacist organizations had clashed with them on more than one occasion. So far, their battles had consisted of shouting and a few beatings. They seemed to give as good as they took. But all that would change tonight. The RLF was about to learn just who they were fucking with.

Mize and Slone pulled up their neck gaiters, covering the lower portions of their faces. They both had blank black baseball caps on, and plain black clothing. They pulled on tight black gloves. Mize checked his Beretta M9, ensuring it was loaded. Slone did the same with his Smith & Wesson M&P Shield pistol. They were both wearing bulletproof vests under their loose-fitting clothing.

"You good?" Mize asked.

"Fuck yeah," Slone said.

They opened their doors and got out, concealing their pistols in their waistbands before heading down the sidewalk.

The narrow two-story townhouse on Freeman Street was brick, sandwiched between two similar houses on either side. The front porch light was on, so Slone reached up to unscrew it while Mize pulled out his set of lock picks and knelt in front of the door. He'd been practicing on an identical lock for weeks, and he'd gotten to where he could unlock both deadbolt and knob in under two minutes.

But that was under ideal circumstances, in the safety of his room. Now, he found that his hands were shaking and slick with sweat inside the thin gloves.

Two minutes came and went, and he'd been working on the deadbolt the whole time.

"What's up, man?" Slone whispered, sounding very much like the teenager he was.

"Shut up and keep watch," Mize whispered back.

Finally, he got the deadbolt unlocked. Before he started on the knob, he tried it to see if it was locked. It wasn't.

Stuffing the picks in his pocket without putting them back in their case, he stood up. "We're good," he said. He felt sick with excitement as he pulled out his gun.

Slone turned to face the door. They'd planned their entry, practicing it several times in the apartment they shared back in Connecticut. Mize had his gun up in his right hand while his left hand was on the doorknob. He was standing aside, ready to throw open the door and let Slone rush inside.

"One," Mize whispered. "Two. *Three*." He twisted and pushed, opening the door. Slone was through a split second later, sweeping the entryway with his gun. Then Mize stepped in after him, trying to be as quiet as possible. He shut the door behind him. They both stood for a moment, listening for movement. They heard none.

They quickly cleared the downstairs, finding no one. All the lights were off, save the microwave light in the kitchen. They knew that the two RLF leaders were a couple—a man and a woman. The man was white and the woman Black, which made what they were about to do so much sweeter. Interracial couples made Mize sick to his stomach. It just wasn't natural.

Since they were a couple, the two men figured they'd be sleeping in the same bed, which would make things easier. There wasn't supposed to be anyone else in the house, according to their intel.

They moved up the stairs quietly, still listening for movement. They heard none. There was an office at the top of the stairs, the door open on the unoccupied room. Then there was a bathroom and a narrow door that surely belonged to a linen closet. The last door in the upstairs hallway was closed. The master bedroom.

Stopping outside the door, they looked at each other. This time, Slone would open the door and Mize would go in first. They readied themselves and nodded to each other. Instead of whispering, Slone bobbed his gun up and down to signify the count. *One. Two. Th—*

The door exploded outward. Mize went flying back, crunching into the drywall before falling down onto his hands and knees, gasping in pain. Before Slone could react, a second shotgun blast blew another hole in the door. Pain erupted in his right arm. He stumbled back down the hall, away from the door. Straightening his arm out in preparation to fire, he couldn't understand what was wrong. Something looked off. Two long seconds passed before he realized his arm had been shredded by the blast. He was no longer holding onto the gun because his hand was hanging off his wrist where the shot had hit him.

As the shock settled on him, he looked past his ruined arm to Mize, who was now standing up in front of the bedroom door. He still had his gun in his hand, but he was clearly in pain. He'd taken a shotgun blast to the chest. His bulletproof vest had prevented him from being killed outright, but he looked to be severely injured.

As Mize was steadying himself, the bedroom door opened and a Black woman in blue pajamas stepped out, holding a shotgun to her shoulder. Mize raised his gun, but before he could get it up, the woman shot him in the head, obliterating his face.

Slone stumbled to the stairs as the woman turned toward him. A white man slipped out of the bedroom behind her, pistol in his hand. He raised the gun, but before he could fire, Slone tripped and fell headfirst down the stairs. He crashed down the stairwell and ended up in a pile on the floor at the foot of the stairs, knocked unconscious and bleeding heavily from his wounded arm.

By the time the EMTs arrived, he'd already lost too much blood. He died on the way to the hospital. All attempts at resuscitation failed.

Chapter 18

I WOKE UP TO hands grabbing my arms and legs, pinning me to the cot. I was surrounded by guys—most of them younger than me—in various states of dress. Some had only their pants and long underwear shirts on. Others were fully dressed. They all stared down at me as I struggled, panic chasing sleep away like a guard dog chasing a crook.

"What the fuck is this?" I said, looking for a familiar face. I didn't see Spencer anywhere. But I did see the guy I'd met outside the barracks last night. Stoll. He was helping two other guys hold my right leg down. It didn't help that I was still in the sleeping bag, which limited my movement even more.

A man who looked to be in his late forties stood glaring down at me at the foot of my cot, his arms crossed. "What's so special about this jacket?" he barked, reaching down to grab my leather off the top of the footlocker. "Is there a GPS chip in it? You working for the feds?"

I looked into his face. He had pale blue eyes and cheeks pocked with old acne scars. His brown hair was styled in an undercut—combed and held in place with gel on top but shaved close to the scalp on the sides and back. "Why don't you check it?" I said.

"Oh, I will," he said. "But I wanted to give you a chance to come clean first. Maybe you can walk away with a few broken bones if you tell the truth. But if you don't . . . well, you won't be walking away at all."

I smiled. "If I was working for the feds, you think they would just let you kill me? That would be the worst thing you could do."

The guy shrugged. "I'm willing to take my chances."

I looked around at the faces staring down at me. "I'm not working for the feds," I said. "I didn't even know this place existed yesterday. *Your* people offered to get *me* out of jail. I didn't ask for any of this. So if you're going to accuse me of shit, I'd just as soon not have anything to do with you assholes."

"What were you doing in Los Angeles?" the guy asked.

"Getting payback," I said.

"For what?"

"Fuck you. I'm not telling you my life story."

The guy nodded, and a man to my left let go of my arm and punched me in the stomach. I flexed, but it still hurt. He was a big guy. And it looked like he was enjoying himself.

"What did Hoffman do to you?" the guy asked.

"None of your goddamn business."

Again the signal. This time, though, the big guy punched me lower. Still in the stomach, but he was getting awfully close to the family jewels. He grinned at me with small teeth. He had the tiny, dark eyes of a rodent, and they glittered with mischief.

"What. Did. He. Do."

"He ran a foster home," I said. "I was one of his foster kids. He made my life a living hell, okay? He beat us kids up, starved us, and made us clean his fucking house all the time. That's why I wanted payback."

"It didn't have anything to do with him being Jewish, did it?" the guy asked.

"What do you mean?" I said. "Why do you think he's like that in the first place? It has *everything* to do with him being Jewish."

The guy stared at me for a moment before saying, "Let him go."

As soon as the guys holding me down stood up, I scrambled up and swung at the big guy who hit me in the stomach. It was clear that they'd been expecting this, so I was quickly subdued before I could land a punch. Again, he showed me his small teeth in a fuck-you grin.

"You done?" the leader asked, smiling slightly.

"Yeah."

"Good. No more of that shit. You fight your brothers, you're gone, you got it?"

"Yeah," I said again. The guys let me go and started to disperse, murmuring quietly to each other. The leader stayed.

"Name's Halverson," he said. "But you can call me sir." We shook hands.

"Terrence Rubble. But you can call me—"

"Trouble," he finished. "That's a hell of a name. I bet you earned it, didn't you?"

"Damn right."

Still smiling, Halverson studied me with his pale eyes for a moment before pointing to my jacket on the footlocker. "I don't want to see you wearing that around camp, got it? Unless we tell you to get into street clothes, you're to wear the fatigues."

I nodded.

His expression changed, growing hard.

"Yes, sir," I said.

"That's better." He turned and walked away.

"Don't you want to check the jacket?" I asked.

"Already did."

Once Halverson was gone, Stoll stepped up to me. "Pretty freaky, right?" he asked. "They do that to all the new recruits. Well, something similar, anyway. Can't be too careful, I guess."

"Yeah," I said, stepping over to the footlocker to put the jacket away and grab my pants. "I guess not. So, what do we do now?"

"Morning PT," Stoll said. He didn't sound happy about it.

"What, like running?" I asked.

He nodded.

"Fantastic," I said. I'd never been a fan of cardio of any kind. Give me a chin-up bar, a place to do push-ups, or a set of dumbbells, and I'll be a happy camper. But running? I wasn't built for it. And I didn't want to be.

I got dressed and followed Stoll outside and down the same trail Spencer and I had taken only a few hours earlier. It was just getting light outside, allowing us to see as we made our way through the trees. We lined up on the dirt road next to the supply tent where I'd gotten my fatigues. Halverson was no longer around, but McCray walked out of the supply tent wearing full fatigues. He came up and did a half-assed inspection, clearly just going through the motions. When he was done, we all did a Nazi salute and shouted out, "White power!" I wasn't ready for it, so we had to do it again, making sure we were all in unison. It was something I was going to have to get used to. It made the back of my head grow cold when I did it.

After we got it right, McCray put a guy from the group named Kilnar in charge and told him to lead us on a run. By the time we were done, I'd counted how many people were in the camp—at least the ones on the run. Including me, there were eighty-two. Add to that guys like Halverson and McCray and any support staff, and I was guessing around a hundred people at the camp. And this didn't account for people who weren't attending any camps but were being radicalized through the internet or groups that only met occasionally. If there were even five hundred organized white supremacists willing to take violent action, there was no telling how much damage they could do. With the right supplies and motivation, five hundred could kill five thousand—or more. If they managed to knock out power by attacking electricity substations, then they could kill a lot more. It was the middle of winter, after all. If they timed it right, they could knock out power to predominantly non-white neighborhoods during a cold snap or in parts of the country that always had below-freezing temperatures during winter. Elderly people and babies would be most vulnerable to the freezing temperatures.

And from what I'd seen so far, these people were pretty organized.

The more I saw of the operation, the more worried I got about the damage they could do if I couldn't help the FBI stop them.

Chapter 19

AFTER OUR RUN, A third of us were served breakfast in a long army tent similar to the one at the front of the property where we'd hauled all the supplies the previous night. This one had long white banquet tables inside it, and it was set up about ten yards away from a modest two-story cabin that was located at what I assumed was the rear of the property. There were several vehicles parked in front of the cabin, including McCray's truck. It looked like headquarters to me. And when the food was served—scrambled eggs and thick slices of ham—I understood why the mess hall tent was set up next to the cabin.

The only women I'd seen so far in the camp were the ones who brought the food into the tent and set it into chafing dishes. They were mostly young women in their late teens or early twenties, but I saw a couple of middle-aged women as well. I realized that they were using the kitchen in the cabin to cook all the food. That was also why they couldn't serve us all at once; they didn't have enough room in the kitchen. They had to cook the stuff in shifts.

Before we were allowed to sit down, we had to do the Nazi salute and the white power shout again. It left a distinctly bad taste in my mouth. While I ate, sitting next to Spencer, I thought about getting inside the cabin. If there was any information worth having in this place, it was probably in there. Most likely on a computer. Or among paperwork, if these guys were really paranoid.

Nez and Hudson had given me the rundown on what to look for if I got the chance to go through any files. They said financial information or communication logs would be ideal. But the goal was to get usernames and passwords for any or all of the encrypted chat services these guys used to communicate. The FBI had already gained access to a couple of encrypted white supremacist chat rooms, the logs of which I'd read in preparation for this mission. But there didn't seem to be any vital information changing hands in those rooms. The theory was they had other chat rooms to which only specific, thoroughly vetted people were allowed access.

One thing was for sure: there was no incriminating communication going down over the phone. At least, not over the phones belonging to those people the feds had identified as power players in the white supremacist scene. The problem was, they didn't know if there were other people they didn't know about. They'd gotten wiretaps on a number of well-known names, but they also thought that maybe they were listening to the wrong people.

I was storing names away in my head to give to Nez and Hudson. Halverson was the most promising so far, but there was also McCray. I figured he was a bit player, though. Still, I didn't want to rule anything out. Maybe it would be that easy. Maybe I could give them Halverson's name, they could get a tap on his phone, and it would blow the whole thing wide open.

I doubted it would be so simple. Nothing in my life ever was. But a guy could hope.

Of course, getting my new fed friends any information at all would be tricky. I had memorized a phone number to call, but I didn't have access to a phone. McCray had taken mine back in Santa Clarita. I wondered if it was still in the glove compartment where Spencer had put it after taking it apart. Nez had figured they would take my phone, so she told me that they would approach me when and if they could. Or, if I could get away and use a phone I was sure was safe, then I should call them.

That was all fine and good, but what if they kept me here in this camp right up until the attacks? I didn't know what I would do if a week went by and I was still stuck here. How long could I wait? How long did I have? Hudson and Nez thought three weeks or so, but they weren't sure.

I had to keep my eyes open for an opportunity, and I had to take advantage without getting myself caught or killed. The problem was, there were eyes everywhere. And a lone guy—especially a new guy—wandering around would surely raise eyebrows. I had to figure something out, and fast.

***

After breakfast, we stayed in our smaller groups and did training and team-building stuff. Before and after each exercise, we lined up and did the Nazi salute again, and yelled, "White power." The first exercise after breakfast consisted of us running back and forth along a stretch of dirt road holding logs. The road wasn't perfectly level, and one of the guys twisted his ankle pretty badly.

Our instructor, a guy named West who clearly had military training, urged the kid to tough it out. But when it was clear the guy couldn't put weight on his ankle, West had a couple of other guys help him back to headquarters. "One of the women will help him," West said scornfully.

I watched the three kids walk away, the injured one limping along as he put most of his weight on the other two guys. I figured they had an impromptu nurse's station in the cabin. *Maybe that's my way in*, I thought before West snapped at me to resume the exercise.

Afterward, we had a class on hand-to-hand combat, but it was clear that the rest of the recruits had already been taught some stuff. They were building on what they'd already learned. Luckily, I had plenty of experience to pull from, so I easily held my own.

I also realized that I was among the oldest recruits of all eighty-two of us. Most of them were just slightly older than the kids you'd find at a real military boot camp. I figured out over the course of the day that their median age was around twenty-four. That made me over ten years older than most of them.

I was pleased to learn that experience certainly counts for something. It quickly became apparent that I could get most of these kids on the ground in short order during the hand-to-hand combat exercises. Pretty soon, West was standing aside and letting anyone who wanted to come up and grapple with me.

The only guy I had trouble with was the big guy who'd taken pleasure in punching me in the stomach earlier. His name was Pennington, he was twenty-five, and he was built like a concrete shithouse. He was a couple of inches taller than me—six-five or so—and outweighed me by a good thirty pounds, putting him somewhere in the two-thirty range. I put up a decent fight, but he ended up getting me on the ground after a few minutes. Granted, this was after I'd already gone against seven or eight other guys. Between that and the running, I was gassed by early afternoon.

As we headed back to the mess hall for lunch, Pennington was talking shit about getting me on the ground. I smiled and said nothing, just listened to him jabber behind me. If I had managed to get him down, I would've made an enemy for life. He was one of those kinds of guys. Big ego, small brain.

"Where'd you learn to fight like that?" Stoll asked, walking next to me.

I shrugged. "Just living, I guess."

Stoll mulled that over for several long moments. "What, did you just get in fights a lot or something?"

"When I wasn't on the street, I was in and out of juvenile detention centers," I told him. "You learn real quick how to hold your own that way."

Stoll seemed in awe of that kind of life. In fact, as I listened to their chatter and asked questions of the guys, I learned that most of them were from the suburbs. They didn't know much of anything about living on the streets or fighting to survive every day. Most of them had wanted for very little growing up. I couldn't understand what would draw them to a white supremacist organization like this one. Was it isolation? Restlessness? The urge to belong?

I didn't understand it. The only thing that made sense was that they had no idea what they were really getting into. They were playing soldiers, thinking that they could call timeout and run home when things got too rough. But that wasn't going to happen.

For lunch, we had peanut butter and jelly sandwiches with little cartons of milk and one protein bar each. It wasn't much of a meal, but we didn't have much time to ruminate on it. Pretty soon, we were headed toward the firing range to practice our shooting.

We spent two hours at the shooting range, firing Ruger AR-556 rifles at targets at various distances. When we were done, we had to return the rifles to the small armory building back behind the cabin, which I thought was unfortunate. I would've loved to hang onto one of them, just in case.

As the sun was going down, our group was headed back toward the barracks when McCray approached from the other direction. "Trouble, Spencer, Pennington, and Everett, come with me," he said. "The rest of you, head to the parade ground."

The four of us broke off and followed McCray to the barracks. We stopped at the front door and the burly man turned to us. "You have five minutes to shower and get dressed in street clothes."

"Where we going?" I asked.

"Recruitment drive," McCray said, smiling.

Chapter 20

LIAM TANNER WAS AT work when he got the news. The night was just getting started. The two-story bar he worked at called Irish Abe's was slowly beginning to fill up. Liam and the other barback, a Puerto Rican guy named Alex who was actually pretty funny, had finished stocking up the bars with beer, ice, napkins, fruit wedges, and all the other stuff the bartenders would need for the shift. Now was the time, before it got crazy, that Liam could take a few minutes to himself.

Pulling his coat on, he went to the back alley, leaned against the brick wall, and pulled out his phone. The first thing he saw were the news alerts. And the first headline he read gave him chills: *Two Men With White Supremacist Ties Killed After Invading Brooklyn Home.*

Liam's mind reeled. He wondered if this had anything to do with the WPA and whether it would affect what he'd been asked to do when the time came. He opened the article and read it quickly once, then forced himself to slow down as he read it a second time, gleaning more information.

Although authorities hadn't yet released the names of the two men, someone familiar with the case verified that both men had matching tattoos that related their affiliation to the white supremacist organization The New Order. Liam was familiar with them and didn't think they had anything to do with The White Power Alliance. In fact, if he was remembering correctly, their leader had taken to social media in an attempt to discredit those joining the WPA.

It didn't matter what organization these men had belonged to. Not in Liam's mind. They were down for the cause. They were fighting the good fight. They deserved to be treated as heroes. But as he read the rest of the story again, a white light of fury ignited deep inside him.

The two men had been killed by known members of The Revolutionary Liberation Front. While the district attorney's office hadn't yet decided whether charges were going to be filed, the two were walking around free. Their lawyer said it was a clear case of self-defense, and he was confident that prosecutors weren't going to seek charges.

There was even a picture of the two murderers. It was taken at a protest, the caption said, in 2020. The Black woman held her fist up, a defiant look on her face. Next to her, the white man—her husband, according to the story—had his hands cupped around his mouth and was in mid-shout when the picture had been taken. Liam fixated on the Black woman as he stared at his phone, his fingers white where he gripped the device tightly. She was going to get away with killing a white man. *What kind of a world are we living in where a nigger bitch can kill a White man and walk free?* he thought.

But her husband wasn't much better. In fact, in some ways, he was worse. Subs couldn't help it, he thought. They were just dumber than whites. But this guy should've known better. He was a race traitor. And the fact that he would actually sleep with a black woman was beyond the pale in Liam's mind.

He realized he'd been holding his breath, and he let it out with a low growl. His jaw hurt from clenching it, and his hand was sore from clutching the phone. Getting a grip on himself, he navigated to one of the encrypted chat apps and opened it up. He wanted to see what his brothers were saying about this. He wanted to share his sense of injustice with someone, even if they were essentially strangers he'd never met in real life.

The first chat he opened, titled Lynchers Anonymous, was full of people expressing their rage over the incident. As he read all the comments, he started to feel a little better. He wasn't the only one who felt this way. Far from it.

Then he saw one message that made him nod his head in vehement agreement. It read: "Impromptu gathering at 94th Precinct in Brooklyn to protest this bullshit. Tomorrow at six pm. Come on, brothers! We must stand against this injustice!"

There were at least two dozen replies to the comment, most of them from people saying they'd be there and to spread the word.

It didn't take Liam long to decide to go. As he stood in the alley, with the reek of dumpsters and trash water, he made a promise to himself that he'd go. He had to be ready for the go-ahead from WPA leadership, but he could just load up all his equipment in his car to have it on him if he needed it. He was scheduled to work tomorrow, but he'd already been thinking about quitting. He wouldn't be alive for much longer. In less than a week, his name would be in the news for killing a bunch of subs. Maybe it would even be the last story before the Jew-controlled media crumbled as the WPA took over. *Wouldn't that be something?* he thought with a smile as he walked back inside the bar to say "fuck you" to his boss before leaving to never come back again.

Chapter 21

ONCE AGAIN, I FOUND myself in McCray's truck. But this time, I was jammed in the back with Pennington and Everett. Being the smallest, Everett was sitting in the middle. But he wasn't exactly a tiny guy. Our shoulders were all bunched up against each other. McCray had his window open while he smoked, the cool air blowing in my face.

I wore brand-new blue jeans and a black long-sleeved shirt, along with my leather jacket. The jeans and shirt had been in my footlocker when McCray took us to the barracks and told us to shower. They fit well and were comfortable enough, although the jeans were a little stiff. I wasn't complaining. It was better than wearing a uniform.

We stopped at a fast-food joint and got a quick meal on McCray's dime. He said something about us needing our strength. I didn't know what the hell he was talking about. But half an hour later, when we pulled onto a small college campus, I realized why he'd said that. Suddenly, it made sense why he'd selected the biggest and most experienced guys from the group. We were surely going to take some shit at this place.

I'd never heard of the College of the Siskiyous before, but I knew enough about Northern California to realize that it was probably the closest college to Mount Shasta. Located off the 5 in a town called Weed, the community college campus was dotted with evergreen pine trees around low, rustic-style buildings. The place looked more like a low-end ski lodge than a college campus.

It was nearing eight o'clock as we pulled in, which I found strange. Surely there wouldn't be a bunch of classes in session at this time of night. "Is there going to be anyone here for us to recruit?" I asked. "I mean, this is a community college, right?"

"They have on-campus housing here," Spencer said from the front seat. "There will be people at the student hall. Trust me."

McCray turned into a parking lot and, sure enough, I saw the student hall up ahead. There were students milling around out front in coats and jackets. As we got out, a few kids went into the hall and others came out.

As we'd been loading up back at the training camp, I'd noticed a plastic storage container in the back of the truck. Now, McCray said we needed to grab it and bring it with us. Pennington reached in and lifted the thing out easily. He looked right at home wearing jogging pants and a hoodie, along with a black baseball cap with a white Celtic cross on it.

McCray leading the way, we all walked up the sidewalk toward the student hall. I could see through the double set of glass doors as we approached. There were pool tables and lounge chairs and a snack bar. The place wasn't what I would call packed, but there were plenty of people inside, chatting and flirting and laughing and craning their necks to stare at their phones.

There were five people still outside as we approached—two girls and three guys. I guess they were technically women and men, but I couldn't really think of them that way. They all looked like kids to me. And I probably looked like an old man to them. But as we slowed outside the doors and the five students looked at us with open curiosity, I tried to make the mental shift to see them as men and women. Because I had a plan. And for it to work, I would probably have to hurt one of them.

"Good evening, ladies and gentlemen," McCray said. Suddenly, I realized that all five of them were white. I had obviously noticed this before, but it hadn't crossed my mind as a conscious awareness. Now, it did. And I wondered what the approach would've been if one or more of them had been non-white. I guessed time would tell.

"How would you like to learn something useful for a change?" McCray said, continuing to talk to them.

"Uh, no thanks," one of the girls said, turning away from him.

Pennington set the plastic storage bin down. McCray opened it up and grabbed a handful of flyers from inside. I looked over and saw Spencer with his phone out, held up and fixed on McCray. He was shooting a video.

"Here," McCray said, holding out a flyer to one of the guys standing in the little group.

"What's this?" the guy said, taking it and reading it.

"It's time you saw the light, kiddos," McCray said. "The revolution is coming. Which side do you want to be on?"

The guy who took the flyer looked up at McCray, his face screwed up in disgust. He crumpled the flyer up and dropped it on the ground. "Why don't you take your hateful bullshit somewhere else?"

"What is it, Darren?" another one of the guys asked him.

"Neo-Nazi bullshit," Darren said, eyes still fixed on McCray.

Pennington and Everett stood near me, several feet away from the confrontation, watching. I noticed Spencer, who was off to the side, his phone out. He was filming.

"Haven't you ever heard of free speech?" McCray said. "Haven't you heard that white people are disappearing in this country? Did you know we'll be a minority in just a few years?"

"Who cares?" Darren said. "Seriously, why does that matter?"

"Come on, Darren," one of the girls said, grabbing his arm and trying to pull him inside. Darren wasn't having it.

"What the hell is wrong with you people?" he asked, looking at all of us in turn. "You're disgusting."

"And *you're* part of the problem," Everett said, stepping forward. "You don't care about your own culture, your own heritage!? You've been fucking brainwashed into turning your back on your own culture."

"There's no talking to these people," the other girl said. "Let's just go inside."

This seemed to get through to Darren. His expression changed from anger to sadness. He shook his head and went inside with his friends.

I watched them go, wondering just what the point of this little visit was. It was clearly not for recruitment. So I could only think it would be for one thing: manipulation. If we could get one of these kids to swing on us—and get it on camera—it would make a great piece of propaganda. I knew that white supremacist groups loved to claim discrimination, like their rights were being trampled on. And there was nothing like a video of white people being attacked to get their followers riled up.

If that was the case, then I was more than happy to facilitate. And I knew I would get a chance because I could see Darren and his friends inside. They were spreading the word about the neo-Nazis outside. It didn't take long for a large group of mostly guys to form in the student hall and head out toward us.

Chapter 22

"KEEP THAT CAMERA ON US," McCray said to Spencer as the group approached the door. I shook my arms out and loosened up my neck. No need to pull a muscle if you can help it.

"Whatever you do," McCray said to us, "make them throw the first punch."

I counted ten people coming out the doors, and even more coming up to the pair of interior doors to watch the drama play out. Most everyone in the group was white except for two Black guys. As if by some unspoken agreement, the two Black guys were leading the pack. I saw Darren nearby, coming out with the group while the girl who'd pulled him inside stood behind the glass doors, looking worried.

I sized up all the men, trying to determine who was most likely to throw a punch first. It's hard to tell these kinds of things just by looking, but I figured I would peg them once we started jawing at each other.

They walked out the door, stopped a good ten feet from us, and stared. I wasn't about to let this opportunity pass me by, so I stepped up, putting myself in front of the other guys—even McCray.

"You guys need to go," one of the Black guys said after sizing me up. He looked to be maybe twenty years old. He was wearing a dark green sweatsuit and had slippers on. I figured he'd come over from the residence hall to get a snack and hang out. Despite his footwear, he seemed confident enough. Of course, he had a reason to be confident; he had the numbers on his side.

"I thought this was a free country," I said. "Why do we have to leave? Just because you don't like what we're saying?"

"Because you're a racist fucking prick," Darren said. A few of their group laughed nervously.

"So what?" I said, raising my arms in a taunting gesture. "This country protects my right to say whatever I want. Isn't that what's great about America? Freedom of expression. Freedom of religion. Freedom to oppress white people."

"Oppress white people?!" the Black guy said, scoffing. "You've got to be fucking kidding me. You have to be blind *and* fucking stupid to think that white people are being oppressed in today's America."

"Every time one of my white brothers or sisters opens their mouth to advocate for white people, it's considered racist," I said, calling up the rhetoric white supremacists used to make it seem like they were victims. In the days leading up to the torching of Hoffman's house, I had done my best to memorize it. Honestly, it wasn't all that hard. I'd been hearing white supremacist talking points in the news for years now, thinly veiled and spouted by talking heads and "influencers" alike. "How is that not oppression? They're silencing our voices in favor of voices like yours."

"You know full well there's a difference between how Black people go about advocating for their people and how white supremacists go about it," the guy said, stepping closer to me and leveling his finger at me. "You people think the only way to stay on top is to stand on everyone else. But my people believe that we can all enjoy the view from the top. We don't have to step on anyone to get there. I'd say that's a pretty fucking big difference."

I laughed without humor in his face. "Ah, bullshit. Blacks want to see folks with white skin dead in the streets and you know it. But we can't say that. If we do point out the truth, we're punished for it."

The man stepped even closer to me and started shoving his finger in my face. "I can't speak for every Black person in this country," he said in a harsh whisper. "But I sure as hell wouldn't mind seeing your dumb ass dead in the fucking street."

I could see the effect I was having on this guy, and I didn't relish it. But I was so close. I just needed to give him a little push. So I said, "Then do something about it, *boy.*"

His finger curled in as he balled his hand into a fist. But, after a moment, he shook his head and stepped back. "Nah," he said. "Fuck you all. I'm not going to jail for you."

He turned around, and I felt some of the tension go out of the air as he told the rest of his group to head inside. We weren't going to come to blows. Not unless I did something quickly. And I had one more thing to try. It was the simplest thing of all, but something about it seemed to drive men of all kinds crazy. "That's what I thought," I said. "Fucking pussies."

Darren was the first one to break ranks. He spun around and lunged at me, leading with his fist. I turned on instinct, unable to help myself, and he hit me in the ear. But by the time his fist struck me, several of the other men were over the edge. The Black guy I'd been talking to tackled me to the grass next to the sidewalk. I let him hit me twice in the face.

"Get him, Dom!" Darren shouted.

McCray, Everett, and Pennington were all in the fight now, too, while Spencer recorded the whole thing.

One woman was screaming about calling the police as I blocked Dom's third punch. Then I sensed Darren next to me, and there was nothing I could do to block his kick. He hit me in the ribs, sending a shock of tremendous pain up my rib cage. As he reared back to kick me again, I managed to roll Dom off me, tripping Darren up in the process. Scrambling to my feet, someone came at me from the side, punching me in the back of the head. My vision went blurry as I stumbled and fell again.

I started to worry that I would take too much damage. My plan was to get hurt just enough to get taken to the cabin back at the camp, but if this kept up, I could end up in the hospital. Or, worse yet, we could all end up in jail.

As I hit the ground, I rolled onto my back and kicked out instinctively, hitting one of my assailants—a third man—in the stomach. He doubled over and I kicked him in the face, sending him falling to the ground. Although my vision was blurry, I saw Spencer grabbing up the storage container and heading toward the car. McCray was already running that way. "Let's go!" he shouted.

Both Dom and Darren were rushing me, and it was clear that no one was going to help me—Everett and Pennington were still occupied—so I got to my feet and faced off against them. They slowed, then started going in both directions to flank me. The last thing I wanted to do was put these guys in the hospital, but I couldn't let them get me down again. I probably wouldn't be getting back up without help. As it was, my vision was still swimming. With the three decent blows to the head, combined with the exhausting day I'd already had, I didn't have much left in the tank.

I backed up, preventing them from flanking me and moving toward the parking lot at once. I could turn to run, but my legs were a little wobbly and I'd never been all that fast. I was sure one of these guys would catch me. So I had to put them down. If I could.

Raising my hands to my jacket's lapels, I shifted my leather off my shoulders, slipping my left arm out of the sleeve and then swinging it around in front of me. I pulled my right arm out and gathered the jacket up in front of me, holding it by the sleeves.

Darren was to my left, Dom to my right. I had to make a move.

I whipped the jacket at Dom's face, causing him to flinch back. At the same time, Darren saw his chance and moved in. But I'd been counting on this. I jackknifed my left arm up and lunged to my left, smashing Darren in the face with my elbow. He went down hard in the grass. Turning back toward Dom, I got hold of the leather jacket with my left hand again and pulled it up just as Dom swung at me. The taut jacket caught him under the elbow of his outstretched arm, throwing his punch off, his fist narrowly missing my face.

The move and his momentum spun him, turning him slightly away from me. Once his arm was clear, I wrapped the jacket around his neck from behind even as I was turning my back to him. As I pulled on the jacket, I finished turning my back to him. We were now back-to-back. Using what strength I had left, I whipped my torso forward, levering Dom onto my back with the jacket and then throwing him over. He flipped backward, landing hard on his hands and knees in the grass.

I pulled the jacket free from his neck as I straightened up. The flip hadn't hurt him, as far as I could tell, but it bought me a moment to put him down. As he moved to get up to his feet, I kicked him in the head, pulling the hit at the last moment so I wouldn't do too much damage. He flopped onto his back, and I wasted no time before running out to the parking lot.

Glancing over my shoulder, I saw Pennington and Everett running after me. Everett was leaning heavily on Pennington, bleeding from his face. Behind them, I counted five men down on the sidewalk or in the grass, in addition to the three I put down. I wondered how many of those had been Pennington's doing. He didn't look like he had a scratch on him. In fact, he was grinning.

McCray's truck screeched as it reversed over to the sidewalk. Spencer opened his door and the suicide door behind it. He was no longer recording; he'd gotten all he needed. "Come on!" he shouted.

As I clambered into the back of the cab, I looked over and saw a couple of the women running toward us, cellphones held out.

"Pennington, the back!" McCray shouted. "Get in the back and cover the plate!"

Pennington nodded, nearly throwing Everett into the back of the truck before jumping in himself. I slammed the suicide door and Spencer did the same with his door as we sped off. I looked into the back of the truck to see Pennington leaning over the tailgate to obscure the license plate with his hands. Meanwhile, Everett had pulled the top off the plastic container and was tossing sheaves of the racist pamphlets out of the truck, laughing like a madman.

I collapsed down onto the seat, putting a hand to my bloody nose.

"You good?" Spencer asked, mirth in his voice.

"They fucked me up," I groaned. "Goddamn subs fucked me up."

Chapter 23

"HEY, TROUBLE. YOU ALIVE back there?"

I kept my eyes closed, pretending not to hear McCray.

"He took a couple good shots to the head," Spencer said. "It's great fuckin' footage, if I say so myself. Black dude beating up on him like that. Gonna get some people *pissed*."

"Good," McCray said. "Give the phone over."

"Oh, yeah. Right," Spencer said. I could hear noises indicating Spencer pulling his phone out and giving it to McCray.

The truck was stopped, and everyone had already gotten out. Everyone but me, anyway. When we were safely away from the campus, McCray had pulled over to let Pennington and Everett get into the cab. I had ended up behind the driver's seat, leaning against the window. I found a nearly finished roll of blue paper towels near my feet and had grabbed a couple to staunch the flow of blood from my nose and the gash on my eyebrow. Then I'd leaned against the door and closed my eyes.

Now, I wanted to make sure I got to the cabin, and I figured having them check me for a concussion was the way to go. So I stayed quiet and still until McCray reached in and shook my shoulder. I opened my eyes and groaned.

"We're here," he said. "Get your ass out of my truck."

I stumbled out of the truck and saw that we were parked next to the cabin. The lights were on inside, and I could see people moving around through one of the lower windows. Everett leaned against the truck, his face as bloody as mine. He had his mouth open and was wiggling a loose tooth with a finger.

Pennington stood at the back of the truck, next to Spencer. Both men looked unharmed. Of course, Spencer hadn't been involved in the fight. Pennington had been, but it looked as if he hadn't even taken a punch. Suddenly, I didn't feel so bad for letting him get me on the ground earlier. Not only was he a giant of a man, but he knew what the hell he was doing.

"Get back to the barracks and get yourselves cleaned up," McCray said.

My heart plummeted into my stomach. I didn't have time for this shit. I needed to get inside the cabin so I could get some intel to give to Nez and Hudson.

The other three men started off while McCray turned toward the cabin's steps.

"Hey, McCray," I said. "I think I got a concussion. My head's killing me, and I can't see straight. Can you get me something for it? Some Advil or something?"

McCray turned and looked at me, his features hard. "Come on, then," he said, waving me after him.

"I could use some Advil, too," Everett said. I resisted the urge to stare daggers at him.

McCray sighed. "Alright, follow me."

"Aww, poor little bitches," Pennington said from behind us.

"Cut that shit out," McCray told him.

Everett and I trudged up the stairs after McCray and waited while he used a key to unlock the front door. We stepped into the warmth of the cabin. A man I'd never seen before poked his head out from a doorway to our right. "Just me," McCray said. The guy disappeared without a word.

The interior was a perfect match for the exterior. The walls were covered with richly colored wood panels. The floors were polished wood adorned with rustic-style rugs of earthen colors. There were animal antlers displayed on walls, along with pictures detailing what looked like several generations of a white family.

McCray led us down the entryway hall and toward a log-and-timber staircase but turned into a sitting room before we got to it. He took us through the sitting room and into a small den that had been converted to a makeshift first aid station. There were four cots there, each with a TV tray set up at its foot. Basic first aid supplies sat atop each wooden tray. Other than the three of us, there was no one in the room.

McCray told us to stay put and then walked through the room's second doorway, which led past what looked like a basement or closet door. I sat on one of the cots, still holding the wad of bloody blue paper towels. My nose and eyebrow had stopped bleeding, but I needed to sell my injuries if I didn't want to only be in here for a few minutes. My plan was to try and stay the night here. I just didn't know exactly how I would pull that off.

After a few minutes, McCray came back the way he'd left, leading a woman in her mid-twenties. I'd seen her earlier in the day when she was bringing food out to the mess hall. She had long auburn hair secured behind her head with a couple of hair clips. Her brown eyes were big, and her pretty, freckled face came to a point at a sharp chin. The modest floral-print dress she wore would've looked right at home a hundred years ago.

"Clean 'em up, check 'em out," McCray said to her. Then he looked at both of us—me sitting on a cot, Everett standing up and messing with his loose tooth with one thumb. "If I hear you so much as fart around Lorena here, the beating you took tonight will feel like a massage. Get me?"

"Yes, sir," Everett and I said in unison.

McCray nodded and snapped off a Nazi salute. "White power!"

We both returned the gesture and the words. Then, he went off into the house to do whatever it was he did.

"Who wants it first?" Lorena said, stepping forward and putting her hands on her hips.

"You can do him first," I said, gesturing at Everett, who smiled at her with bloody teeth.

"Sit down," she said to him. And as Everett sat down, I stood up, wobbling as I did. Lorena saw it, turning to grab my arm.

"I'm okay," I said. "I just need to use the bathroom. Where is it?"

"Down that way," she said, studying me with furrowed brows. "Right at the hallway and first door on your left," she said.

I trudged that way, bracing myself against walls as I went. It wasn't an act at this point. I was starting to feel like something was really wrong with me.

Up ahead was the kitchen. Through the doorway I could see a couple of women, dressed similarly to Lorena, performing food prep. It was approaching midnight, so I assumed they were preparing tomorrow's breakfast.

I turned right, into the hallway bisecting the cabin. I could see the underside of the staircase and, beyond it, the front door. There was a door on my left which I assumed was the bathroom, but I continued, curious about what was going on in the room the man had stuck his head out of when we came in.

I stepped up to the doorway, which was not built to contain an actual door—it was called a cased opening, I remembered from my construction days. The room was divided in half by a cubicle-like divider, preventing me from seeing half the space. The half I could see was occupied by two desks, each with a desktop computer on top. McCray was sitting at one desk and the curious guy was at the other. My angle was wrong for seeing the curious guy's computer screen, but I could see McCray's. He looked to be editing the video footage of the encounter.

Curious Guy looked up at me. "What the fuck are you doing?" he said.

McCray turned in his seat. "What is it?" he snapped.

"Sorry," I said. "Bathroom?"

"Behind you. On the right," McCray said.

"You can't be wandering around in here," the other guy said.

"Relax," McCray said. "Look at his fuckin' face. He just took a beating for us. Besides, this is the Jew Burner."

The guy's face lit up at that. "That was you?" he said.

"I didn't actually burn the guy, much as I wanted to," I said.

"If you had, you wouldn't be here with us," he said. "Still, I laughed my ass off when I saw that shit on the news. You got some balls on you, man."

"Yeah, thanks," I said. "So, back this way? I must have passed it." I turned and went back the way I came, stepping into the bathroom and locking the door.

I took a minute to catch my breath, leaning on the countertop and looking into the mirror. As I looked into my eyes—my left half-obscured by my swollen eyelid—a wave of nausea swept through me. I realized my arms were shaking. I straightened up and raised my hands to look at them. They trembled noticeably.

My stomach convulsed. I spun around and flipped the toilet cover up just in time to vomit half-digested fast-food into the toilet bowl.

Shit, I thought between stomach convulsions, *maybe there really is something wrong with me.*

Chapter 24

"ARE YOU OKAY IN there?" Lorena asked from the other side of the bathroom door. On my knees in front of the toilet, I told her I was and that I'd be out in a few minutes.

I heard her walk away, knowing I had nothing left to throw up. That didn't keep me from feeling nauseous, though. Breathing deeply, I tried to get myself under control, telling myself everything was fine. As I stood up to drink a little water from the faucet, I heard heavy footsteps coming down the stairs. It sounded like three or four people. I pressed myself up against the closed door and listened.

The footsteps seemed to stop at the bottom of the stairs. Men's voices came through the door, just loud enough for me to strain to make out the words.

"We're heading out now," a familiar voice said. It was Halverson. "Should be back tomorrow."

"Just keep things as they are," another man said. I didn't recognize his voice. "Make sure these men are ready and that they can fire their weapons with some kind of accuracy."

"They won't need to be *that* accurate," Halverson said. This elicited some laughter from the other men.

"You want me to just keep everyone here?" McCray asked. "No more propaganda or recruitment drives?"

"Right," the mystery man said. "Use this time to make sure all the men you have are willing to do what's asked of them. If they seem like they're fucking snowflakes or too scared to kill for the cause, get rid of them."

There was a moment of silence before McCray spoke again. "Do you mean what I think you mean?"

"We're not going to have one of these idiots blowing this whole thing for us. So yeah, I mean *get rid of them*. Obviously, I would prefer it if you don't have to. We need all the good white men we can get. But I'll leave it up to your judgment. You know these guys better than us."

"Yes, sir," McCray said.

I listened as the men said their goodbyes. The front door closed and, a few moments later, I thought I heard an engine starting up outside.

After flushing the toilet, washing my mouth out, and cleaning up, I stepped out of the bathroom and headed back to the little first-aid room. Lorena was sitting on one of the cots, looking at her phone. She glanced up at me as I walked in.

"Where's Everett," I asked.

"The other guy?" she said, standing up. "I sent him back to the barracks. Wasn't much I could do for him but clean his cuts and tell him to see a dentist."

"Right," I said. "My turn, I guess."

"Were you vomiting in the bathroom?"

"I'm fine," I said, sitting down.

"Not what I asked," she said, putting her hands on her hips. "Were you vomiting in the bathroom?"

"Yes."

"That other man—Everett—told me what happened. How many times did you get hit in the head, and how hard?"

Suddenly, I saw my opportunity. I had to play this right. If I did, I could stay in the house overnight for observation. If I didn't, she would probably insist I go to a hospital. I had some idea of the kinds of complications that could arise from head injuries, but I wasn't exactly sure what the various symptoms were. After thinking about her question, I said, "I don't know. Maybe three or four times. Not super hard, but they weren't love taps, either."

Lorena pursed her lips and stared down at me. "I saw you wobble when you got up to go to the bathroom. Have you experienced any vision problems?"

I had been, but it seemed like she was checking off a list. So I took a chance and lied. "No, not really."

She glanced down at her phone. "What about difficulty keeping your eyes open?"

"No."

"And headache? Has it been getting worse or better since the fight?"

"It's about the same," I said. "Are these concussion symptoms?"

"Well, that's the tricky thing. They can present after a concussion, but they may also indicate a subdural hematoma."

I gave her a puzzled look.

"It means bleeding in the brain where blood collects between the brain and the skull. It can be life-threatening if not treated."

"Huh," I said. "Well, I doubt my brain is bleeding."

"Oh, yeah? And how would you know?"

I shrugged. "It's my brain, isn't it?"

That got a smile from her. But it faded quickly as she studied me. I looked into her big eyes, appreciating her beauty. I'd always had a thing for brunettes with big eyes.

After a moment of deliberation, she shook her head and muttered, "Damn niggers."

And just like that, any appreciation I had for this woman or her beauty popped like a balloon in a cactus field. Her words shouldn't have surprised me, given where I was, but they did.

"I think I'll ask McCray to take you to the hospital," she said. "I would hate for you to die on my watch."

My throat thickened. I shook my head. "Please, don't. I feel like I'm finally right where I belong, and if I go to the hospital, I may never get to come back here. I know something big is happening soon, and I want to be around for it."

She bit the side of her bottom lip, clearly thinking.

"Isn't there another way?" I asked. "Can't you like . . . keep me here for observation? If I don't get better in a few hours, I'll go to the hospital willingly. I'll do whatever you say."

"And you won't lie to me about your symptoms?" she asked with narrowed eyes.

"I swear," I said, raising my right hand as though in a courtroom.

"Okay," she said. "Fine."

"Thank you."

Lorena nodded as she gathered the supplies to clean the cuts on my face. Ten minutes later, I had a couple of over-the-counter painkillers in my stomach and a clean, although still swollen, face.

"I'll come down to check on you in a few hours," she said, getting ready to leave.

"Where will you be? If I need you."

"I'll be with the other women in an upstairs bedroom," she said. Then, seeming to realize something, she glared at me. "But the door will be locked, so don't try anything," she said, only half joking.

"Wouldn't dream of it."

"But if it's a real emergency, you can come up and knock on the door. Second one on the left in the upstairs hallway."

"Thank you," I said, lying back on the cot.

"You're welcome." Lorena flipped off the lights and headed out of the room. Sometime during our little treatment session, the women in the kitchen had finished up. The house was quiet for the most part, save for someone still in the room near the front door. I figured it was McCray or the other guy—or both.

Lying on the cot, I kept my eyes closed but my ears perked. I waited for the place to go completely silent. Then I would check it out. Hopefully I'd find something Nez and Hudson could use.

As I lay there, waiting, I willed the painkillers to work. Despite what I told Lorena, my headache was getting worse. Much worse.

Chapter 25

TIME PASSED. THE SOUND of computer keyboard keys clacking was replaced by the sound of snoring from the sitting room. I didn't know how much time had passed since Lorena had left, but I guessed two hours or so. I should've looked at a clock when I'd gone to the bathroom, but it hadn't occurred to me.

Lorena said she'd check on me in a "few" hours. It could be any time now, or I could be waiting for another hour or two. Figuring now was my best chance, I got up from the cot and untied my boots, slipping them off so I wouldn't be clomping around the place. It would mean I couldn't run if I was caught snooping, but it wasn't like I could get away even if I did run. No, I knew that if I was caught, I'd either have to do some verbal gymnastics to get out of it or I would be killed. After all, if McCray had standing orders to kill recruits whose hearts weren't in the fight, they surely wouldn't hesitate to remove my brains from my skull with a well-placed bullet.

But the way my head was aching, it wouldn't be the worst thing in the world.

The drugs hadn't made a noticeable difference. And as I straightened after taking off my boots, a wave of pain swept through my skull. I jammed the heels of my hands against my eyes, but that only made things worse. I forced myself to breathe deeply for a few moments before taking off my jacket—which had zipper pull tabs that rattled a bit—and standing up.

The first thing I did was move into the sitting room, looking down at McCray on one couch and Curious Guy on the other. I hadn't caught the man's name during our brief exchange earlier. They both looked to be sound asleep.

Padding past them, I snuck across the hall and into the room with the computers on one side and the divider partitioning the other. Both computers were dark. I didn't want to get on them unless I had to. My plan was to look around and see what I could find before I went snooping around on computers. I was no hacker, so I hoped it wouldn't come to that.

I moved over toward the edge of the partition and peered around at the other side of the room. There was a light on in the hallway, which provided some illumination, but not on this side of the divider. I could see two desks pushed up against each other so if two people sat at them they would be facing each other. Both desks were littered with items and tools. I moved closer to get a better look.

When I got close enough, I realized that the items on the desks were bomb-making supplies. There were steel pipes sitting on the near desk. Each of them had been fitted with a steel cap on one end. The other ends were open. Lined up nearby was a corresponding number of steel caps with holes drilled in their tops. That was where the fuses would go.

On the other desk, there were lengths of wire, batteries, and square black devices that had to be simple timers. I didn't see any evidence of actual explosives that would go inside the pipe bombs. This didn't surprise me, though. These people clearly weren't stupid, and that's just what it would've been to be assembling explosives in this house with so many people around. I figured they would take these prepared components somewhere isolated to finish the construction. So if something did go wrong, it would only kill the one or two people doing the assembly.

After looking around for anything else of value, I moved back into the hallway and started up the stairs. Keeping to the edges of the steps, I made my way up without making a noise louder than a whisper. As I stood at the top of the stairs, looking down the hallway, I heard movement from downstairs. Stepping quickly toward the wall, I pressed myself up against it, hoping the deep shadows there would keep me hidden. I was able to look over the railing next to the stairwell as McCray walked out of the sitting room, clearing his throat and muttering to himself. He walked past the stairwell, heading for the bathroom. I held my breath—all it would take was a glance up for him to see me. But he didn't glance up, and soon he was lost from sight as he passed under me on the floor below.

Not willing to press my luck any further, I turned to the nearest door and tried the knob. It was unlocked. I opened it slowly, willing the hinges to stay quiet, and peered inside. It was an office. And there was no one inside. I closed the door behind me and stood there, waiting for McCray to finish in the bathroom. Finally, I heard the toilet flush and the door open. I didn't hear him walk back out to the sitting room, but after about two minutes, I figured he'd done just that.

Then I wondered what he'd do if he went to check on me and saw I wasn't there. Would he raise the alarm, or would he stalk quietly around the house looking for me?

I had no idea. But I couldn't let my fear get the better of me. My steady hum of a headache was doing enough to keep me from thinking clearly, and I didn't need any more stress. So I turned my attention to searching the office.

There was a window in the wall opposite the door, but there simply wasn't enough starlight or moonlight coming in for me to search by. I contemplated flipping the light switch until I made out a floor lamp next to a seat in the corner. Moving to the window, I lower the shades. Then, as I was about to turn on the lamp, I looked toward the door, thinking about the light. There was a cardigan hanging over the back of the seat, so I grabbed it and put it across the bottom of the door, hoping it would be enough to keep anyone passing in the hall from spotting the light.

I just hoped Lorena wouldn't come to check on me in the next ten or fifteen minutes.

With the cardigan in place, I moved back to the lamp and clicked it on. My attention went immediately to the desk, which was positioned against the wall next to the door. It was a modest one, although it looked fairly new. There was a computer on it, along with an old coffee mug with pens, pencils, and markers in it. Sticky notes were stuck to the computer monitor and at various places on the desk's surface.

I read them all, looking for names or addresses. Most of the stuff seemed innocuous enough, but I wasn't about to take the chance. I had no phone to take pictures of them and my memory was far from infallible. So I opened the thin, wide drawer above the knee hole and found a blank pad of neon green sticky notes. Grabbing a pen from the coffee mug, I started copying down anything and everything I saw written on the notes. Most of them had only been used for a single idea, so I was able to fit nearly all on a single square paper by writing small.

Once done with the surface of the desk, I went through the drawers. In the top right drawer, I saw a .22 Ruger pistol. The urge to pick it up and pocket it was almost unbearable. For much of my adult life, I'd carried guns on me as a matter of course. Being without the comforting weight of one in my jacket pocket, or stuffed less comfortably in my waistband, was a feeling I didn't relish. But I resisted the urge, knowing that taking it would eventually alert the brass that someone had been in this room.

If I had some secure knowledge that the information I was collecting would be enough to stop whatever insane, hatred-inspired plot they had cooking up, I would've taken the gun, stolen McCray's truck, and booked it off the property. But as it was, I wasn't sure if I would need to stay undercover for a day or a week or a month longer.

Using the hem of my shirt, I picked up the gun and moved it off the small brown notebook it was sitting on. Setting the gun momentarily on top of the desk, I grabbed the notebook and flipped to the first page. There was a line of names on the page. But they weren't normal names. They looked to be usernames.

I read the first few.

E-TurnEr

WLPierce$

AndyM@c

They all looked familiar to me, but I couldn't think why. My head throbbed and my vision blurred as I stared down at the page. Wrenching my eyes shut for a moment, I took a deep breath. Then I opened them and flipped further into the notebook. I stopped at a page that had only two lines of text, one under the other:

Key: EugenFischer.org

1, 3, 5, 7

Realizing all this stuff was likely important, I set the notebook down and went about copying all that I could onto pieces of paper from the green notepad. First, I copied the most recent page down—the one with only two lines of text. Then I flipped back to the first page and got through the first four usernames before I heard something outside in the hallway. There was a creak. And it was close. Someone was in the hall outside the office.

I froze, looking toward the closed door. My heart slammed against my rib cage as my vision blurred.

The doorknob turned.

Chapter 26

THERE WAS NO PLACE to hide in the office. Not that I would've had time to hide anywhere. Not even close. The door opened as I stood frozen on the far side of the desk. I'd been using the little rectangle of free space on this side of the desk as a writing surface, and I still held the pen I'd been using. The little sticky notepad sat on the desk, next to the notebook I'd pulled out of the drawer.

It took a moment for the man to see me. I recognized him immediately. It was Stoll—the friendly guy I'd met with Spencer outside the barracks last night. He was looking down as the door opened its first six inches, surely trying to figure out what was obstructing the door. But the cardigan I'd placed there didn't do much to keep him from opening it. And a half-second after opening the office door, he looked up into my face.

He looked as surprised to see me as I was to see him. I had a moment to wonder if he was supposed to be in here. But before I could follow this train of thought, Stoll's eyes left mine and moved down to the Ruger pistol on the corner of the desk nearest him. Since the door was right there, he was slightly closer to the weapon than I was.

A sneer transformed his features as he went for the gun. I had no idea whether it was even loaded, but I wasn't about to leave it to chance. I lunged forward, bracing my left hand on the desk as my upper body leaned over the chair I had pulled a few inches out from the knee hole when I'd opened the drawer there. Stoll got his right hand on the gun just before I jammed the point of the pen down into the back of his palm. I felt the pen puncture skin and sink into his flesh, causing Stoll to cry out. But he didn't pull his hand back like I'd hoped. He kept it on the gun, bringing his left hand forward to assist his now-injured right.

I slipped my hand off the pen and onto his right hand, holding it down as I maneuvered my feet around the desk chair. We wrestled for the gun, each with both our hands. All my attention was placed on the Ruger, so I didn't see the headbutt coming. Stoll whipped the curve of his forehead into my face, sending a blinding white explosion of pain through my already tormented head.

My legs went rubbery, and a black curtain seemed to fall over my eyes for a moment. I went down, but I still managed to hold onto the gun. Stoll wasn't a big guy by any means, so I pulled him with me as I fell to my butt and then rolled onto my back. Stoll was bent awkwardly over me, still on his feet, while I was on my back. The gun was between us, neither one having the better grip.

Stoll tried to use his leverage to wrench the gun away from me, but his hand was bleeding, making the appendage slippery. As he yanked up, his right hand's tenuous grip slipped off the gun and he stumbled upright.

It gave me an opening.

He still had his left hand around the barrel, but with his right hand gone, I was no longer blocked from the grip or the trigger assembly. I yanked on the weapon, slipping my finger into the trigger guard even as Stoll tried to keep the barrel pointed away from himself.

Someone yelled from downstairs, drawn by our scuffle and Stoll's cry of pain.

The Ruger had a safety lever on either side of the gun, and I thought the odds were pretty good that one of us had slid the mechanism from Safe to Fire as we wrestled with it. I pulled the trigger to find out.

The gun fired, the bullet hitting the open door to the room. Stoll's hand had been on the slide as it fired, and now he pulled it away as though it had been burned or pinched—or both.

He no longer had a hand on the weapon.

I pointed it at his face and had just enough time for the word "Don't" to form in my mind and travel to the tip of my tongue. As all the muscles necessary for speech fired into action, Stoll threw himself at me.

I pulled the trigger again.

This time, I didn't miss. The bullet obliterated his left eye. Although I couldn't see it, I was sure it did massive damage to his brain. But he didn't die right away. He landed on me, his hands going for the gun again. But now they didn't have the same strength or urgency. The sneer stayed on his face for a long moment as I held him off me with my left hand while pointing the gun at his chest with my right, unsure if I would need to fire again.

Blood poured out of his wounded eye and onto my shirt. He made a few sounds, his mouth moving like that of a half-asleep drunk. If he spoke words, I couldn't understand them. Then his face went slack, followed shortly by his body. I threw him off me just as McCray and Curious Guy arrived in the office doorway, both pointing pistols at me and looking around in confusion.

I looked up at the two men, my own half-swollen face surely matching the shock they were feeling. But I was sure there was something else on my face: fear.

McCray straightened his arms, pointing his weapon toward me and slipping his finger into the trigger guard.

I was about to die.

But there was one thing I could try. One thing that just might work. One thing that, if I was lucky, would keep me alive for just a little longer.

I dropped the Ruger and said the only three words in the world that had any hope at all of saving me from a bullet to the head.

Chapter 27

"He's a rat."

I pointed at Stoll as I said this. "He's a rat. I followed him up here. Just look at what he was doing. He was going through the desk."

It was the only chance I had. But if Stoll was supposed to be in here—if he was a trusted member of the organization who had a reason for coming up to the office—then I was a dead man. But I had nothing to lose. When you're five pounds of trigger pull weight away from death, you take what you can get.

McCray rested his finger against the trigger, his eyes bouncing from me to Stoll's body to the desk and back again. Meanwhile, Curious Guy's thin and angular face became thinner and more angular as his mouth dropped open and his eyebrows went up. He stared at Stoll's body as though he'd never seen a dead person before. Maybe he hadn't.

McCray stepped forward into the room, telling me to keep my hands up as he continued pointing his gun at me. His .45 would make a much bigger mess of me than the .22 had of Stoll. "Pete," he said to Curious Guy, "check out the desk. Tell me what you see."

Pete swallowed and nodded absently, but he kept staring at Stoll's body.

"Pete!"

Pete snapped out of it and stepped over to the desk.

"What's going on in there, Wyatt?" a woman's voice asked from down the hall.

"Everything's under control, Mary," McCray said without moving his gaze from me. "Stay in your rooms till I tell you to come out."

I heard women whispering and then a door shutting down the hall.

The vision in my left eye was blurry and my headache had gotten worse since Stoll had headbutted me. I settled my head back on the carpet, telling myself not to speak unless spoken to. I wanted time to think my story through, and the last thing I needed was to blurt out something that would later come to bite me in the ass. So I started asking myself questions, putting myself in McCray's shoes.

How had Stoll gotten inside the house? Did he break in? Was a door left unlocked for him? How had I heard him? What prompted me to follow him up the stairs?

There were too many unknowns. I had to be very careful. If I said I'd heard him come through the back door, but it later came out that he'd come in through a window, I would be dead.

So I pushed past the pain and the cloudiness in my head, thinking, and doing it fast.

"He was copying stuff down from Cotter's notebook," Pete said, looking at the evidence on the desk. "Or, *someone* was, anyway."

"Cover him," McCray said. "If he moves, kill him."

"I'm telling the truth," I said. "I'm not gonna move."

Pete and McCray switched places.

I thought about the pen that I'd stabbed into Stoll's hand as he went for the gun. It was still there, sticking out from the bloody wound. It was a major crack in my story. If he'd been the one writing stuff down, wouldn't he have had the pen?

McCray did something on the desk and then turned around, pointing his gun at me again. "Get up slowly," he said.

I did as I was told, getting first to my knees and then to my feet, keeping my hands up.

"Step over to the desk," McCray said, moving out of the way, something cupped in his left hand.

I had to step over Stoll's body to get there. I looked down and saw McCray had taken the top sticky note sheet off the pad, revealing the blank one underneath.

"Write something down," McCray said. He wanted to see if my handwriting was the same as the samples he now had in his left hand.

"What do you want me to write?" I said, trying to keep the fear out of my voice.

"I don't care. How about you write the fourteen words?"

I nodded, my throat thickening. Grabbing a pen out of the mug on the table, I thought about how I'd been careful to copy down the words from the notebook slowly. I'd never had the best handwriting, and I'd known that I would likely be giving the paper off to Nez and Hudson. I wanted to be sure they could read it without issue. But it was still my handwriting.

As I touched the pen to paper, I decided to write larger, in a kind of swooping script halfway to cursive. If I'd remembered actual cursive from my occasional stints at public schools, I would've gone for it. As it was, I hoped it would be different enough to give McCray pause. After all, he couldn't ask Stoll to provide a sample.

I wrote the fourteen words down on the paper, trying not to go too fast or too slow. *We must secure the existence of our people and a future for white children.* When I was done, I set the pen down and stood up.

"Sit in the chair," McCray said, pointing at the seat with the standing lamp next to it.

I sat down, resting my arms on the chair's arms. McCray stepped over, set his gun down, and picked up the pad I'd been writing on. He inspected the words, comparing them to the ones on the sheet from earlier. Pete kept his pistol trained on me.

After nearly two minutes of this, he set the papers down and picked his gun up again, turning to me. "Tell me exactly what happened," he said.

"I was downstairs, sleeping on one of the cots," I said. "You knew that, right? Lorena told you?"

"What happened with Stoll?" McCray asked.

"That's what I'm getting at. I was downstairs, but I couldn't sleep. And a little while after I heard you get up and go to the bathroom, I heard someone else moving through the house. But it wasn't like when you went to the bathroom. I could tell they were trying to be as quiet as possible. So—"

"How'd he get inside?" McCray interrupted.

"I don't know," I said. "I just heard him moving around. He might've come from the back, but I couldn't be sure. You probably would have heard him if he came from the front, right? Besides, the front door stays locked, doesn't it?"

McCray glanced at Pete, who nodded and said, "I locked it. I know I locked it."

"He must've gotten in another way," I said. "Anyway, I heard him—I didn't know who it was at the time, though—I heard him go up the stairs really slowly and quietly. So I got up from the cot and moved down the hall to see if I could see what was going on."

"Why didn't you wake us up?" McCray asked.

I shrugged. "What if it was nothing? What if it was one of the women, just trying to be quiet after she went and got some water or something? I didn't want to wake you up for nothing, you know?"

"Fine. So what happened next?"

"By the time I got to the stairwell and looked up, I couldn't see anyone. But I thought I heard a door close. So I went halfway up the stairs and stopped. I was about to go back down—I didn't want anyone to think I was snooping around—but then I heard something. It sounded like a lamp clicking on." I gestured at the lamp next to me as I said this.

"So I went to the top of the stairs and looked for light under any of the doors, but I didn't see any. I thought that was strange. Then I heard movement in this room. So I came to investigate. I opened the door, noticing that something was in the way." We all looked at the cardigan that was now jammed up behind the door and against the wall. "And then I saw Stoll standing right there where you are but leaning over the desk. I didn't know what he was doing, you know? I thought maybe it was normal for him to be in here. But before I could think of what to do, he came at me with the pen he was writing with. The same one that's still sticking out of his hand."

"What about the gun? Where did that come from?"

Here's where I had to change things a little bit to make the story fit. I shook my head. "I didn't even know there was a gun. Not at first. It was sitting in that drawer, but I didn't see it until after I got the pen away from Stoll. He shoved me away and went for the drawer, and that was when I knew something important was in there. But as he brought the thing out, I stabbed him with the pen and then we fought for the gun. I won."

"Why not go for the gun first?" McCray asked. "Why go after you with the pen at all?"

I shrugged. "Maybe he panicked. Maybe he didn't want to make a bunch of noise because he was still hoping to get out of here with the information. I don't know. If he had gone for it first, he might've killed me."

McCray studied me for a long moment. Hope sparked in my chest. I thought he was buying it. But then he stepped forward and put his gun against my forehead. "I don't believe a fuckin' word you've said."

Chapter 28

"HERE THEY COME," BOVE said from beside Coakley. They stood on the porch of Bove's Cape Cod-style house, shaded from the morning sunshine by the awning. It was an unseasonably warm and cloudless day in Oregon, and both men were in shirtsleeves. They were looking toward the entrance to the little valley they called their home, watching two SUVs turn onto the dirt road. This was their little slice of white heaven. It was the conception place of a new country, the equivalent of Philadelphia during the kicking-and-screaming birth of America.

A dozen houses had already been built on the two gently sloping sides of the narrow valley, and there was room for two dozen more. If all went according to plan, this would be the seat of the new government. The Pacific Northwest would eventually become a white mecca. That was the ultimate aim. But to accomplish this goal, they would need to plunge much of America into chaos. While the Zionist Occupied Government was busy elsewhere, trying to restore electricity to millions, take down rampaging men with military-style weapons, and deal with the assassinations of several elected officials, the rest of The White Power Alliance would be taking over much of Oregon, starting with the capital. Once they established that as their base of operations, they could worry about expanding to Washington and Idaho.

They didn't have the numbers at their immediate disposal for such a task, but they were confident that when the call went out—when their brothers and sisters saw that the revolution was upon them—then the whites would rise up against the inferior races. Not all of the whites, of course. But they didn't need all of them. They didn't even need half. If even a quarter of the white people in the Pacific Northwest took up arms—and there were plenty to be taken up—then they could secure the borders of their new country.

Then they would cleanse it. They would hang interracial couples from trees, execute anyone who stood against them, and slaughter anyone who wasn't white. After that, they could breathe easy. They could thank God for delivering them from evil. For guiding their hands, helping them do the things no one else wanted to.

But they were realists, above all else. Even if they didn't take all of Oregon, they could still take a chunk in the northwest corner. And even if they didn't manage to take *any* land, their show of force would be enough to strike terror into the hearts of all the subhumans in the country, and their race-traitor brethren. Besides, the more subhumans eliminated during their attempted revolution, the better. As Bove had expressed many times, even one less Black or Jew or chink or Muslim or beaner in the world was a step in the right direction.

Coakley had to agree. He wondered how he had ever thought differently. He wondered how he had ever gone through life lying to himself, telling himself that all races were equal. Well, the last decade or so had dispelled him of that notion. He'd watched white culture being destroyed with glee as Blacks had cried and moaned about systemic racism when all they had to do was look at their own culture of laziness and addiction.

He'd seen white families destroyed by the opioid epidemic while Jew-controlled pharmaceutical companies recorded record profits.

He'd seen the percentage of white people in America slowly tick down as non-whites continued to grow and grow. He'd seen health insurance prices skyrocket—along with prices for everything else—squeezing the white middle class down to nothing. All while the Jews at the top continued getting richer.

He had felt helpless to do anything about it. Until he met Bove. Since then, they'd come so far, done so much. And now they were on the cusp of doing something great. Something that would truly matter.

But they weren't there yet. These next steps were the most tenuous. There were so many moving parts and so many egos at play. They had to be very deliberate. And very careful.

As the two SUVs turned off the main road, heading up Bove's driveway, Coakley stepped out from under the awning and looked up at the sky. He wondered if there was a drone up there, looking down at him right now. If so, things would simply get harder. But they had a plan in place just in case they were arrested.

The government had to play by certain rules. And Coakley was well aware of those rules. Which was why he had been in charge of drafting Plan B. They could still accomplish their goals if he and Bove were arrested. While the system was somewhat centralized, with Bove in command, they had an alternative system set up. A decentralized system that would take effect if something should happen to Bove.

Still, he preferred that they stay free. Things would go much smoother if they did.

"See anything?" Bove asked, stepping down from the porch and standing beside him.

Coakley shook his head. "Not that I would even if one was up there."

"Well, let's hope there's not," Bove said. "We've been careful. Very careful."

Coakley nodded. "Yes, we have."

There was a moment of silence as both men studied the sky. Then Bove sighed. "Let's go greet our guests."

***

The six men sat around the table in Bove's dining room. The children, Stephen and Brandon, were joining another family for their home-school lessons today. Bove was as careful as possible about not letting the children hear his plans. Of course, it wasn't always possible. Kids were curious by nature, and Bove often discussed things with his wife when the children were in the house. But today, the last thing they needed was Stephen and Brandon around.

Sarah brought in doughnuts, coffee, water, and other finger foods as they were all getting situated. She wouldn't stay for the meeting. There were very strongly ingrained notions about women in the white supremacy movement. They were to serve support roles, never as decision-makers. Their primary function was to birth and raise white children who would grow up to continue the struggle. Of course, if all went to plan, any new children would be born into an Aryan utopia of sorts, where they wouldn't have to commingle with lesser children.

Coakley watched casually as she placed the items on the table. In fact, most of the men were watching her. She was a beautiful woman and an ideal Aryan. He thought about their conversation from last night, after she'd snuck out of her house when Bove was asleep and came to see Coakley in his house across the valley. She'd told him that Bove was angry at her for not becoming pregnant again. Bove wanted five children, she said. And her biological clock was ticking.

But the last thing Coakley wanted to hear about when they were together was the relationship issues between her and her husband. He had no doubt that he loved Sarah like he'd never loved another woman before, and listening to her talk about Bove made him feel sick. But the conversation was quickly forgotten minutes later as they made love. Sex with her made the world fade away, if just for a short time.

Now as she came around to his side of the table, he struggled to contain his anger at her as she bent over to place a glass of water before him, brushing her breast against his shoulder. She would often do little things like this, as if she was daring her husband to notice. As far as Coakley could tell, the man was oblivious. Which was good. Coakley had no idea what would happen if Bove found out he was sleeping with his wife. Nothing good.

"Thank you," Coakley said in a flat tone.

"You're welcome," she said, placing a glass next to Frank Cotter, who sat next to Coakley.

Next to Cotter was Gene Halverson, both of them from the Mount Shasta camp. Bove was at the head of the table, hand resting on his prized black-and-silver Ernst Rohm SS dagger. Sitting across from him was Damian Griffith, who represented nearly half of The White Power Alliance numbers. Griffith had been the leader of a self-proclaimed white isolationist group called the White Aryan Coalition before he'd agreed to join his group with The White Power Alliance. Still, most of his people answered only to him, despite Bove being the de facto leader of the alliance. Griffith had an enormous ego and had to be coddled. Many times he'd threatened to pull his support if he didn't get something or other, and Coakley figured today would be no different.

The fact of the matter was, Bove controlled the purse strings. Griffith's people donated to the cause, as was one of the requirements, but it was likely that Griffith was skimming off the top. This would've been an issue if Bove didn't have access to a seemingly unending source of funds. Coakley had no idea about the identity of the generous donor or donors. Bove wouldn't discuss it. Even Sarah had no idea where the bulk of the money was coming from. Although Coakley was curious, he'd ultimately decided that it didn't matter. So long as the cause was being furthered with the money. And it was. Without these mysterious funds, there was no telling where the WPA would be now.

It had paid for everything: the camps, the weapons, the powerful computers, and the training on how to use the computers without raising law enforcement red flags. And it had paid for the house they now sat in, on the land that belonged to them through an opaque consortium of shell companies.

Sure, the donations from those within the movement covered some of the costs, but nowhere near all of them. And Griffith knew this. He also knew that the manpower at his disposal was a significant bargaining chip. Coakley had argued that, no matter what Griffith said, the White Aryan Coalition would take up arms once it was clear the revolution was underway, but Bove insisted they couldn't take the chance. They needed the manpower up-front to accomplish their goals.

So as the meeting got underway, Coakley waited for Griffith to make his demands in his roundabout way. It would be coming sooner or later. He just hoped they could get it out of the way and move on with things.

"I want to start with some bad news," Bove said after thanking them all for being here. "There's a reason I've moved this meeting up two weeks. It's the same reason I say we need to shorten our timeline. And it has to do with our attack on the PGE Beaver power plant."

Chapter 29

COAKLEY HAD INSISTED ON frisking and wanding everyone before the meeting, so he was able to relax a little as Bove talked about the reason for moving up the revolution. He knew there were no recording devices in the room. It was his job to be paranoid, even if their distinguished guests didn't like being frisked.

"It sounds like your people fucked up," Griffith said in his heavy Southern accent. He was a corpulent man who always wore dark suit jackets over long sleeve dress shirts unbuttoned at the collar. If he was feeling casual, he would wear jeans. Today, he had slacks on. His small, bright eyes shone across the table as he leaned back in his chair, hands clasped over his belly. The thinning hair atop his head was light blond with expanding patches of gray here and there. "Why should we have to drop everything and scramble because your people couldn't tail a guy without getting caught?"

"I take responsibility for my men," Bove said, fidgeting absently with his dagger. "But that doesn't change the fact that waiting another two and a half weeks is a risk we can't take. Authorities are already searching for this man, and the longer we give them, the more likely it is they'll zone in on my men and this place."

"Where is this man, anyway?" Griffith asked, glancing around. "You have him in the kitchen, helping your wife cook?"

Griffith's right-hand man, Wayland Otto, snorted laughter at the joke.

"The man is already taken care of," Bove said. "He won't be talking."

"Did we get what we needed out of him?" Cotter asked.

"Yes," Coakley put in. "We did. Which is what Bove is getting at, I believe."

"Right," Bove said. "I'm confident that we can knock out power to Portland with a couple of small and well-placed devices at the Beaver power plant—so long as we hit a couple of essential substations as well. That will work nicely as a diversion while our men make an example out of the city."

"You mean *my* men," Griffith said.

"*Our* men. If they're for the cause, what's the difference?"

"And where will I be during this?" Griffith asked, dropping it.

"I hope that you'll be by my side as we take the Oregon State Capitol," Bove said. "But you can be wherever you like. Wherever is most comfortable for you."

Griffith knew he was being baited as well as the next guy, and he sat up straight. "Taking the capitol is exactly where I'd *like* to be."

"Good. So are we in agreement?"

"Who will be handling Portland, then?" Griffith asked, not yet done nitpicking the plan, even though they'd gone over it all before. The question of whether they could cut power to Portland was the last major issue. If they had deemed it wouldn't be possible, they would've concentrated everything on the capital, Salem. But symbolically Portland was much better. It stood for everything they stood against. And there were more subhumans living there per capita than elsewhere in the state.

"Cotter and Halverson," Bove said, gesturing to the two men from the Mount Shasta camp. Then he pointed to a third. "Oldham will be in charge of organizing the hit on the Beaver power station and the three substations."

Griffith looked at them each in turn, nodded, and turned his attention back to Bove. "Okay. And what about the attacks in the rest of the country? Have you already told your 'lone wolf' gunmen that the time is coming sooner than expected?"

Bove waved a hand. "I've sent out the word for them to be on standby. But whatever happens outside of this part of the country is a bonus as far as I'm concerned," he said. "It will simply show how serious we are. But the crux of the thing will be on us in Salem. So long as we can get our mission accomplished and get our message out, the true Aryans of Oregon and Washington and Idaho will step up and do their part."

Griffith grinned at this. "And even if they don't, we'll sure put the fear of God into the niggers, spics, and chinks," he said, his belly shaking as he chuckled. "They'll be fleeing the country in droves."

"How many incidents do you think will happen in the rest of the country?" Wayland Otto asked after biting into a doughnut.

"I don't know," Bove said. "I'm sure some of the young men will chicken out when the time comes. But if I had to guess, probably around fifty."

"No shit?" Otto said. "So if each of them kills even five subs, that's twenty-five hundred dead."

"Two hundred and fifty, you idiot," Griffith said to his underling.

"Oh, right," Otto said, face flushing red. "Still, that's pretty good."

"What about that group you were telling us about?" Bove asked Griffith. "The one in Kansas? Any word on whether they're going to join? Can they be counted on to create some chaos?"

Griffith nodded. "Oh, yes. The Homeland Heroes Militia is sympathetic to our cause. And they're well-trained, too. I'll make sure to tell them the night and time."

"I actually wanted to say something about that," Halverson said. "There's going to be a march in Portland on Monday for MLK Day. Word is, plenty of RLF people are going to be there. It should be pretty big. We could do a lot of damage if we hit that."

Bove nodded. "As attractive and poetic as it would be to do this on Martin Luther King Jr. Day, I just don't see it happening. I think Monday is too soon. Saturday would give us enough time to fully prepare. What does everyone think? Can we do Saturday?"

Cotter and Halverson looked at each other. Then they nodded. So did the others.

Bove leaned back and crossed his arms. For the first time in a long time, Coakley saw a smile on his face. "Saturday it is," he said. "We've got just under six days to get everything and everyone in place."

The smiles were contagious, and Coakley found himself grinning until the phone in his pocket buzzed with an incoming call. His smile fell when he saw who it was.

Bove noticed this. "Who is it?"

"McCray," Coakley said, looking at Cotter and Halverson.

"Why would he be calling Coakley and not one of you two?" Bove asked the men.

"I told them all to leave their phones in the cars," Coakley said, answering for the two men.

"Well, answer it," Bove said.

Coakley answered the phone.

Chapter 30

I WAS KIND OF surprised to still be alive when the sun came up. Although McCray had put his gun to my head and told me he didn't believe a word I'd said, he didn't pull the trigger. And that was enough for me to think that some part of him *did* believe. But I was pretty fucking far from out of the woods. In fact, I couldn't see anything *but* woods.

Although not literally. All I could see literally was the inside of a pillowcase McCray had put over my head after leading me out of the upstairs office and throwing me on one of the two couches down in the sitting room. He made me get on my belly and then secured my ankles to my wrists behind me before shoving my head in the pillowcase.

Shortly after that, I heard him and Pete arguing outside. Meanwhile, the women were milling around, whispering, until McCray came back inside and yelled at them to clean up the mess in the office.

Hours passed. It seemed that McCray wasn't sure what to do with his bosses gone. He kept coming into the house and asking me the same questions over and over again. I kept giving him the same answers. Finally, minutes ago now, he decided that he had to call for some guidance. It was clear that he thought he had a rat on his hands. Whether that rat was already dead or not was a question he badly wanted answered. And so did I, as long as that answer wasn't punctuated with a bullet to my head.

"Come on, pick up," he said from outside. I could hear him because apparently one of the windows was open; it got hot in the house when there was cooking going on in the kitchen. I could even hear his boots crunching on the dirt and pine needles as he paced in front of the cabin.

"Pick the fuck up," he said after more crunching.

Seconds passed.

"I need to talk," he said. I couldn't hear the other side of the conversation, but there were things I could glean without much effort. "Yes, now, goddammit . . . Sorry. No, I'm sorry. It's just that there's been a clusterfuck here. Okay. Okay, yeah. Fine. Okay. I'll call you right back."

McCray came rushing back into the house. "Pete!" he called. "Where are the fucking burner phones at?"

There was no answer.

"Pete left to bury Stoll's body," I said.

"You shut the fuck—wait, what? Who told him to bury the body?"

"You told them to clean up the mess. What else would they do with it?" I asked.

"Fuck."

There were a few moments of silence as McCray did something. Then I realized he was calling Pete. "Hey," he said, "stop what you're doing right now. Because we may need him for something. I don't know. Just stop and bring it back here. Or . . . no, no, just wait there. I need to call Coakley back and get some fuckin' instructions. So where are the burner phones? Okay. Okay. Just wait for my call before you bury it."

He stomped up the stairs and came back down a few minutes later, heading out the front door and slamming it behind him.

Not for the first time, I tried to get out of the binds, but I already knew it wasn't going to work. My shoulders were killing me, and my feet were numb. Given the day I'd had yesterday, I barely had enough strength to stay awake. But there was good news. My headache was slowly fading. I didn't feel like my brain was swelling anymore—if it ever had been.

"So here's the deal," McCray said from outside. "I woke up to shouting and a gunshot in the house in the middle of the night. I can tell it's from upstairs, right, so I go runnin' up there and find two fuckin' recruits in Cotter's office. One of them had just shot the other one in the fuckin' head with Cotter's Ruger twenty-two. And, according to that guy, he heard the dead guy sneaking around in the house and followed him up to the office. Then he walked in and saw that the dead guy was writing down some shit from one of Cotter's notebooks. They both went for the gun, the bigger guy won, put a bullet into the smaller one's eyeball."

There was a long silence as McCray listened. *Tell him that I was supposed to be in the house*, I thought, trying my hand at telepathy.

McCray said, "Well, I don't know. Could've been the other way around, for all I know. Only one of them is alive to tell his tale. But there is one thing I forgot to mention. The one guy who lived, he was allowed in the house. He took a beating for us during an outing and one of our girls wanted to make sure he didn't have a concussion or some shit."

He listened again.

"The other guy was supposed to be in the barracks sleeping with all the other soldiers. Yeah. Yeah, okay. That's what I thought. Sure. Yeah,

I'll have Pete send them right over. Okay . . . No, he's tied up. He's not going anywhere . . . Fine."

McCray came back in the house and marched over to me. "Okay, motherfucker," he said. "Moment of truth. We're gonna take your fuckin' prints. If we find anything we don't like, I'm gonna kill you myself."

"You taking the dead guy's prints, too?" I asked.

"What the fuck do you think? 'Course we are. Now hold still while I cut you loose. If you make a sudden move, I'll shoot you."

***

When McCray shoved me back onto the couch, my hands were bound in front of me and covered in fingerprint ink. My ankles were also bound together again, but at least I wasn't hogtied and blinded with a pillowcase anymore.

My favorite person, Pennington, was tasked with watching over me as McCray and Pete took Stoll's fingerprints outside. The guy was sitting across from me on the other couch, sneering at me. He was a big guy, sure, but he was also dumb. I mean, you have to be pretty dumb to join a militant white supremacist group, but this guy was a few shaved IQ points away from a Furby toy. I knew that antagonizing him would only get me hurt, so I kept my eyes averted. At least for now. If I came out of this clean, I would have to deal with him somehow. The good news was, he didn't have a gun. McCray told him to yell if I moved. I wasn't planning on moving.

From what I had heard, Pete was going to scan the fingerprints and send the images to someone named Coakley, who was going to check them against a national database somehow.

I didn't think it would be such a big deal to call in a favor from someone in a law enforcement agency or even the military. It was clear that white power groups tried hard to recruit those with training, which meant cops and soldiers. And when they couldn't recruit them, they sent their people into these organizations to learn tactics. I was pretty sure the guy teaching us yesterday had official military training. So the fact that they could run the prints without much effort wasn't really surprising. I was more concerned with what they would find out.

Presumably, the backstopping Nez and Hudson had done would prevent these people from learning anything concerning about me. After all, they'd apparently already checked my file, so I wasn't really worried about that.

What I was worried about was what Nez and Hudson would do. I figured anyone running my prints might raise a flag, possibly alerting them something was wrong. The last thing I wanted was for them to come swooping down on this camp like an invading force. It would cause the mysterious leadership and the rest of the WPA to close ranks. And I doubted it would delay their overall plan much, if at all. Hell, it might even move it up. Sure, the loss of manpower would hurt, but I didn't think it would be a killing blow.

No, I didn't want the FBI interfering. Now that my head had cleared and I'd been listening to McCray trying to figure stuff out, I didn't think I would be killed. McCray wanted to believe me, he just had to be sure.

In the meantime, I was busy going over in my head the usernames I'd seen in the notebook, along with the key and the numbers. And as I did this, puzzle pieces were falling into place. The first username I'd seen in the notebook was something like *ETurner*. I thought there was a dash in there somewhere, and maybe a capital letter. *E-TurnEr*, maybe. And that made sense. Because Earl Turner was the protagonist in a nasty little white supremacist wet dream novel called *The Turner Diaries*.

Published in the late seventies, the novel had been turned into a kind of handbook for white supremacist organizations sowing hate and calling for the overthrow of the American government. I hadn't had time to read the thing before my fiery little stunt at Hoffman's house in Santa Clarita, but I'd read the Wikipedia page and an article on how the novel had been used by various domestic terrorist groups over the years. Pages of it had been found in Timothy McVeigh's car after he murdered 168 men, women, and children with a bomb at the Alfred P. Murrah Federal Building in Oklahoma City. He was also known to sell copies of the book at gun shows around the country.

And the author's name led me to the second and third usernames I saw in the notebook. The second one was something like *WLPierce$*. William Luther Pierce was the name of the absolute genius who wrote the book, probably salivating at his wit the whole time. But, perhaps afraid of being called out as a hate-spewing racist, he used a pseudonym to publish the book: Andy Macdonald. This was the basis for the third username: *AndyM@c*.

I couldn't remember any of the other usernames, so I was hoping that the three would be enough. I just needed to get them to Nez and Hudson, along with the only other pieces of information I could remember from the notebook. The first was a website with the word key in front of it: *Key: EugenFischer.org*. I had no idea who Eugen Fisher was, but I thought it a safe bet that he was someone famous for promoting racist ideas. The next piece of information, found on the same page as the key, was a series of four numbers: 1, 3, 5, 7. Odd numbers.

I thought it likely that if I went to that website and looked at every first, third, fifth, and seventh word on every line of the home page, another piece of the puzzle would fall into place.

I repeated these bits of information silently in my head, freezing them into my memory as best I could. And I hoped that I would get a chance to contact Nez and Hudson sooner rather than later. If I was lucky, it was enough to get a glimpse into the inner workings of the organization. If I wasn't, then I had to keep digging.

But there was one thing still bothering me. Something I couldn't quite make heads or tails of. Just what the hell was Stoll going into that office for?

Chapter 31

McCray was grinning at me as he came into the house after taking a call. He stopped in the doorway to the sitting room, glancing between me and Pennington, who'd been trying to get a rise out of me for the last hour or so. I looked up at the bearded man expectantly, raising my bound hands slightly.

"You know who you killed?" McCray said, still grinning.

I said nothing.

"You know who you fuckin' killed? He was a goddamn rat, that's for sure. He was a member of The Revolutionary Liberation Front."

Pennington's face fell as he heard the news. I guess he was looking forward to killing me, or at least watching me die. "How do you know that?" he asked.

McCray turned toward him. "Because he was arrested three years ago in connection with an RLF plot to rob an armored truck. You remember when that string of bank and armored car robberies happened in Portland three years ago? That was them, apparently. They killed a couple of security guards in the process."

"So why wasn't he in prison?" Pennington asked.

"The cops caught them *before* they hit the car. And then some Jew lawyer got him off with only a year," McCray said.

"You guys didn't check him out when he joined?" I asked.

"He's been with us since before we started recruiting widely," Mc-Cray said, shaking his head. "He's been feeding information to his people the whole time. No wonder those RLF assholes always seem to show up when we go out in public."

I knew little about the RLF, but enough to know that they had violent tendencies just like the WPA did. They weren't responsible for nearly as much turmoil and bloodshed, but they tried their best. Still, I didn't feel great about killing the guy. Not that I'd had much of a choice. It was him or me, and that was that.

"So can you let me out of these binds now?" I asked. "You checked me out again, right?"

"Yeah, yeah," McCray said, coming over while pulling out his pocketknife. "But I wanna remind you of something. I wanna remind you that we have your fingerprints on the Ruger that killed Stoll. We can put that murder on you if you get cold feet."

"Do I look like I have cold feet?" I snapped. "What the fuck else does a guy have to do to earn your trust? I took a beating for you and now I've killed a man to protect this movement. Even before I met you, I was on this path. You people recruited *me*, remember?"

"All right, calm down," McCray said, smiling. "Just telling you how it is. Because you're going to help us see if we have any more rats in our presence. And if so, you'll help us get rid of them."

Oh shit, I thought, but I made sure to keep my face neutral. "Fine," I said. "Happy to do it. Just get me out of these fucking zip ties."

***

"If you try to run, we'll have to assume you're guilty, and we'll kill you," McCray bellowed out in his scratchy smoker's voice. I was standing next to him just inside the barracks door. All the men were gathered, standing at attention in front of their bunks. "If you have nothing to hide, you have nothing to worry about. But if you're working for the ZOG or for the goddamn Revolutionary Liberation Front, why don't you just tell us now so we can get this over with?"

No one answered. I didn't think anyone would.

The camp was now on lockdown. I wasn't sure if McCray was the paranoid one or if the order had come down from the other two guys: Cotter and Halverson. It was probably both. People involved in massive criminal conspiracies are generally pretty paranoid.

For that matter, so are undercover operatives, if my experience was any indication.

My face and head still hurt from last night, but both were feeling much better. Which was good, because I had to think clearly about what I would do if we found another snitch on the premises. McCray had made it sound like I would be in charge of eliminating them. That wasn't something I could do. Killing Stoll had been in self-defense. This would be straight-up execution.

"That's what I thought," McCray said. Then he pointed at the man nearest, a pimply faced kid of eighteen or nineteen. "You, come with us."

The kid's face got whiter than I thought possible. He made no move, but McCray was already turning to leave. I had been given a gun—one of the Ruger AR-556 rifles they had on hand—and I held it in my right hand as I grabbed the kid by his arm and pulled him toward the door with my left. We walked into the cold winter evening behind McCray. Spencer stood by the door outside the barracks, holding his own Ruger 556. We exchanged nods.

The kid was stiff with terror as we moved down the trail toward the cabin. It was like trying to get a mannequin to walk beside me. I stopped and pulled the kid close. "Are you a rat?" I asked him.

He looked at me, eyes brimming with tears, and shook his head.

"Talk to me, dammit," I said. "Are you a fucking rat?"

"N—No," he said, voice cracking.

"Are you a man?"

"Yes," he said.

"Then what the fuck are you worried about?"

The kid stuck his jaw out and nodded, something other than fear coming back into his eyes. He resumed walking, this time on his own. I fell in step behind him, both hands on my rifle. Up ahead, McCray had stopped to watch the little exchange. He looked at me for a long second before leading the way again.

I had earned his trust. All it had taken was killing a man. And even though I saw The Revolutionary Liberation Front as similar in many ways to the WPA, I was determined to make Stoll's death mean something. If it could help me thwart their plan, then some good would come of it.

Pennington was pacing in front of the cabin, his own rifle held casually across his body. He glared at me as I walked up. I met his gaze, knowing I'd have to deal with him sooner or later. I wanted to see how riled up I could get him.

He waited until McCray was inside before trudging up to me and leaning over to whisper in my ear, "You wanna go against me again, bitch?"

"Wow, you really have a thing for me, don't you?" I said. "Why is that? I mean, I know I'm good-looking, but damn."

The kid ahead turned and glanced at us, his gaze lingering on Pennington for a long moment. This seemed to infuriate the big man. "The fuck are you staring at, asshole?" he snapped at the kid.

McCray, who'd left the front door open a crack, yanked it all the way open. "Pennington, knock it the fuck off, goddammit," he yelled. Then he looked at me and the kid. "Both of you, get in here!"

I winked at Pennington as I moved up the porch steps and then into the cabin.

"You're fucking dead," Pennington whispered behind me, his voice choked with rage. He was an angry guy. And I thought I could use it to my advantage.

Inside, McCray and I stood around while Pete took the kid's fingerprints. Once he had them, I took the kid back to the barracks to get the next person. It wasn't a very efficient system. We could've done five guys at a time, bringing them up and having them wait outside the cabin. But that's not how McCray wanted it done. And I wasn't in any rush.

I used the time to think about what I would do if we found a snitch. I was also wondering if my phone was still inside McCray's truck. And, if it was, what it would take to get it out.

Chapter 32

LIAM TANNER FELT A sense of freedom that even the search for a parking spot in Brooklyn couldn't dampen. After quitting his job at the bar last night, he'd been walking on clouds. He found it amazing what the surety of his impending death could do for his mood. But it wasn't just any death. It was the fact that he was going to give his life for The Cause. If he'd gotten the news that he had some terminal disease and only had a week to live, he probably would've been miserable. That, he reflected as he pulled into a parking garage off 13th Street, was the power of Purpose.

As he found a spot in the garage, he considered bringing his Colt LE-901 rifle to the protest. There was no law against carrying long guns openly in Brooklyn, but Liam decided against it. He didn't want to give the cops a reason to harass him. Although it was legal to open-carry the gun, it could single him out if something did go down with counter-protesters. The last thing he wanted was to be locked up in jail when the call came for him to do his part.

So he left the Colt in the trunk as he prepared for the gathering. The sun was nearly down now, and it was a chilly day in Brooklyn. This was good because Liam sure as hell wasn't going there unarmed. He was taking one of his two Smith & Wesson M&P Compact .45s. While it was a compact, it wasn't exactly the smallest of guns. The layers of clothing Liam wore as protection against the cold would help to hide its bulk. Funnily enough, it was illegal for him to conceal carry a pistol in New York without the proper license. Still, he didn't think it was as risky as carrying his rifle because he probably wouldn't even need to take it out. And if he did, well, then the shit was going down. He'd rather have it and not need it than the other way around.

Word was that there were going to be counter-protesters from the RLF there, and he knew tempers would be flaring. You never knew what would go down at one of these things.

Liam left his car with his M&P tucked into his front waistband and hidden by a t-shirt, a baggy black hoodie, and a brown suede jacket. He wore black boots and a pair of black cargo pants. In his backpack, he had a rudimentary first-aid kit, snacks, and some water. He also had some fliers a guy in one of his chat rooms was passing around for people to download and print. They outlined how the Zionist Occupied Government was preventing the immigration of white people to the United States in favor of browns and blacks and yellows. People needed to know this stuff. They needed to open their fucking eyes.

He took a left off 13th onto Wythe and followed it down to Norman, which he took to Lorimer. He took a left and, about halfway down the block, spotted a group of white men gathered on the sidewalk. His heart rate increased as he approached, the streetlights providing illumination along the route. Three- and four-story buildings lined the road, most of them apartment buildings.

As he approached the group, he counted fifteen men, most of them around his age or younger. They were hanging back from the front of the police station, where a gated alley led to the back of the building. He moved up to them tentatively, looking around for evidence of RLF people and seeing none. One guy with trim orange hair and a freckled face turned and looked at him. Liam acknowledged him with a nod.

"Here for the protest?" the guy asked.

"Yeah. You?" Liam said.

"Well, yeah, obviously," the guy said, smiling.

Liam felt foolish. He was nervous. He'd only been to two other protests, and those had been over a year ago. But then the guy proffered his hand and said, "Joe."

"Liam," Tanner said, shaking his hand.

"Hey, we got one more," Joe said, turning to the group of milling men.

A tall, muscular man with a bushy black beard and shaggy black hair looked over and said, "Welcome, brother. We should have some other purebloods showing up soon. I say we get started at 6:30. How's that sound to everyone?"

There were murmurs of assent. After the initial excitement of seeing the group, Liam was beginning to realize that, unless many more people showed up, this would be a bust. Such a small group would make them look stupid and weak. But worst of all, if a sizeable number of RLF counter-protesters showed up, they would be outnumbered.

A couple of the men had signs. One of them read, "Justice for Our Brothers!" and another read, "Hang the Bitch," clearly referring to the woman who'd killed one or both of the white men who'd broken into her apartment.

As they milled about, Joe and Liam talked a little bit more, asking each other the usual get-to-know-you stuff. More people arrived—mostly men but a few women—and joined their group, bringing their numbers to around thirty.

It was 6:25 when Liam decided he wanted to walk up to the corner and see if he could locate any likely counter-protesters. Joe said he'd come with.

The sky was fully dark by the time the two men reached the front of the three-story police station. They looked down Meserole Avenue, past the main entrance to the building. A couple of uniformed officers were near the front door. They stared. Liam and Joe looked away, scanning for anyone who looked like a snowflake cuck.

There were people walking down the street, but there were no large groups. They stood there for a minute, looking in every direction. "I don't know, maybe they're not coming," Joe said.

"No media here, either," Liam said with a hint of sadness.

"Let's go back," Joe said.

They turned that way. But as they started back down Lorimer, Liam spotted a group two blocks down Meserole, in the direction of the East River. "Hold up," he said, pointing. Joe looked. They stood there for a long moment, waiting as the group got closer. Then they saw black skin and white skin and brown skin above cloth masks pulled over noses and mouths. They saw dyed hair and ratty clothes and skinny jeans.

"That's them," Joe said.

"No shit," Liam responded.

"There's lots of them."

Liam just nodded.

Without another word, they headed back down toward their people.

"They're coming!" Joe shouted when they were still fifteen yards away. White faces turned toward them, eyes growing hard. The guy with the shaggy black hair asked, "Any media?"

"Not yet," Joe said.

"Okay, Joe," the man replied, "get your phone out and start recording. You too, Adam. Let's do this!"

Following his lead, the small crowd started in the direction Liam and Joe had just come. They quickly fell to chanting, "White justice! White peace! White power!"

As they were coming to the corner, the crowd of counter-protesters appeared at the intersection, crossing the street. They started chanting, "Nazi punks, fuck off!"

The two groups converged near the corner in front of the 94th Precinct.

Chapter 33

LIAM QUICKLY REALIZED THAT they were outnumbered at least two to one. He was pressed backward as the counter-protesters surrounded them, forcing the white supremacists back against the side of the building. He hadn't been able to see the full extent of their numbers earlier, thanks to the darkness and the distance.

Most of the counter-protesters had gaiter masks or bandanas pulled over the lower halves of their faces, but he could still see their eyes. He could see the hate there as they pressed in, yelling and forcing the smaller group back, quickly overwhelming them. They weren't getting physical yet. No one was throwing punches. Liam looked around wildly, panic building. He saw thinly veiled fear in the eyes of the young white men around him.

People from both sides were yelling and screaming at each other.

"Go home and kill yourselves, you racist pricks!"

"Fuck you!"

"Race traitors!"

"Fucking subs!"

"Fascists are not welcome here!"

He was near the front of the group, barely able to move. It was like being in the front row of a standing-room-only concert. He swayed with the crowd, constantly moving his feet to keep his balance. A white woman no older than twenty pulled her mask down and spit in Liam's face. He felt his face go red as anger exploded inside him. "Fuck you, cunt!" he screamed, but it was just another shout among many.

The screams were getting louder, the tension growing. Faintly, Liam wondered if the police would come out and break it up. He saw no sign of them. Of course, he couldn't see around the corner of the building, where the entrance was. For all he knew, there were riot cops standing there, protecting the entrance.

Then all hell broke loose.

One of the white supremacists shoved a Black man, yelling, "Kill you, nigger!"

That was it. That was all it took. The counter-protesters exploded, no longer holding back. Fists started flying. The guy in front of Liam jerked his head back to avoid a punch, slamming the back of his skull into Liam's forehead. Pain erupted and the world went hazy for a moment. And when it came back into focus, a skateboard was flying at his face, swung by a young Hispanic man. The edge of the board caught him in the temple, whipping his head sideways. His legs gave way, and he crumpled down.

There was a forest of legs around him, moving constantly as chaos prompted the two groups to intermingle. The sounds of fighting and yelling and screaming were deafening. He could smell blood in the crisp winter air, along with sweat and deodorant and fabric softener. Someone stepped on Liam, then tripped, falling backward and landing on a small patch of sidewalk right next to him.

It was the Hispanic man who'd hit him with the skateboard. The board was nowhere to be seen as the two men looked each other in the eye. Liam moved first, scrambling to get his M&P .45 out of his waistband. The Hispanic man kicked out, hitting Liam in the chin with his heel.

As Liam was knocked back off his elbows, he looked up to see one of the white supremacists jamming a small knife into the abdomen of the white girl who'd spit in his face. The girl wasn't screaming. Her mouth was caught in a silent O, her eyes wide in disbelief.

The savagery of the assault, combined with the three blows to the head, gave everything a sense of unreality. It was as if he was in a dream. A nightmare. The reality of violence suddenly became apparent to him. It was wholly different than how he'd imagined it.

But as he felt hands grabbing his own, the threat he was under came quickly back to him. He raised his head to see that he'd pulled his gun from his waistband, although he couldn't remember doing it. His finger was in the trigger guard, which he couldn't remember doing, either. The Hispanic man was on his right, trying to wrestle the weapon from him. Liam pulled himself upright and yanked on the weapon, the movement jerking the barrel to point down toward his legs. Since he'd opted for the version of the weapon without an external safety, the gun fired. The bullet hit him in the right shin at an angle, snapping his tibia in half as the projectile barreled through his lower leg.

The pain didn't register at first. Not for a long moment. But the pressure and the resulting change in the structure of his leg were unmistakable. He looked down at the bloody hole in his pant leg, feeling like he was going to vomit.

The shot had caused some people to scatter, but the Hispanic man was still fighting for the pistol. He yanked it away from a shocked Liam. Not two feet away, the white supremacist with the knife turned his attention away from the girl, who dropped to the ground, bleeding profusely. The man lunged at the Hispanic guy, bloody knife held out. He was rewarded with two bullets to the chest as the Hispanic man pulled the trigger even as he was scrambling to his feet to run away.

Liam reached out and grabbed the man's foot as he tried to run. He didn't know why he'd done it—the move was driven by instinct. As the white supremacist with the knife stumbled against the building and collapsed, the Hispanic man turned back and shot Liam twice. One bullet went into his chest at a downward angle, causing extensive damage to his lungs and heart, while the other went through his neck. The shooter pulled his foot free and ran off down the street as police officers rounded the corner, guns drawn.

As pain became all and consciousness faded to a sharp hole, Liam was filled with a crushing sense of regret. This wasn't the death he'd wanted. It wasn't aligned with his Purpose. It was a death that didn't *matter*.

It's not fair, Liam thought.

It was the last thing to cross his mind before he died.

Chapter 34

THE SMELL OF CHICKEN cooking made my stomach rumble as I led another recruit into the cabin. It was fully dark outside now, and none of us had eaten lunch—except for McCray and Pete. I'd changed out of my street clothes and back into my fatigues and cold-weather gear once the temperature had started dropping. Now I was nice and cozy, wearing the waterproof coat and gloves they'd given me. We were almost done fingerprinting all the recruits, so I was looking forward to the hot meal I assumed would come when we finished.

As I waited around in the warm cabin while the latest guy was printed, McCray took a quick phone call. When he hung up, he picked up a radio and told the guys at the gate to expect an SUV. Then he looked up at me. "Does Pennington have a radio?"

I shook my head. "I think Spencer is the only recruit who has one."

"Step out and tell him there'll be an SUV coming soon, would you? Wouldn't want the idiot to start shooting."

"Yes, sir," I said, heading out to the porch. I stepped down the stairs, spotting Pennington off to my right near the side of the cabin. I hustled over to him. "McCray says he wants you to go get the next recruit."

"What? Why?"

"How the hell should I know? That's just what he told me. You can go question him if you want to, but I'm not doing it."

Pennington looked over toward the front door, clearly debating what he should do. "What about the guy you just brought back?"

"He didn't tell me his every thought," I said. "I guess he wants him to stay in there until you get back. I don't know."

The big guy grumbled, but he started off toward the barracks. I watched him go until he was out of sight. Then I hurried over to McCray's truck. Before I tried the passenger side door, I looked for headlights coming down the dirt road. Nothing yet.

The truck door was unlocked. I opened it, propped my rifle nearby, and popped the glove compartment. My phone was still there, still in pieces. I grabbed the body, the battery, and the cover, but I couldn't find the SIM card. There was too much junk in the compartment, so I had to go digging. But I didn't want to make it obvious that someone had been rummaging through it. So I tried to remember how everything was placed in there as I pulled it out, searching for the small golden computer chip.

Headlights pierced the trees lining the woods, drawing my attention. Halverson and Cotter, coming back from their meeting. I still hadn't found the card. And, to make matters worse, McCray suddenly called my name from inside the cabin.

Shit.

I pulled out the last thing in the compartment. It was a folded piece of paper—proof of insurance—and there was nothing under it. No SIM card.

The SUV was getting closer. I could hear its tires crunching on gravel. I couldn't let them see me digging through the truck. They would have questions I couldn't answer. I was out of time.

"Trouble?" McCray shouted. "Where the hell did you go?"

As I went to put the piece of paper back in the compartment, giving up my search, something small and golden fell out of it. The SIM card. It had made its way inside the folded-up paper. I grabbed it and shoved it in my pocket with the rest of the phone, then quickly tossed everything back into the glove compartment. I had no time to put it back in exactly the way I found it.

Just as I was closing the door to the truck—quietly—the front door of the cabin opened, revealing McCray's face. He was looking in the opposite direction, giving me just enough time to grab my rifle, turn, and step away from the truck. He looked at me, a question on his face. "What the hell are you doing by my truck?" he asked.

I donned my best confused look just as the SUV rolled up to the front of the cabin.

"Your truck?" I said. "No, I was looking for Pennington. I don't know where he went."

McCray looked from me to the newly arrived SUV. "Well, come get this kid out of here and bring the next one."

"Yes, sir," I said.

Cotter and Halverson were stepping out of the SUV. I looked at each of them in turn, nodding, as I walked up to the porch steps.

"Hey," Cotter said. I turned and waited while the two men came over. I'd met Halverson yesterday morning when I woke up with him standing at the foot of my cot while Pennington and some other guys held me down. But I hadn't yet interacted with Cotter. He was one of those wiry guys who would be skinny as a post until the day he died. His arms dangled and his joints were all knobby, but there was a definite strength there. And a stamina that only skinny guys seemed to have. He was gray-haired but far from wrinkled. He couldn't have been more than ten years my senior.

Cotter stopped next to me and put out a hand. I shook it.

"I hear you did us a great service this morning," he said.

"Honestly, sir, I didn't know what I was doing. Not really. I just knew something was off. And when he went for that gun, I knew he meant to kill me."

"Well, it just goes to show you that *God* is on our side," Cotter said, putting emphasis on the word God, as if to make sure the right one heard him.

I nodded. "Yes, sir," I said, taking my hand back. "I'm just happy to finally have a purpose. I'd like to do whatever I can to help the cause."

Cotter glanced at Halverson, who was standing nearby looking at me like I was his son and I'd just graduated racist asshole finishing school. Then he looked up at McCray, who had stepped out onto the porch to greet his bosses.

"Well, I think that's something we can manage," Cotter said. "Don't you think, boys?"

Halverson and McCray nodded.

"Well," he continued, "let's get in out of the cold. It's downright frigid out here."

The four of us went inside, stepping through the door just as Pennington arrived with the next recruit to be fingerprinted. "Sir," Pennington said, "here's the next one."

McCray stepped back out onto the porch. "Where the hell did you get off to?" Before Pennington could answer, he said, "Never mind. I think we're done for the day. Why don't you take these two boys back to the barracks." He gestured for the kid still waiting in the house to step outside.

"What about him?" Pennington asked, pointing at me.

"What about him?" McCray asked. "Do as you're told. I think dinner's about ready. You and spencer bring the first group over to the mess tent to eat. Trouble's gonna eat in the house tonight."

I'd been standing just inside the door, watching this interaction. And just before McCray closed it, I winked at Pennington.

The look of fury on his face was priceless.

***

"Saturday," Cotter said with a beaming smile. "It's all happening on Saturday."

"*This* Saturday?" McCray asked. "I mean, a week from today, Saturday?"

Halverson and Cotter nodded.

The five of us—Pete, McCray, Cotter, Halverson, and I—were sitting around the dining room table, plates of chicken, veggies, and rolls in front of us. Suddenly, I wasn't feeling so hungry. Saturday. That was way sooner than Hudson and Nez thought. Here it was Saturday night, so we were talking a week. I feigned ignorance, looking at the men. "What are we going to do Saturday?" I asked. "Are we doing a protest or something? More recruitment tapes?"

Cotter, who was sitting at the head of the table to my right, shook his head. "I know you just got here, but many of us have been training for this for a long time. We're going to change the world on Saturday. We're going to take the power back after so many decades of oppression. But we've got a lot of work to do before then to prepare."

"Jesus," McCray said. "It's really happening. Finally. We'll finally be free."

"Have you ever tried speaking out for the white race, Trouble?" Halverson asked. "Have you ever tried to say, 'What about white culture? What about the things that *we* value?' Well, I have. And you know what it gets you? Fired. I lost my job because I spoke up online for the rights of white people to not be exterminated by other races. Does that seem right to you?"

I shook my head, chewing a mouthful of chicken. I sensed a sermon coming, along with a whole lot of justification for the violence they were planning.

"You suggest that white people and other people should be separate, and people freak out," Halverson continued. "Why *can't* we be separate? Races aren't supposed to mix. Even today, Black people tend to stick with their own. They live in their rundown houses and drug-infested neighborhoods, and then they try to blame white people for their problems. I guess they just want us to be as miserable as them. But that's not right. Just because they can't get off their lazy asses to make something of their lives, doesn't mean my kids should have to go to a second-rate school. It doesn't mean I should have to pay extra taxes to support people who don't even respect themselves. And then, when their drugs and violence spill over into our neighborhoods, they get mad at us for wanting to live separately. Does that make any sense to you?"

None of this made *any* sense to me. A little logic and a dash of American history could tell any reasonable person that his argument was about as sturdy as a house of cards in a hurricane.

Then it hit me like a pair of brass knuckles. All these people, these so-called white warriors, were nothing but professional victims. And like victims who perceive themselves to have been knocked around and pushed down their whole lives, they were lashing out.

These people—those who made up the WPA—seemed to think that every missed opportunity, every job loss, every stroke of bad luck was thanks to some Black or brown American stepping up to take that opportunity, that job, or prosper off the finite share of good luck that was floating around for grabs.

By this logic, they thought that if they could make America the way it was supposed to be—all white—then it would be a utopia where everyone had everything they could ever ask for.

It was a fantasy. And a dangerous one.

Anyone with any kind of sense knew that killing people wasn't the answer. I knew that shooting up crowds or planting bombs or spreading hatred wouldn't do it. If anything, it would keep progress—true progress, the kind that lifts everyone—from happening. It would make things harder in the long run. And if it got bad enough, it would be a self-fulfilling prophecy.

In their misguided and wholly ignorant search for justice for perceived wrongs, they'd turned themselves into a group that *could* be pointed to with confidence as a cancer. There was no one group to blame for their imagined misfortunes. But there was now a group to blame for a lot of hurt in America. The White Power Alliance.

But wasn't that always how it went? The greatest villains in history thought they were really heroes. They saw themselves as saviors, persecuted for beliefs that would be proved worthy through the lens of history.

They felt hurt, and all they wanted to do was give that hurt back to their supposed oppressors.

Of course, I knew this wasn't only a white phenomenon. There were extremist groups of all shapes and colors, and from all sides of the political spectrum. But it was the white supremacist groups in America that seemed the most willing to take action. And that meant killing innocent people by the thousands if they had their way.

Halverson hadn't really been looking for an answer. He continued his diatribe, with Cotter and McCray chiming in occasionally. They really thought that killing a bunch of innocent people was going to get them what they wanted, which was a white ethnostate.

Saturday. It was happening Saturday.

As I ate and agreed every so often with the three men, I thought about how fast I'd have to move to prevent this from happening. The first step was calling Nez and Hudson and giving them the information I'd gathered. Then, we'd have to go from there.

The first chance I got, I would find a place to be alone and put my phone together.

I had to warn the FBI. And I had to do it soon.

Chapter 35

ROGER INMAN SAT IN his garage-turned-mancave, stewing in his own drunken hate as he watched the news. First, two perfectly good Aryan boys were killed in Brooklyn. Sure, they should've been better prepared when breaking into the house, but it didn't change the fact that they were dead. To add insult to injury, at least one of them had been killed by a *black bitch*.

Now, two *more* Aryan brothers were dead after two groups of protesters clashed in *Jew York City*. The movement was a laughingstock. Strong Aryan men were dropping like flies. It was making white men look like peckerwoods who didn't know how to handle themselves. And they still hadn't caught the guy who'd done the killing. *Probably a black guy*, Inman thought as he grabbed his glass of whiskey and took a swig. *Probably a rapist. Probably raping a white woman right now.* The image he conjured in his head sent bright colors swirling through his brain. The rage wasn't coherent. It was a burning ball of static, bright as the sun. He felt hot all over, and realized he was tensing his muscles.

He looked at his gun cabinet. His rage shifted directions, and a picture of Darla Greenberg flashed in his mind. He imagined emptying a thirty-round magazine into the esteemed governor of the state of Kansas, feeling giddy with the possibility.

Right this very moment, a couple of his best men were keeping an eye on the governor's house. Everything was in place. Everything was ready. They'd been working for months, finalizing plans and practicing their entry at their militia camp outside of Topeka. The mansion backed up to the Kansas River, separated from the water by a thick swath of trees. But Inman's men had worked under cover of darkness all through the late fall and early winter to clear a path through the thick vegetation.

Everything was ready. Inman could taste it. It was so close. After his Homeland Heroes Militia hit the governor, everyone would realize how serious the movement was.

But Griffith told him to wait, the fat fuck. Wait until Saturday. Do it Saturday. Do it for the cause.

It was bullshit. A pipedream. There was no way the WPA would succeed in creating a white ethnostate in the Pacific Northwest. They were delusional.

But he had to give it to them, they were planning something big. They would kill a lot of people and cause a lot of damage. It would be delicious. Of course, Inman knew he likely wouldn't be around to see it. He'd be killed by police shortly after killing the Jew governor. And that was okay with him. He'd made his peace with the fact. Actually, he was kind of excited about it. His name would be remembered for something other than the abysmal governor's race he'd just lost. It was embarrassing. And it proved that the Jews controlled it all. Pretty soon, every single governor in every state would be a Jew, even if they didn't have berg or stein in their last name. Even if they didn't have beady eyes and big noses. They would all be Jews just the same. And that would be the end for hard-working white people like him. They would be squeezed out. Eliminated. Maybe even put in some of those concentration camps the government was building. He'd seen the pictures all over social media.

Behind him, the door to the garage opened. Inman was so lost in his daydream that he barely registered the sound. That was, until his wife spoke.

"Drunk again, huh?" she said.

Inman's face fell, and that ball of rage that seemed to be always there lately tripled in size. It felt like it was swirling at the base of his brain, sending red tendrils of anger across his mind. He stood from his chair and turned around. "What did you say?" he asked her.

Patricia scoffed, shaking her head. Inman could barely look at her. She'd been pretty once, back when she was a different person. Her brown hair, once full of life and bounce, hung around her chunky face like she was wearing a wet mop head. She'd certainly let herself go since the kids were born. But worse than all that was the way she'd been treating him. She was always talking back, criticizing, telling him in underhanded ways that he was just a rube who'd been taken in by the bad actors spreading disinformation all over the internet.

She wasn't the kind of wife he wanted. The kind he deserved. The kind that kept her mouth shut and let the men do the thinking. The *white* men. She was nothing but a Dumb Bitch. That was how he thought of her. Dumb Bitch Wife.

"Are you going to come in and eat something, or you just stickin' to a liquid dinner tonight?" she asked, not even bothering to hide her disdain.

"I'll be in when I'm goddamn good and ready," he said, slurring his words and swaying on his feet.

"Fine," Patricia said. "Just don't expect the food to be warm when you do."

"It better be warm, you dumb bitch," he said, the words just spilling out.

Her eyes grew hard for a moment, then the fight seemed to go out of her. "I'm not doing this with you again," she said. "I'm over it. You're a sad excuse for a man. I'll be leaving in the morning to go be with the kids at my mom's house. You can expect divorce papers soon after."

"You can't leave," Inman said, his voice a high whine. He tried to walk around the chair and the TV tray he used as a side table, but his motor functions were all over the place. He stumbled and knocked over the TV tray, sending his glass of whiskey spilling onto the thick rug on the floor. Mumbling, he reached down to try and pick up his glass, but he tipped too far forward, tumbling sideways and smacking his back into the corner of the mini fridge against the wall. Even in his drunken state, the pain was immense.

"Jesus, you're pathetic," Dumb Bitch Wife said as she turned and walked back into the house.

That ball of rage in his head went supernova, the explosion blasting all reason from his mind. He got to his feet, grunting at the pain in his back, and wobbled over to the gun cabinet. He pulled out his favorite revolver, a 44-magnum Colt Anaconda. It was loaded. He always kept it loaded.

Inman had thought about doing this very thing so many times, it didn't have the impact it should have. After every argument over the last six months, every squabble, every shouting match, and every poisonous word whispered in his ear just before the booze took his consciousness away, Inman had thought about grabbing his Anaconda from the cabinet and ending Dumb Bitch Wife once and for all. In his drunken state, it was almost as if he was imagining it. Almost. But the weight of the gun and the pain in his back and the rage that just couldn't be contained any longer all made it real. Real as life and death.

He lurched over to the door, shoving it open as he went through. His head was full of bright swirling lights, so hot they seemed to be burning the backs of his eyeballs. But he knew just what would make them go away.

Roger Inman bumped into the dryer on his way through the laundry room, careening off the doorway as he stumbled into the kitchen. Dumb Bitch Wife was just serving herself a plate of pasta at the stove. She turned and looked over her shoulder, seeing the revolver in his hand.

In his barely coherent state, he wanted to see the fear on her face. He wanted to see it distort her features. He wanted her to beg and plead with him not to kill her.

She did none of these things. She scoffed, shook her head, and went back to loading her plate with carbs that would go straight to her fat, cottage-cheese ass.

He raised the weapon, aimed it at the back of her head, and pulled the trigger. The sound was immensely loud, and the microwave to the left of his wife's head popped as the bullet smashed through the door.

Patricia screamed, dropping her plate and turning to run toward the living room. Swaying, Inman aimed again and fired, missing again, instead blasting a hole through the cabinet where they kept the good dishes.

He ran after her, turning into the living room to see her rounding the corner toward the front door. His only thought was one of making her dead. And even that wasn't explicit in his mind. He was operating on some sort of primal instinct, fueled by the booze and the anger and the betrayal.

He turned and went back the other way through the kitchen, grabbing the keys to his truck as he went. He verified that the keys to the minivan were still there, smiling at the knowledge that his wife wouldn't be able to leave in her vehicle. Then he hustled down the hall and out the open front door, into the cold night. Patricia was running down the dirt road toward the front of their property, which was a good quarter mile away.

Roger Inman got into his truck and fired it up, reversing out of his spot in front of the garage. His tires spat gravel as he shifted into drive and tore off after Dumb Bitch Wife. She veered off the road, but there was nowhere to run. The woods were too far, and she was too out of shape to run fast. There was nothing but a field of empty Kansas grass for several hundred yards.

Laughing insanely, Inman rolled down his window and transferred the pistol to his left hand. He slowed the truck, his wife about twenty yards away, swerving as she ran, as if that would help anything. She was screaming. "Please," and, "Stop," and, "Help."

The dumb bitch.

He leaned his head out the window and lined up his shot, his running wife caught in the headlights ahead. He fired.

Missed.

He fired again.

Missed again.

"Goddammit," he said, slamming his foot on the gas.

Patricia Inman's last scream was cut off as the front bumper struck her. The truck's momentum tossed her forward several feet. A moment later, the right-side wheel bumped over her, snapping bones and crushing major organs. The back tire on that side finished the job.

But that wasn't enough for Inman. He put the truck in park and then got out, stumbling back to look at the bloody mess that had once been his wife. She was still breathing, but it sounded wet and raspy. He still had two shots left in his gun. From this range, he wouldn't miss.

"You dumb bitch," he said, just before he put a 44-caliber bullet into her half-crushed skull. He shot her again, expecting to feel something, expecting the rage to dwindle. But it didn't. It was still there. He just felt tired.

Looking around the property he'd inherited from his parents, he was thankful they didn't have any close neighbors. The kids were at Patricia's mother's house, taken there after a particularly bad fight three days ago. That was good, too. It would give him time to do what he needed to do.

But he'd have to make it quick.

Chapter 36

THE PHONE BATTERY CLICKED into place. I was sitting in the downstairs bathroom, putting the thing back together so I could text the number Hudson and Nez gave me. I wasn't sure whose number it was, but I guess it didn't really matter.

I had thought about waiting until everyone went to bed—Cotter had already told me I could sleep in the house tonight—before calling the number. But that was just too risky. Someone could hear me talking, and that wouldn't be good. I wasn't supposed to have a phone, after all. Sneaking outside wasn't an option either. If I got caught, I would have to come up with some explanation. And I couldn't think of one that would be legit enough to avoid suspicion.

So I was in the bathroom. The phone was powering up. I waited, tapping my foot up and down in anticipation.

After dinner, I had tried to gently pry some specifics out of the four other men at the table with me. I didn't want to seem too eager, but I was also wary of seeming too disinterested. After all, I was supposed to be down for the cause. So I paid attention to the level of excitement projected by Cotter and Halverson, then toned it down a bit and gave it back.

But it was all to no avail. They said the time would come when they could tell me more, but it wasn't yet.

"We don't even know all the specifics yet," Cotter had said. "It's safer that way."

I had to hope that the information I did have was enough to get the ball rolling.

The phone finished booting up and I unlocked it, immediately tapping on the message app. I drafted a long message:

It's happening Saturday. Not sure of specifics. Won't tell me.

Found some info though:

Names: Coakley, located elsewhere. Cotter, Halverson, McCray, and Pete, all located here at Mt Shasta.

Possible Usernames: E-TurnEr, WLPierce$, and AndyM@c

Found this on a separate page in a notebook:

Key: EugenFischer.org

1, 3, 5, 7

Nearly 100 people here. No children, few women. Lots of new recruits. Military training basics. AR-15s and fatigues.

Will check message when I can.

I read it once over before hitting send. I knew that telling them about the thing with Stoll wasn't a good idea. I didn't know how they'd react to that. And I sure as hell didn't want them getting all weird on me, trying to pull me out. So I left it out.

I'd already been in the bathroom too long, so I shut the phone off and then shoved it down my pants into my boxer briefs. I figured it would be safe there until I could use the bathroom again in a couple of hours to see what the response was.

After flushing the toilet and washing my hands, I came out of the bathroom and found McCray watching the news in the sitting room. "Anything you want me doing right now?" I asked him.

"Get some rest. The next week is gonna be busy as shit," he said without looking up.

"Yes, sir," I said, walking through the sitting room and into the makeshift first aid room where the cots were set up.

I took off my boots and then remembered that I'd left my coat in the dining room, draped on the back of one of the chairs. I walked out the other doorway, passing next to the kitchen on my way to the dining room. As I turned the corner, I was surprised to see six women sitting at the table, eating their dinner. They all looked up at me as I walked in.

"Excuse me," I said, reaching for the coat. Lorena was sitting on the opposite side of the table, and our eyes met. I grabbed the coat, thanked them for dinner, and made my way back to my bedroom for the night. But as I went, something about the way Lorena looked at me stuck in my mind. It was a knowing look. I wondered if it was possible she'd seen what had really happened last night. Maybe she'd seen Stoll coming up the stairs and opening the door. Or maybe she'd come down the stairs and found that I was not where I was supposed to be.

I shrugged it off as I got comfortable on the cot. Reaching down with my right hand, I adjusted the phone in my underwear. It wasn't the most comfortable thing in the world. Thankfully it wasn't one of those giant phones that could barely fit in a pocket.

Comfortable as I was going to get, I took a deep breath, looked up at the ceiling, and waited for everyone to go to sleep.

***

The house had been mostly silent for fifteen minutes when someone came into the room. I tensed, sitting up before the figure rushed through the dark toward me and pushed me back down with two hands. Then there were lips on mine, and hands pushing up into my hair, and a very nice, very womanly smell filling my nostrils. The smell of clean hair and mild deodorant and nervous feminine anticipation.

I pulled back, seeing that it was Lorena. She was on her knees next to my cot. Suddenly, the strange look she'd given me earlier made sense. It *was* a knowing look. It was her knowing that she was going to do this when she thought the time was right.

"It's okay," she said in a breathy whisper, shoving her face into mine again.

No, it's very much not okay, I thought. But she did smell good. And her lips were soft. And I could *feel* her excitement. So for a moment, I gave in, against my better judgment.

She pulled her left hand down and dragged it along my chest and down my abs, and she kept on going. A sudden thought came racing into my mind as her hand ventured down toward my crotch. I pictured her saying, "Is that a phone in your pants, or are you just happy to see me?"

I had grown momentarily used to the phone being down there, but now panic surged through me. I shot my right hand out and caught her wrist just before her fingers could brush the device. At the same time, I pulled my head away from hers again. And I remembered her casual racism from the night before. Any excitement I'd felt was gone in an instant.

"This is not okay," I told her. "I'm sorry, but I can't do this."

"If you're worried about them, they won't mind," she said, gesturing toward the sitting room where McCray and Pete were no doubt sleeping. "They'll understand," she continued. "It's a woman's duty. I want to do my part."

"What part is that?" I asked, truly confused.

"I want to bear white warriors," she said. "We're each expected to bear at least five white children. More, if we can. And I saw the way you were looking at me last night. So don't worry. We can make it quick."

As she pulled my head toward her with her free hand, I grabbed her wrist and used her arms to push her away from me. "No," I said. "That's not happening."

As her face changed, I knew I had to step carefully. Hell hath no fury, and all that. "It's not that I don't find you attractive," I said. "It's just that I . . . am waiting until marriage."

"Really?" she asked, incredulous.

"Yes, really," I said, becoming more serious. "Are you going to criticize me for my faith? I thought the people in this movement had more traditional values. Or is that not the case?"

The anger went out of her eyes. I had her on the defensive. "No," she said. "No, I'm sorry. I just thought . . ."

"I'm flattered, really. But if I can't keep that vow with God, then how can I call myself a true Aryan man? It's this breakdown in traditional values I'm fighting against. I mean, it's half the reason I'm here."

Lorena pulled her arms back and I let them go. She set her hands in her lap. "I'm sorry," she said. "I feel like such a . . . slut. It's just . . . what you did for the cause . . . what you did for all of us . . . I'd be proud to raise your children."

"Maybe, when the time is right, we can get to know each other," I told her. "You're very beautiful. But I would need to do things the right way, okay?"

She nodded sadly. "Sorry," she said again, standing up.

"It's okay, really. Don't worry about it."

She turned and walked out, shoulders hunched and head hanging. I listened hard, hearing the stairs creak faintly as she went upstairs. Then I let out a long, heavy breath. *Christ,* I thought. *That was way too close.*

I gave it another half an hour before getting up and heading to the bathroom again. I pulled out the phone and powered it on. There was a message waiting for me:

Good work. Looking into info. Check back for updates every couple of hours if you can. Find out targets! Be careful.

Before deleting the conversation, I replied with an *OK*. Then I shut down the phone again and stuffed it back down my pants. I would need to find a better place for it if we would be doing any sort of active training tomorrow. But for now, I wanted to keep it close. I just had to hope that McCray wouldn't need anything out of his glove box anytime soon.

I went back to my cot and settled in to get some sleep, hoping, for perhaps the first time in my adult life, that I wouldn't attract any further attention from the fairer sex.

Chapter 37

RIYA DESAI, A COMPUTER forensic specialist for the New York Police Department, had been given the task of finding a way into Liam Tanner's phone. And she was close. In fact, it wasn't the first time she'd broken into a murder victim's phone. It certainly wouldn't be the last.

Although there had been several eyewitnesses to the shooting, the suspect hadn't been caught in all the chaos. He was still out there. And whatever information they could glean from Tanner's phone might help them. It was likely that the killer hadn't known Tanner personally, but they weren't ready to rule anything out. Besides, there was a three-letter agency interested in the contents of the phone.

The detective in charge of Tanner's case was Reyland Winston, and he'd already called her twice today to see if she'd gotten into the phone. Apparently, the FBI had been breathing down his neck ever since they'd learned about the murder. Desai was kind of surprised they hadn't just bigfooted the thing and commanded the NYPD to give the phone over. The FBI surely had ways to crack fingerprint-protected phones. Of course, they didn't have any real authority over the NYPD, but it wouldn't have been the first time some Special Asshole in Charge *thought* he did. Regardless, Desai was happy to do it. It was kind of fun.

It wasn't all that complicated, really. The hardest part was making sure the recreated fingerprint was detailed and filled in enough for the phone to recognize it. Of course, she had no idea which finger Tanner had used for the lock. Most people used their index finger, so that was the one she'd started with.

She'd seen a show once in which one of the characters used a dead man's hand to unlock his fingerprint-protected phone. Unfortunately, it wasn't that easy. The technology relied upon a completed electrical circuit, which a dead person couldn't provide. Neither could a severed finger.

But there were ways around that. So Desai had gone to work.

First, she'd had Detective Winston provide her with Tanner's fingerprints, which she scanned and uploaded into a tool that allowed her to go in and clean up the prints. The tool had actually been created by a computer forensic specialist in Michigan for this very purpose. She connected broken ridges, filled in the valleys, and cleaned up smudges. The details needed to be there, so she was careful not to go too crazy, enhancing without removing any details.

When she was satisfied with that, she printed off 2-D replicas of all ten fingers, using a special conductive ink to trick the phone sensor. That way, it would create the electrical circuit required for unlocking the device.

She tried all ten fingers, but the phone didn't unlock. So she went back to the original prints that Winston had sent her. Studying them, she thought she saw the problem. It was a slight smudge on the right index finger. She called Winston and asked him to redo the print for the finger. And she asked him to do it carefully. He'd delivered the prints to her personally.

Since then, he'd been hanging around in her lab, quietly pacing.

She printed the revised index fingers off. As she retrieved them from the printer, Winston came up to her. "You think it'll work this time?" he asked, his mustache twitching.

"Let's find out," she said, moving back over to the desk. Winston followed along. She carefully cut the right and left prints out of the special paper and then grabbed the phone, placing it face down in front of her. She used the right-hand print first, aligning it over the fingerprint reader and then pressing down with her own index finger. The phone vibrated once, a short, decisive vibration.

Desai smiled. She set the print aside and picked up the phone, turning it over to show that it was awake and unlocked.

"That's what I'm talkin' about," Winston said.

"Now, let's take a look at what's on it, Desai said.

"Gotta be a white supremacy thing," Winston said. "Maybe look for that app those guys use . . . Telegraph?"

Desai nodded. She read the news, just like Winston did. Sure enough, she found the icon for the Telegraph app on the home screen. She tapped it with her thumb, prompting it to open and fill the screen.

There were a lot of chats on the home screen, all of which Tanner had recently participated in, even if just to read the posts and not respond. They were all private chat rooms.

She opened the very first one on the list, which had a white star on it, denoting it as a favorite. She started scrolling along, scanning the conversations.

Winston, looking over her shoulder, voiced what she was thinking. "Jesus Christ," he said.

Desai nodded. "Yeah."

"No wonder the FBI wants this."

"I guess we better give it to them," Desai said, navigating to the settings to unlock the phone for good.

***

In Lowell, Massachusetts, off Liberty Street, Special Agent Dezba Nez was approaching Liam Tanner's house in an SUV with a couple of local cops. She had a warrant on hand to search the premises and confiscate Tanner's computer and any other electronic devices at the house, since the warrant covered the IP address and not just select devices.

It was nice to be *doing* something again. When she'd heard about the first two white supremacists who'd been killed in Brooklyn, she immediately called her boss and asked to get involved. It was the kind of thing investigators hoped for, and she had a good feeling about it. Then, shortly after she got to New York, Liam Tanner had been killed outside the 94th Precinct. It quickly became clear that the two men who'd attempted to kill RLF leaders in Green Point were part of a group that had no direct ties to the WPA. The man who'd been killed along with Tanner was clearly part of that group. It hadn't taken her long to find that out.

But Liam was an unknown quantity. He hadn't been on anyone's radar. Which meant he could go either way. So she quickly zoned in on him, hoping there was a trail of digital breadcrumbs to follow.

She'd been going stir-crazy in California, waiting to hear from Rubble. Then, less than twenty-four hours after she left the West Coast, Hudson called her in the early hours of the morning and told her he'd got a message from Rubble. *Of course.*

The first thing he'd said was, "Saturday. Rubble says it's happening Saturday. I told him to find out about targets. But he did manage to send some info. Looks like usernames and possibly a key for a simple code. I have Kim going over them right now."

They'd talked for another five minutes or so, but Nez was now concentrating on that first portion of the conversation. If there was some evidence of Liam interacting with the website or the usernames Rubble had uncovered, they would be on to something. They could use that to get a much broader warrant, maybe even allowing them to uncover other potential lone wolf operators who'd been interacting with the WPA from afar.

As the SUV slowed outside Liam Tanner's house, Nez put her game face on, clearing her head. The cop driving the SUV pulled over in front of the house. Nez had convinced the local cops to let her go in with minimal force. The last thing she wanted was a big to-do with SWAT officers and military tactics. She wanted to keep this off the evening news for as long as possible. The NYPD hadn't yet released Tanner's name to the public, which would work to her advantage. Besides, she'd done research on the two roommates and found no evidence of extremist involvement. And she knew one of them was at work right now; they'd had people watching the house for almost twelve hours.

"All right let's do this," the cop driving said in a heavy Boston accent.

"Follow my lead," Nez said, getting out of the car.

"Yah huh," the two cops confirmed as they opened their doors.

Behind them was another unmarked police SUV. Several plain-clothes officers got out and gathered on the side of the vehicle opposite the house, just in case.

Nez walked up to the door and knocked. "FBI, we have a warrant to search the property," she said.

"What the fuck?" came the reply from inside the house. There was the sound of someone coming to the door. "I'm opening the door and I'm unarmed," the voice said from inside. "And I'm Black. Don't shoot me."

The door opened, revealing twenty-five-year-old Tyler Simpson.

"Mr. Simpson, is there anyone else in the house?" Nez asked as the man looked with wide eyes at the police milling in the street in front of his house.

"Uh, no," he said. "Seth is at work. I don't know where Liam is. Is that what this is about? Did that crazy fucker do something? I haven't seen him in a couple of days."

Nez pulled a copy of the warrant out of her jacket pocket and told him to step out of the house. She handed him the warrant and said, "Stay out here while we search the premises."

"Come with me," one of the cops backing her up said, taking Simpson by the arm over toward the SUVs.

Nez and the other cop quickly cleared the house. It wasn't hard to tell which room was Liam's. He had a copy of *The Turner Diaries, The Camp of the Saints*, and *Mein Kampf* on his bookshelf, along with other materials, including a Celtic cross flag on the wall.

Her priority was Liam's desktop computer, but she looked around the room first, searching for anything else that might be important. If she was lucky, she would find a book of passwords, usernames, and notes about what, if anything, Liam had been planning.

She could hear the other officers in the house, searching the place for digital devices and anything that could be reasonably related to extremism or planned attacks on civilian or government targets.

Nez knew it was going to take some time to determine whether anything of importance was here. But at least she was doing *something*. They were making progress. But it was Sunday morning. And they had to hurry.

Chapter 38

MANY OF THE RECRUITS were not happy. They'd been cooped up in the barracks building for the entire day yesterday, save for eating dinner after the sun went down. They didn't seem to understand what was happening. Sure, some of them were scared shitless, but most of them seemed to be under the impression they were playing a game. They acted as if they could call timeout or hit pause or simply ask to leave whenever they wanted. But they were sorely mistaken. And I had an increasingly bad feeling in my gut as the morning crept toward noon.

As I escorted the very last man to be fingerprinted, I wondered if anyone knew where any of these guys were. If they had all been recruited similarly to the way I had, then I doubted it. As far as I had gathered by listening to them talk and asking the occasional question, many of them had been pulled out of jails after committing petty offenses during protests or marches. Before that, they'd been remotely radicalized through the internet.

Some of them had been out on their own, living with roommates they despised or struggling to afford their own places. Many of them were estranged from their families for their racist and extremist beliefs. But some of them had come from families with these same beliefs. Those were the true believers. The ones really down for the cause.

But what about the other ones? Was there anyone out there looking for them? If they went missing off the face of the earth, how long would it take for someone to notice?

That made me think of my own situation. Sure, Nez and Hudson knew I was here, but no one else did. I didn't have a family. The few friends I had were used to going weeks or even months without hearing from me. It was kind of sad to think about what would happen if I died in this place, at the hands of these people. I almost had once already.

But as we approached the cabin, I told myself to cut the shit. End the pity party. I was here to do a job. It was important. It mattered.

The really sad thing was, I knew that all of the people in the cabin and many of the recruits were thinking exactly the same thing. They were here to do a job. And to them, it was important. It mattered.

I escorted the guy inside and stood around in the foyer until they were done printing him. Pennington was no longer on guard duty because he'd disappeared last night. Instead, it was a guy named Dickson. I had been there when McCray had told Pennington to stay put in the barracks. The big guy immediately pointed the finger at me, whining as he tried to tell McCray what happened. But the boss man wasn't having it. He cut Pennington off, saying he didn't want to hear excuses.

I'd kept my face blank during the interaction because the entire barracks building was looking at us. If Pennington had disliked me before, he really hated me now. But it had been worth it to get my phone out of the truck. Still, I would probably have to deal with the consequences sooner rather than later. For all I knew, Pennington was back in the barracks, spewing venom and getting all the other recruits to turn against me. If he was smart, that would be the thing to do.

Then he could wait until the time was right and shoot me, then claim it was an accident.

Then again, I didn't think Pennington was all that smart. Still, I needed to watch myself.

When McCray and Pete were done fingerprinting the guy, they told me to escort him back to the barracks and then return to the cabin.

Spencer was on guard duty outside the barracks building, and he looked shaken when I escorted the guy back. As soon as the man was inside, Spencer stepped over. "What's the plan here?" he asked. "These guys are getting pissed. We're about to have a fucking riot on our hands if we don't do something."

He was right. I could hear shouting from inside the structure. They were chanting, "Let us out!"

I shared a look with Spencer then pulled out the radio McCray had given me that morning. He told me not to use it unless it was an emergency because it was too easy for third parties to listen in on the frequency. But I thought this qualified as an emergency.

"Hey, boss?" I said into the radio. "You there?"

There was a long moment of silence before McCray's voice came over. "What is it?"

"We've got a problem at the barracks. You should probably get down here."

"Be right there," he said.

I clipped the radio back to my belt. I still had the phone on me, but I had moved it down to a cargo pocket. I felt confident I wouldn't be searched today. And keeping it in my boxer briefs would've been way too uncomfortable with all the walking I was doing.

"So you're the golden boy, huh?" Spencer said. "What happened? Word is you killed a guy. Must've been Stoll, because he's the only one missing. What did he do? Was he working for the cops or something? That why they're all getting fingerprinted?"

I shrugged. "I'm just doing what the bosses tell me."

"Who would've thought that you would climb the ranks so fast," Spencer said. He didn't seem mad, though. He seemed proud. "I knew I saw potential in you back at that jail."

"Yeah, well, I've been around the block a few times. I know how to handle myself."

"You don't have to tell me," Spencer said, pointing up at the bruises on his face. He was a good sport about it, I had to give him that much. Maybe because he'd felt firsthand how hard I could hit.

A branch snapped and I turned my head toward the noise, seeing McCray and Cotter coming down the trail to the bunkhouse. Cotter was hurrying, and he had longer legs than McCray, who was kind of waddling to keep up while carrying one of the AR-556 rifles. Neither man had heavy coats on despite the morning chill. That bad feeling in my gut got suddenly worse.

They stopped in front of the doors, facing Spencer and me. "How long has this been going on?" Cotter asked in a clipped tone. He was bent forward at the waist, his shoulders tensed.

"Maybe ten minutes?" Spencer said. "They just want to be let out. They've been in there for most of the last twenty-four hours."

Cotter turned to McCray. "The one you told me about, what does he look like?"

"He looks like a skinhead," McCray said. "Shaved head with a thin beard. Got a scar through his left eyebrow."

Cotter turned back toward the door, pulling his pistol out of his holster. He opened the door and held it. "Go," he said to us. "I want you to see this."

The chanting faded as soon as the guys inside saw McCray walk in behind Spencer and me. Then Cotter came in and the chanting died altogether. I wasn't sure if it was the look on his face or the pistol in his hand that did it. Either way, the place went quiet.

Cotter scanned the room for a moment, then he fixated on the guy McCray had described. He was standing over to the right, between the first two cots on that side of the room. He was smirking, a mischievous look in his eyes.

Cotter stalked over to him and raised his pistol, the click of the safety disengaging loud in the quiet room. The guy's face changed, his look morphing into one of pure fear. He opened his mouth to speak, but before he could get a word out, Cotter pulled the trigger. I flinched at the shot, my ears ringing as I watched the contents of the man's skull splatter all over the wall behind him. He stepped backward before stumbling and falling over the cot, ending up with his limp legs on the bed and the rest of his body on the floor.

Stunned faces stared at Cotter. "Everyone sit down!" he shouted.

Everyone but Spencer, me, McCray, and Cotter himself quickly found a seat. Some of them sat on the floor right where they'd been standing while others shuffled to sit on a cot.

"You think this is a game?" Cotter asked, stepping out into the aisle, pistol now held down at his side. "You think we aren't serious people here? Is that what you think?"

No one answered. Eyes bounced between the dead man and Cotter.

"You are here for a reason," Cotter continued. "You are here because you have a duty to your race. You aren't here to be coddled. You aren't here to be babysat or to learn to play soldier. You *are* soldiers. And in this army, mutiny gets you killed. So you will do what you're told. You will do your part. You can decide, right here and now, to fight for the Aryan race, or we can bury you out in the woods. What are you going to choose?"

Still, no one answered.

"What are you going to choose?" Cotter screamed, putting the gun into a kid's face.

"Fight!" the kid screamed, tears streaming down his cheeks. "I want to fight!"

"Fight!" many other guys screamed. But not everyone voiced it. Several young men were sobbing, heads in their hands. Cotter looked around the room for several long moments. All but two of the sobbing men stopped. Still, Cotter waited. Then, he stepped over and whispered in McCray's ear. The shorter man nodded.

Cotter stepped over to me, putting his left hand on my shoulder. "I don't ask this of you lightly," he whispered in my ear. "But I know you can handle it."

He let go of my shoulder and walked out the door. I looked after him, confused. My gut was screaming.

"Okay, listen up!" McCray said, pulling out a piece of paper. "I want the following men to come with me. Dewey, Scanlan, and Sommer. Let's go!"

The guys still sobbing looked at each other. No one made a move.

"Let's go, goddammit!" McCray said. "Time's wasting. We have a lot to do today!"

Finally, the three men he called stood up and walked forward.

"You three, wait outside with Rubble," McCray said, turning and nodding to me. "The rest of you, get ready for exercises, okay?"

Hesitantly, I walked outside and gathered with Dewey, Scanlan, and Sommer. They were all kids, maybe twenty years old. And they all looked scared shitless.

I heard McCray continue talking inside. "Spencer, select four men to take care of this mess," he said. "Pennington, get your ass outside. Oh, and you two, come with me."

I wasn't sure who that last sentence was directed at since I couldn't see inside from where I was, but I had a feeling I knew. Sure enough, McCray came out of the building leading the two kids who couldn't stop crying. Pennington came out after them, and McCray handed him the rifle he'd been carrying.

"Let's take a walk," McCray said.

This isn't happening, I thought. *This can't be happening. We're not really going to execute these kids, are we?*

Deep down, I knew the answer.

Chapter 39

THE WORLD WAS SO quiet. Everything seemed muffled. The crunch of fallen pine needles under our boots. The birds chirping. Even the sound of my breathing sounded far away as we walked away from the main portion of the camp. Pennington walked next to me. Ahead of us were the five recruits who'd been called out of the barracks building. Leading us through a path in the woods was McCray.

The two kids who'd been crying were deathly silent now. One of them kept glancing over his shoulder at us. The third time, Pennington snapped at him. "The fuck you looking at? Face forward. Keep walking."

"Relax, Pennington," McCray said from up front. "We're just going to get some wood some of the guys chopped out here."

It was a poor excuse for a lie. McCray didn't even sound like he believed it. And all five kids knew what was coming. After the showing back in the building, there was no way they didn't know.

But I couldn't let it happen, could I?

The debate had been raging in my head since we'd left the building.

What if I did let it happen? How many lives would I save if I did nothing and let these five kids die? Fifty? A hundred? A thousand?

Because the only other choice was to blow my cover. I would have to kill Pennington and McCray to save these guys. And even then, I had no idea what I would tell the five guys. That they could go home? That they should run as fast as they could away? What guarantee would I have that they wouldn't turn on me the first chance they got? After all, just because Cotter and McCray had decided they should die didn't mean they weren't true believers. For all I knew, if I kept these guys from getting killed, one of them might show up at a supermarket next year with an AR-15 and start killing people who didn't have the right skin color.

But could I stand by and watch them die?

Sure I could. Inaction is the easiest way to let the world go to shit. It's taking action that's hard. I could absolutely stand by and watch them get executed. I wouldn't like it, but I could sure as hell do it.

And I knew that if I killed McCray and Pennington, it would only be a matter of time before someone from the camp came looking for us. Then what would happen? What would Cotter do when he found out that I had run off with five recruits? What would the WPA leadership do? Would they move their plan up? Would they go on Tuesday or Wednesday? Could they even do that if they wanted to?

There were too many questions and too few answers. And I didn't have much time.

As we continued, moving deeper into the woods, I fell back a little bit, getting out of Pennington's peripheral vision. Holding my AR-556 with my left hand, I reached down to my cargo pocket with my right and pressed the power button on the phone through the cloth of my pants. I knew it wouldn't make a sound upon turning on, but I wasn't sure how I was going to find a moment to do what I needed to do.

Pennington turned his head to look at me just as I was bringing my right hand back up. "What're you doing?" he said.

"A guy can't scratch a fuckin' itch without you getting in his business?" I said.

His face turned red, but he turned back around and didn't say more about it.

Up ahead through the trees, I could see a clearing. I figured that was where we were headed. Not much longer now.

Suddenly one of the kids bolted, sprinting left away from us and out into the woods. "Hey!" Pennington yelled, lifting his rifle to his shoulder and aiming down the sights.

Seeing my opportunity, I bolted after the kid, running right into Pennington's line of fire.

"Get out of the way!" he yelled.

Then McCray yelled something next, but I couldn't make it out. I was running as hard as I could after the kid. The next thing I knew, gunfire crackled behind me. It only took me a moment to realize it wasn't directed toward me. The sound was all wrong for that. Someone—Pennington, I guessed—was firing in the opposite direction. One or more of the other guys had run.

"Stop!" I shouted at the kid running from me. I didn't really want him to stop. But I needed to make it seem like I was trying my hardest to catch him. He didn't slow, didn't stop. I thumbed the fire selector on the rifle down and then fired several shots into the woods, pointing my rifle up so there was no chance of hitting the kid.

I kept going for a dozen more yards or so before I stopped running. Pretty soon, the kid was lost from my sight. I turned around, looking for any sign of the others, but saw only trees.

Crouching, I pulled out my phone and dialed the number I'd memorized. It was answered after two rings.

"Hello?" Hudson said.

"Hudson, I got a situation," I said quietly. "And I don't have much time."

***

"I'm coming out!" I shouted.

"Rubble? That you?" McCray shouted back.

"It's me," I said. "The kid got away."

"Well, come on, then," he called.

I moved through the trees, bringing five men into view on the trail near the clearing. The three recruits, Dewey, Scanlan, and Sommer, were sitting down. Dewey and Sommer were crying while the Scanlan looked like his brain had just shut down. He stared at the ground blankly. Pennington was standing nearby, weapon pointed at them. McCray was on the other side of the trio, his pistol in hand.

I shook my head as I approached. "I shot at him, but he was too far ahead. Too many damn trees in the way."

"Goddammit," McCray said. "Now we're gonna have to go find him. We need to hurry."

"Please," Dewey, said, turning his wet face up to McCray. "Please, I won't tell anyone. I swear."

McCray stepped toward the kid and smacked him with his pistol across the cheek. The kid went limp and fell onto his side on the ground, knocked unconscious by the blow.

"Where's the other one?" I asked.

Pennington grinned and pointed out into the woods. "*I* can actually use *my* weapon," he said.

I looked where he was pointing and spotted the dead kid sprawled awkwardly next to a thick pine trunk.

I turned back to McCray. "What do we do with them?"

"What do you think?" McCray said.

"Okay," I said. "Here or in the clearing?"

"Let's just do it here," McCray said, stepping off the trail to get in a better firing position. Pennington was slightly ahead of me and to my right, which put McCray about five yards further on. I nodded, stepping back as if to get some distance between me and the kids on the ground. This put me behind Pennington.

"Pennington," I said.

The big guy turned toward me. "What?"

I looked him in the eye as I raised my rifle and pulled the trigger. The bullet obliterated his nose and put a hole in the back of his head.

I shifted and pointed the weapon at McCray, who still had his pistol down by his side.

"Drop it," I said as Pennington's body came to rest on the ground with a thud. McCray looked at me, utter confusion written all over his face. He was still holding the gun.

"Put it down, McCray," I told him, taking better aim.

He dropped the weapon, anger transforming his features.

Sommer twitched, getting ready to run. "Don't you move either," I said, looking toward the trio. "Not unless you want to get shot."

Turning back to McCray, I asked, "Where's the nearest road?"

"Back the way we came," he said, hands held out at his sides. "Only one road in."

"I didn't ask you where the nearest road *out* was. I asked where the nearest road was. Period. If we were to walk from here, how long would it take to get to the nearest road?"

McCray shook his head. "Not possible. We'd have to walk for ten miles or more to get to another road. No, you're fucked, Rubble. You're done. Pretty soon, Cotter and Halverson will come looking. And they'll find you wandering around in the forest."

"You," I said, looking at Sommer. "What's your name? Your first name?"

"Mike," he said. He had short and fuzzy brown hair, acne on his forehead, and the skinny frame of a teenager.

"What about you?" I asked Scanlan. Dewey was still unconscious from when McCray pistol-whipped him.

"Owen," he said. He looked slightly older than Mike, with darker hair, a large nose, and a small mouth.

"Okay, Mike," I said. "McCray's going to pull out his phone and bring up a satellite map of this place. Once he has it up, he's going to show you exactly where we are on the map. Then, you're going to bring the phone to me and show me. Got it?"

"Yes," Mike said, sniffling.

"Fuck that," McCray said. "I'm not doin' it."

"Okay," I said. "Fine. I'll just shoot you in your fat head. I'm sure we can figure it out. I know generally where we are anyway. Might take me a minute longer, but that's a compromise I'm willing to make." I stepped closer to McCray, stiffening and bending my head down to aim.

"Okay!" McCray said.

"Good. Now we're getting somewhere."

Chapter 40

McCray had been lying about the nearest road. No big surprise there, really. Once Mike had helped me figure out which way to go, I directed him to use Pennington's boot laces to tie McCray's hands behind his back. Dewey came around during this process.

When we were all ready to go, I grabbed McCray's pistol from the ground and stuffed it into a coat pocket. Then I looked at the four people with me. "Here's what we're going to do," I said. "Owen, you're gonna help Dewey on the hike. Mike, you're going to hang onto the phone and follow our progress, making sure we're going the right way. McCray, you're going to walk just ahead of me. You better believe that if you run, I will not hesitate to shoot you in the back. Besides, we don't need to kid ourselves here. You've really let yourself go. You wouldn't get very far even if you did run."

"You some kind of race traitor?" McCray asked. "The man loves niggers, spics, and Jews," he said to the other three. "You really going to let him do this!?"

I smiled at him. "Five minutes ago you were about to execute these guys. You really think they don't remember that? Are you really that fucking stupid, or do you just think *they're* that stupid?"

McCray shook his head.

"Yeah, I figured as much," I said.

I took McCray's radio and turned it off, sticking it in my back pocket. I still had my radio, and I left it on to listen for signs that those back at the camp knew something was amiss. So far, there was nothing.

We started through the forest, heading past the clearing we'd originally been going to and moving up a hill beyond. I paid close attention to which way Mike was taking us. I'd studied the satellite image and so knew we should be heading southwest to get to the dirt road.

"What's going to happen when we get to the road?" Owen asked after we'd been walking for fifteen minutes or so.

"We're going to hitch a ride and go our separate ways," I lied.

"How are we going to do that?"

"We'll borrow a car from some camper or hunter. Don't worry about it. Just be happy you're not dead." I clearly couldn't tell them the truth. I didn't want to put them on edge, so I just strung them along and hoped we wouldn't have to wait long when we got to the road.

We'd been walking for another ten minutes when my radio crackled to life. "Mac, where the hell are you?" Halverson asked.

Ahead of me, McCray looked over his shoulder. "You better let me talk to him," he said. "If you want to buy some time."

"Not a chance," I said. I knew it would only take one or two words to give Halverson an idea of where we were. I wasn't willing to take that chance. Too risky. I thought briefly about answering myself, telling him everything was good, and that we were about to head back. But if I did that, I would be giving up the game in the long run. This way, I might be able to convince the WPA that I was still on their side. It was a card up my sleeve that I didn't want to play just yet. Unfortunately, I wouldn't know if it was an ace or a deuce until I actually had a chance to lay it down—*if* I had a chance to lay it down.

We walked on. Both Halverson and Cotter got on the radio again, fear in their voices. I figured it was a matter of minutes before they sent someone out to investigate.

"Let's pick up the pace!" I called ahead.

Fifteen minutes later, Mike called from ahead, "There it is!"

We hurried down a gentle slope, me prodding McCray to go faster, and out onto the dirt road. Pine trees created an alley which the tan-colored road wound through. I couldn't see more than a couple of hundred yards in either direction, thanks to the curvature of the road. There was no sign of anyone.

"Come on," I said under my breath. It had already been too long. Surely Cotter and Halverson had found the bodies out in the woods by now. I wasn't sure what their reaction would be, but I didn't think it would be good. And the last thing I wanted was for the WPA to get even more paranoid or change their communication tactics.

"Which way do we go?" Mike asked.

Right was toward town, left toward the mountain. "Right," I said. That was when I heard the sound of an engine. It was growing louder.

"What do we do?" Owen asked. "Should we hide?"

"Just stay where you are," I told them. "Nobody move."

A black SUV appeared, coming from the right, toward town. It was moving fast, and it kept coming, only slowing when it was bearing down on us. It came to a skidding stop about ten yards away. Through the windshield, I could see Hudson's face. I smiled as all four doors opened and four plainclothes FBI agents jumped out, all of them but Hudson yelling for the others to get on their knees.

The three of them ran past me and started dealing with the captives while I strolled up to Hudson. We shook hands. Hudson looked past my shoulder and said, "Oh, they don't like this at all."

I turned and looked at the four of them, on their knees while the three feds dealt with them. They were glaring at Hudson and me. Apparently, the fact that I was shaking a Black FBI agent's hand was all the confirmation they needed as to what side I was on. It was the embodiment of everything they stood against.

I was somewhat surprised to see the three kids glaring at me like they were, given what they'd just gone through. I hoped I hadn't made the wrong decision. I hoped I hadn't just blown this whole operation up to save the lives of three dyed-in-the-wool racists who would never be able to overcome their ignorance.

But they were just kids.

And I thought they deserved a second chance.

***

I watched over Hudson's shoulder as the FBI SWAT team he'd brought up from the San Francisco office approached The White Power Alliance camp. We were standing outside the SUV just down the road from the camp, watching the body camera and drone feeds on a laptop.

Apparently, he'd brought the team up to be on standby shortly after they'd gotten good drone footage of how many people were at the camp. Now, after several days of waiting around, the thirty-eight-strong SWAT team was rushing to do what they did best.

A small group of them had gone in through the woods I had come out of. Once they were in position, they radioed in. The rest of the team—who'd been waiting just down their road in their vehicles—headed in.

The lead vehicle was something Hudson called a Ballistic Armored Tactical Transport. It was big, black, and heavily armored. We watched the drone feed, seeing the bulky vehicle speed up to the simple live-stock gate. The vehicle barely slowed as it came to the closed gate, smashing through. I'd told Hudson about the two guards who'd appeared out of the darkness on the night I'd arrived. I had seen similar guards the one other time we left the property, although I hadn't been paying much attention on the way back, thanks to the head injuries I'd suffered.

Three out of the four SUVs following powered through the busted gate. The fourth came to a stop, and four armored officers jumped out, rifles pointed at the woods on either side of the gate. I half expected to hear shots, but there were none. Not yet, at least. Maybe the show of force had sent the two guards running scared.

The other three vehicles approached the tent near the front of the property, where I'd gotten my fatigues the first night. The last of the three vehicles in the line skidded to a stop, armored SWAT officers jumping out just as two men stepped out of the tent, unarmed and with their hands up.

The lead vehicle continued up to the cabin, coming to a stop right near the front steps. The rear doors opened, and ten officers poured out. The other one drove around the cabin, heading toward the trail to the barracks building.

Hudson and I looked closer at the screen as we heard the distant crack of gunfire.

"Shots fired," a man said over the radio. "Second-floor windows."

Hudson switched to a body cam feed, seeing one of the men behind the armored vehicle as he leaned out and fired his M4 carbine at one of the broken windows on the second floor of the cabin.

While several officers laid down covering fire from the vehicle, the rest of them ran up the porch steps and broke the door down. Hudson switched the feed to let us see as they moved into the house. I saw

Pete on his knees with his hands up in the computer room. An officer moved forward to secure him.

Cotter suddenly appeared at the top of the stairs with a rifle in his hands. Before he could get a shot off, the SWAT officer whose body cam we were watching shot him in the chest twice. I could hear women screaming through the laptop's speakers.

They quickly cleared the house, finding no other armed individuals inside. Cotter had clearly been the one firing from the second-floor window.

Switching feeds again, we watched as the officers approached about a dozen recruits who were heading for the armory to get weapons. Spencer was the only one of them armed, and when he refused to put his weapon down when first commanded, he was killed. The rest of the recruits gave up quickly after that.

The team who'd gone through the woods secured Halverson and a couple of armed recruits without a shot fired. Apparently, they'd gone out to investigate after not hearing back from McCray.

By the time it was all over, only Cotter and Spencer had been shot. No one else, including the SWAT officers, had been injured. The two guards at the front of the property had given themselves up. The only person unaccounted for was the kid I had gone after into the woods. I knew he'd turn up sooner or later.

As the afternoon waned, I stood near the side of the road, a flurry of FBI activity around me. So far, the press hadn't gotten wind of the raid. That was due to the location of the camp. It was just a matter of time until this thing was all over the news. And I had no idea what the WPA leadership would do when they found out that the camp had been raided. At worst, they would accelerate their plans, hitting targets within days. At best, they would go into hiding, licking their wounds until they decided it was time to terrorize America again. Maybe it would be next month. Or maybe next year. Maybe in five years.

In a way, the latter scenario would be worse. Right now we knew many of the players. We had the will and the resources to go after them. If they went back into hiding, the whole landscape would change. It would be like starting from scratch.

As I thought about the way McCray and those kids had looked at us when Hudson and I were shaking hands, I knew I wasn't done. I needed to end this. I needed to rid the world of these men, one way or another.

I just hoped that the feds would continue giving me support.

If not, I'd just have to do it without their blessing.

Chapter 41

ROGER INMAN PACED IN his front yard as the sun went down. He kept looking at the road in, waiting for his men to show up. Time was wasting. It wouldn't be long before Patricia's dumb bitch of a mother started making a fuss. She was used to talking to her daughter every day. But not today. Not ever again.

After murdering his wife, he'd passed out for several hours in his recliner, waking up with an awful hangover and the sure knowledge that he'd done something terrible. It took him several groggy minutes to remember exactly what it was. And along with the recalled details and sensation of the murder came the justification for it.

After stumbling to the kitchen to get a glass of water, he stood over the sink, looking out the picture window toward the back of the property. The sun was just rising over the field of yellow grass and the woods beyond. He waited for the shame and regret to come. He waited to break down in tears and cry out, "What have I done!? Dear God, what have I done?"

But it never happened. He didn't feel shame. There was no regret. He knew exactly what he'd done. If anything, he felt a sense of elation. But he also felt the time ticking by. There was much to do before he could leave his mark on the world. Much to do before he could actually make a difference. Before he could show that Jew governor who she was fucking with.

After forcing down another glass of water, he got to work. The first thing he did was drag his wife's body into the woods. He didn't have time to bury her, especially with the ground as hard as it was during winter. But even more than that, he didn't *want* to bury her. She didn't deserve a Christian burial. She deserved to have her carcass ripped apart by animals and eaten by bugs.

He attached a rope to her leg and secured it to the ball hitch on his truck. Then he dragged her over into the woods along one of the lesser-used dirt tracks. Once deep in the woods, he took the rope off and pulled her off the track. He smiled as he thought about the hell of a time the feds would have finding her.

After getting back to the house and cleaning up, he sat down and sketched out the whole thing with paper and pen. It was not the first time he'd done it. But he wanted to get it all fresh in his mind, allowing him to make final preparations. This took him several hours. When he was done, he gathered supplies.

Then he made the calls. It took some convincing to get the men to drop their Sunday plans and come over. The last thing he wanted to do was say anything over the phone that might alert the feds to their plan. Not when he was so close. So he just told them it was important. He said it was an emergency. And, eventually, they all relented.

Now he paced in his front yard, watching for a vehicle coming down the road. He had his phone in one hand, and when he wasn't looking at the road, he was looking at the phone. Patricia's mother had called him twice so far. He hadn't picked up either call. She had left a message on the second call, saying that she couldn't get ahold of Pat and that she would appreciate it if he could have her call. The dumb bitch.

Finally, he saw movement ahead. It was a truck, coming down the road. A few moments later, he was able to identify the vehicle. It was Allen's. And Ben always rode with Allen. That was two. Four more to go.

***

"I don't know, Roger," Tony said, sitting with long arms propped on his knees. "I thought we were going to have a little more time to prepare. I mean, *tonight*? That seems awfully fucking fast."

"What the fuck have we been training for?" Roger said. He was standing in the living room while the other six men sat on the couch or the two recliners flanking it. "We know the plan. We know we can do it. So what's the big deal, dammit? Are you just not up for it?"

Heads turned toward Tony, who raised his hands. "That's not what I'm saying. I just thought we were going to have a couple of days at least to get our affairs in order. I mean, what if something happens to us?"

"What, you don't have a will? You don't even have any fuckin' kids, Tony," Roger said, pacing in front of the flatscreen television on the wall behind him, which was turned off.

"I'm thinking about my sister," Tony said. "That's all. I'd like to give her what little I have saved in my account if something happens."

"Immediate family will get it regardless," Allen said, camouflage hat pushed high on his forehead.

"I can't be the only one who thinks this is fast," Tony said, looking around.

The other men glanced at each other and at Roger in turn. This was the moment of truth. It could go either way.

"Well, you know my vote," Roger said. "I say we do it. If the WPA is going to hit their targets tonight, we need to do our part. This is history in the making, boys. Don't you see that?"

"Why did they suddenly move it up to tonight?" Tony asked. "What's the hurry? I thought you said Saturday. I was planning on Saturday."

"I don't know," Roger said. "Something must have happened, but that's just what Griffith told me. He said tonight."

"Fuck it. I'm in," Ben said, standing up from the couch and chugging the rest of his beer. "I can't stand to see all these niggers taking over our country. I'm sick of it."

Dustin, whose pale blue eyes betrayed no emotion, stood up from his spot in a recliner. "Hell, I've been impatient for this ever since we started talkin' about it."

Roger smiled as Dustin joined him and Ben in front of the television. He thought for sure the tide was about to break. But as seconds passed, it seemed he was wrong.

"I'd like to talk a little more about this," Clint said, his eyes fixed on the floor.

You fucking pussy, Roger thought.

In the other recliner, Hugh's phone pinged. He grabbed for it quickly, as though thankful to have something to divert his attention from the matter at hand.

"What do you want to talk about?" Roger asked, rolling his eyes.

Clint looked up, then glanced around. "You sure no one's here?"

"Jesus, Clint," Roger said. "My wife is gone with the kids. They'll be gone all day, okay? So let's figure this thing out. What did you want—"

"Turn on the TV!" Hugh shouted, looking up from his phone. Everyone looked at him. "Turn it on! Find a news channel."

Seeing the look on his friend's face, Roger grabbed the remote and powered it on. After a few moments, he found a 24/7 news channel. The headline at the bottom of the screen read, "White Supremacist Camp Raided." Above this, two news anchors—a Black woman and a white man—were discussing the news.

"Now, we don't have any official word yet on the dead," the white man said, "but unconfirmed reports suggest that several of the suspects in the camp were killed during a short firefight. We can confirm that one of the officers who raided the camp has been killed. We now go live to WCAN news correspondent Darren West in the town of Mount Shasta, California. Darren?"

The screen switched from a shot of the studio to one of a Black man standing on a dirt road. Official vehicles rolled past in the distance over his left shoulder. Trees dominated the frame over his right.

"Yeah, thanks, Simon," Darren said. "You mentioned the unconfirmed reports of those suspects killed during the raid. We've actually just gotten word on three of those individuals. The Federal Bureau of Investigation has released the names of Frank Cotter, Gene Halverson, and Wyatt McCray..."

"Holy shit," Roger said as he stared at the television. "Holy shit, it's happening. This is why they moved it up from Saturday," he said, even though he'd made the whole thing up about the WPA changing the date. Still, he saw an opportunity when it was right in front of his face.

"Look at the smirk on that nigger's face," Clint said. "He's loving it. He'd probably piss on their bodies if he had half a chance."

Roger muted the television. "The war has started," he said slowly, looking at the other six men. "So what's it going to be? Stay home and wait for them to come and execute you like a sick dog, or bring the fight to their fuckin' doorstep?" Even before he finished getting the words out, he knew what their answers would be.

Chapter 42

"WHAT HAPPENS WHEN THEY find out McCray and Halverson are still alive?" I asked.

"They won't," Nez said. "Not before Saturday, anyway." She'd only just returned from her trip to the East Coast, and she looked more than a little upset at having missed all the excitement.

"The laws that came into effect following 9/11 give us a lot of leeway when it comes to holding those suspected of terrorism," Hudson said.

We were all sitting in a hotel room at the Inn at Mount Shasta. Nez and I were sitting on a couch while Hudson perched on the edge of a bed just to our left. Shortly after the raid was over at the WPA camp, Hudson had assigned an underling to bring me here. He wanted to make sure I wasn't seen by any of the media. And I was only now coming to realize why.

"Okay," I said. "So if these guys at White Power Asshole headquarters think the three guys who held all their secrets died in the raid, they may still go ahead with their plan?"

Hudson nodded, reaching into his jacket pocket. He was still wearing the same dusty and rumpled suit from earlier. "That's the hope. And when you tell them you have this—" he pulled Cotter's little notebook out of his pocket— "they should breathe a sigh of relief just before coming to get you."

I slumped into the couch, examining the logic from all angles. It wasn't the best plan I'd ever heard, but I'd also never been much of a planner. Most of the time I just got by on gut feeling, grit, and nerve. But I wanted to think about this. I wanted to do it right.

Then again, it's not like I would've refused. There was no way. These assholes had touched a nerve. Maybe it was because I'm white and I felt it was my duty to stand up for all the other white people who weren't racist pieces of shit. But it was more than that. It was that I was an American. And because of that, I believed in the land of opportunity. Not as it was, with its myriad problems including government corruption and entrenched systemic racism, but as it *could* be. As it was *supposed* to be.

I knew in my heart that Americans had it in them to make real, meaningful change. I knew we could turn it into the land we wanted it to be. But we had to keep striving for those heights. We had to keep holding that vision up high and working toward it.

And anyone who was willing to stand in the way of that America with hate, derision, and violence had to be stopped. There was no place for them in the country. There was no place for them in the world. Because the freedom to threaten, intimidate, and oppress was no freedom at all.

"But you're going to start working through that book, right?" I said, sitting back up to look past Nez at Hudson. "What happens if you trip some sort of alarm while I'm there with them? They'll know I'm the one, because I brought them the book."

"We won't trip any alarms," Nez said. "Believe me. These guys might have some smart people on their side, but our people are better. The team that's working on this right now is fantastic. They're already connecting the dots, finding likely lone wolf actors, and they haven't even had to talk to anyone in these chat rooms yet. Trust me, the danger will not come from some digital tripwire."

"What she said," Hudson quipped.

"And you don't think you'll be able to find out who the leaders are that way?" I asked.

"That's the problem," Nez said. "We don't know what we don't know. It could be that everything we need to take down the whole organization is in this notebook. But if it's not, then we'll be in it deep. We need you on the inside. You're our insurance policy."

I sighed. "Good enough for me. So how do I contact these people? What was the name I texted you? Coakley?"

Nez and Hudson shared a look. It was quick, but I saw it. "What?" I asked. "You guys know him?"

Hudson shook his head. "No. I mean, we're looking into him, but we don't know him."

I looked at Nez, who met my gaze easily. It was like trying to read a brick wall.

"Okay," I said, but I wasn't convinced. There was something they weren't telling me.

"We're going to have you write an email in one of the accounts from that book," Nez said. "And then save it as a draft. That's the way these guys have been communicating."

Hudson grabbed his laptop and gave it to me. He gave me the little notebook and pointed to an email address and password on the page. "That one," he said.

"Just type it out on your laptop?" I asked. "They won't be able to tell where it came from?"

"You watch too many movies," Hudson said. "It's fine. We know what we're doing. Just sign in."

I opened a browsing window and navigated to the email service provider. When I was inside, I hit the New Message button, then looked up at the two feds. "Okay, what do I say?"

***

Sarah moaned with pleasure as Coakley continued his pumping rhythm. She tightened her legs around his hips, mouth open as she grabbed handfuls of sheets. It was only when they were having sex that Coakley managed to forget all about Bove. It was as if Sarah was *his* wife. It was as if she would be able to stay here after they finished. Spend the rest of the evening with him. Sleep in his bed. Wake up and eat breakfast with him.

It was all make-believe, but it felt good while he was in it. He thought about what their kids would look like. Not that they would have any. Sarah was on the pill. And besides, the fact that Bove never fucked her anymore would make a pregnancy awkward. She would have some explaining to do. Right before Bove put a bullet in her head—and, of course, her lover's head.

There was a noise from downstairs, so faint Coakley wasn't sure he'd actually heard something. But he stopped mid-thrust and turned his head.

Breathing heavily, Sarah pushed herself against him. "Why are you stopping?"

"Did you hear that?" he asked.

"I didn't hear anything."

Then it came again, this time unmistakable. It was quickly followed by Bove shouting, "Bob?"

"Oh shit," Coakley said, extricating himself from the woman's embrace and clambering off the bed. The trance broken, Coakley felt his erection quickly fading. Nothing like the sound of Sarah's husband to dampen the mood.

Sarah jumped up as well, grabbing her clothes just as they heard the knock again, this time louder.

Coakley pulled some gym clothes on before ducking into the bathroom to spray cologne on, hoping to cover the smell of sex. Then he rushed downstairs and opened the door.

"Something's happened," Bove said, stepping through the door and marching into the house.

Coakley shut the door and turned to follow the man. "What is it?" he asked as he glanced up the stairs, willing Sarah to stay as silent as the grave they would surely be in if Bove found out about their affair.

"The fucking feds," Bove said, stepping into the den and grabbing the TV remote off the table next to the couch. As he waited for the device to power on, he turned and looked Coakley up and down. "Were you exercising?"

"Yeah," Coakley said. "Just a quick weight workout in the gym." He had turned a small downstairs bedroom into a basic gym with some free weights, which had been a gift from Bove. Paid for with the mysterious money that only Bove knew the source of.

"I thought I heard you come down the stairs," Bove said.

"You did. I'd just finished my workout and was about to get in the shower when I heard you knock. In fact, I barely heard you over the water." The lie came easy. It was second nature to him.

Bove turned back to the television and navigated to a live news channel on one of the three streaming apps on the device.

"Jesus Christ," Coakley said, staring at the aerial coverage of the Mount Shasta compound. "Do we need to worry?"

"If they were coming here, they would have already hit us."

"It's just a matter of time before they get Cotter or Halverson to spill," Coakley said. "We have to move. We have to get out of here."

"Cotter and Halverson are dead," Bove said. "So is McCray. They were executed by foot soldiers of the ZOG."

Both men fell silent, listening to the talking head explain what had happened, sliding into conjecture and editorialization as he did so.

Bove pressed the mute button and set the remote down. Then he leaned down, both hands on the back of the couch, staring at the television.

"What do we do?" Coakley asked.

"I don't know," Bove said. "This changes things. We needed those soldiers."

"Do you want to postpone it for now? Re-group and gather our wits?"

Bove stood and turned around, stepping toward Coakley, eyes bright with fury. "We're not postponing it," he said. "If anything, we need to hit them harder. We need to show them what happens when they mess with true Aryans. I'm so fucking sick of this shit. Being treated like second-rate citizens. Getting walked all over. This country was built for us, goddammit. I will not stand by and watch it slip through our fingers."

Coakley stepped back once and nodded. "I'm with you. All the way."

Bove seemed to regain his composure, turning and looking back at the television as he inhaled deeply. "Check to see if there's a message. Maybe Cotter or Halverson drafted one before they were killed. Maybe they know how this happened. You said you couldn't find any dirt from running the prints they sent us?"

"Not exactly," Coakley said. "I couldn't find any direct ties to law enforcement or any other ties to the RLF—other than the one who was killed. But there were three men I recommended they terminate."

"Why?" Bove asked. "If they didn't have any direct ties, why would you have them killed?"

"All three of them had essentially no history I could pull up. In this day and age, that's strange. So I decided to err on the side of caution. I told them to get rid of the three. It's possible that one or all of them were working for the feds or the RLF."

Bove considered this. "That seems the most likely possibility. When they were about to be executed, the feds swooped in to save them."

"Right," Coakley said. "That was my first thought."

"Well, check the messages anyway," Bove said. "Just in case."

Coakley nodded and went out of the room. His cellphone was upstairs, so he decided to use his laptop, which was on his desk in the office. He sat down and opened the computer, then quickly navigated to the email provider. There was a draft there. He opened it up and read it. Then he read it again, eyes narrowing. "Bove," he called. "You should see this."

Bove came into the room and leaned down to read the message over Coakley's shoulder.

"That's the one who killed the spy?" he asked. "Rubble?"

"Yeah," Coakley said. "Also the one who was on the latest recruitment video McCray posted. What do you make of it?"

"Seems awfully convenient that he got away with the book," Bove said. "I don't know."

"Could you see Cotter doing that? Giving him the book and telling him to run?"

Bove considered this for a moment. "Yes, actually. He knows—knew—how important that book was. If the feds got it . . ."

"Yeah. So what do you want me to do?"

Bove stood up and paced in the office. "Take someone and go meet him. Take precautions, though. Find out if he's being watched. If he is, then just get out of there and come back. If it looks legitimate, then get him and see what he knows."

"If it is legit, do you want me to bring him back here?"

"Only if you can verify he's not a spy."

"And if he is a spy?"

"Then make sure to lose his tail before you kill him."

Chapter 43

As I was standing in line at the Mount Shasta Greyhound station, I glanced up at a television in the corner and saw my face on the screen. It was a mugshot from when I'd been arrested in Compton the last time I'd come to California. Even though Nez and Hudson had told me it was coming, it was still a shock to see myself on the news, wanted for questioning in the murder of the FBI agent who'd died in the WPA camp raid.

Only there was no dead Fed. The extent of injuries to the good guys during the raid was a couple of twisted ankles. Just as the news about Halverson and McCray being killed was made up, so was the news about me killing a fed. It was all designed to help me cozy up to the WPA leadership. The only thing was, the general public didn't know that. If I was spotted and the cops were called, there was a good chance I would end up dead. Law enforcement didn't like it when one of their own was killed.

Luckily, I had shaved my beard stubble—which I sported in the mugshot—and I was wearing a baseball cap with the bill pulled down to my eyebrows. The hat, along with the rest of my outfit, was from a Goodwill in Mount Shasta. The blue jeans were a little baggy and the black coat a little threadbare, but the sweater fit well. I still wore the same trusty boots I'd had for several years.

Ahead of me, the line shuffled toward the door and the waiting bus outside. I'd bought a backpack and some extra clothes at the Goodwill, mostly so I didn't look suspicious when I got on the bus. People traveling without bags raised eyebrows, and the last thing I wanted was for anyone to take a second look at me.

When it was my turn to load onto the bus, I handed the driver my ticket. He tore it and gave my stub back without looking at me. As I passed the people who'd already sat down on the bus, I kept my head down, hat bill blocking half my face. Most of the people didn't look at me, anyway. I found an empty pair of seats, setting my backpack in the window seat while I sat at the aisle. Judging by the number of people in line, the bus wouldn't be full. So I pulled my hat down, leaned back, and pretended to be sleeping. When the bus started moving, I knew my little ploy had worked. Everyone had boarded and no one sat next to me.

I settled in and went about calming my mind down. I hoped sleep would come. It was a long ride up the 5 to Salem, where I was supposed to get off. I'd had a long conversation with some unnamed man through the draft function in the email account. I told him that I regularly carried fake IDs and could use one to get a bus ticket to wherever he wanted. He said Salem, so that's what I did.

I was sure they would be skeptical about my story, but figured my face all over the news would help to quell their fears. If not, then I was walking into a very bad situation indeed.

***

"I still think we should've told him," Hudson said from the car as they watched the Greyhound bus pull out of the station. It was dark and cold out, the exhaust pipe creating clouds of vapor as it drove away.

"Too late now," Nez said from the driver's seat.

"I just don't like it."

"He's fine," Nez said. "He's a natural. Better than any newbie I've ever seen."

"I just think we're pushing this thing."

"What else are we supposed to do? Wait and hope they don't attack?"

"Surely we'll get something from the notebook," Hudson said.

"Yeah, given enough time. But we don't have time. We're doing the right thing, hedging our bets. If he doesn't work out, then hopefully we'll have solid intel from the copies we made of Cotter's notebook."

"You mean if they just decide to kill him?" Hudson asked. "Is that what you mean by 'doesn't work out'?"

"He knows the risk. Why all the sudden feelings for him? I mean, I like the guy. I'm not saying I don't. But this is so much bigger than one guy, no matter how much he's grown on us."

"Bullshit," Hudson said. "You may want to think that way, but I know how you really think. I mean, do whatever you have to do to prepare yourself for the possibility of getting that man killed, but don't talk to me like he's just another asset. He's a fucking human being. And he just wants to do what's right."

"All the people in the WPA are human beings, too," Nez said as she guided the car out of the parking lot across from the station. The bus was out of view now, but that was on purpose. They had a couple of agents on the bus, so they weren't worried about losing him. They were going to pass the slower vehicle on their way to Salem, anyway.

"Yeah, they are," he said. "But they've given up their chance to be a part of the human race. They've made their choices."

"So you're saying that you'd rather see Rubble live even if it meant the attacks went ahead?"

"That's not at all what I'm saying. Of course not. I just feel we should've been straight with him about Coakley."

"It only would've muddied the waters," Nez said. "If anything, we've made things easier on him by not telling him. Now he doesn't have to worry about that. He can concentrate on getting us intel on the leadership and their exact targets. Halverson and McCray sure aren't talking. I'm betting we can get through to them eventually, but they only have to wait it out for the next six days."

Hudson was quiet, looking out the window as they approached I-5. "You think it really is Coakley, or just someone using his name?"

"I don't know," Nez said. "But I hope to God it's the latter."

They drove on in silence, merging onto the northbound lanes of the highway, headlights spearing the dark.

Nez's phone, which was perched in a holder next to the steering wheel, rang. She swiped the screen to answer it and then put it on speaker. "Nez," she said.

"Hey, Nez," a woman said over the phone. "It's Wilson. Got a minute?"

"Yeah," she said. "You got me and Hudson."

"Okay, good. We're making progress. We've managed to locate nearly sixty potential lone wolf shooters across the country. They've all posted to various chats on Telegraph, and they've all responded to the phrase, '*Stand by. It will not be televised*,' posted on Friday. We've also confirmed that almost all of them legally own at least one AR-15-style rifle, not to mention several other weapons. We're drawing up a proposal for cooperation from all these state agencies."

"Good. You have all the overtime you need," Nez said. "I want to get eyes on these guys as soon as possible. There's no telling how many of them might jump the gun with all the white power news these last few days."

"Got it. We'll keep digging, but the priority right now is the proposal, which I'll send to you and the SAC as soon as I get it done."

"Great work, Wilson," Hudson put in. "Thank you."

"Thanks. Good luck to you guys," Wilson said before hanging up.

"Progress," Nez said. "That's good. If we can stop the lone wolf shooters, all we have to worry about are the targeted attacks—whatever the hell those are."

"Cross your fingers that Rubble comes through," Hudson said, sighing.

"He will. Like I said, he's a natural."

Chapter 44

THE MAN STEERING THE rigid inflatable boat cut off the engine when they were still three-quarters of a mile upstream from their optimal landing area. The other four men all retrieved their paddles from nearby and stuck them in the water.

The Kansas River moved them steadily east under the star-splashed night sky. There was a new moon tonight, which was a happy coincidence. The men were all dressed in black. The boat was black. Even the paddles were black. But all five of the Hometown Heroes Militia members were wearing NODs—night optics devices. They saw the night as though it were day.

There was the trickle of water and the occasional splash as the men paddled downstream. And there was the sound of them breathing heavily with the effort and the excitement. Trees with barren gray branches lined both sides of the river, still months away from sprouting new leaves.

There was a clearing on the right side of the river. A gap in the trees. Roger Inman saw it and signaled back from his place on the front right side of the RIB. The other three men pulled their paddles out of the water and watched silently, their heads turning as they came abreast of the state park boat ramp. There were no vehicles parked in the parking lot. No one to see them as they floated by. When they were past, the men breathed easily again. One potential obstacle passed.

On Roger's signal, they put their paddles back into the water and rowed with purpose toward the right riverbank. The bottom of the RIB's rigid skeleton scraped ashore a quarter of a mile past the boat ramp. As soon as they were ashore, they discarded the paddles in the middle of the craft.

The first two men—Roger and Ben—jumped out and pulled the boat further onto shore, holding their slung semiautomatic rifles away from their bodies. The next two men— Allen and Tony—did the same, but Dustin, who was in the very back, stayed in the RIB. He turned around, sitting on one of the two inflatable bench seats and facing the water, pulling his rifle up. He scanned the visible section of the river, his back to the trees separating the river from the target property.

Tony retrieved a small, four-step hook ladder from the boat. He followed the three others into the trees, carrying the ladder in his left hand while holding his rifle in the retention position with his right hand, the stock clamped in his armpit.

Part of the reason for picking this time of year for the assault had to do with the trees. In the spring and summer, the three-hundred yards of woodland would've been too thick for reasonable ingress. Even as it was, Roger had been sending men up all winter to clear a path a little bit at a time—to within fifty yards of the fence line.

Now, as the four armed men moved through the woods, they did so with little noise and relative ease. When they came within fifty yards of the fence line, they had to slow down. To take their time maneuvering over and around branches, roots, and uneven ground.

They made it to the fence fifteen minutes after landing the boat. Within acceptable parameters.

The fence was wrought iron, leaving four-inch gaps between posts. But it wasn't topped with barbed wire or anything else to prevent people from climbing it. There were, however, cameras beyond the fence, observing the area around the mansion. And the camera feeds were watched by members of the state highway patrol.

But they had planned for that. Clint and Hugh, the other two members of the seven-person team, were in charge of knocking out the power to the mansion by hitting a power substation several miles away. One of the more casual members of the Hometown Heroes Militia worked for the power company and had told them which station it was and how to hit it by shooting through the fence at certain components. He probably didn't think they would ever actually do it. Or if they did, it wouldn't be much more than a highly illegal and expensive prank.

Roger knelt next to the fence and pulled his sleeve up over his watch. Ben, Allen, and Tony knelt and waited, looking through the black fence slats at the well-lit mansion just over a hundred yards away. The lights appeared as a washed-out white-green, with the darker areas around the mansion appearing in darker shades of green through their NODs. They concentrated on their breathing, on keeping their heads clear. They'd been training for this.

Replacing his sleeve over his watch, Roger raised his hand, ready to give the signal. They peered at the house, waiting. Seconds ticked by. Roger began to wonder if Clint and Hugh had gotten pulled over or had been otherwise prevented from hitting the substation. If so, he wouldn't let that stop him. He would attack the house anyway. He was ready to kill. Ready to die.

Suddenly, the mansion was plunged into darkness. Roger gave the signal, his excitement growing. Tony stepped forward and hooked the ladder over the top crossbar of the fence. The men made their way over the fence one at a time. Tony, the last one over, turned the ladder around so they could use it on their way out. *If* they made it out.

They moved forward in a line, the order pre-determined and practiced until it was second nature. Cedar Crest, the name for the Kansas governor's mansion, was designed in a style imitating French and English country houses. It had three visible stories, aside from an offset garage built below ground level on the east side of the house. The light tan color and the multi-colored shingles simply appeared as various shades of green through the NODs.

They approached the back of the mansion, skirting a covered seating area just beyond a wide patio. They came to the back doors, which led to the library. The doors were wood and glass—a lattice of wooden frames holding small glass windows. The house was quiet inside. They hadn't been spotted yet. But things were about to get loud.

The lights came back on, the on-site generator kicking in. They knew it would happen. They also knew it would take nearly two minutes for the security system to boot back up.

Roger pulled out a compact black tool designed for breaking car windows in an emergency. It featured a spring-loaded metal pin inside that would retract and then shoot forward when the retractable tip of the tool was pressed up against the glass.

Among the many things he had found out about Cedar Crest was the fact that the library doors were original. The mansion was gifted to the state of Kansas with a will in place that required certain structural elements to remain in place. So while there had been certain security upgrades recently—including the wrought-iron fence replacing a low wooden fence—the library doors had not been significantly changed in decades.

Roger aligned the tool with the glass pane nearest the doorknob and deadbolt, and he pressed on it. The metal pin inside retracted under tension and then released, delivering a large amount of energy into a small area of the glass. White cracks exploded from the impact point, but the glass didn't shatter. The sound of the tool was surprisingly quiet in the still night air. But they had to assume it had been heard by one or more of the security detail inside.

Roger stepped away while Allen stepped forward and used a screwdriver to bust out the damaged glass. He had the door open in less than five seconds.

They were in the house.

As they moved into the library, a man in a suit came around a far doorway and leveled a gun at them. It was clear to every member of the team that this man hadn't seen them before that moment. The surprise on his face as he saw their tactical gear and heavy-duty equipment was unmistakable.

There was a moment of stillness as the situation unfolded in each man's mind. The team stared at the man, a plainclothes Kansas Highway Patrol officer, seemingly frozen with the reality of the situation. But it was only the briefest of moments.

As Roger brought his gun up to fire, the cop fired first, hitting Tony in the chest. Roger and Ben fired on him, one after the other. Six bullets hit the cop in quick succession. He went down hard.

Everyone moved quickly, leaving Tony in the library for the time being. They moved up the stairs, firing on and killing another patrolman in the hallway outside the governor's bedroom.

As Roger, Ben, and Allen stopped outside the closed bedroom door, they could hear frightened voices from inside. Allen stepped forward and, keeping his back to the wall next to the door, reached out for the knob. As soon as he turned it, someone opened fire from inside the room. A bullet went through the bedroom door and into Allen's forearm, shattering his radius bone. He cried out and stumbled back.

"Fuck it," Roger said, pulling the trigger on his Smith & Wesson Sport II AR-15 rifle, putting rounds through the door indiscriminately. One of the bullets hit the doorknob, sending a spray of fragments toward Ben. The man recoiled as several fragments tore into the left side of his face.

Roger stopped firing with half a magazine left and kicked at the door. It took two kicks to get the door open, and when he stepped into the room, he saw a man in a suit dead on the floor just inside the doorway, a bullet hole in his head.

He swiveled to find the Kansas governor and her husband cowering next to their bed, whimpering.

Ben, who'd been hit in the face with the ricochet fragments, came into the room behind Roger. Allen was sitting in the hallway cradling his arm, looking at all the blood coming out of him.

"Get the camera out," Roger said.

Ben pulled a phone from a vest pocket and started filming.

"Please," Darla Greenberg said. "Please, don't hurt us." Her auburn hair was disheveled from sleep. Her dark eyes brimmed with fearful tears. She had expensive-looking red and white pajamas on.

The governor's husband, a balding man who looked a decade older than his wife, was dressed in blue boxers and nothing else. He looked even more frightened than her, although he had positioned himself in front of her.

"You recording?" Roger asked without taking his eyes off the pair.

"Yes."

"This is what happens when you fuck with us, you Jew cunt," Roger said, raising his weapon. "We're done letting people like you run our fucking lives. This is for the cause. This is how we will secure the existence of our people and a future for white children."

He pulled the trigger, unloading the rest of his magazine into the governor and her husband.

Ben stood nearby and filmed the slaughter, a smile on his bloody face.

Chapter 45

The Salem bus station shared space with the Amtrak station. I got off the bus next to a small tan-and-white wooden building and then walked over to the larger tan-and-white brick building that was the station proper. It was just after three o'clock in the morning on Monday, Martin Luther King, Jr. Day, and the place was nearly deserted.

As I was told, I stopped and checked my phone again for a new draft message. There was one waiting for me. It told me to walk down the street toward some soccer fields and then take the footbridge across.

Securing my backpack on my back, I walked down the road. A low ceiling of thick clouds reflected the dim glow of the city. I could see the footbridge in the distance, and I figured the whole point of this exercise was to make sure I wasn't being watched.

Hearing footsteps behind me, I looked over my shoulder to see a woman who'd been on the bus walking after me. I wasn't sure if Nez and Hudson had put someone on the bus with me, but it wouldn't have surprised me to learn that they had. If they did, I didn't think that person would be so stupid as to follow me around. And as I passed the station parking lot, a man got out of a white midsize sedan and greeted the woman. They kissed before the man took her bags and started loading them into the car.

While my new fed friends hadn't told me all the details of their plan to track me, they said it was possible I'd be on my own until I could contact them. I'd asked about drones and teams of cars following me after I met up with whoever I was supposed to meet, but Hudson had shook his head. "Drones only work with clear line of sight. And this time of year, in Oregon, I can bet it'll be cloudy. We'll try to follow you with a small team if we can, but I think there's a reason they put you on the bus they did. The streets will be dead when you get there. We'll do our best, but there's no guarantee we'll be able to stay with you. Just keep that in mind."

I replayed this conversation in my mind as I continued on, counting only three cars passing me on the street as I walked toward the footbridge. My breath plumed in front of me in the chilly Oregon air. I had to detour off the main road to get to the mouth of the footbridge. I took it over the street and walked into a deserted university parking lot on the other side. There was a red SUV idling nearby, just like the message said.

I went up and looked inside, but there was no one there. Looking around in the parking lot, I wondered what I should do.

I waited several minutes, leaning against the car, before a faint sound caught my attention. I turned toward one of the buildings bordering the parking lot and saw a man walking out from the landscaped bushes around the structure. He was wearing a bandana over his face and pointing a semiauto rifle at me. Another sound in the opposite direction had me looking that way. Another similarly dressed man was coming toward me, also armed. They were positioned in such a way that there was no threat of shooting each other on accident if they had to fire.

Holding my hands out from my body, I waited for them to approach. This wasn't exactly the welcome I'd been hoping for. But I figured they would be taking some precautions. I worked to get my heart rate and breathing under control as they approached.

"Drop the backpack on the ground," the first man I'd seen said.

With deliberate slowness, I did as he told me.

"Now step away," he said. The other guy had yet to speak.

I moved away from the backpack, keeping my attention on the first guy. I heard the second one stop about fifteen feet behind me. On the distant road, beyond one of the college's buildings, a car drove past. Once it was gone, the town was silent again.

"Very warm welcome," I said.

"Shut up," he said, grabbing my backpack and taking it around to the other side of the idling SUV. He opened the door and set the bag on the seat before going through it.

"What are you looking for?" I asked.

"He said shut up," the guy behind me said. He sounded younger than the first guy.

When the guy was done going through the bag, he came over, pulling his weapon around to his back on its strap. Then he frisked me, pulling out my phone, wallet, and Cotter's little notebook. Setting the items aside in the vehicle, he then produced an electronic bug sweeper and waved it up and down my body, looking for bugs. When he found none, he stepped back and told me to get in the driver's seat.

"Can I talk now?" I asked.

"In the car," he said.

I got in the driver's seat while the older guy got in the front passenger seat. He pulled a pistol out of the glove compartment and held it down near his lap, keeping it pointed at me. The other guy got in the back seat, situating himself directly behind the older guy so he could point his rifle at me.

"Why are you treating me like a sub?" I asked. "I'm on your side."

"Drive," the guy in front said.

I put my hands on the wheel and shook my head. "No. Fuck that. Not until you tell me your names at least. I didn't come up here to be treated like some common criminal. I fucking killed a cop for you people, and this is the way you treat me? That's two bodies I've dropped for you. And you treat me like this?"

The guy in the front seat raised the pistol and put it against my temple. "For all we know, you're a fucking rat. I've never seen you before in my life. All I know is what Cotter and Halverson said. Maybe you're this Rubble guy, maybe not. But I'm tempted to kill you right now. We got what we came for. Why should we let you live now?"

"You have my license. Someone in your organization has my prints on file. There's even video of me online getting into it with some subs on a college campus. So if you want to kill me, go ahead. But don't tell yourself it's because you don't know who I am. That's bullshit. Really, I don't care. I've *been* ready to die. But if you do pull that trigger, you'll be killing a brother. One who's willing to kill for you. So hey, that's your loss."

The SUV was silent for a long moment save the low hum of the engine and the sound of the heater circulating warm air. The man still pressed the pistol against my temple.

Then he withdrew it, bringing it back to his lap but keeping it pointed at me. "Coakley," he said. "That's Dyer in the back. Now fucking drive or I really will shoot you."

I looked at him, jaw jutting out to show him that I was still pissed. But then I turned and put the vehicle in gear. "Where am I going?"

"North on the 5," Coakley said.

I navigated out of the parking lot and toward the bus station, then back the way the bus had come to get to the highway.

"So how did you out of everyone at that camp manage to get out?" Coakley asked.

"It wasn't just me," I said. "There were several of us. Me and three others."

"News didn't say anything about anyone else."

"I don't think they knew. They'll find out eventually since we were fingerprinting everyone, but they didn't see the other three. They almost didn't see me."

"Run it down for me," Coakley said.

I told him the story just as I'd rehearsed it with Nez and Hudson. I told him how me, McCray, Cotter, Pennington, and Halverson were escorting five recruits out to the woods to execute them when we heard something up ahead. Then Pete from the house radioed us, saying the cops were there. I said Cotter ordered me and Pennington to fall back into the woods with the five recruits. And that shortly after we did, there was gunfire. We hunkered down in a divot and waited. Then Cotter came running through the woods, all shot up and barely able to stand.

"He got down with us and handed me the notebook," I told Coakley. "And he told me and Pennington to run. Said that if we made it out, we should contact you through the email draft function in that email address. Seeing their chance, the five recruits started running while we were occupied. Pennington, that dumbass, started firing at them. Put two of them down. That brought the feds down on us. I guess McCray and Halverson were still putting up a fight because I heard firing from up ahead. But this one fed came running up and shot Pennington. Then I shot him. That's when I ran."

"And how did you get back to the city?" he asked.

"I stole a car from a cabin out there in the middle of the woods. Some rich couple. I tied them up. I'm sure they got free pretty quick and called the cops. But I took their car and stopped at the first thrift store I could find. That's when I bought these clothes. I had to get out of the fatigues."

"And you just ditched the car there?"

I nodded. "I knew it was only a matter of time before they found it. So I left it in that parking lot. Left my rifle in there, too."

"So how did the cops know you were there? Sounded like the only one who saw you got killed."

"I spent the night in the cabin—two nights, actually. My prints were all over the place. With my record, it wouldn't take them long to get a hit."

Coakley studied me as we drove on the highway. "So where do you think those recruits got off to?"

I shrugged. "I don't know. But I didn't see any of them on my way out of there. If they made it out, they might've gone to the cops. They knew they were about to die before the feds showed up. That was pretty clear."

"Okay," he said. "I'm going to check out your story. And if I hear different, I'm going to kill you. How's that sound?"

How the hell are you going to check it out? I thought. But I shrugged and nodded. "Fine. Sounds fine. Because it's the truth."

Chapter 46

"Turn right here," Coakley said. Both he and Dyer had long since taken their bandanas off, allowing me to see their faces. I thought that was a sign in my favor.

I did as he instructed, turning off Highway 202 and onto a small country road with widely spaced homes on either side. We'd just passed through a small town called Jewell after almost two hours of driving. The dash clock read quarter after five in the morning. The sky was still dark as night. The sun wouldn't be up for at least another hour and a half. Maybe two hours.

"Keep going until I tell you to turn," Coakley said.

Dyer, in back, hadn't said more than a dozen words during the trip. He was still pointing his rifle at me, although he held it down near his hip. Coakley still held his pistol, but it wasn't pointed at me. It was on his right thigh, held there casually. The only time he'd put it away was when he got a text message on his phone. He opened the glove box and set the gun inside while he messed with his phone for several minutes.

I thought there had been a subtle change in his mood after that, but I couldn't tell one way or the other. Maybe I was reading too much into things. I was anything but calm inside. Now that I was getting close to the leadership, I was struggling to contain my mounting fear. There was too much at stake and too many moving parts. I felt like

I was living in a house of cards, just waiting for a breeze to send it crashing in on me.

"Left here," Coakley said.

I made the left onto a narrow asphalt driveway, passing a black mailbox with the number 634 on it. There were some trees around, and a few low hills that I could see. Judging by what I'd glimpsed out the windows, we were in a broad and somewhat flat river valley. Where there were no trees, there were fields with winter crops growing. The driveway went on for a good half mile before we came to an old farmhouse. I slowed as we approached, but Coakley told me to keep going.

We passed the house and went a little over a hundred yards to an old barn of faded and warped wood. I guessed it had been built before the second world war. It was tall and windowless, and the front doors were closed.

"Park in front," Coakley said.

Something wasn't right about this. There were no other cars around, no sign of light coming from around the edges of the barn doors. I suddenly had a feeling I was about to be killed.

"What are we doing here?" I asked, putting the vehicle in park.

"Turn it off and leave the keys in," Coakley said. He still wasn't pointing his gun at me, which I wanted to take as a good sign. But maybe he just wanted me to think I wasn't in danger until it was too late for me to do anything about it. "We're going to stay here for the night."

"In the barn?" I asked.

"Yes, in the fucking barn," Coakley said. "It's set up for us. There's space heaters and everything."

I turned the vehicle off and left the keys in the ignition, then opened the door. Coakley reached over and took the keys out before opening his door.

It was below freezing, my breath turning to vapor as I breathed. I looked back toward the house, seeing that there was a light on in one of the back windows.

Dyer stepped up behind me, clearly waiting for me to head to the barn doors. I looked around even though it was too dark to see much of anything. Trying my best to silence the clatter of fearful voices in my head, I listened to my gut.

It was telling me to run.

"Let's go," Coakley said, waiting at the barn doors. "It's freezing."

I took a deep breath and stepped forward, knowing that if this was my time, there was nothing I could do about it. Dyer was far enough behind me that it would take me too much time to make a move on him. Coakley held his gun by his side, and he could get it up in a moment. If I ran, I would surely be shot in the back.

They had me good. I'd known that death was a possibility. It always was. Whether you were trying to thwart a bunch of racists planning a slaughter or just heading to the grocery store, death was a possibility. And as I stepped up to the barn doors, I just hoped that Nez and Hudson could finish the job without me, whatever it took.

Coakley opened the right-hand door and stepped aside. "There's a light switch to the right," he said.

Throat thickening, I stepped inside and searched for the light switch, finding it after a long moment. As I flipped it on, I illuminated two men with rifles standing in the barn. They had their weapons trained on me.

"Sorry, pal," Coakley said from behind me. "Plans have changed. Can't take the chance."

I put my hands up and stared at the two young white men standing fifteen feet away from me. I heard a door on the SUV open and then shut, followed quickly by the engine turning over.

"Step inside," Dyer said from behind me.

I did. I heard the barn door shut behind me while the SUV drove away, back the way we'd come. Coakley was leaving. And I was staying to face the fate everyone must face eventually.

***

As soon as Coakley was past the house, he stopped the car and pulled out his phone. He re-read the draft message Bove had sent him in a newly created email account. The one telling him what to do with Rubble. But it also told him to check the news when he had a chance. And now that he wasn't concerned about Rubble making a move, he typed "Breaking news" into the search bar.

The first several headlines were about the same story. The governor of Kansas was feared dead after a group of men attacked her at the governor's mansion in Topeka. Coakley felt his stomach roil even as he clenched his teeth in anger. He clicked on a headline from a news organization he trusted and read the story. It was only a few paragraphs because the situation was ongoing.

According to the story, shortly after a call went out from one of the highway patrol officers on the governor's security team, a video showed up on Telegraph. A video that was still in the process of being authenticated by the authorities. It showed the shooting murder of Governor Darla Greenberg and her husband Lester in their bedroom. People in the white supremacist Telegraph chats had been sharing the video around on various social media platforms that were now racing to remove it. But every time it was removed, someone else posted it from another account.

It was unknown how many perpetrators were involved, but the police had the place surrounded and were attempting to make contact with the people inside. When the first police officers showed up on scene, they'd been fired upon from the house and forced to retreat to a safe distance.

The last paragraph of the story mentioned how law enforcement had been hearing chatter about a potential widespread white supremacist attack. State and federal officials were now on high alert all across the country.

"You fucking idiots," Coakley said through clenched teeth. "You goddamn fucking idiots!" He dropped his phone and slammed the heel of his hand into the steering wheel before grabbing it with both hands and rocking back and forth, shaking the vehicle.

When he got control of himself again, he thought about how the plan would change. Because there was no turning back. Not now. It was clear from Bove's message that he still planned on doing something. How much the plan had changed he had no way of knowing. But they were still going to do something. Even if those fucking hicks in Kansas had just made it ten times harder.

It was a thirty-minute drive back home. He could make it in twenty at this time of the morning. He shoved a hand through his hair to put it back in place and took a couple of deep breaths. Then he took his foot off the brake and started down the road.

Hell, maybe now we can hit that MLK Day celebration scheduled for today in Portland, he thought as he drove. That, at least, made him smile.

Chapter 47

"WHAT THE HELL IS this?" I said. "You guys serious right now?"

"Get on your knees," Dyer said from behind me.

"Can you at least give me a minute to get my head around this?" I paused. "One of you wouldn't happen to have a smoke, would you?"

"We're not gonna kill you," Dyer said. "Just get on your knees, man. We gotta tie you up. That's the orders."

"Seriously?" I said, laughing nervously.

"Yeah, seriously," Dyer said. "But if you try to run, we will."

"Why would I run?" I got to my knees on the cold dirt floor. Despite what Coakley had said as we'd pulled up, there were no space heaters. The barn was only a few degrees warmer than outside. "I mean, where the hell would I go? I'm wanted by every fucking pig in this country right now."

"Exactly," Dyer said. "Robbie, you got the flex cuffs?"

Robbie, who had a large swastika tattooed on the side of his neck, stepped forward. He was wearing tan Shit-Kicker boots, black jeans, and a brown rancher coat. I thought maybe this was his family's property. He moved toward me, still holding his rifle with one hand while he reached into a jacket pocket with his other.

"Put the gun down first," Dyer said. "Over there."

"Oh, right," Robbie said, shaking his head. "Sorry." After propping his rifle against a support beam, he came over and stepped behind me to bind my hands.

"Hey, Robbie?" I asked. "You mind if we do it in front? That way I can sit down without my hands in the way. And I can take a piss by myself when the time comes."

Robbie paused. I had a feeling he was turning to look at Dyer. "Yeah, all right," Dyer said. "Do it in front."

"Thanks, guys," I said. Then I looked up at the third man. He had his rifle pointed at the floor, his brown eyes fixed on me. Thick-set and with considerable facial acne, he was probably in his early twenties. He was dressed in a camouflage outfit like the one I'd been given at the Mount Shasta camp. "What's your name?" I asked him.

"Layton," he said.

I nodded. "Layton. Robbie. I'm Terrence, but you can call me Trouble."

"We've heard about you," Layton said.

"No shit? What did you hear?"

"That you burned a Jew's house down and shot a race traitor in the face," Layton said. "And then we heard you killed a fed."

Robbie finished up with my hands and stepped away. "Well, most of that's true, anyway," I said.

"Get to your feet," Dyer said. I was pleased to hear that his voice had mellowed. This was a babysitting job, and I was counting on my reputation to help me get on their good side.

I got to my feet and followed Robbie deeper into the structure. There was a hayloft on stilts splitting the back half of the barn into two levels. Underneath the loft, there looked to be four small rooms with simple latching doors, two on each side. I knew next to nothing about barns, but I didn't think these were animal stalls. I was pretty sure animal stalls weren't completely closed off to where you had to open the door to see inside. So maybe they were for storage. Maybe they had been stalls before and were now just small rooms. It didn't really matter. What mattered was that Dyer had been telling me the truth when he said they weren't going to kill me.

Robbie stopped at the first room on the right and opened the warped wooden door, which swung outward on its hinges. I moved inside, seeing that it was completely empty. There wasn't even any hay on the floor, like you always see in movies or TV shows.

"You guys have really rolled out the red carpet, huh?"

"Yeah, well, this was all kind of last minute," Dyer said. "Something went down, and we had to change plans. I'll see about getting you a chair and maybe even a book to read or something."

I nodded in appreciation. Then he told me to sit down so Robbie could bind my ankles together.

"Is that really necessary?" I asked. "I'm not gonna run. Why would I?"

Dyer shook his head, red beard swaying slightly. "Gotta do it. So sit down."

I chose a spot against the interior stall wall, thinking it would be slightly warmer than the exterior wall. Robbie put the flex cuffs around my ankles and secured them.

Dyer and Layton waited while Robbie got his gun and stepped back into the stall with me.

"Stay here," Dyer said to Robbie. "Layton and me will be back in a few. We'll have some coffee and a chair and hopefully a goddamn space heater. It's freezing in here."

The two of them left, leaving me and Robbie in the stall.

I wondered if Nez and Hudson knew where I was. They hadn't wanted to risk putting some kind of GPS tracker on my person. Coakley had taken my phone back in Salem, and I wasn't sure what he'd done with it. Given how careful he was, I assumed it was lying in the parking lot back in Oregon's capital city.

While I got as comfortable as possible, I considered my next move. It was early Monday morning, so I ostensibly still had five days until the attacks. But I needed to figure out what Dyer was talking about when he'd said that 'something went down' that made them change their plans. Plus, I still had to figure out where exactly they were going to hit. It didn't take me long to decide that I couldn't wait to see if Hudson and Nez would come to my rescue. For all I knew, they had no idea where I was. So I decided to try to get some information out of these guys.

I looked up at Robbie, who stood by the door, awkwardly averting his eyes.

"What were you doing before this?" I asked him, keeping my tone casual.

"Huh?" he said. "Before what? Before I joined up with these guys?"

I shrugged. "Yeah. Or before you were assigned to babysit me."

"Oh. Yeah. Well, I was in prison for two years after I turned eighteen. I got in a fight with a guy who went to my school. A nigger. I fucked him up pretty good. Took one of his eyes." Robbie smiled. "And I only got two years. Probably because he's a nigger. The judge was white. Probably looking out for me, you know?"

This outpouring caught me off guard. Not counting the swastika on his neck, Robbie seemed like an awkward young man just shedding the mindset of a teenager, getting comfortable in his own skin. It was clear that he'd been nervous when putting the flex cuffs on me, which had made me feel some kind of sympathy for him. But his words were a sobering reminder that violent racism was the entire reason for his presence here.

"You get that in prison?" I asked, lifting my bound hands to point at the swastika on his neck.

"Yeah," he said. "You like it?"

"It's good work," I said. "Most prison tattoos don't look half as good."

"Yeah," he said, grinning now. "I wouldn't have made it through my time if it weren't for the AB."

I knew he was talking about the Aryan Brotherhood. It wasn't surprising that he would join the infamous prison gang. Some white guys sided with the AB in prison as a survival tactic. This guy had probably been happy to join.

"It's a reminder," Robbie continued.

"Of what?"

"Of my purpose on this earth. I see that in the mirror, and I think about why God put me here."

"Why did He?"

"To help rid the world of all but the pure Aryan race. Which is why this kind of sucks. No offense."

"What do you mean?" I asked.

"I mean, we're probably not going to be able to kick off the revolution," he said. "From what I hear, they've moved it up to today."

I swallowed, my mouth suddenly going dry. "Today? No shit?"

Robbie shrugged. "What I heard. I mean, it makes sense. It's nigger day, after all."

"Damn. Do you know where they're going to hit?"

He shook his head. "I don't think anyone but the top guys know. Actually, Dyer might know. He's one of the top guys, I think. Seems that way, anyway."

My throat thickened. *Today?* I had only hours to find potentially hundreds of white supremacists and stop them from attacking innocent civilians. I fought a sudden bout of nausea as I shook my head. "Damn, man. That does suck. I was hoping to participate. More than I already have, anyway."

Robbie laughed. "Yeah, you've seen more action than most of us have so far. That must've been crazy, shooting it out with the feds like that. I wish we could just nuke them all, man. All the fuckin' idiots who work for the government. You know most of them think it isn't controlled by Jews? I mean, how stupid do you have to be?"

"Pretty fucking stupid," I said. Then, before Robbie could ramble on more, I said, "Hey, I gotta piss. Where's the bathroom?"

"Oh, uh . . . I guess you can just go in here. In the corner. Dyer didn't really tell me about that."

I scrunched up my face. "Dude, I don't want to be smelling my piss all night. At least let me go across to one of the other stalls."

Robbie considered this for a moment. "Alright," he said. "That's cool."

"I appreciate it." I pulled my bound feet toward me and tried to get up, using my hands to steady myself. I struggled for a moment, moving intentionally slow. Then I looked up at him. "I don't suppose you'd be willing to cut the ties around my ankles, would you? Otherwise, I'm going to have to hop over there."

"Sorry, bro," Robbie said. "No can do."

I shrugged. "That's cool. Just thought I'd ask." I flipped around so I was on my hands and knees, which made it easier to get up to my feet. Robbie was standing by the door, and he moved into the opposite corner to give me room. He still held his rifle casually down by his waist with both hands.

"Actually, could you get the door for me?" I asked. "Gonna be hard to hop and open the door at the same time."

For a moment, I thought Robbie was going to refuse my request. But his face changed, and he nodded. I stood near the stall door, waiting for him to come open it. As he walked over, I bunched my right hand up into a tight fist and gripped it with my left hand. He stepped up in front of me, stopping at the stall door. I was facing him side-on, and as he reached up to unlatch the door, I made my move.

I swiveled my upper body right at the hips and brought my arms out, my joined hands making one big fist. Then I swung the fist up and left, keeping my arms straight and leading with the knuckles of my left hand. I knew that if I interlaced my fingers and hit him, I would probably break a couple of them. This way was better. I hoped.

I put everything I had into it. I didn't want to have to hit him again. I wanted him down in one go. My knuckles connected with the back of Robbie's neck right where skull meets spine. Something crunched as his head jerked savagely backward even as it was moving forward with the momentum of the hit. His face slammed into the warped wood of the door just before he fell to his knees, dropping his rifle and then falling into a pile on the cold dirt floor.

I went to my knees next to him, raising my arms for another hit. But there was no need. He was out. I started feeling around, patting his pockets, hoping he had a knife on him. I was moving to the pockets on his right side when I heard the door to the barn open.

Dyer and Layton were back.

Chapter 48

LEANING OVER A STILL-UNCONSCIOUS Robbie, I heard the barn door shut. Dyer said something innocuous. A moment later, Layton replied. It sounded like Layton was the nearer of the two. Their footsteps moved closer.

Heart slamming in my chest, I dug into Robbie's right pants pocket but found no knife.

The footsteps got closer.

"Hey, you guys asleep or something?" Dyer called.

I had only seconds.

I checked his other pockets. There was no knife. Nothing to cut the flex cuffs with.

Giving up on getting my hands free, I grabbed Robbie's rifle from the floor. It was the same kind I'd used back at the Mount Shasta camp. A Ruger AR-556.

The adjustable stock was pushed all the way in for some reason I couldn't comprehend and didn't have time to think about. With my hands bound together, I couldn't easily adjust the stock to where I needed it to be. I couldn't hold the rifle as it was meant to be held, with one hand on the pistol grip and the other on the handguard.

As the footsteps approached the stall door, I pushed the radial safety from Safe to Fire. Forced to hold it with both hands around the pistol grip, I needed some way to steady it. With my hands bound at the wrists, pulling it back against my shoulder wouldn't provide enough accuracy. So I splayed my elbows out and pulled the gun back and to the right, closing my right armpit around the stock. I was sitting on my feet, knees together next to Robbie, pointing the barrel at the door. I rested my finger on the trigger.

The footsteps stopped on the other side of the door. If it had only been one of them, I would've fired through the door. But there were two of them, and I wasn't exactly sure where Dyer was. Since I was at a significant disadvantage, I wanted to see where they were before I opened up. After all, if Dyer ran, I couldn't exactly run after him. Not with my ankles bound together.

I waited, trying not to breathe heavily despite the adrenaline and cortisol flooding my bloodstream, making my heart beat harder and my breath faster. The door didn't open. They were just standing there. *What the hell are they doing?*

I knew I had to go for the one nearest the door, the most immediate threat. I was pretty sure that was Layton.

"Robbie?" Layton said from just outside the door.

Shit. They know. "Yeah, we're here," I said. As soon as the words were out, I knew I'd fucked up. My voice was shaking.

"Move!" Dyer yelled at Layton just a split-second before I heard something metal clatter to the ground outside the stall door. I shifted the weapon and fired four times, moving in the direction I thought Layton was headed. There was a sound like a body falling to the ground in the direction I'd been firing.

I thought I'd heard footsteps over the sound of the gun firing, but I couldn't hear them now. I listened hard, shifting the gun the other way, toward where I thought Dyer would've been.

Small portions of the wall exploded in flying splinters as bullets punched into the little room. I threw myself down on my side, flinching as bits of wood hit me in the face. I pointed my weapon awkwardly to where I thought the firing was coming from and pulled the trigger three times. The firing from the other side stopped, and I heard footsteps running away, followed by the barn door opening and slamming shut.

Still on my left side on the ground, I listened hard. When I heard no movement, I got to my knees and listened again. Still nothing. Thinking briefly about trying to shoot the flex cuffs off my ankles, I quickly dismissed the idea and got to my feet, still holding the gun ready. I hopped around Robbie's body, thankful that the door opened outward instead of inward. Regardless, I had no way to open the latch without adjusting the gun. I took it out of my armpit and managed to hold onto it with one hand while unlatching the door with the other. I shoved the door open and waited to see if anyone would shoot at it. No one did.

Getting the gun back into position, I readied myself to hop out of the room. Just as I was about to move, a hand wrapped around my left leg. Reflexively, I jumped away. The hand held tight, and I fell forward, twisting as I went to land on my side. The rifle stock in my right armpit sent pain thrumming through my ribs as I landed on that arm, compressing the unyielding stock.

I yanked my legs away from Robbie, who let them go as he got to his knees. Shifting my upper body, I got the gun up and pulled the trigger just as he was getting to his feet. The bullet punched into his stomach and out his back. He stumbled, looking down at the wound before anger turned his face red. He stepped toward me. I fired again, hitting him in the chest. This stopped him, and he turned, stepping back to the wall and sitting down hard.

We looked at each other for a long moment through the doorway, my feet preventing the door from falling closed on its own. Robbie's eyes slowly lost their luster, then his head tilted down to his chest.

He didn't move again after that.

Wincing at the pain in my ribs, I rolled over, looking the other way. Layton was lying face-down on the dirt floor. Pulling my legs toward me and letting the stall door close, I sat up and got a better look at him. His head was turned to the right, his gun awkwardly under him as though he'd fallen mid-run. His eyes were open and unseeing. There was a spreading pool of blood around him from a bullet wound just under his right ear. Given the trajectory, I figured the bullet killed him immediately when it entered his skull at an upward angle. Massive trauma to the brain will do that.

I got up and hopped over next to him. Getting to my knees and setting the gun down outside the pool of blood, I pushed him onto his back and got to searching. It didn't take long to see the knife which was clipped to a front pants pocket.

A minute later, I had freed my arms and legs. I picked the rifle up and adjusted the stock. Then I looked up the central passageway toward the front of the barn and saw the space heater Layton had dropped. It was what I had heard clattering to the ground. And that noise had apparently covered the sound of Dyer dropping a folding chair and a disposable cup of coffee, the contents of which were still steaming on the floor.

What I didn't see on the ground leading toward the front door was blood. I hadn't hit Dyer. He was still out there. Maybe getting help. Maybe just waiting for me to come out of the barn so he could shoot me.

There were no windows on the AR-556 magazine, so I had no idea how many rounds I had left. But it was a thirty-round mag, so I was betting I had twenty-one good to go. Still, I took the magazine from Layton's rifle, and, after wiping the blood off, put it in my back pocket.

Although it felt good to have my arms and legs free, I didn't think my situation was much improved. I didn't know how many people were in the farmhouse. If it was just Dyer, I could probably handle it. But if the place was currently surrounded by people with guns, I would be hard-pressed to get out of here alive.

Regardless, I had to do something.

Walking to the back of the barn, I looked around for another door. There wasn't one. There were some old rusty farm tools hanging in the rear of the barn, past the four stalls. Otherwise, there was nothing. Just the metal-and-plastic folding chair, the propane space heater, two rifles, and two dead terrorists.

I noticed a damaged board at the rear of the structure. Using my left hand, I got my fingers under the board and managed to pry it out a few inches, wood cracking and nails screeching. Looking out the hole, I saw a truck parked directly behind the barn. There was no one in the truck. The sky was brightening enough for me to see beyond the vehicle, but I saw nothing but farmland. No people.

I turned and moved toward the front, thinking about what to do. Just as I was considering turning the lights off at the switch near the front door, I heard some movement from outside. "Put it down!" a familiar voice yelled. They sounded like they were a good thirty yards on the diagonal away from the barn. I paused and listened.

"I've got you from over here," another familiar voice called, this one more distant.

Nez and Hudson.

"Set it down slowly!" Hudson called. "That's right. Now turn around and put your hands on your head. And step toward me. Keep coming."

I moved up to the barn door. "It's Rubble!" I called. "Coming out!" I shoved through the door and looked over toward the sound of the voices. The sun hadn't yet peeked up over the horizon, but the east was putting off a pretty good glow, allowing me to see the situation. Off in the field of some sort of winter crop were Nez, Hudson, and Dyer. I couldn't see their car, so figured they'd parked somewhere down the road and come up on foot. And it had worked. Given their positions, they'd taken Dyer from two sides. The man with the red beard looked even angrier than Robbie had just after I shot him. But as I approached, his eyes darted over toward the house.

My guts coiled like a snake about to strike.

Just as I was turning my head to follow Dyer's gaze, the sound of the shot reached my ears. Out of the corner of my eye, I saw Hudson stumble and collapse to the ground.

"Sniper!" I shouted.

Chapter 49

THE SHOT HAD COME from the only rear-facing second-floor window on the farmhouse. I jumped onto my stomach and aimed at the window. I knew I was too far away for accuracy, but I needed to lay down covering fire. I needed to buy us time to get Hudson and get to safety.

I fired six times in quick succession. To my left, Nez fired too. But she wasn't firing at the house. I turned my head to see Dyer, who'd been running toward the house, go down hard. It wasn't clear where she'd hit him, only that she had.

"Get Hudson!" I screamed at her. "Get him behind the barn!" I turned my attention back to the house, firing four more times at the window. If the shooter was smart, he'd be moving downstairs or out of the house for another shot. Which would give us some time.

In my peripheral vision, I saw Nez run to Hudson. I fired three more times. Eight rounds left in the magazine.

Nez screamed out. For a second, I thought she'd been hit herself. But I hadn't heard a shot.

"Rubble!" she yelled. "Move!" She fired on the house, and I jumped up and ran over toward her. "No!" she called. "To cover!"

I knew what that meant. Bile gathered in my throat as I changed directions, fury swarming inside my chest. I got to the corner of the barn and knelt, then shouted for Nez to run as I fired five times at the house. She booked it toward me, jumping over the lines of crops as she left Hudson behind. When she was safely behind me, I stood up and ran, meeting her near the truck parked behind the barn. "He's dead?"

Nez nodded, eyes hard.

I removed the magazine from the rifle and replaced it with the one from Layton's gun. Nez had a similar weapon in her hands, and she was wearing a tactical vest with extra magazines in the pockets. I had no idea how they'd found me or if they'd ever even lost me, but it wasn't important. Not right now. "Did you kill Dyer, or is he still alive?"

"I shot him in the leg once. Maybe twice," she said.

I nodded. "Keep watch. Tell me if you see anything." Standing, I moved up to the truck door, trying the handle. It was unlocked. I sat inside, looking out the windshield to see Nez standing, peering past the back corner of the barn, toward where Dyer went down. The problem was, she couldn't see the entire house from there. So she moved over to the other corner and stood there watching for a moment.

Meanwhile, I was searching for the keys. After checking all the likely spots, I gave up and decided to move to plan B. Putting my rifle across my lap, I gripped the wheel with my left hand and the gear selector with my right. I depressed the brake pedal with my foot.

There are ways to override the shift lock, which prevents the car from shifting out of park unless there's a key in the ignition and a foot on the brake pedal. Most of these ways took more time than we had and required a bit of finesse.

But there's one sure way to override the shift lock quickly. Breaking it.

I pushed against the brake pedal and pulled down on the gear selector with my right arm. The shift lock kept the selector in place. I pulled harder. The shift lock broke with a pop, and I pulled the shifter down into neutral.

"We need to get to Dyer," I said to Nez, who was back over at the near corner. "You ready to move?"

She nodded and then put a fresh mag in her rifle. It was plain to see how angry she was. I was pissed off myself, and I'd only known Hudson for about a week. I couldn't imagine what she was feeling.

I grabbed the rifle out of my lap and stepped out of the truck. The ground behind the barn was fairly level, but the field sloped gently toward the house, with the lines of crops parallel to the barn. Both of these factors made my plan possible. Setting the rifle down on the seat, I positioned myself with one hand against the door frame and the other against the steering wheel. Looking up at Nez, I said, "Just let me know when you're about to reload. I'll cover you."

I leaned down and pushed. The truck rolled past the corner of the barn. As soon as it was fully past, Nez stepped behind it and walked slowly along in a half-crouch. A moment later, she rose and fired at the house. Just a couple of shots. She knew as I did that the shooter had probably moved.

The truck bounced diagonally over the first lines of crops, slowing its progress. I leaned further and pushed harder, and I felt Nez put her weight into it. With my right hand, I moved the steering wheel, turning the truck slowly until its tires were lined up in the crop divots. Suddenly, the going was much easier, and I barely had to push the truck, thanks to the slope.

The bullet hit the windshield a split second before the sound of the shot reached my ears. I ducked, even though it wouldn't have done any good if the bullet had been on target. I didn't hear it pass by, but I did get pelted with some glass from the windshield.

"You see where it came from?" I asked, grabbing my rifle from the seat now that I didn't need to steer anymore.

"No," Nez said. "Probably in those trees down past the house."

I wasn't about to risk looking over to see if Dyer was still there, but I recalled where he'd gone down and was aimed for that general area.

A bullet punched into the truck again, this time blasting through the open door I was hiding behind and hitting the side of the truck bed behind me and to my right. "I think you're right," I said. "It's coming from that direction."

Nez answered with a volley of shots toward the trees. The shooter was clever. He'd gone further away from the house because he had a long-range rifle and knew that ours weren't. It didn't bode well for us. Especially because we were getting closer. And he was zeroing in on me.

We had to be coming up on Dyer. As soon as she was done firing, I asked Nez if she could see him.

"Ten yards. He'll be on your left."

Which meant we were coming up on Hudson, too.

Nez fired a few more shots again. It seemed to be working. She was preventing the guy from shooting.

"Will we hit Hudson?" I called when she was done.

"Just keep going. Don't worry about it. He's dead."

"I'm going to get this motherfucker," I said to myself.

Suddenly I saw Dyer. He was trying his best to crawl away from us, and he was a good ten feet to our left, about five yards ahead.

I straightened and fired toward the trees a couple of times before tossing the rifle back down on the front seat. I put both hands on the steering wheel and wrenched it to the left as we came abreast of Dyer. The tires bumped up over two lines of crops before the truck lost momentum and stopped. Now the truck was between us and the trees, but Dyer was still about six feet away from the truck, out in the open.

Nez came up beside me. "I think he's moving," she said, talking about the sniper. "We better make this quick."

"Where would you go if you were him?"

Clearly, Nez had already considered this because she answered without delay. Her dark eyes shifted to the low, wooded ridge off to our left. "There." It was maybe five hundred yards away, putting it a hundred yards out of effective range for our AR rifles. Even that was being generous. I knew I couldn't shoot accurately with my rifle more than three hundred yards. I just hadn't practiced enough. Plus, I didn't know if the rifle had even been properly sighted.

I moved to the front of the truck and popped my head up over the hood quickly to get the lay of the land. The trees he'd been shooting from did not stretch to the ridge. So the shooter would have to cross open ground to get there if he took the quickest way. Which he wouldn't. There was another way, but it would involve going away from us to get on the other side of a distant hill before arcing around to come up on the ridge from behind.

I calculated the movement in my head, thinking about the last shot from the shooter. If he got up and moved right after that shot, he still wouldn't be halfway to the ridge yet. I hoped.

"Cover me," I said, getting up and running over to Dyer. He looked half-dead and was moving like he was on his last ounce of energy. I just hoped he wouldn't die before we had a chance to pry some information out of him. I grabbed him by the legs, prompting a tortured scream from him. Nez had shot him twice—once in each leg. His pants were caked with blood and dirt. I dragged him back and dropped him near the back corner of the truck, where there would be a little cover from both the trees and the ridge.

"See what you can get from him," I said, stepping over and grabbing my rifle from the front seat. "I heard they're doing it tonight. Something happened and they moved it up again."

"I'm not telling you shit," Dyer said weakly.

Nez shoved his head down into the dirt with one hand. "Where are you going?" she asked.

"To kill the asshole who shot Hudson."

Chapter 50

I RAN AS FAST as I could, head swiveling between the ridge and the woods, looking for movement. If Nez's assumption was wrong, or if I had made a mistake in my mental calculations, I would be running directly toward a waiting sniper, making it that much easier for him to put a hole in me.

Sitting and waiting behind the truck wasn't an option. For all I knew, more white supremacists were on their way. Besides, I'd always been a fan of the direct approach. The do-or-die approach. The either-incredibly-smart-or-ridiculously-stupid approach. There would be no telling which it was until the moment of contact.

If the shooter had stayed in the copse of trees, the shot would be difficult, but not impossible. If that were the case, I would be running from left to right through his field of vision.

But I saw no movement from the woods. And I saw no movement from the ridge, either. The sun, rising behind me, penetrated the cloud cover, giving the whole area a watery winter glow. Thanks to this, I was confident I would spot any movement. Whether I would have time to react was a different story.

My lungs heaved as I sprinted, high stepping over the rows of crops so I wouldn't trip and give the shooter a stationary target. I held the gun close, ready to pull it up and fire in a matter of seconds. Behind me, I heard Dyer scream. That sound might've made me cringe in other circumstances. But now it served to strengthen my resolve.

I'd covered a hundred yards, and I could feel my legs weakening. But I pushed on, breath rasping in and out of my lungs, heart beating in my temples.

And then I saw movement from the ridge. It was a person's head and shoulders poking up between two trees as though climbing up the hill on the other side. I saw them jerk back as if in surprise. I knew what came next.

I moved to my right as I slowed down, then quickly back left before falling to my knees and raising my rifle. I could tell the shooter was preparing his shot, about four hundred yards away. I wasn't close enough. It was the very edge of my rifle's effective range.

But I had to try.

I lined up the front and rear sights and put them just over and to the right of the shooter. And I pulled the trigger.

It was a miss. And I couldn't tell where the bullet hit. I didn't know how to correct my aim.

I lined up my next shot just before I saw a muzzle flash from the shooter's rifle. The bullet struck the dirt three feet in front of me. A moment later, the sound of the shot reached my ears.

It was close. Which would mean an easy correction. I couldn't give him a second shot.

I fired again, this time aiming down and left. Then I shifted the rifle to fire up and left. Once again, I adjusted, aiming down and right and firing.

The shooter jerked. The last shot had hit home. Down and right, which meant my rifle was pulling up and left.

I waited a beat for him to go down, but he didn't.

And he fired again.

I flinched, expecting the impact of a bullet traveling at somewhere around 2600 feet per second.

When that didn't happen, I knew the shot had gone wide. A moment later, the shooter fell out of sight.

I got to my feet and ran again, still not letting my guard down as I approached the ridge. I took it a little slower, not only because my legs were tired and I had a stitch in my side, but because I wanted to be able to react faster if the whole thing was a ploy.

Finally reaching the wooded ridge, I moved up toward where the shooter had been, taking it slow, rifle up and ready. I saw the blood before I saw the shooter. There was a small pool on the ground next to a cedar tree. Stepping up next to the blood, I brought the backside of the ridge into view.

The shooter was a woman. She was early-middle-aged, her brown hair held up in a bun. And she was dead.

I'd hit her in the chest, near the bottom of her rib cage. I could tell by the frothy pinkish blood around her mouth that she'd likely drowned in her own blood when it filled her lungs.

I leaned against a nearby tree trunk and slid down to sit on the ground. I stared at the woman, Browning .308 hunting rifle with attached scope lying in the dirt next to her.

That she was a woman shouldn't have made a difference to me. She'd killed Hudson. And there was no mistaking him for anything but an FBI agent. Both he and Nez were wearing vests with big white letters on the back and front.

Or maybe her gender *should've* made a difference. I wasn't sure.

Would I have done anything differently if I'd known?

It didn't take me long to decide that, no, I wouldn't have.

Still, seeing her brought the true scope of this whole thing down on me. As much as I wanted to believe these people were through-and-through monsters, I knew that wasn't the case. Very few humans were. They were not much different from the nearly eight billion other people on this planet. They had friends and family members. They felt kindness and love and, to a certain extent, even empathy. But these things didn't extend beyond people with similar European ancestry.

Fine. So what. That in itself was disappointing, but it wasn't enough to make me hate them. All humans had prejudices. That was common enough.

The problem was that they took their beliefs and prejudices and weaponized them. They found like-minded others and started devising plans to force their hateful ideology on the world. And they'd decided to do it in the most extreme way possible.

That was all I needed to know. If they were willing to use violence as a means to accomplish an ideological goal, there was only one word for it. Terrorism.

When I'd heard Dyer scream earlier, I'd felt no sympathy for him. No remorse. Not a twinge of empathy for my fellow human being. But not because of the color of his skin or even his beliefs. But his actions. That was what mattered.

This woman was no different. She decided to pick up the rifle and kill a Black FBI agent. Whether the color of his skin factored into it or not, I had no way of knowing. Maybe she'd chosen him because he'd been closest to Dyer. The most immediate threat.

But whatever thinking processes had brought her to that specific decision didn't matter so much as the thoughts and actions that had led up to that point. She was a terrorist. It was as simple as that. No different than any other terrorist, when it came down to it. No different at all.

I stood up and walked out of the woods, feeling a strange mixture of numbness and determination. My job wasn't done. But I wanted, more than anything, for this to be over. I wanted it to have never happened in the first place.

The whole thing was sickening.

As I stepped from the trees and into the field, I looked up and saw Nez off in the distance. She was waving at me. I shook my head, pushing the image of the dead woman out of my mind, and worked up to a jog.

My job wasn't done.

Not yet.

***

Dyer was dead. He'd bled out. As I stood there looking at him, I said, "Please tell me you got something before he died."

"I got an address," Nez said.

"Where?"

"Not far, I don't think. I haven't had a chance to look it up yet."

"Okay," I said. "Give it to me. I'll go."

"I have people coming," Nez said. "Let them handle it."

I looked up toward the farmhouse, and then over toward Hudson's body. "How long until they get here?"

"We're keeping the locals out of this one, so maybe another hour? It was half a miracle that Hudson and I found this place at all."

"How did you? Were you following me with a drone?"

She shook her head. "No, the cloud cover was too low and too thick. Given how empty the roads were, we didn't want to follow too closely. But we managed to keep track of the direction in which you were headed. I had my research team start looking into Telegraph usernames we got from the notebook, finding associated IP addresses. They found that one of them belonged to this house."

I nodded, only half listening. I was thinking about waiting around here for an hour and then letting the feds take over. I knew I couldn't do it. It was an hour I was afraid to waste. Plus, I knew that the feds would take another few hours to prepare to raid the house or the compound or whatever was at the address Dyer had given up.

"What if there's no one there?" I asked. "What if they're already gone?"

"Then we'll gather intel," Nez said. She'd been crouching next to Dyer's body, but now she stood. "Surely there will be something there that will tell us about their plan of attack."

"And what if he was lying? Maybe it's just an empty lot."

"I don't think he was lying," she said.

"Give me the address and a radio. I'll go check it out and let you know what I find. See if anyone's there."

"Just wait. They'll be here soon."

"They're planning on hitting *today*, Nez," I said. "*Today*. That means they're already moving to prepare. They're scrambling, running around to set up bombs and mass shootings and who the hell knows what else."

Nez's dark eyes grew hard, but she didn't say anything.

I shook my head and stepped over, kneeling beside Dyer. "I don't know why I'm arguing with you," I said, patting the man's pockets. "I'm going. If you don't give me the address, I'll have to go tear the farmhouse apart looking for it." I found a set of keys and pulled it out of Dyer's jacket pocket. Then I did the same with his wallet.

I stepped over to the still-open truck door and sat inside, trying the key in the ignition. It worked. I'd broken the shift lock, but it was nothing vital. I fired up the engine and turned to look at Nez.

We stared at each other, neither wanting to budge.

Finally, she sighed and told me the address. Then she pulled her radio off her belt, handing it to me.

I took it, nodding at her. "What about you?"

"I'll get Hudson's," she said.

I shut the door and rolled down the window, which got stuck about halfway down, thanks to the bullet hole in the door. "I'll let you know what I find."

"Don't approach," she said. "Just gather intel, okay?"

"Thanks," I said, grabbing the gearshift and moving it down one notch into drive. I eased the truck out of the field, getting it onto the driveway before punching in the address Nez gave me on the built-in GPS system in the truck. The system was maybe six years old, but it worked fine for my purposes, since I didn't have a phone or a map.

As I passed by the farmhouse on my left, I saw a small face staring at me through the bottom of one of the windows. A child's face. A little boy.

"Damn," I muttered under my breath.

Before I was off the property, I radioed Nez about the child. And as I followed the GPS prompts, turning onto the main road, I had to sit with the knowledge that, in all likelihood, I'd killed that little boy's mother.

Chapter 51

I SLOWED AS I approached the address marked on the GPS system in the dashboard. The drive had only taken me about twenty minutes. Thanks to the early hours, I passed very little traffic on the Oregon back roads. Which was a good thing because there was a bullet hole in the truck's windshield and the rear window. If a cop had seen either hole, I surely would've been pulled over.

There were very few houses on the road, and most of them were tucked up on the wooded hills on either side. But as I approached my destination, there was a stretch without any houses at all. I'd been hoping to park on a side road or someone's driveway and head the final stretch on foot. There were no side roads here. And the driveways were all behind me. Unless I wanted to drive back nearly a mile and park the truck, I only had two choices. I could leave the truck on the side of the road and hope it wasn't noticed by someone coming or going. Or I could drive onto the property like I was supposed to be there.

The only problem with these options was that they were both terrible. I had no idea if Dyer had called or messaged to let Coakley know what had happened on the farm. He'd certainly had a few minutes to do just that while I was still in the barn and before Nez and Hudson showed up.

This meant that parking on the side of the road was the best of the two options. Anyone who recognized it would be on alert. Especially with the bullet holes in it. But I really had no choice.

I slowed and pulled over, the passenger-side tires crunching on the twigs and leaves on the side of the shoulderless road. About two-hundred yards ahead, beyond a shallow downward curve in the road, I could see the mouth of a dirt driveway. But that was all I could see of the property. There was a hill blocking my view of anything else.

I turned the engine off, stepped out of the truck, and pocketed the keys. There was no traffic coming down the road, so I took the rifle with its twenty-four rounds left and hurried into the woods. I moved straight away from the road for about fifty yards before turning left and heading up the hill.

As I neared the top, I stopped and listened for any movement. I thought about possible sentinels patrolling the grounds. But after two minutes, I hadn't heard anything but birds and wind and the occasional squirrel. I continued on, slowing as I got to the top. I could see that the hill I was on comprised one half of a small valley, the other side of which had houses built onto the hill facing me. I counted six houses, all widely spaced and brand-new. Their driveways arced down from the garages, leading to the dirt road that ran along the valley floor.

Moving further up, to the crest of the hill, I looked down through the trees at the backs of six more houses built on this side of the valley. Crouching, I settled myself against a tree and waited. There was no movement that I could see. It looked like a nice little upper-middle-class neighborhood. I wondered if Dyer had lied about the address.

Then the garage door on one of the houses across the way opened. And a familiar red SUV pulled out. It reversed down the driveway, preventing me from seeing who was driving. But as it backed onto the dirt road, pointing out, I saw through the window. *Coakley.* I was in the right place.

Then the implications dawned on me. He was leaving. If he drove past the truck, he would surely raise the alarm. I raised the rifle to my shoulder and aimed, but I knew there was no chance of a shot that would keep him from pulling out. There were too many trees in the way. And I wasn't a good enough shot to hit one of his tires from this distance, anyway. Besides, firing a gun would be just the same as raising the alarm.

I stood from my spot, unsure what to do. I still didn't know if anyone else was here. And I had a fifty-fifty chance that Coakley would turn right out of the property instead of left. If he did that, he wouldn't pass the truck.

But if he went left . . . I would have to retreat into the woods and radio Nez. Then sit back and hope the feds did things fast enough to prevent the attacks.

I held my breath, watching the red SUV approach the main road. The brake lights flared as it slowed.

He didn't use a blinker.

The vehicle came to a stop and sat there for what seemed like a full minute but was really just a few seconds.

It turned right, speeding off down the paved road.

I breathed a sigh of relief. I had some time. I could figure things out and determine whether I needed to tell Nez what I'd found.

There was movement across the valley, at the house Coakley had just left from. I watched a short-haired blonde woman step out the front door, shutting it gently behind her. She moved down the porch steps and then down the hill, looking left and right as though afraid she'd be seen. Soon after she got to the dirt road, I lost her from sight behind one of the nearer houses. When she didn't show up on either side of the house blocking my view, I knew that was where she'd gone.

So that was where I would start.

***

Looking through a back window, I saw the blond woman in the kitchen. She was alone in the room, her back to me as she used one of those single-cup machines to brew a cup of coffee. Ducking down, I gazed around, looking for a way into the house. There was a wooden deck to my left, a covered grill and lawn furniture on it. The sliding glass door was closed, the curtains inside drawn over it.

Faintly, I heard stirring from inside—metal spoon on ceramic mug. I glanced up and saw the woman finish stirring her coffee before putting the spoon down in the sink. Then she walked away, turning down a hallway of which I could only see a sliver.

I walked lightly as I moved up onto the wooden porch and under the narrow awning. The house and the neighborhood were just secluded enough that I thought I might get lucky with an unlocked door. With my left hand, I tried to open the door. It was locked. I looked at the track and saw that they had a broomstick for extra security, but it was propped up against the frame, as though someone had forgotten to put it down to block the path of the door.

Looking at the type of lock on the door, I knew immediately that I could unlock it in less than ten seconds. It always amazed me that sliding glass door makers still used the simple locks that were so easy to defeat. I didn't need anything but my hands to do it.

Setting the rifle down next to the door, I placed both hands under the bottom edge of the outside handle. I pulled the door away from the frame, so the locking mechanism was hard up against its counterpoint on the door frame. Then I lifted and dropped the door by the handle several times in quick succession, watching the simple flip-down lock lever move up with every repeated action. It made some noise, but not much. I knew the closed curtain on the other side would serve as a damper. After eight of these quick lifts-and-drops, I had moved the locking mechanism up enough so that it was no longer secured. Grabbing my rifle, I opened the door and stepped inside, batting the curtain away as I did.

The kitchen and adjacent dining room were empty. From here, I could see the hall down which the blond woman had walked. It was empty, too. I listened for a moment, hearing quick and light footsteps upstairs. Then I heard a child's laughter.

"Come here, Brandon!" a woman said from upstairs.

I turned around and closed the sliding glass door before venturing into the house, rifle up and ready. As I moved through the rooms downstairs, I saw nothing to indicate that these people were white supremacists. But then I came around to the front door and looked into a nearby room, seeing a standalone blackboard in front of two desks. There was a single quote on the blackboard:

"This is a white man's country: Let white men rule." -Horatio Seymour

I didn't know who Horatio Seymour was, but I knew I was in the right place. There were still sounds from upstairs of the woman talking with a child. It sounded like they were getting ready for the day.

Having cleared the downstairs, I moved up the stairwell. There was an open door on my right at the top of the stairs, but I could tell it wasn't where the woman and child were. Further on down the hall was another open door, but I could see from where I was that it was a bathroom. I approached the door on my right and spun around the door frame, rifle up. I quickly saw that it was unoccupied. There was a desk with three monitors and a couple of white supremacist flags on the walls. A bookshelf was stacked with MREs and gas masks and water filtration devices.

I turned and moved down the hall. There was a closed door on my right. I figured it led to a bedroom. But I could tell that the woman and the child were in a room at the end of the hall. So I moved past the closed door and into the bedroom without delay.

The blond woman saw me first. She was sitting on the bed, leaning down to tie the shoes she'd apparently just changed into. Her eyes came up first, traveling up from my boots and legs to the gun I was pointing at her. I gestured toward the attached bathroom, where I could hear the kid running water.

The woman swallowed, sitting up straight and placing her hands on either side of her thighs. "Brandon?" she called out, a little louder than she needed to. "Are you done in there?"

"Coming!" the kid said.

"Is there anyone else in the house?" I asked, stepping so my back was no longer to the hall.

She turned her head to follow me, eyes blank.

"I would hate to be surprised and shoot someone," I said.

The woman shook her head. "My other son. He's in his bedroom."

"How old is he?"

"Ten. Just ten."

"Okay, call him in here."

The kid came out of the bathroom, his brow furrowed. He'd heard my voice. He stopped and looked up at me. "Go to your mom, Brandon," I said.

As soon as the kid was sitting next to his mom, the woman called for her other son, using first, middle, and last name.

There was no answer.

"Where is he?" I asked.

"Stephen Browning Bove!" she called. "Come in here now!"

Still no answer. I didn't like this. Maybe the kid had heard me, even though I'd been trying to talk in a low and calm voice.

"Let me go find him," the woman said, moving to get up.

"Don't move," I said, stepping toward her. Once she settled back on the bed, I asked, "What's your name?"

"Sarah."

"Okay, Sarah. I just need to know one thing from you. Where are they going to hit? What are their targets?"

Out of the corner of my eye, I saw a dark-haired kid step into the bedroom doorway. He held a Browning pistol in his hands, pointed up at me—making me think Browning wasn't his real middle name. His eyes shifted from his mother to me repeatedly.

"Do it!" his mother shouted.

The kid had his finger on the trigger, but he didn't fire. The gun shook in his little hands.

"Shoot him!" Sarah yelled.

I started toward him.

"Don't hurt him!" Sarah screamed. This time she was talking to me.

Ignoring her, I moved up to the kid, my eyes fixed on his, and snatched the gun away from him. "Go sit down with your mother, Stephen," I said. He dropped his head and did what he was told. When all three of them were sitting there, I looked at Sarah. "I wouldn't hurt a child. No matter the color of their skin. Too bad I can't say the same about your people. Now, are you going to tell me what they're planning on hitting?"

One arm around each boy, Sarah shook her head.

"I don't want to make this difficult," I said. "I really don't. But if you don't tell me, I'll have to get creative."

"You just told me you won't hurt a child," she said with a sudden resurgence of hubris. "What can you do to threaten me?"

I looked at her for a moment. "I said I wouldn't hurt a child. I never said I wouldn't hurt a woman."

The truth was, I had no plan to hurt her. That wasn't really in me. Not after what I'd done to that woman back at the farm. Not after seeing that child's face in the farmhouse window. And not if I thought there was any other way to go. But it was the most obvious card I had to play. So I played it.

I waited, staring her down, willing her to believe me.

And she opened her mouth to speak.

Chapter 52

COTTER HAD BEEN THE one to communicate with the lone wolf shooters, with Bove giving him strict instructions on how to do it. But now that Cotter was gone, it fell to Bove to message them directly. And he had sent the message out early that morning. Only time would tell how many of the lone wolf warriors he'd been cultivating for years would take action. It was a numbers game, Bove knew as he drove toward a town on the outskirts of Portland. Those who were serious about the cause—who truly felt in their hearts that white people were superior to all others on Earth—would answer the call. Those who didn't have it in them would skirt their responsibility. But maybe, once the news reports started rolling in about the coordinated violence, this latter group would get the push they needed to go out and kill for the cause.

In Bove's mind, every nigger or spic or chink or race traitor who died tonight would be a feather in his cap. He wasn't stupid enough to think that his original plan would work. Every politician in the country, no matter their affiliation, would be on alert, thanks to the idiots in the Hometown Heroes Militia. If he and his hand-picked group showed up at the governor's mansion in Salem, he was sure the place would be unoccupied by anyone of importance.

But that didn't mean all was lost. It didn't mean he was going to give up. He knew this was his last chance at doing something great. If he put it off, the feds would surely close in. So he had spent the early morning hours formulating a new plan. The loss of the Aryan soldiers at the Mount Shasta camp hurt, but he still had several dozen men at his disposal. Now, his only hope was to light a spark that would ignite an inferno of white justice across the country.

And, in a way, the timing was perfect. The MLK Day celebration in Portland was such an attractive target, and it was scheduled to start at noon and go until four, according to what he read online. It would make things much easier for him now that the timeline had narrowed significantly.

The idea had come to him while watching the news one day over a year ago. It was a report about yet another white supremacist rally being interrupted by counter-protesters. They seemed to show up whenever white people got together to exercise their first amendment rights.

Suddenly, it clicked. He'd been struggling with the problem of creating a target-rich environment in Portland when the time came. At first, he thought he'd simply have to wait for a protest or a rally to happen and scramble to find good positions for his men to take their shots. This complicated things. In order to do the most damage, his men couldn't just be on the streets with the protesters. They needed to have the high ground.

But what if he could get the race traitors and subhumans gathered at a place of his choosing? The pattern that was emerging gave him hope. He could simply announce a white supremacist gathering at a specific place and watch the counter-protesters—race traitors and subhumans all—show up with their ridiculous signs and chants and disregard for traditional values.

Shortly after that, he'd started searching for office space at suitable locations. Money was no object. Not with his wealthy benefactor. It didn't take him long to find the third floor of an office building for rent in Portland. A floor with windows overlooking Pioneer Courthouse Square.

Not only would it give his people a good place to fire from, but it might even allow a few of them to escape after the deed was done.

He had his place. And he'd kept it empty since signing the lease, waiting for the day that he could make use of it.

That day had come.

Shortly after sending out the go-ahead to his network of lone wolf shooters, he also sent out an emergency message about a white supremacist gathering at Pioneer Courthouse Square that day. And he made sure that his people "accidentally" leaked it. With the MLK Day celebration already planned, Bove was sure a lot of counter-protesters would show up at the square, even if the parade wasn't scheduled to go anywhere near it. They'd be sitting ducks.

Some minor people from the white supremacist cause might be caught in the crossfire, not knowing that the protest was a farce. But that was a price Bove was willing to pay. All the important players—those committed to the cause with their lives—would know not to show up unless they did so ready for war.

But he wouldn't just hit the subhuman counter-protesters. No, he was planning on striking a crippling blow to Oregon's most populous city. A city that stood as a bastion of white oppression. Much of the population was already homeless, and after tonight, the rest would be without power. There would surely be police on hand, and they would make excellent targets as his men fired on them from the windows.

To kick everything off, one trusted man would park a bomb outside the Portland police station on 2nd Avenue. One big enough to blow half the building apart.

The IRS building right down the street was an attractive target, but they just didn't have the ordnance or the manpower to hit it.

No, the police station was the main target.

Then, when the other groups hit the power plant up north and three essential substations around the city, the police would have their hands full. The city would fall into chaos. Officials would be scrambling to get the power restored. There would be looting once people realized what was happening. By then, Bove would be out of the city, having slipped out in the middle of the attack from the building overlooking the square. He would meet up with Damian Griffith and his group from Idaho. They would work to take control of the very northwestern tip of Oregon. The dividing line to the south would be Highway 26, which ran northwest from Portland. The Columbia River would make a nice border to the north and east. Then, of course, the Pacific Ocean to the west.

It would simply be a matter of putting roadblocks in place and getting the word out to both the citizens living in the area and the rest of the country, bypassing the *national Jews media* and going straight to the internet.

Once they took credit for the chaos in Portland, the feds would think twice about messing with them. Then the negotiations could begin. Sovereignty would be the ultimate goal, but that probably wouldn't happen in Bove's lifetime. Still, he was confident that the move would be the spark to ignite an Aryan revolution. Proud white people from all over the country would flock to the area—once Bove eliminated all the undesirables, of course—and he would welcome them with open arms.

It would be the beginning of a new era signifying a blow to the oppression of whites in America. Maybe it would even result in legal changes reintroducing the segregation laws of pre-Civil Rights Act America. If that happened, or something like it, Bove could die a happy man knowing that his fellow Aryans could make their own way in peace and safety instead of having to put up with subhumans in their neighborhoods, their children's schools, and their places of business.

Eventually, as the Revolution continued, they could expel all subhumans from the whole of America, making it a great place to live again. Or better yet, they could house them all in prisons, and only bring them out to work. Slave labor was a big part of how America came to be an industrial nation in the first place, and they could do it again. The infrastructure was already there for it, the template already in place thanks to the proliferation of for-profit prisons.

It would take a long time and a lot of hard work, but he knew the Aryan race had it in them. He knew, because it was in *him*. And it was the most important thing in his life. For his wife. And his children . . . including the one just starting to grow in Sarah's uterus.

As Bove navigated through the streets in the morning rush hour traffic, his thoughts turned to Coakley. The time had come to talk with the man. To talk to him about Sarah and the child taking form inside her. He was sure his friend would be surprised at what he had to say. What he had to do. Perhaps Coakley would even be shocked and dismayed.

But that was to be expected. There was no way around it. And it was best to deal with Coakley before everything started in just a few hours.

Chapter 53

THERE WAS A KNOCK at the front door, clearly audible from the bedroom. I grimaced but didn't take my eyes off Sarah. She'd just finished telling me to fuck off for the third time. She didn't believe I would hurt her. But I was starting to think that maybe I would. I didn't want to, but if she was determined to play this part in the deaths of hundreds or thousands of innocent people, I wouldn't have much of a choice. I couldn't let the attacks happen.

"Who is it?" I asked. "Who are you expecting?"

"Probably my neighbors with a bunch of guns," she said. "I bet they saw you breaking in. You better run while you still have the chance, race traitor."

"From where I'm sitting, there's only one race on the planet, and you're the only person in the room who wants to kill them. Now stand up. All of you."

The three of them got up from the couch and I directed them toward the door. "If either of you try anything, I will shoot your mother," I told the kids. "So don't." I looked up at Sarah. "Now call down and tell them you're coming."

She looked angry, but she did as I ordered. Then I stepped around behind them and grabbed Sarah by the hair with one hand and pointed the rifle at the base of her neck with the other. We moved out into the hall like that, and then down the stairs.

I pulled them into the makeshift classroom and whispered for the youngest—Brandon—to go answer the door and let whoever it was inside. I really didn't think it was a bunch of guys with guns. I was confident all the men were gone, out preparing for their big day. Besides, if it was a bunch of guys with guns, they wouldn't be knocking on the door. They'd be trying to get the jump on me.

Brandon moved to the door looking pale and frightened. He unlocked the deadbolt and opened the door a crack, looking out. "Hello," he said. "Oh, Brandon, what's wrong?" a woman said. "Are you okay? Where's your mother?"

Brandon looked toward us. I gestured at him with my head, motioning for him to get the woman inside. He looked back out the door then stepped aside, opening it to allow entrance.

A red-headed woman in her twenties stepped inside carrying a cloth grocery bag in one hand. She shut the door behind her before glancing to her right and seeing us in the other room. Her face blanched and she dropped the bag, turning to the door to run.

"Stop or I'll shoot her," I said.

The woman didn't stop. She wrenched the door open and ran out, screaming for help as she went.

"Seriously?" I said. "That's some friend you've got there." Now time was definitely not on my side.

Sarah said nothing. Brandon still stood by the door, staring at us. Stephen was next to his mother, holding her hand.

There was a chair by the blackboard, and I shoved Sarah down into it, leaving Stephen where he was. "Where do you want it?" I asked. "Which arm?"

"You won't do it," she said. But her face said otherwise.

"Your friend just forced my hand. I have no choice," I said, raising the gun and pointing it at her right arm. "What targets are they hitting?"

Sarah pressed her lips together and shook her head once.

"Fine," I said, slipping my finger into the trigger guard, silently willing her to take the bait, to believe that I would do something I wasn't actually prepared to do, even now.

"It's on his computer!" Stephen blurted. "It's all on there! I've seen it!"

I stopped and turned to the boy. "You know the password?"

He nodded.

"Show me," I said, grabbing Sarah again and moving toward the stairs.

After I locked the front door, the four of us moved up the stairs and into the office. Outside, the woman's screaming had stopped. It was only a matter of time until the house was beset by angry racist white women with guns. Maybe there were even a couple of men still around. Either way, I didn't want to be around to deal with that. But if I could get information on the targets, I could at least radio Nez. If that was the last thing I was able to do in this life, it would be worth it.

I told Sarah and Brandon to get on the floor while Stephen sat at the desk. Sarah made no effort to stop her son from getting into the computer. I thought she seemed relieved, maybe because she believed I was really going to shoot her.

Brandon entered the password and unlocked the computer. The three screens came to life, and the kid used the mouse to click on a desktop file labeled "Previous Tax Returns." A password box popped up.

"You know that password, too?" I asked.

The kid shook his head.

I bit down on my tongue, trying to quell my mounting anger. This was getting me nowhere. Maybe the kid was just killing time. I looked at the folders and programs on the desktop, seeing nothing that caught my eye. I could spend hours searching through the computer files and still not find anything.

Straightening, I looked at Sarah again, shifting the gun barrel toward her. "What's the password?"

She shook her head, hugging her younger son to her chest. Rage swirled inside me, seeming to crash against my rib cage with every beat of my heart. "Goddamn you," I said in a low voice. "Innocent people are going to die today because of you. Don't you understand that?"

She swallowed hard, but kept her eyes fixed firmly on me, her lips clamped together.

My control broke down. I stepped over to her and raised the rifle. I wanted to hit her until she told me something I could use. And if she didn't do that, I wanted to hit her until she left this world, taking her hate along with her.

But I didn't. For better or worse, I didn't.

Instead, I slammed the butt of the rifle into the wall, punching a hole in it. I let out a savage yell and slammed it down again, right next to her head.

Swinging away from her, I pulled the shelf down, sending it crashing onto the floor. Gas masks and MREs and water filters spilled across the carpet.

Both the children were crying now, and it looked as though Sarah was barely keeping it together. Stepping back over to her, I bent down and wrenched Brandon out of her arms, setting him on his feet by his brother, who was still sitting in the desk chair. I got the rifle lined up on Sarah and tried one more time.

"What. Are. The. Targets."

"A police station!" Brandon called out. "They're gonna blow up a police station in Portland!" He wrenched his eyes shut and started bawling.

I looked at the kid for a long moment before turning back to Sarah. "That true?"

"No," she said. "He doesn't know anything."

"You're lying," I said. And I knew she was. I saw it on her face. It was a look of disappointment that only a mother can manage when her child has done something beyond the pale. "What station is it?"

No one answered.

Someone banged on the door downstairs, making all three of them jump. It wasn't a knock. Someone was trying to break the door down.

"Which police station?" I said.

No answer. I'd gotten all I could out of them. Now, it was time to go.

Downstairs, another bang came from the door.

Moving over to Sarah, I put out my hand. "Phone," I said.

She stared up at me, flinching slightly as another bang came from downstairs. It sounded like the door frame was coming apart.

I grabbed my rifle with both hands and made like I was going to hit her with it. "Okay!" she said, putting her hands up. "Okay." She reached into a pocket and pulled out the phone, handing it up to me.

"Unlock it," I said. I watched while she punched in a four-digit code, committing the numbers to memory.

Then I grabbed the phone away from her. As I ran out of the room, the sound of the front door crashing in reverberated up the stairs.

Chapter 54

I RAN TOWARD THE back bedroom, hoping I could get out a window before they got up the stairs. Shoving Sarah's phone into a pocket, I stopped at a window that looked out over the back deck. Frilly lace curtains let limited sunlight through, the thicker curtains already pushed aside. I had to put my rifle down to use both hands to open the window upward. I got out onto the small portion of the roof overhanging the back door and grabbed my rifle.

A white-haired man and a middle-aged woman rushed into the room, both armed with rifles like mine. They saw me immediately, raising their weapons. I rolled backward and dropped off the roof as one of them fired, twisting my body to get my legs under me just before I hit the deck. My legs took the brunt, collapsing and dumping me hard onto my butt and then my back. My head and shoulders crashed into a patio chair, sending bolts of pain through my spine and skull.

I ended up facing toward the sliding glass door and the narrow gap I'd left when I batted away the curtain on my way inside. Through the gap, I could see a woman with a rifle staring straight at me. I raised my weapon, which I had managed to keep hold of through the fall, and pointed it at her through the glass. She stared at me, rifle held down by her waist, not making a move.

There was a commotion from upstairs, pulling my attention up toward the second-floor window, which was now mostly out of view. From my angle, I could still see a sliver of the very top pane. But I didn't need to see the whole thing to know that one or both of the people who'd come rushing into the room were now looking out the window for me.

I bounced my vision back down, looking at the woman through the glass door. She raised one hand and backed away, shaking her head. I let her go, feeling grateful that she didn't want to shoot me. She could've had me dead to rights. Maybe it was the color of my skin. Maybe she just wasn't as into the whole movement as the other people in the house.

Either way, she'd just made it possible for me to escape. I raised my rifle up and shot four times at the small sliver of window I could see over the edge of the roof. The glass shattered. I jumped up and ran off the porch, into the woods behind the house. I booked it to a large western hemlock tree about ten yards from the porch, ducking behind its trunk and peering back at the house. When I saw movement in the upstairs window, I fired a few covering shots again before running further up the hill, ignoring the pain in my head.

As I approached the next tree I was aiming to hide behind, I heard a shot. Bark from the tree flew off and struck me in the chest just as I was coming up to it. Ducking behind it, I prepared to fire again. But before I moved out from cover to take my shots, I heard sirens approaching the property. I gazed around the trunk, toward the entrance to the little valley, and soon saw a line of black SUVs appear, barely slowing as they turned onto the dirt road. The lights located inside their windshields were flashing as they pulled in, the lead vehicles heading all the way to the furthest houses in the valley.

I managed a smile as I pulled out and turned on the radio Nez had given me.

"You down there, Nez?" I asked.

"Rubble, where are you?" she replied.

"There's people in the fourth house on the right," I said. "Watch out, they're armed. Three or four hostiles that I saw. But there are kids in there. I don't know about the other houses. Use caution."

There was silence from the radio. I figured Nez had switched to another channel to relay the information. I took a moment to stick my head out and look back at the house. There was no longer anyone in the back window. The greater threat was now coming from the front of the house.

I used the opportunity to move up the hill and diagonally away from the valley entrance. I wanted to see what was going on in front of the house. Although the cavalry was here, it didn't mean I could go running down the hill to greet them. Not until the area was secure and I had assurance some trigger-happy fed wouldn't shoot me by accident.

Picking a large tree near the top of the hill, I knelt and looked down the sloping hill between the trees. There were four SUVs gathered on the dirt road in front of the house I'd just left. Two more were at the far end of the valley on the road, and two were sitting near the entrance.

I watched Nez get out of one of the gathered SUVs, kneeling behind it and pointing a rifle up at the house. Behind her, on the other side of the road, other feds were doing the same thing, pointing at the house on the opposite side of the valley.

Surveying the scene, I looked for any hostiles that could be a threat but saw none. Bringing my attention back to Nez, I saw her pull out a radio and bring it to her mouth. "Talk to me, Rubble," she said over my radio. "What happened? What's going on?"

I brought the radio out and was opening my mouth to tell her about the plan to hit a Portland police station when gunfire started up. It was coming from the first two SUVs that had pulled in and stopped in front of the two adjacent houses furthest from the entrance.

Looking that way, I saw an old but well-maintained Subaru SUV appear from behind the house to my right. It was tearing down the hill toward the dirt road, not bothering to use the driveway. Most of the trees had been cleared from the front yards, so it had no problem getting down. I could see the guy driving it. He was bent over to his right, his upper body practically in the passenger seat. His head was raised just enough to see out the bottom of the windshield.

Nez and the others at the four SUVs fired at the vehicle as it barreled toward them.

Eyes going wide and terror seizing my heart, I dropped the radio and raised my gun. I led the vehicle slightly and fired. The driver's side window shattered, but the guy kept driving. I'd missed.

The feds kept firing as he closed the distance.

I shot again, and the man twitched. I'd hit him.

But he didn't slow. He didn't stop. Half a second passed.

Nez and the other agents scattered, but it was too late. They'd waited too long.

As soon as the Subaru reached the gathering of the four SUVs, the driver sat up in his seat. And that was when I realized he had something gripped in his right hand.

The Subaru exploded, the briefest flash of fire coming from the back of the vehicle before the air was filled with nothing but dust and smoke and debris. The explosion ripped the two nearest SUVs apart and sent the next two in line flipping onto their roofs.

Debris rained down all over the valley as I watched in stunned disbelief. The air cleared, revealing a crater in the dirt road. The two

SUVs that had been nearby looked like soda cans that had been blown up by fireworks, all twisted metal and smoldering upholstery.

I could only see evidence of three of the agents who'd been there. One of them had no legs. Another one was missing a head and an arm. The third was limping around in a daze.

Bile rose in my throat as I scanned the area for Nez. But I knew it was hopeless. She'd been too close to the explosion.

Nez was gone.

The other agents were running over to do what they could for the victims.

I leaned my forehead against the tree, my entire body shaking. The taste of blood filled my mouth, making me realize I'd bitten into my tongue.

Images rushed through my head. Memories of all the hurt these people had caused. Of the bombing in Cleveland, the aftermath of which I'd seen on the news. Of Hudson stumbling down in the crop field as a shot rang out. Of Nez disappearing in a flash of explosive violence.

But it wasn't just those. It was the images of white police beating peaceful Black and white protesters in grainy footage from the 1960s. It was men in white hoods burning crosses or hanging people from trees. It was Americans wearing swastikas or carrying tiki torches and shouting their ignorance into the night air. It was a man plowing a car into a crowd of protesters, killing one and injuring thirty-five.

Each one of these flashes seemed to click something into place inside me. Each of them took a little piece of that rage inside of me—a rage so pure and potent it threatened to overwhelm me—and put it into a little cell. Each of those little cells clicked into place next to each other, bringing together the scattered swirl of emotions and harnessing them in a way I could never have imagined.

I loosened my jaw, letting my tongue free. I stopped shaking all at once, like a toy whose batteries have suddenly fallen out.

Glancing down at the scene below once more, I stood up. I added what I saw to that place inside that had once been so chaotic but now was so orderly and ready to be harnessed.

But I was not numb as I turned and hurried up the hill. I was anything but numb.

I was mad. Madder than I'd ever been in my life.

And I felt like a one-man kill squad.

Chapter 55

COAKLEY SAW BOVE'S TRUCK as he pulled his SUV into the IHOP in Hillsboro, thirty minutes outside of Portland. He also saw Damian Griffith's SUV parked nearby. He headed inside and saw the men at a corner booth. It was the breakfast rush, and the diner was crowded with all types of people. Barely anyone paid attention to him as he headed over and took off his coat before sliding into the booth next to Bove.

Griffith and his man Otto were across the way. Oldham and Whitmer were sitting in the middle of the semi-circular booth. They'd be in charge of knocking out the power to Portland, now that the plan had changed. After that, they'd rush over to help secure the northwest corner of Oregon.

Everyone seemed subdued, but none more so than Griffith. He glanced up at Coakley before returning his gaze to his coffee mug on the table.

"You ditch your phone?" Bove asked.

Coakley nodded. "Everyone else?"

The rest of the men said they had. It was radio silence from here on out. They would only be communicating in person, especially since the fiasco in Kansas. The feds would be paying close attention to anyone with even the loosest ties to white supremacist or militia groups.

They just had to hope that the morning's final messages hadn't been flagged by anyone in the Zionist Occupied Government. They had no other choice.

"How did everything go?" Bove asked.

"Fine," Coakley said. "We got him to the farm. We weren't followed. The guys will keep him until this is all over."

"I still don't understand why you didn't just kill the guy," Whitmer said, a green trucker's cap pulled down on his head.

"You don't have to understand everything," Bove said. "We're going to need all the competent and capable white men we can find once things get rolling. What we do tonight is only the beginning. It's the easy part. What comes next will be difficult. Which is why I don't understand why the hell the Hometown Heroes jumped the gun." He glared at Griffith.

The overweight man shrugged his shoulders. "They didn't tell me they were gonna do that," he said. "I don't know why. But it's over and done with now, ain't it?"

"And how the hell did they find out about the Mount Shasta camp?" Oldham asked.

"The Revolutionary Liberation Front," Bove said. "They infiltrated one of their people into the camp. Apparently, Cotter's initial screening didn't catch it. And he paid for it with his life."

"You're saying the RLF told the cops? They hate the cops," Oldham said.

Bove gave him an exasperated look. "They hate us more. I'm guessing that when their man didn't report back to them, they went to the cops. Or hell, maybe they've been working together all along. Anything to keep white people down in this country."

Whitmer shook his head. "Fucking RLF. I can't wait to kill those goddamn social justice—"

"Shut up," Coakley whispered. "Stop saying kill, goddammit. Last thing we need is some bumpkin overhearing us in fucking IHOP of all places."

The table went silent as the men glanced around at the occupied tables on either side. A young Hispanic server came up to the table. She looked at Coakley. "Can I get you something to drink?"

"Coffee and a water, please," Coakley said.

"And are the rest of you ready to order?"

The men all ordered food. When they were done, the server smiled and walked away.

"Fuckin' spics," Griffith said. "Why did we have to get the spic waitress when there's some perfectly good white waitresses in here?"

"Can you just keep your goddamn mouth shut for half an hour?" Coakley said.

Bove elbowed Coakley, catching his attention. "Let's go outside and have a chat."

Coakley glared at Griffith as he slid out of the booth. The man smirked back with his fat face.

Bove and Coakley pulled on their coats as they stepped outside into the chilly morning air. Low winter clouds sat in the sky, a soft wind blowing through the parking lot. They walked away from the door, stopping on the sidewalk next to 25th Avenue and the steady traffic rolling by.

They looked at each other as Coakley waited for the admonishment. But there was something in Bove's dark eyes that hadn't been there inside. He couldn't place what it was, but it immediately made him uncomfortable.

After several long moments of unbroken eye contact, Bove spoke. "Sarah's pregnant."

Not possible, Coakley thought. *She told me she was on the pill.* Then another, more worrying thought rushed to mind, along with a surge of fear. *He knows.* "Congratulations," he said, smiling softly.

Bove's expression remained unchanged. "Problem is, we haven't had sex in three months."

Coakley swallowed. "Hey, look—look. It's uh—"

A grin spread across Bove's face.

Confusion crashed inside Coakley's skull like a tsunami wave.

"Your face," Bove said. "Letting you fuck my wife was worth it just for that."

Coakley laughed nervously. "Ethan, what the hell—"

"You really thought I didn't know?" Bove asked, smile disappearing like the vapor coming out of his mouth as he talked.

Coakley's mouth moved, nothing but a strangled sound escaping.

"You really think I didn't know that you were an FBI informant?" Bove said.

"I don't know what you're—"

"Come on, man. I'm not an idiot."

"But . . . Jesus, Ethan. What the hell is going on here?"

"Let me ask you this: Are you with us?"

"Yes. Of course I am."

"Right," Bove said. "I know that. You know that. So you can just relax. I'm just telling you this now because things are going to change after today, okay? I'm not going to kill you. I'm not going to hurt you. I expect you to be a valuable member of the Aryan community, provided we make it out of Portland alive tonight. But you will not be sleeping with Sarah any longer, do you understand that? That's over with now. It has served its purpose."

Coakley's legs felt weak. The world around him narrowed to a point that was focused only on Bove's face and words. "Served its purpose?" he asked.

"Something's wrong with me," Bove said. "My reproductive system. Doctors were even surprised we had Brandon and Stephen. We'd been trying for more kids for years after Brandon was born, but nothing was working. Birthing white children is one of the most important things we can do. Do you see what I'm getting at?"

"You *wanted* me to get Sarah pregnant?"

Bove nodded. "Yes. That was a big part of it. But I also saw an opportunity to get you completely on our side . . . with Sarah's help. I knew you would be an asset, thanks to your FBI and law enforcement ties. I mean, you've made a career out of being an informant, haven't you? Anyway, I figured you'd be a great asset. And you have been. It worked out better than I could've imagined. You know how much we love to get ex-cops and soldiers on our side."

"You told Sarah to sleep with me?"

"If it makes you feel any better, it didn't take much convincing. She put up some token resistance, but that was all. You're a handsome man, Bill."

"But what about Hearn? I watched you kill him. You knew he wasn't the informant? You knew it was me the whole time?"

"Hearn was useless," Bove said with a wave of his hand. "Once I thought you were with us, I orchestrated that final test to see what you would do. And you didn't disappoint. How long did you torture him? Four hours? And you made Dyer think Hearn was the informant. Hell, you even planted that recording at Hearn's apartment to start the whole thing off. That really sealed the deal. Pretty impressive. When you did that, I knew there was no turning back for you. I knew you actually believed in the cause."

Coakley thought about everything leading up to that first time with Sarah. How she had subtly initiated it, always staring and smiling shyly at him. He cringed as he remembered confessing his love for her only months after their first afternoon together. "It was your idea?"

"I know you two developed a bond," Bove said. "But that's over now, okay? Is that clear?"

Coakley shook his head. "I need to call her."

"No, you don't. It's radio silence, remember? Even if you managed to find a pay phone, she wouldn't pick up. Not today. Not until it's over."

Coakley felt sick.

Bove smiled and stepped up, wrapping an arm around his shoulders. "Everything's going to be okay," he said. "We'll find you a nice young wife when this is over. You'll have lots of kids and you'll be an important figure in the community. It'll be much better than the alternative."

He didn't need to spell it out. Coakley knew what the alternative was. Still, he couldn't believe he'd been played so well. This whole time, he'd been terrified his secrets would come out. The only thing that made the constant tension worth it was Sarah.

His chest tightened as he grimaced. *I thought I was in love.*

"No more secrets between us, right?" Bove asked.

Coakley managed a nod.

"Good. Now pull yourself together. I bet our food's waiting for us in there."

Bove walked inside, leaving Coakley on the sidewalk, still processing the shock.

Chapter 56

In Dallas, Texas, a young man named Scott Lee had just finished calling into his job at a local grocery store. He wouldn't be in for his shift today. Or ever again.

He had his weapons and ammunition laid out on his bed. He was about to clean his AR-15 rifle again, just to be sure he had no problems when the time came to do his duty.

He had two one-hundred-round drum magazines and six thirty-round magazines, all loaded with 5.56 NATO rounds. He also had a pistol and a tactical vest ready to go.

Surprised at how calm he was, he gathered his cleaning kit and got to work, sitting on the floor with a towel spread out before him. As he worked, he went over his plan again. Where he was going to go. Where he was going to set up. How many people he figured he could kill.

It was going to be a good day.

***

In Phoenix, Arizona, a middle-aged divorcee and father of three was also preparing for his shooting spree. He was planning to go to a local Mexican cantina to kill as many illegals as he could. Maybe it would make them think twice before flooding into the country and getting on welfare like they did.

A man in Mesa was preparing to do something similar.

And so was one in Tucson.

***

There was a man in Denver, two in San Antonio, and one in Atlanta. There were seven of them across Florida, two in Alabama, one in Hawaii, and dozens more scattered around the United States. All their heads were filled with lies or half-truths or bad personal experiences. They'd been living in a bubble, the algorithms controlling their social media and search engine feeds only giving them information that bolstered their racist tendencies or enraged them with misinformation.

Many of them hadn't thought of themselves as racist five, three, or even two years ago. Some of them had friends or acquaintances who were of a different skin color. But after living in the modern echo chamber that passed for culture, after consuming white supremacist propaganda and steeping themselves in the hate of like-minded individuals, they had come to a place where they thought killing innocent people was a good idea.

With very few exceptions, they were under thirty years old. Most of them had casual friendships, but no meaningful relationships. They'd been drawn into the white supremacist movement slowly and carefully with promises of camaraderie and a sense of community. 95% of it happened online, in chat rooms on Telegraph and other platforms that did little or nothing to monitor hate speech, citing first amendment rights and decrying any form of censorship.

There had been no overt racism in the early stages of the recruitment process. Not at first. But after the "moderators" had felt them out a little bit, there had been an occasional racist remark, just to see how they would react. If there was no pushback, then the remarks would continue, getting more and more blatant as time went on.

In this way, the moderators weeded out those who were not ready for the next steps. The young white men who objected to the subtle or overt racism were removed or left the groups on their own. Those that remained were guided down a very deliberate funnel, given access to other "elite" groups where members regularly talked of violence and shared information on the Great Replacement conspiracy. A conspiracy that insisted the Zionist Occupied Government was slowly replacing white people with people of color.

Current events were twisted to fit the needs of the moderators so that they could hold them up as an example of the Great Replacement. Crucial facts were left out or disregarded as lies broadcast by the Jew-controlled mass media machine.

All of this was orchestrated by Bove, and all of it was designed to swell the ranks of soldiers for the coming revolution.

The time was near.

Chapter 57

IT TOOK ME TWO hours to get to Portland because I stopped to have the windshield replaced. It took considerable self-control to make the stop. I wanted nothing more than to get to Portland and find some kind of lead I could use to figure out what they were planning besides the police station bombing—if that was even the truth. I felt like a dam getting ready to burst. Or a bomb getting ready to detonate.

Still, I knew that I wouldn't last long driving around in a truck with bullet holes in the windshield and the back window. The first cop to see them would pull me over, no question. There were also bullet holes in the door and the side panel, but they weren't nearly as noticeable.

So I tipped the auto glass guy a hundred bucks so he would expedite the job. I wanted him to replace the back window, too, but he didn't have the right size in stock. Said he'd have to order it. I told him just to do the windshield.

I no longer had my wallet, but I had Dyer's. There wasn't enough cash inside, but there was a debit card and a couple of credit cards. I used a credit card.

Once that was done, I found a secluded spot on the side of the road and used a wrench from a basic tool set that was in the truck to break out the back window. Driving around with no window was better than driving around with a clearly visible bullet hole in the window.

On my way into the city, I listened to the news, waiting to hear if I was too late. If a police station had already been bombed or if there were mass shootings going on all around the country. Nez had said something about getting close to tracking down all the lone wolf guys thanks to the information in Cotter's little notebook. I couldn't worry about that. I just had to hope the feds would stop them. I had to focus on what I *could* control. What I *could* change.

But there was nothing on the news to indicate the attacks had started. Not yet. The big news of the day was an attack on the Kansas governor. I realized what had happened in Kansas was the "something" that had gone down and forced Coakley to change plans, putting me in the barn. Someone had fucked up and gone ahead with their part of the plan too early. Now the whole country would be on edge.

That gave me hope. Maybe the authorities could stop this thing before it got started. But I couldn't count on that happening.

The news also mentioned the MLK Day parade in Portland. I knew it would make an attractive target. But the problem was, the parade would cover so much ground, it would be half impossible for me to find out where the attack was going to be until it was too late. Not unless I could locate one of these Aryan assholes and make him tell me.

With that in mind, my first priority was figuring out which police station was the most likely target. It was my best and only lead. So while I'd been waiting for the guy to replace the truck's windshield, I'd used Sarah's phone to look up all the stations in the city. The one I figured the WPA would hit was the Portland Police Bureau building on 2nd Avenue. As far as I could tell, it was the headquarters for the entire department.

There was no public parking in the building itself, but there was a parking garage right across the street. I pulled into the garage and took a ticket. It was an underground garage, so I couldn't look across at the police station. I had to get out on the street and find a place to watch. I left the AR-556 in the truck and headed out with the Browning .22 pistol I'd taken from Stephen tucked in my front waistband.

I came out on 2nd Avenue under a cloudy sky. Directly across the street was the police station. The tan-colored building took up the entire block between Main and Madison streets. It was over fifteen stories tall and shared space with the Multnomah County Justice Center.

I took stock of the building entrances and exits as I ambled along the sidewalk. There were two narrow vehicle doorways at opposite ends of the building. One was an entrance and the other an exit. But it was clear they weren't for public usage. They were for police cars and city employees who worked in the building.

Unless the WPA had convinced an insider to blow up their own building—which I found unlikely—whoever was tasked with the job would have to find some other way to get the bomb into the building. I thought the most likely option was a car bomb. I'd already seen one in action, so I knew they had the capabilities. It was how these things were done all over the world. Timothy McVeigh had done it in Oklahoma City, and Islamic terrorists had done something similar at the World Trade Center in 1993, although that one didn't claim nearly as many lives as the one McVeigh perpetrated.

I supposed it was possible that one or two members of the WPA could drive into the garage and detonate immediately. If that was the case, I wouldn't have much time at all to stop them. Then all would be lost.

Between the two vehicle doors, there was a designated pull-through parking area that was occupied by six marked police cruisers. There were a couple of cops milling on the sidewalk next to these cars, and one female officer sitting in a cruiser looking at her phone. Otherwise, the cars were unoccupied.

I walked over to Main Street and looked down the side of the building. There was another pull-through area there, about a quarter of the way down the side of the station. It was unoccupied by any vehicles.

That would be the place to do it, I thought. There were cameras on the corners of the building, but that wouldn't matter. It would be easy for someone to pull up there, get out of the car, and walk away. Once they got a safe distance, they could detonate the bomb. It would all happen before anyone inside had a chance to do anything about it.

I strolled around the entire building, looking for other possible areas where a car bomb would be effective. The best one was still the abandoned pull-through off Main Street. There was a no parking sign on one of the little metal posts flanking the area, but that wouldn't deter a terrorist. If the bomb was powerful enough, it would do some serious damage to the building from there, killing untold cops and civilians.

Should I tell the police? I asked myself as I jaywalked across Main Street to the sidewalk opposite the pull-through area. There were certain implications to that. I mulled it over as I leaned against a tree growing in a little square of dirt surrounded by concrete. I pretended to be killing time on my phone, but I glanced up at every vehicle that slowed as it passed.

I had a decision to make.

Potentially thousands of lives were in my hands.

Chapter 58

THIRTY MINUTES PASSED AS I waited across Main Street. Hundreds of vehicles passed by, going from left to right through my vision down the one-way street. But none of them stopped in the pull-through.

I spent the time trying to keep my thoughts in order. I was all but vibrating with barely contained rage. I wanted to do something. I felt that each minute I spent standing here was a minute wasted.

In a search for clues or something that would lead me in the right direction, I looked through Sarah's phone. Her background was an image of her, her husband, and their two children. I studied her husband, wondering what part he was playing in the attacks. He was bald except for a horseshoe of closely cut dark hair around his head. Dark eyes under heavy lids. A thin nose and prominent lips. Her messages contained nothing incriminating that I could see. Most of her texts were to someone named Ethan. Same with her calls. I figured it was her husband's name.

I also learned that their last name was Bove. And if Ethan Bove was important enough to have terrorist attacks discussed at his house, where his kids could possibly hear, then I figured he was in the top echelon. He was one of the top assholes. And I figured he was in Portland right now.

I looked for one of those tracking apps that some couples use for each other's phones, but I found none. I thought briefly about calling Ethan but discounted the option for the time being. It would accomplish nothing good.

Then again, I figured that Sarah had probably already contacted him. And if that was the case, then he knew at least one person was aware of the plan to blow up the police station. Would he change plans? Would *they* change plans? Would they choose another police station to hit? Would they call it off?

I didn't know. The parade was supposed to start at noon, and it was a quarter of. I was running out of time.

Just as I was about to use Sarah's phone to call 911, a yellow moving truck caught my eye, coming down Main Street.

I had spent some of the time waiting doing research on car bombs. While the one the guy had exploded back in the little neighborhood certainly did plenty of damage to the vehicles and agents there, it wouldn't have done much to a building like the one I was standing across from.

The bomb that Timothy McVeigh constructed was so big he used a moving truck like the one that was approaching me now. The bomb Islamic terrorists used to try to topple the North Tower of the World Trade Center in 1993 was housed in a large van and exploded in a parking garage under the building. It didn't come anywhere close to toppling the building, but it did some serious damage and killed six people.

I stared at the truck as it closed in, unable to help myself. And as it approached the 2nd Avenue intersection, I saw that there was a Black man driving it. It passed the building without slowing and continued down Main Street.

I returned my attention to the phone to call the police. As I pulled up the correct app, the sound of a big engine came to my ears. I glanced up and saw a UPS truck at the intersection. It was on 2nd Avenue, its blinker on to turn left onto Main when the light changed.

Not thinking much of it, I put my attention back on the phone and punched in 911. The light changed and, in my peripheral vision, the truck turned. Just as I was about to hit the button to send the call through, I glanced up to see the UPS truck pulling into the little pull-through area across the street.

I stared at the delivery truck, blood rushing in my ears. From my angle, I couldn't see the driver. And I couldn't remember if he was white or not. Although I had looked at the truck, I had discounted it as soon as I'd seen what it was.

But that was stupid. How hard would it be to steal a UPS truck? Or to buy a stepvan and paint it brown?

Staring at the truck over the traffic going down the street, I waited for the driver to step out with a package in his hand. When nothing happened, I shoved the phone away and looked for a break in traffic. I saw a narrow gap and darted across the street, one of the cars honking at me just before I stepped foot on the sidewalk.

I looked down the driver's side of the UPS truck and saw a white guy looking back at me, his attention likely drawn by the honk. He wore brown slacks and a brown button-up shirt under a black jacket. And he looked like any other white delivery driver you'd see on a daily basis. Just another person, trying to make his way through the world.

But then our eyes met, and I knew immediately. I could see it on his face. It was the face of a man who was getting ready to detonate a bomb that would kill hundreds.

He'd been facing the truck, in the middle of locking the sliding door, when the noise had drawn his attention. Now, he dropped his hand and turned away from me, leaving the keys hanging in the door. He reached under his shirt for something as he darted away.

I ran toward him, reaching under my own jacket and shirt for the Browning .22 in my waistband.

He moved around the front of the truck, and I lost him from view. I stopped, now right beside the midpoint of the long truck, gun held out in front of me. Up near 3rd Avenue, a pedestrian saw me and turned to run the other way. I inched forward and away from the truck, aiming at the front edge of the vehicle.

Two horns honked on Main, and I suddenly realized what he was doing. He was running. Running so he could detonate without killing himself. It seemed he didn't have the courage to give his own life for the cause. But I aimed to change that for him.

Then something occurred to me. What if the bomb was on a timer, like McVeigh's?

Changing direction, I ran for the back of the truck again, bringing the guy into view just before he rounded the corner of the building across the street.

He was fast. Faster than me. There was no way I could catch him. Not on foot.

Changing direction again, I ran back to the truck and unlocked the door with the keys he'd left in the lock. I jumped into the driver's seat, trying to ignore the fact that there was a massive bomb just behind me in the package compartment. I shoved the pistol under the outside of my right thigh and stuck the key in the ignition. The truck fired up immediately. I put it in drive and checked my mirror. The street was momentarily clear. I cranked the wheel and hit the gas.

Even with the bike lane extending the road another four feet or so, I didn't have enough room to turn around. I put the truck in reverse and backed away from the curb to give myself some room. Even if there hadn't been trees in the way, I probably wouldn't have gone up on the curb. I didn't know what kind of explosives were in the truck, or how stable they were. For all I knew, a violent bump would set them off.

The memory of the SUV exploding came to mind, putting me slightly at ease. That vehicle had bumped over plenty of rough ground and had been shot at, and it didn't detonate until the guy driving set it off.

As I gunned it the wrong way down the one-way street, the light changed again to allow the traffic stopped on the other side of 2nd Avenue to continue on. I laid on the horn as I came to the intersection and turned left to follow the man. I grimaced as the truck bumped into a black sedan whose driver apparently hadn't been paying attention. The truck took part of the sedan's front bumper off as I put the pedal to the floor.

I was now on 2nd Avenue and going with traffic. I could see the man running down the sidewalk two blocks distant, dodging around pedestrians. The light on Salmon Street turned yellow when I was still some yards back, and the truck in front of me slowed. I jerked the wheel, getting into the middle lane and streaking through the intersection a full second after the light turned red.

Gaining on the man, I flew through the Taylor Street intersection. He looked over his shoulder, eyes widening when he saw me. Behind me, sirens started up. The police were coming.

The man ducked into a business, slamming through the door to an art gallery.

I slammed on the brakes and threw the truck in park. When I'd first gotten inside the truck, the sliding door had automatically latched itself open, and I'd left it like that. Now I had no obstructions in the way as I lunged out of the vehicle, dodging between two parked cars at the curb.

The few other people on the sidewalk shouted as they saw me jump out of the truck, gun in hand. As I approached the glass gallery door, trying to peer inside to see the man, the glass shattered in time with a gunshot. I flinched, resisting the urge to look down at my body. I didn't think I'd been hit, but I also didn't know how he could've missed.

Then, as I looked through the now-shattered door, everything made sense. There was an Asian man with graying hair in the gallery, wrestling the guy for the gun. I jumped through the glassless door and ran across the polished concrete floor toward the pair, trying to stay out of the gun's way. I shoved the Browning's barrel hard into the guy's throat and told him to drop it. With my other hand, I reached up and grabbed the barrel of his gun. He froze, and so did the Asian guy. Both of them were looking at me.

The white guy released the gun, and I shoved it in a jacket pocket. Saying thanks to the Asian man, I kept the gun on the man and gripped his collar, shoving him toward the back of the gallery. Outside, the police were pulling up.

"Tell them there's a bomb in the UPS truck, would you?" I called to the Good Samaritan. "Should probably evacuate the area."

The guy was still in shock. He looked at me like I was speaking Latin.

"I'm serious!" I yelled. "There's a bomb in that truck! Tell the cops."

That snapped him out of it. He headed toward the door.

"And keep your hands up!" I shouted after him. "You don't want them to shoot you!"

He put his hands up as he stepped outside, glass crunching under his feet. I heard him shout, "There's a bomb on the truck!"

I knew that would most likely keep me from getting arrested in the next few minutes; the cops would be busy with the bomb. For better or worse, law enforcement agencies took all bomb threats seriously. And a few minutes was all I needed to find out what the hell was going on.

"How were you going to detonate it?" I asked the guy as I shoved him toward what looked like the back door.

"I want a lawyer," the guy said.

"So I guess it won't be going off anytime soon," I said, smiling a little. "Otherwise, you'd be saying a prayer to whatever fucked-up god you worship."

"There's only one God—"

"Oh, shut up," I said, hitting him in the head with the butt of the Browning—but not too hard. I needed him conscious.

We moved through a back storage area and toward a metal door. As we approached the door, I said, "I'm not a cop. You know that, right?"

"You're a *fed*," the guy said, spitting the last word.

"Not that either. So if you don't tell me what I want to know, I can do whatever the fuck I want to you. I don't give a shit if I go to jail for the rest of my life. As long as I can rid the world of one more racist piece of shit, I'll die a happy man. But I can guarantee you this: if you don't tell me, your last moments will be filled with the worst pain you've ever imagined. Do you understand me?"

He said nothing. I shoved him against the door, and it popped open, revealing a narrow alley. There was construction going on at one side of the alley, so there were no delivery vans or cars in it at the moment. It was just the two of us.

"How were you going to detonate it?"

"By phone," he said. "Call the number and boom. Bunch of dead race traitors."

I shoved him against the wall next to a dumpster and got him to turn around to face me. "When?"

"When I get back there. Which better be fucking soon, or they'll come looking for me."

"Get back where? Where are the rest of them?"

Realizing he'd said too much, he clamped his jaw and shook his head.

I shifted the gun to point at his foot. And I pulled the trigger. The loud pop of the .22 echoed off the alley walls, followed quickly by his scream. He dropped down onto his ass and gripped his boot-clad foot with both hands. "Fuck!"

I looked around. So far so good. "Where are the rest of them? What's the plan?"

"Fuck you!" he screamed.

I shot him in the other foot—*pop*—and he screamed again.

"What did I tell you?" I said. "I thought you understood."

"The American Bank Building!" he said, gasping. "Across from Pioneer Courthouse Square."

"Why there?"

"Because the square. There's gonna be a gathering. Fucking niggers and race traitors, okay? We're gonna shoot them from the windows."

"How many at the building?"

"Twenty, including me," he said. "On the third floor. The whole floor is ours. Please, man. Plea—"

"What else?"

"Damn, man, my feet! I need to go to a hospital. It hurts so fuckin' bad." He was crying, blubbering. I felt no sympathy for him. None at all.

"What else?"

"They're gonna shut the power down to the city. It'll be chaos."

"When? When is this supposed to happen?"

"Twelve fourteen," he said. "For the fourteen words, you fuckin' race traitor!"

"And you think you'll actually make it out of the city after you slaughter a bunch of people? Or are you all ready to die tonight?"

The guy looked up at me, tears streaming down his face. And then he smiled. "You can't stop us all. We brought pipe bombs with us to kill us some cops on the way out—if they follow us."

"Where are they keeping the bombs?" I asked, a sudden idea coming to mind.

"Fuck you. I'm done talking to you."

"After you spill half the plan, you're done?" I said. "How about this?" I jammed the pistol barrel into his crotch and looked into his eyes. I was having a hard time not just emptying the entire magazine into him. There was nothing I wanted to do more. It didn't take him long to see I wasn't messing around.

"They're in a van," he said quickly. "A fuckin' blue minivan, okay? In the parking garage. But it won't do you any good. There's no way you'll stop us. Even if you bring the cops."

"Maybe not," I said. "But I can sure as hell stop you." I brought the gun up and shot him in the head. His body slumped down to the alley floor. Just so much trash, ready to be disposed of to keep America clean and safe.

I stood and pulled out Sarah's phone. It was one minute until noon.

Chapter 59

In Dallas, Scott Lee was loading his truck up to go to war. He'd already put his two one-hundred-round drum magazines on the back seat of the truck, which sat in his driveway. He was bringing his rifle out, along with his tactical vest, weighed down with four of his thirty-round magazines, when something put him on edge.

He looked across the street at the tan-colored ranch-style house. Then he peered at the other houses in his field of view. They were silent. The whole street was silent. Then he realized what had caught his attention. There were no cars driving down the street. There hadn't been any since he'd started loading up the truck. But he lived on a main artery that fed a large housing development. There were always cars driving by. One every minute or two, anyway.

Shortly after renting the house, he'd asked the landlord permission to put up privacy trees along the sides. With the trees in the way, he couldn't see down the street in either direction. Not from where he was.

He propped his Armalite rifle against the front passenger seat and set the tactical vest down, sure that he was being paranoid. He had to admit that he was nervous about what came next. After all, he'd never gone out to slaughter as many Blacks and Hispanics as he could before. First times could be scary.

He walked to the edge of his driveway like a man going to check the mail. But once he cleared the trees and looked down the street to the right, he jerked back, adrenaline spiking. He looked left and saw an identical scene; dozens of cop cars blocking the road about seventy yards away. He ran back to his truck and pulled on the tactical vest, then grabbed his rifle, no question in his mind that the police were there for *him*. It was a shame things weren't going to plan, but he could still kill some foot soldiers of the Zionist Occupied Government.

As he moved away from his truck, sliding the selector on his rifle from safe to fire, he caught a glimpse of something on the top of a two-story house three blocks over. A little glint of sunlight.

He looked that way just in time to see the sniper fire. The bullet hit him just below the base of the neck, above the hem of the tactical vest.

Lee knew he'd been hit, but it took a moment for his body to catch up with his mind. He dropped his rifle and stumbled forward, clawing at his neck, suddenly unable to breathe. He fell to the concrete of his driveway, still clawing, suffocating, panicking.

Before he died, he saw squad cars coming to a rocking halt in front of his house, boots stomping toward him.

And an impossible sadness settled on him, adding itself to the terrible pain he was feeling. He died confused and angry. But mostly he died asking why. Why him.

***

In Phoenix, Arizona, the middle-aged and divorced father of three stepped out of his house to find SWAT officers in his neighbor's yard. He didn't see them until he was a good ten yards from his front door. He was going to check the mail for the last time—force of habit. He wasn't planning to do his shooting until early evening.

And as the police officers screamed at him to get on the ground, he made the split-second decision to run back into his house and shoot it out with them.

He never got the chance. He was shot in the back six times as he reached his front stoop. He died moments later.

A lone wolf shooter in Mesa was arrested as he left his house to get an early lunch.

One in Tucson saw the police coming and took his own life.

***

Nez's team had done an excellent job of tracking down every potential shooter and liaising with local law enforcement to take them down.

Police and FBI all across the country were busy surveilling these potential shooters and waiting for them to make some kind of move. With the information gathered by the FBI, the idea was to wait until they were leaving their homes armed to the teeth. That, in conjunction with the information the FBI had gathered, including transcripts from supposedly encrypted chat rooms, would allow prosecutors to put these men away for years without having to catch them in the act.

Police in Denver arrested a man. Two men in San Antonio were taken into custody, as was one in Atlanta. Seven men in Florida were targeted. Two of them tried to run and were caught quickly. Three more tried to shoot it out with police and were killed in short order. Two were taken without incident.

The police found manifestos in many of their homes, which only added to the evidence against them. Most of these documents were poorly written and full of conspiracy theories and parroted racist rhetoric. They all provided insight into the minds of men who saw themselves as both victims and warriors in a culture war for the soul of America. They were oppressed. Their way of life was under attack. They were fighting for a just cause.

But when it came down to it, they were nothing more than cowards. And they had no one to blame but themselves.

Chapter 60

THE AMERICAN BANK BUILDING was over fifteen stories tall, white, and bland. I stood on the sidewalk of an adjacent block, next to a Nordstroms, and observed it. There were several businesses on the ground floor, including two different banks, which were both closed because of the holiday. There was some traffic through the front doors, which were across the street from the square.

Directly across the two-lane Morrison Street from the building, Pioneer Courthouse Square took up the entire city block. There was a large open area in the middle and steps leading to raised areas on two sides where food and coffee kiosks sat near tables where people could sit and eat or enjoy their lattes. And many of the tables were occupied, along with much of the square.

As I'd passed it on the side opposite the American Bank Building, I'd tried to get a headcount. There were probably five hundred people standing around. Many of them were holding signs opposing racism and fascism. About two thirds of them were white, but that was to be expected in the Pacific Northwest, where the vast majority of the population was Caucasian. Not that it would matter to the WPA. They'd kill them all the same. Unless I did to them what I'd just done to their pal from the UPS truck.

After killing the would-be bomber in the alley, I'd ducked through a restaurant's open back door, headed away from 2nd Avenue, where the UPS truck was parked. I had put my gun away, and the spoil-of-war 9mm Ruger pistol was safely in my pocket as I moved through the kitchen. I got some strange looks, but no one bothered me.

I came out on 3rd Avenue. To my left, at the intersection of 3rd and Taylor, was a small crowd gathered around a police roadblock. I went the other way, toward Yamhill Street. As I walked, I'd taken out Sarah's phone and looked at a map, seeing that the square was a short walk away.

Now, as I stood between Broadway and Park on Morrison Street, gazing at the building, I knew I had to move fast. It had taken me just over five minutes to get here. I had about ten minutes left. If the guy had been telling the truth, his people were on the third floor. But there was something I needed to check before I went up there.

There was an underground garage entrance down the side of the building on Broadway, so that's where I headed. There was a booth between the entrance and exit ramps, but it was empty. Everything was automated. I skirted the barrier arm blocking vehicle entrance and hustled down the ramp into the parking garage.

I scanned the cars on the first level, looking for a blue Chrysler minivan. I didn't see one, so I kept going, down to the next sublevel. There were many empty spots on both the first and second levels—most of them reserved for bank employees. I saw no blue minivan. I was starting to worry that the bomber had lied to me. But when I rounded the ramp to the third sublevel, I spotted a blue Chrysler van. Looking around to make sure I was alone, I made my way down toward it and looked through the tinted back windows. There were three duffel bags in the vehicle's cargo area. The rest of the van was clean. And, of course, it was locked.

The sound of a metal door opening caught my attention. I ducked down and moved between the van and the silver Honda crossover parked next to it. Peering over the Honda, I looked toward the stairwell entrance to see a pair of white men hurrying in my direction. I didn't recognize either of them. They were both dressed in comfortable, casual clothing. But the way they moved and the concentrated look on their faces gave me an inkling that they were coming for the supplies in the van.

I ducked all the way down behind the Honda and pulled the Browning .22 out. There were still eight rounds left in it, and I wanted to save the larger caliber Ruger 9mm for when I got up to the third floor.

Kneeling behind the Honda and listening to their footsteps, I finally had a moment where I wasn't trying to accomplish something. I was just waiting. And with the waiting, the visions came back. The memories. Hudson getting shot. Nez getting blown up. All those FBI agents dying or getting blown apart. Images from the news of all those people in the community center in Cleveland.

And while these visions burned the brightest inside me, causing those little boxes of fury to rattle and shake and beg for release, other visions joined them. Visions of planes crashing into towers. Visions of people jumping to their deaths from those buildings so they wouldn't have to go through the torture of burning alive or suffocating. Every single piece of news footage I'd seen of the towers falling flashed through my mind. So did images of the aftermath of the Oklahoma City bombing, and the Boston Marathon bombing, and every one of the thousands of mass shootings that had occurred in America over the last decade.

These men were no different than the perpetrators of all those heinous crimes. They didn't deserve to have their day in court. Not in my mind. They didn't deserve to live out their lives in jail cells, where they could infect other young white men with their lies.

They needed to die.

But I had to be sure that these men were part of the WPA. I couldn't shoot first and hope that they were the bad guys. And I had to be sure that what I needed was in the van. Otherwise, I would be forced to come up with a new plan.

I waited for them to come to the vehicle. As they got closer to the Honda, I moved around to its front. There was just enough space for me to fit between the front of the vehicle and the concrete wall while maintaining my crouch. Shifting around the Honda, I moved to the other side as they stopped at the back of the van. I peered through the crossover's rear windows, watching them open the van's cargo door.

Now was the time to move. While they were busy.

I moved to stand up and step out from between the cars, but before I could complete the movement, I heard the stairwell door open again. Ducking back down between the vehicles, I looked through the windows of the Lexus sedan parked next to the Honda and saw a third white man heading in my direction.

"Hurry it up, Otto," one of the guys at the van called up.

Otto wore jeans and a green-and-black plaid shirt. He had dark, patchy facial hair and a crooked nose that had no doubt been broken once or twice. He muttered something I couldn't hear. I wasn't listening hard, anyway. I was thinking about what to do. Moving around the Lexus while Otto came up would put me at risk of being seen by the other two. Plus, it would put me further away from them than I wanted. Covering three guys was exponentially harder than covering two. But I had no choice.

So I stayed put, my heart rate increasing until it felt not so much like a series of beats but more like a steady thrum. I waited for Otto to come up to the gap between the Honda and the Lexus. If he noticed me, I would make my move. If he didn't, all the better. It would make things that much easier.

I heard the sound of a zipper being retracted, and I was sure that the men at the van were checking the supplies. Maybe making sure they wouldn't suddenly explode when they moved them. I figured it was why they'd kept the bags in the van at all. If one of them happened to go off, they wouldn't be in the same room with them when it happened. The would-be bomber had said that they would use them to get out of the city. But maybe plans had changed. Maybe since their guy hadn't showed up, they were improvising. Maybe they'd even tried to detonate the truck bomb by calling the phone attached to it, only to find that there was no explosion rocking the city to the southeast.

Otto's footsteps approached at a steady clip. I counted down in my head to the moment of truth. The moment I would make my move.

Three.

Two.

One.

Otto glanced between the cars, looking me in the eye. I jumped up on heavy legs, leading with the Browning.

"Nobody move a goddamn muscle," I said.

Otto froze where he was, which was exactly why I'd been hoping he wouldn't notice me. Now, the other two guys were to my immediate left, and although I could see their shapes in my peripheral vision, it was not enough. I needed to get them all together. I swiveled my head toward the two guys at the van. And as soon as I did, Otto rushed me.

It was all or nothing now. And what happened next happened in the span of four or five seconds.

I pulled the trigger twice, shooting Otto in the chest before swiveling and firing four quick shots at the two other men as they scrambled away. One of them was pulling a gun out as he turned to run, but he lost his legs and went down hard before he got the gun up. The other one got his pistol out and fired four shots back at me blindly as he ran down the row of cars, stumbling but keeping his footing.

There was only one of his shots I couldn't account for almost as soon as he fired. Two of them thumped into the Honda to my left. A split-second later, I felt a sickening impact on the left side of my abdomen and knew I'd been shot. My mind was so occupied with the shock of this realization that I had no idea what happened with the fourth shot.

Otto, somehow still up, plowed into me, knocking me into the back corner of the Honda. My head whipped back and cracked the rear window before we went down onto the hard concrete. I got the Browning jammed into his gut and pulled the trigger twice, firing the last two shots. It did the trick, and I was able to shove Otto off me, dead with four .22 caliber bullets in him.

There was no pain yet. Not from where I'd been shot. And I couldn't look at the wound. If it was bad, there was nothing I could do about it anyway. And if it wasn't, then it would hold. But if it *was* bad, I could spend the last moments of my life doing what I came here to do. Or trying until the life left me for good.

I got up into a crouch, tossing the Browning and getting the Ruger out of my jacket pocket. I'd checked it after killing Asshole Bomber in the alley behind the art gallery. It had started out with eighteen rounds, but Asshole Bomber had fired one in the gallery, so now there were seventeen left. I hoped it was enough.

As I moved to get up, my legs turned to rubber, and I had to lean against the Honda. My vision blurred, and I reached up to feel the back of my head. My fingers came away bloody. I shook my head and blinked, and my vision cleared momentarily. Lurching upright, I peered around the back of the vehicle, looking for the other two guys. One of them—the one who'd gone down while trying to pull his gun out—was twitching on the ground where he'd fallen. There was blood pouring out of him, although I couldn't tell where from. I just saw it gathering underneath him. Apparently, I'd hit him with one or both shots from the Browning.

Looking beyond the twitcher, I saw a trail of blood leading down toward sublevel four. I'd hit the other guy at least once. Shaking my head to clear my vision again, I looked for signs of the guy. I couldn't see far enough to follow the blood trail from here. I'd have to go find him.

I didn't have time for this shit. Warm blood ran down my left side, soaking into my underwear and jeans. Already feeling lightheaded, I wasn't sure how much longer I would be on my feet.

Wincing, I moved out beyond the cover of the Honda, then quickly back, waiting for gunshots. None came. So I moved out again and went directly to the van. One of the bags was unzipped, revealing a half dozen pipe bombs like the ones I'd seen at the Mount Shasta camp. I zipped it back up and snaked my right arm through the straps. With my left hand, I held the straps in place on my shoulder as I turned toward the sloping ramp down to the fourth level.

"I've got a bag of bombs with me," I called out. "If you shoot me, we both die. How's that sound, you piece of shit? I don't know about you, but I'm ready. It's been a long, hard life, dealing with assholes like you, and I think I deserve a rest."

As I spoke, I walked down, following the trail of blood as I went. It seemed to end at the terminus of the row to my left. There was a concrete wall there, next to a white Tesla Model X. But as I got closer, I realized the blood trail didn't stop. It went down the gap between the Tesla and the wall.

"You hear me?" I called while I was still several cars away, making sure to stay where he wouldn't have a shot at my feet under the vehicles.

"Fuck you," he said. "You can't stop it all. No one can."

There was a gunshot, and I ducked down, even though I was sure he didn't have a shot at me. When I raised back up, I saw blood splatter on the concrete wall beyond the Tesla's hood. I moved up warily and glanced around the side of the vehicle. The guy was slumped against the wall, legs splayed, brains painting the wall above his head. He'd shot himself. And after a moment, I saw why. I'd hit him in the liver with one of the .22 shots. He'd pulled his shirt up to inspect the wound, and the blood coming out was nearly black.

I probably would've done the same thing in his position.

Turning around, I moved back toward the van, pausing to lean on the back of a truck while I tried to gather myself. The pain was here now. And it was bad. Really bad.

I couldn't catch my breath, and I felt lightheaded. My vision swam and blurred. I wanted to just sit down for a minute. Or to lie on the concrete and close my eyes. To make the pain go away.

Gritting my teeth, I grabbed a second bag from the back of the van after verifying that it contained pipe bombs. And I moved up toward the stairwell door.

Just as I was about to open the door, the power to the entire garage went out. It was like a thunderclap, followed by dead silence. All the humming and vibrating you generally hear in a city was gone.

They'd cut the power to the city, leaving an eerie silence. And in that silence, I heard footsteps coming down the stairs toward the garage.

Chapter 61

THE FLASHLIGHT BEAM SHONE briefly through the vertical rectangular window in the door a moment before it was opened. I stood against the wall next to the door, bags of pipe bombs over my right shoulder. I held the Ruger in my right hand, left hand pressed to the excruciating and oozing gunshot wound just above my left hip bone. I blinked constantly, trying to keep my vision from blurring. It wasn't working so great.

A man dressed much like the other guys stepped out, flashlight in one hand. "What the hell is taking you guys so long?" he said, shining the light around.

I raised my gun. He seemed to notice the movement because he flinched and started to turn toward me. But he didn't have a chance to put his eyes on me, because a 9mm bullet from the Ruger ended his miserable life with the squeeze of my trigger finger. His body fell to the ground as the gunshot echoed around the garage.

I reached down and grabbed the flashlight from him with my bloody left hand. Then I used the same hand to open the stairwell door. I turned off and pocketed the flashlight, allowing the battery-operated emergency lights to guide my way.

As I limped up the stairs, I wondered about getting my hands on a rifle. There weren't any in the van, and none of the men had come down with rifles—only pistols. So I was guessing they'd just left the weapons upstairs, thinking they wouldn't need them and that it would be easier to carry the bombs without them. But then I realized I hadn't checked the last bag in the van. I wasn't about to go back and open it up. The way I was moving now, it would take all I had to get up to the third floor.

I paused as I came to the door to the lobby. I couldn't see much more than a corridor and a couple of bathrooms nearby. Several people walked by, chatting about the power outage, their phones adding to the illumination provided by the emergency lights.

Continuing up, I wanted nothing more than to pause on every landing. Each step sent a bolt of sickening pain through my side. Nausea swirled in my stomach. I forced myself to continue, thinking about all the people gathered in the square across the narrow street. Although I couldn't hear them any longer, I had to assume they were still there. The gunfire from the parking garage probably wasn't loud enough to be heard at the square—or even throughout the building.

As I came to the second floor, the door to the stairwell came open. A man and a woman in business-casual clothing froze as they saw me. "Call the police," I said, continuing up. "And stay off the third floor."

I figured all the people in the offices were simply waiting for the power to come back on. But they would only wait so long before they had to take the stairs down. I hoped to be done by then.

I reached the third-floor landing and listened by the door for a minute. I heard nothing. Then I gently set the bags of pipe bombs down and got on my knees to open them up. I picked one of the bombs up in my left hand, my right still holding the Ruger. It was constructed of an eight-inch-long section of steel water pipe with steel caps threaded onto each end. Two wires—red and white—snaked from one cap to a simple digital timer affixed to the outside with black zip ties. All the other bombs I could see were identical to the one I held in my hand. But when I opened the other bag up, I noticed that the pipe bombs in that bag had screws and nails taped to their exteriors. Not only would the pipe itself break apart to become potentially deadly shrapnel, but the nails and screws attached would also do damage. Thrown into a crowd of people, these twelve bombs could kill and maim dozens.

I thought about this, wanting to feel those little cells of harnessed energy that had clicked into place after I watched Nez get blown apart. Images of racism-fueled atrocities paraded across my mind, but I didn't feel that energy swelling in me or begging for release. I didn't feel much of anything but sadness, despair, and exhaustion. But I needed that energy. I needed it to fuel me across the finish line. I had no idea how many men were waiting on the third floor. Twenty, like the bomber said? Minus the five I'd already killed, it would make fifteen. In the state I was in, I didn't think I'd be able to take even three or four.

But what was the alternative? Sit here and die, so close to accomplishing my goal? No. No, that wasn't an option. Even if sitting down against the wall and letting darkness take me sounded like the most attractive thing in the world. I'd lost so much blood, I didn't think it would be long.

Better get to work then, I told myself. *Better get going before you do die.*

Setting the Ruger down, I found and pressed the power button on the timer for the pipe bomb I was holding. Its slate-gray digital face came to life with segmented black numbers: 00:00. All I had to do was punch in a time and then hit start. Once that time was up, it would go boom—if it was constructed correctly. There was always a chance one of them would go off before it was supposed to. At which point, I wouldn't have to worry about a slow death.

I stuck the pipe bomb in my right jacket pocket. And, after powering the timer on, I stuck another in my left. And I put one each in my back pockets, and then one more in my left front pocket. They were all powered on and ready to go.

I picked up a sixth bomb—this one with nails taped to the outside—and then got the Ruger in hand. I stood up, leaning against the wall for a moment when I got lightheaded. Then I pushed through the door to the third floor, leaving the bag with five shrapnel-laden pipe bombs on the landing. I stepped into a short corridor with a couple of bathrooms to my left and a wide hallway to my right. I moved right, leading with my gun, rounding the corner to see that I was right next to the bank of four elevators that served the building.

The elevators were separated from a large, empty area by a thin wall. I figured the area was designed to be used for cubicles. There were outlet fixtures in the floor here and there. To the right of the empty area, down a short hallway, was a kitchen/break room. Faint wintery light illuminated that area.

There were no windows letting light into where I was, but I could see by the emergency lighting fixtures that there were three sets of wooden doors off the wide cubicle area. I knew from the layout that all three of the office areas behind those doors would have windows looking out on the square. The terrorists would be in one of those three offices—maybe all of them. I stepped to the nearest set of doors and put my ear to it. I heard low talking inside.

I moved to the next set of doors and heard the same thing. Men's voices. Talking low. Sounding impatient.

At the third set of doors, I heard nothing. I listened for several long seconds before moving back to the first set. It sounded like there were more men in there than in the middle office.

With my left thumb, I found and pressed the seconds button on the pipe bomb's timer. It beeped faintly ten times. Ten seconds.

Holding the Ruger in my left armpit, I pulled the pipe bomb out of my right jacket pocket and set it for five seconds before returning it to the pocket. With my free right hand, I gently tried the office doorknob. It turned freely. I unlatched the door and pushed it open about an inch before keeping it open with my foot while I got the Ruger back in my hand. Taking a deep and shaky breath, I readied myself for what I thought would be the last few minutes of my life. And I pushed the door open.

Chapter 62

I STEPPED INTO A furnitureless rectangular area that was probably designed to house a large desk for meetings. Beyond that, there was an open door leading to a small office that had windows looking out over the square. I counted six men visible—four in the office and two in the meeting area. They all held semi-automatic rifles. And they all stopped talking as I stepped inside, their eyes piercing the gloom to gaze at me.

I pressed the start button on the timer and threw the bomb into the middle of the meeting area, realizing that ten seconds was much too long. In an effort to counter this, I fired the Ruger wildly four times, hitting the two nearest men while the rest of them took cover in the small office.

I then stepped back out of the room, slamming the door and putting my back against the wall next to it. Awkwardly, I pulled the second bomb out of my right jacket pocket just before the first one—the one with shrapnel affixed to it—exploded. The floor shook with the resonant concussion, and I could barely hear the sound of glass shattering over the ringing in my ears. I had to move quickly now, even though my feet felt heavy, like they were wrapped in giant chains.

Sticking the Ruger in my left armpit once again, I stepped back and opened the door to the office with my right hand, pressing the start button on the second bomb, which I threw inside underhand.

Moments later, it exploded. But I was already moving to the next office in line, setting the next bomb for five seconds.

As I came to the set of office doors, one of them opened. In my weakened and dazed state, I hadn't thought things through. I had wasted too much time throwing the second bomb into the first office. I should've moved to the other occupied office first. Even if the men in the first office had not all been killed or injured by the first explosion, it would've taken them time to gather themselves and decide on a course of action.

So when the office door I was approaching opened, I reacted without thinking. I was still holding the pistol in my armpit, and the man peering out at me had his rifle up, although his left hand was on the door, so he wasn't quite ready to fire.

I pressed the start button on the bomb and threw it at the man in the doorway. But he was quick. He shut the door, and the device bounced off. I turned around and lurched for the other office door, shouldering it open just as the pipe bomb exploded behind me. I heard pieces of the exploded pipe hit the door and felt something strike the inside of my right leg at the calf. I reached up and pulled my pistol out, but I was unable to keep my balance. I fell to the floor in the smoky room, the smell of spent explosives still pungent.

Peering through the haze, I saw the bodies of the two men I'd shot, but I couldn't see into the office beyond. The door was closed—damaged, but intact. Since it hadn't been open when I had thrown the first bomb, I knew some of the remaining four men were likely still alive.

I got to my feet, wincing at the pain in my right calf. I'd been hit with a piece of shrapnel. Limping to the wall, I put my back against it, looking right toward the still-open door I'd come through, and then left toward the closed inner office door. My ears were ringing, but

I thought I could hear commotion from outside as people fled the square.

The inner office door opened slightly. I aimed my pistol at the door as a rifle barrel poked out. I was at an angle where they wouldn't see me until they got through most of their sweep, but that also meant I wouldn't see them. The wall was in the way of a clean shot.

I waited, Ruger pointing at the protruding barrel. And then when I saw the man shift out as he swiveled toward me, I fired three times, hitting him once in the head.

As he dropped to the floor, I limped toward the door, deciding on the brute force tactic. I shot twice more, hitting a second man just as he fired a couple of shots from his rifle. But it was clear he'd been injured by one of the bomb blasts, and his shots went wide. I rushed into the room to find that the other two men I'd seen in there were dead. They'd taken some shrapnel from the first bomb I'd tossed into the reception area. Pocketing the Ruger, I grabbed the only rifle in the room I was confident fired and glanced out the window.

There were still dozens of people in the square, filming the building with their phones. "Idiots," I muttered. I limped out of the small office and toward the doors out to the open area, rifle up and trained ahead of me.

I didn't much care if I was shot at this point. I could feel my energy fading fast. I was growing cold and more tired than I'd ever been in my life. There was no time for finesse. No time for anything but quick, decisive action. I stormed into the open area outside the three offices only to find that it was empty. The next set of doors in line was badly damaged from the pipe bomb that had landed right outside. I moved up directly in front of the doors and fired through them with the semi-auto rifle. I fired fifteen shots, then pulled out another pipe bomb and set it for three seconds. I stepped up and kicked the broken door open, taking all I had not to scream from the pain in my calf and my abdomen. I tossed the bomb inside and stepped to the wall as the explosion shook the floor.

As I stood with my back to the wall next to the doors, a man stumbled out of the office, one side of his body a mess of burn marks and bloody holes. I aimed the rifle at him but saw that he was walking dead. He had no weapon. But he turned and looked at me with his one good eye. He wanted mercy, that was easy to see. He wanted me to kill him. I didn't even consider it. I wanted him to suffer. I wanted him to live through what he was ready to do to all the people down in that square—what his organization had already done to people in Cleveland.

He collapsed. And I was suddenly jealous of him. I wanted to collapse and settle in for the big sleep. But I had to make sure I was done. So I stepped over to the door the man had come through and looked inside.

This space wasn't set up like the other one, with the two separate rooms. It was one big room, probably designed for another, smaller bullpen or maybe even the boss's office. From the bomb I'd thrown in and the fifteen rounds I'd fired through the doors, there was no one left alive. The seven men who'd been in the room were all dead.

Breathing heavily, I stepped to the wall, pressing my back against it once again. I let my eyes close and the rifle drop from my hand. I was all out of energy. I felt that coldness seeping deep into my body, solidifying its hold with each passing moment. But I was done. Mission accomplished. I could die now.

Just as I was about to let myself slide down to sit on the floor, I remembered what Asshole Bomber had said. Twenty men, including him. I'd killed four in the garage. Thirteen in the two offices. The bomber made eighteen. Two were missing.

My job wasn't done.

Then I heard something from beyond the last set of doors—the only office I hadn't physically checked yet. And it sounded like two men fighting.

***

Coakley had pulled Bove into the last office at the front of the building while they waited for the men to return with the pipe bombs. Pearson hadn't yet arrived from planting the truck bomb outside the police station, and everyone was getting antsy. But they still had a few minutes before twelve-fourteen.

The conversation they'd had outside the IHOP earlier was driving him crazy. He wanted to talk about Sarah before they got to work. His head was a jumbled mess, and he'd tried and tried to let it go. But finally, just after Bove sent Thurman to go see what was taking the guys so long, he relented. He whispered in Bove's ear, "I need to talk to you." Reluctantly, Bove had followed Coakley out of the middle office.

There was a tree blocking half the view from the last office, so they hadn't planned on using it. But Coakley peered past the leafless tree at the crowd milling in the square, gathering his thoughts.

Instead of using all three offices, they were going to use just the other two, allowing some of the men to fire into the crowd while others waited behind them. When those firing needed to reload, men with full rifles would step up to take their spots.

That had been the plan, anyway.

Shortly after Coakley and Bove stepped into the room, Coakley opened his mouth to talk. But the words wouldn't come. He loved Sarah. Loved her like he'd never loved anyone before. And while he'd previously thought of Bove as a man to be followed, a man to be revered, he now thought of him as a man who was trying to take that love away. He didn't believe that Sarah had only seduced him so she could get pregnant. He didn't believe it for a second. But how to express these feelings in a way that would make Bove understand? How could they come to some sort of agreement whereby Sarah would be shared between them? Surely there was a way. Maybe Bove would want more kids. Maybe he would want five or six. Yes, that could be the tactic to take.

"Bob, listen," Bove began, but Coakley raised a hand.

"Just give me one more minute. I'm going to say my piece."

Bove shrugged and nodded.

Seconds passed while Coakley struggled with the words. Bove waited patiently.

Then, just as Coakley was finally about to say what he wanted to say, they heard gunshots followed by a floor-shaking explosion. Both their faces went pale as they looked at each other. Given the sounds, it was clear the shots and explosion were inside the building and not being directed out toward the crowd. Coakley glanced out the windows to see much of the crowd in the square running away from the building.

There was another explosion, and it shook the building just like the first.

Bove had his black-and-silver SS dagger on his belt, along with his Smith & Wesson M&P pistol at his right hip. He reached for the pistol and stepped toward the door just as a third explosion erupted—closer this time. He heard and felt shrapnel hit the door.

"Christ!" Bove said. "What the hell is going on out there?"

Coakley suddenly saw his chance. How had he been so stupid? How had he not seen it before? He pulled his pistol out and stepped up to the man he'd hoped would lead him to a white eutopia. But, of course, that notion was going tits up like everything else had in the last week. So there was only one thing left to do now.

He pressed the barrel of his pistol to Bove's head. "Drop your gun," he said.

There were more gunshots from the adjacent offices. He had to make this quick. He'd originally wanted to pull the trigger, but now found that he couldn't. Not unless Bove gave him a reason.

"Now, listen here, *partner*," Bove said. "Our men are dying out there."

"Drop the fucking gun, Ethan!"

"All right, all right." Bove tossed the gun to the corner of the room. "What now?"

Coakley shifted his weight from foot to foot. Meanwhile, Bove turned to face him.

"You going to shoot me, Bob? Over a woman?"

"She's not just a woman," Coakley said, hating the pleading tone in his voice.

"She's *my* wife," Bove said. His left hand crept up toward the dagger on his hip.

"I just—"

"I know," Bove said. "It was a nasty trick to pull, I know. But you're not Prince Valiant in this equation, you know? You committed adultery. You slept with another man's wife, Bob."

"I thought she loved me," Coakley said. His eyes were filled with hot tears, and the gun suddenly felt heavy in his hand. Another explosion erupted, and Coakley flinched, dropping the gun a few inches.

It was what Bove had been waiting for.

He reached up, grabbing the gun and shoving it away with his right hand while he pulled the SS dagger out with his left.

Coakley reacted quickly, shifting to bring the gun back up. But Bove was too quick, and he had never let go of the gun. Although his right arm was across his chest holding the gun away, Bove was able to bring the dagger out with practiced ease. With his left hand, he brought it to Coakley's outstretched right arm, jamming the blade up into the meat of his triceps muscle a few inches above the elbow. He yanked the blade down toward the elbow, tearing through muscle and veins and tendons. Coakley shouted and dropped the gun, which Bove tossed away.

With his right hand now free, Bove jammed his forearm into Coakley's neck. He shoved the man back into the wall and then pulled the dagger out of Coakley's arm. The two struggled, Coakley getting his left hand into the fight to block the sharp Nazi dagger from damaging him further.

Screaming sirens approached as they slammed into the walls and finally fell to the floor, landing side by side and still locked in struggle. Bove brought a knee up into Coakley's groin and then managed to yank his left hand away from Coakley. With the dagger free, he stabbed it into the other man's throat, pulling it out to produce a torrent of blood that sputtered and frothed as Coakley gasped for breath.

Bove got to his feet, the sounds of sirens growing closer. Everything was fucked up. The mission was kaput. He had to get out of here. But there was still whatever the hell was happening outside to deal with. Still holding the dagger in his left hand, he went for his pistol near the door. And as he moved, the office door opened. A hand tossed a single pipe bomb inside.

Bove changed direction away from his gun toward the door, which was just two paces away. He slammed into it with his right shoulder even before it could be closed by the bomber. He crashed into the man just before the bomb exploded in the office. The man toppled onto his back, but Bove kept his feet.

The man looked vaguely familiar to Bove, but he certainly wasn't someone he'd met in person. Not recently, anyway. He was badly injured—that much was clear. But Bove wasn't about to stick around to find out just who the hell he was. Not with the sirens growing ever louder outside.

So he ran toward the stairwell, confident he could make it to the car he'd parked several blocks away.

Chapter 63

I RECOGNIZED THE BALDING, dark-eyed man from the photograph on Sarah's phone. He looked down at me after barging through the office door just before my second-to-last bomb exploded. It was Ethan Bove. I had no idea what he was in The White Power Alliance structure, but I knew he was important. Maybe even the top asshole.

I realized with sickening dismay that my job wasn't done. Swallowing a tormented scream as pain erupted all through my body, I got to my feet and ran after the man. It was only when I slammed through the stairwell door, interrupting a small group of office workers coming down the stairs, that I realized I'd left the rifle behind. But I still had the Ruger. I couldn't remember how many shots I'd fired, but I was confident I had at least five rounds left. Maybe six or seven. And I also had one more pipe bomb.

As the four office workers ran in fear away from me and back up the stairs, I remembered the bags I'd left next to the door. There had been pipe bombs in both of them. My heart plunged into my guts as I blinked my vision clear and saw that the bags were gone.

Even though people were still evacuating the building, I didn't think it likely that someone had randomly picked them up. That meant Bove had them. He knew what they were. He knew how to use them.

I could hear Bove's footsteps as he rushed down the stairs. There was no way I could catch him. Not in my condition. I'd already lost too much blood. And although there was a narrow gap between the rails, I couldn't see much more than the man's hand as he rushed down the stairs, gripping the rail at the landing to propel himself around and down.

I thought for a moment about tossing my last pipe bomb down, but I didn't want to risk killing any civilians that were still making their way out of the building.

I pulled the Ruger out of my pocket and aimed it down between the railings. He was nearing the lobby landing, heading down the stairwell between the second and first floors. I only had one chance. If he was going out the lobby to lose himself in the chaos outside, he would have to slow, giving me a chance to shoot him. If he was going to the garage, he could just keep rushing down the stairs.

Swaying, my arms shaking, I leveled the pistol at where he would be, where most of him would be exposed thanks to the angle and the narrow gap between the railings. Blinking rapidly against my blurred vision, I readied myself for the shot. And fired once when I saw his blurry form come into view two floors down.

I rushed down the stairs, thinking I'd heard him fall just after my shot. It was hard to tell with the constant ringing in my ears.

There was no sign of Bove. But as I came to the first-floor landing, I saw two familiar items by the lobby door. Both pipe bomb bags were there. And there was blood on the floor next to them.

I opened the lobby door and stepped out of the stairwell, leading with the pistol. As I swung it around from right to left, Bove emerged from the shadows at a run. He'd been waiting for me. The blade of a knife flashed in his right hand as he lunged for me. I couldn't get the gun on him in time. And as he slammed into me, sending us both to the floor, I lost my grip on the weapon. It went skittering across the polished lobby floor.

An unbelievable symphony of pain racked my body as I hit the floor. Somehow, I got my hands up and jammed one thumb into Bove's right eyeball. He screamed out and wrenched his head away, and I got my leg up to shove him back with a foot. He scrambled to his feet and looked at me. I noticed that his right arm was bloody, but he looked otherwise unharmed. I'd winged him with the shot in the stairwell. A flesh wound. His eyes jumped in the direction of the gun, and then to my left side. He made some kind of decision then. It was in his face. He turned and ran down the lobby corridor, away from the front doors.

I looked down at my left side to see a black-and-silver dagger sticking out of me. It was an SS dagger, the twin lightning bolts and the War Eagle giving it away.

Something came over me at the sight of that dagger. I'd been shot, stabbed, and exploded, and somehow, I was still alive. A short bark of laughter escaped me, and I ignored the sickening pain that it caused.

I laughed as I shook my head and got to my feet, which was a miracle in itself. And I laughed again as I looked down at the dagger.

Job's not done, I thought. *One more to go.*

I limped down the corridor after Bove.

I soon found that he'd gone through a side door. As I stepped outside, I gazed around for the asshole. Looking to the right, I could see a sliver of Pioneer Courthouse Square, and it was mostly empty. There were a few people milling around with their phones out, filming, but that was about it.

Traffic was at a standstill, with cars pulled over and crowds of people blocking the streets in every direction, effectively creating an accidental perimeter around the American Bank Building.

And as I looked to the left, I saw Bove. He was heading toward a crowd of people at the block behind the building. I guessed that the crowd there was made up of people who'd fled both the square and the building and were now warily getting back together to discuss the excitement and possibly wait for the police. From the sounds of the sirens, the cops were only a block or two away. I figured they'd been slowed by the chaotic crowds that had poured into the streets when the explosions started.

Moving that way, I kept my eyes fixed on Bove, who was about to reach the crowd. With every step, the blade stuck in my abdomen caused excruciating pain—not to mention my other injuries. I didn't dare take the dagger out for fear that the blood loss would stop me before I could finish the job.

"Stop him!" I shouted, my voice weak and hoarse. No one paid much attention.

"Stop him!" I tried again, this time managing to get the volume up. Several heads turned toward me, including Bove's. The panicked look that swept his features nearly made me laugh again.

Job's not done, asshole, I thought.

He faced forward again and kept going. No one moved to stop him.

I picked up the pace, even though the pain made me want to puke and my vision blurred between blinks. Suddenly, the world tilted, and my legs went limp. I fell to the asphalt on all fours, unable to stop myself from letting out a ragged scream of agony and anger.

My breath came in gasps, and I felt something seriously wrong inside me. I tried to pull in a breath, but my lungs seemed to spasm, preventing me from doing so. My mouth tasted strange, like I'd been sucking on a rock. Blood splattered the asphalt from my wounds.

He's getting away. Job's not done.

Grunting, I pushed off the street and teetered on my knees and got as much air into my lungs as I could. "White supremacist!" I yelled, pointing at Bove as he stepped among the crowd. People looked at him with furrowed brows. "S—stop him!"

A Black guy in a suit stepped in Bove's path, forcing the man to stop.

Job's not fucking done, I thought, pulling my right leg up so I was only on one knee. *Get up! Finish the job.*

The Black guy said something in a low voice I couldn't hear. Bove seemed to ignore him, stepping to move past the guy. The man put his hand on Bove's chest to stop him.

"Get your fucking hands off me, nigger!" Bove exploded. He reached into a cargo pocket of his pants and pulled out a pipe bomb taped with screws, holding it over his head.

"Bomb!" someone yelled, and the crowd quickly rushed away from him.

Grunting, I forced myself to my feet and stumbled toward Bove. I was the only one moving toward him.

He turned toward me and held the bomb out. "Don't come any closer!"

I kept coming. I could feel the blade in my body, jostled with every step. The bullet wound was a giant ball of pain on that same side, just slightly lower than the knife. My head and leg erupted in pain with every heartbeat. I no longer felt any of that old familiar rage. I didn't have the bandwidth to think about all the terrorist acts that had plagued the country or the world, every single one of them performed by the worst kind of cowards. I didn't have the energy to harness my rage. I'd relied on it so many times before, but it was gone, out of reach.

I just wanted to finish the fucking job. And I wasn't about to get fancy. I wasn't about to practice any finesse. If Bove was determined to blow himself up, and I could facilitate that end, I was happy to do it. Even if it meant he was going to take me with him.

So I kept moving.

"Stay back, dammit!"

The crowd had mostly dispersed, running or hiding behind lamp posts and in shop doors. But a few of them, including the Black guy that had first confronted Bove, were still somewhat close, watching the drama with interest.

I was ten yards away now. Bove still hadn't pressed the start button. And I couldn't see how long the timer was set for. Or if it even was set. It didn't matter. It would only take him moments to set it for one second and press start. And that would be it.

I almost wanted him to do it.

Bove brought the bomb down and went to press a button—or to fake pressing a button to see what I would do. But before he had the chance, a rock the size of a baby's fist came sailing through the air and hit him in the back. He winced and looked in the direction from which it had come. But before he could do more than look, someone chucked a piece of a brick at him, hitting him in the side of the head.

He stumbled, making a little pained noise. Someone threw a bottle at him. It hit the ground and shattered at his feet. My boots crunched on the glass as I continued, getting closer. Another stone struck him, this time in the neck. He whipped his head up to look at me. Then, seemingly remembering what he was doing, he looked back down at the bomb.

As I stepped within arm's reach, I pulled the Nazi dagger out of my side and slashed it down on his wrist, cutting through to the bone. The dagger was sharp. I was fully aware of that.

Bove screamed and dropped the bomb to the street. He looked up at me with eyes full of fear.

As I stepped even closer, Bove brought his uninjured hand up, but I slashed it with the dagger, and he pulled it away on reflex.

I moved quickly, using the last bits of energy I had. The job was almost done. I gripped the back of his head with my left hand and jammed the dagger up under his chin as hard as I could. I aimed it back and up, sending the blade toward his brain stem instead of up through his mouth. It had the desired effect.

Letting go and stepping back, I watched as Bove reached absently for the dagger sticking out of his neck. His hands never reached the dagger's hilt. He fell hard on his butt and then toppled back, cracking his head on the asphalt.

I looked at him for a long moment. Then I walked over to the nearest curb and took a seat with my back propped against a light pole. The crowd edged slowly toward me. Flashing lights appeared in my peripheral vision. The authorities were here. I leaned my head against the pole and closed my eyes.

"Job's done," I said.

Sweet darkness came over me.

Chapter 64

I was dead.

Let me rephrase that. I'd *been* dead. For about a minute, according to the stories I was told when I was no longer dead. You can't hear stories if you're dead, as far as I know. I certainly don't remember hearing any during that time. I don't remember anything. Granted, how good can a story be if you can tell it in a minute?

The paramedics who saved my life were—get this—both people of color. Go figure. It's like they contribute to society just as much as white people. What a concept. Although they tried, there was nothing they could do for Bove. Too bad, so sad. If I'd been conscious, I would've told them not to bother.

I was in surgery for about eight hours, apparently. And it was a close thing. But as I reclined in a hospital bed, I was well aware of how much further I had to go. There would be some serious physical therapy in my future.

Despite all the drugs they had me on, I didn't get much rest. I wanted news, but the television was no help. At first, no one but some cops came to see me, and they were just as much in the dark as I was. In fact, they were so in the dark they read me my rights and handcuffed me to the bed.

Story of my life.

But just a couple of hours later, I knew the feds had arrived because I could hear the raised voices outside my hospital room. The cop tasked with guarding me was arguing with someone out there. And then I heard the three words: Federal Bureau of Investigation. Moments later, a couple of white guys stepped in—one with a horseshoe of white hair around the crown of his head, and the other who looked to be approaching middle age.

They launched into their little spiel about how special they were and what they were in charge of, but I stopped them with a question.

"Did you get the others?" I asked. "The ones who caused the black-outs?" I knew from watching television that there hadn't been a bunch of mass shootings. The feds had made good on getting all the lone wolf actors—or at least enough of them to scare the others for the time being. I also saw that the idiots in the governor's mansion in Topeka were routed and killed when an FBI SWAT team raided the place.

The younger guy looked to the older one, who nodded.

"We got them all, yes," the younger guy said. "Once the news got out that you killed their leader, those we have in custody started to roll on their supposed friends. Not hard to see that coming."

I suddenly realized I recognized him. "Holy shit!" I said. "You're, uh, Gary something, right? We met before. After that thing with the little gang of assholes and the crazy sheriff."

The guy nodded. "That's right. It's Special Agent Gary Jones. And, as we tried to tell you earlier, this is Special Agent in Charge Rodney Whittinger."

I smiled at Gary. "You remember me. How flattering."

"I wish I didn't," he said. "But it's hard to forget a guy literally named Trouble."

"You're so sweet," I said. Maybe the drugs were helping, but I'd always had a penchant for messing with authority figures. Then thoughts of Nez and Hudson floated into my hazy mind, and I knew that I was using humor as a coping mechanism. Not surprising, really. If there wasn't any immediate action I could take, making light of a situation was the next best thing. "So what's up?" I asked. "You guys going to foot my hospital bill, or what?"

"We'd like to know why you didn't call us in when you found out where the attacks were going to take place," Whittinger said. They were standing at the foot of my bed, straight-backed and tight-assed.

I shook my head. "Do you honestly think, with all your protocols and rules and teams to assemble, that you could've prevented more deaths than I did? If you had surrounded that UPS truck with the bomb inside, do you think the guy would've hesitated to blow it up and take a bunch of feds with him? And what about the people in that building? How long would it have taken you to get your people in position, develop a plan, and then execute that plan? By that time, those assholes would've known you were there. And they would've been tossing bombs at your guys. I can guarantee it."

"So your actions were altruistic?" Whittinger asked.

"In a way, yeah. I wanted to end things—for good. I didn't want these people to have the chance to hire lawyers and go through lengthy public trials and write fucking books about how they're victims and the white race is doomed because of some vast global conspiracy. I wanted them dead. And I got what I fucking wanted."

The two men looked at each other, then back at me. Jones rubbed a hand down his face. "This is a mess, but considering that several of ours were killed, we have some serious political capital on our side. And we can use some of that to . . . repay you for your service."

"How are you going to do that?" I asked.

"We're going to control the narrative and use the full weight of the US Government to help you walk away from this unscathed."

"I sense a 'but' coming."

"But you will owe us."

"I will owe *you*?" I said, wincing as I pulled myself up in the bed. "How do you figure?"

"You know how this country looks upon vigilante justice, don't you?" Whittinger said.

I shrugged. "Judging by movies and TV shows, America loves it."

"It's up to you," Jones said. "Take the deal or take your chances. Believe it or not, there are still some politicians out there who, although they would never say so publicly, would've applauded those men's actions. Make no mistake, they will come after you if they think it will be good for their careers."

"What the hell does 'owe you' mean anyway?" I asked. "What, for the rest of my life? For one job? Give me specifics."

"You have a history of certain relationships with people that interest the FBI," Whittinger said. "Some of them we want to arrest and prosecute. Others we want to . . . use, so to speak."

"Still not hearing details about what this means for me," I said.

"I'll put something in writing," Jones said. "How about that?"

"As long as it includes something about paying all my medical bills, I'll consider it."

The two men shared a look again, and then Whittinger nodded.

"Great," I said. "And I want to go to the funerals for Nez and Hudson."

"Of course."

I nodded. "Now, did you ever find out where the WPA was getting all their money?"

"We did, in fact," Jones said. "You'll probably appreciate this. Using information we found on his private computer, we determined that

Ethan Lee Bove was getting money directly from a prominent Middle Eastern terrorist organization. One backed by oil dollars."

"Holy shit," I said, thinking it over. "But I guess it makes sense. If they want America to topple, does it really matter how it happens? Why not dupe some ignorant Americans into terrorist attacks? That way you don't have to worry about getting terrorist into the country. They're already here."

Both men nodded. "That's exactly right," Jones said.

"Did Bove know that's where the money was coming from?"

"Of course he did," Jones said.

"Holy shit. What an asshole."

Both men nodded again.

"So you're going after this organization, right?" I asked. "The terrorists?"

"That's right," Jones said. "And we could use your help."

Thank You for Reading

I HOPE YOU ENJOYED this novel. If so, I would greatly appreciate it if you took a moment to review it on Amazon. Reviews are a huge part of helping other readers decide on a book. So just a minute or two of your time can help me immensely.

If you click here, you'll be taken right to the review page for Kill Squad on the Amazon US store.

Click here for the Amazon UK store.

Thanks!

***

Don't forget you can snag a free Trouble novella at MatthewDoggetAuthor.com/Trouble

That will also get you on my email list, where I send a couple of emails a month, including freebies, deals on my other books, and news about upcoming projects.

Until next time!

-Matt

Afterword

I'VE TAKEN SOME LIBERTIES in this book, mainly to do with the layout of buildings in Portland, Oregon. For example, there is no parking garage under the real American Bank Building. Call it artistic license. But if it really bothers you, feel free to email me and let me know. I'll try to take it with the same calm demeanor as Trouble taking a dagger to the gut. I can't promise anything, but I'll *try*.

On a serious note, white supremacy is making a resurgence in America (and in many other places, as well). This means nothing good. And while opposing racism will look different for everyone, I urge you to find a way to do so. These people will continue to spread their hateful and violent ideology if left to their own devices. More people will die at the hands of racist mass shooters. And that's something a healthy society cannot abide.

Also By Matthew Doggett

The Trouble Series – Gritty Action Thrillers You Can Read in Any Order

Too Much Trouble

When a robbery gone wrong lands him in the middle of a cartel war, Trouble starts running out of options fast. And when these operatives cross the line and go after Trouble's friends, only death will stop him from righting the wrongs and making the cartels pay for what they've done. Available on Amazon and free on Kindle Unlimited.

The Death Dealers

When he prevents a murder, Trouble is thrown into a twisted conspiracy that points to the most dangerous gang in Los Angeles. Available on Amazon and free on Kindle Unlimited.

The Deadly Divine

Trouble's a one-man wrecking crew. When he crosses paths with a charismatic lunatic, can he blow away the murderous brainwashing? Available on Amazon and free on Kindle Unlimited.

Dead Man's Hatch

Trouble works alone, busting heads and bashing bullies. But when he joins a crew of trained professionals, he becomes a target in a deadly revenge plot. Available on Amazon and free on Kindle Unlimited.

Kill Squad

Trouble infiltrates a domestic terrorist ring, posing as a white supremacist. The clock is ticking as he races to thwart their plot to destroy America.

Trouble

When Trouble stands up for what's right, he finds himself in the crosshairs of an insane small-town sheriff with one goal: kill Trouble. Available for free when you sign up for my email list at MatthewDoggettAuthor.com/Trouble

***

The Undead Trilogy

A zombie apocalypse series with a dash of humor and a whole lot of blood. All three books are available on Amazon and free on Kindle Unlimited.

Praise for Undead Annihilation

"A 'Must Read' for end-of-the-world, we're-all-gonna-die, zombie apocalypse story lovers!" -Reedsy Reviewer

"A work of genius. I've read hundreds of zombie books and this is now in my top 2." -Amazon Reviewer

"This book is a MUST!"

"Not to be missed."

"Undead Annihilation starts off fast and just keeps on going."

***

Horror Short Story Collections

3 Volumes with 20 spine-tingling tales each. Available on Amazon.

***

Hole: A Small-Town Horror Novel

A teenage boy and his dog face a gruesome evil in this coming-of-age horror novel.

***